ROAD SEVEN

A NOVEL

KEITH ROSSON

Meerkat Press
Atlanta

ISBN-13 978-1-946154-29-3 (Paperback)
ISBN-13 978-1-946154-30-9 (eBook)

Library of Congress Control Number: 2020938573

This is a work of fiction. Names, characters, businesses, places, events and incidents are either the products of the author's imagination or used in a fictitious manner. Any resemblance to actual persons, living or dead, or actual events is purely coincidental.

Cover design by Keith Rosson

Book design by Tricia Reeks

Printed in the United States of America

Published in the United States of America by
Meerkat Press, LLC, Atlanta, Georgia
www.meerkatpress.com

Praise for *Road Seven*

"A wonderful book—funny, strange, perpetually surprising, aglow with insight and fierce compassion. Keith Rosson is one of my favorite writers; I'd follow him through the haunted woods any day."
—Ben Loory, author of *Tales of Falling and Flying*

"When was the last time I had this much fun reading a novel? Keith Rosson is a mixologist of fiction, and *Road Seven*, with its cryptozoology, Icelandic mysticism, science fiction-ey conspiracy-laden horror, is his craft cocktail. With the forward momentum of a T.C. Boyle novel but a vision wholly his own, Rosson emerges as one of fiction's most exciting voices with a novel unlike any I've read."
—John McNally, author of *The Fear of Everything* and *The Book of Ralph*

"With his unique, preternatural skills, Keith Rosson is back with *Road Seven*. Deeply dimensional characters struggle at their wits' end with the emotional truths of their utterly flawed, conflicted, hapless selves. Dialogue vibrates with subtext in vividly imagined scenes described in always surprising, always apt words. He achieves the goal of so many writers: a style all his own that signifies in all the ways—from the subtlest touches to quick jabs, gut punches, and spin kicks that will floor you."
—Roy Freirich, author of *Deprivation* and *Winged Creatures*

"A well wrought speculative tale that is quirky and creepy by turn . . . the blend of genres, from science fiction to cosmic horror, is masterfully executed. Readers will be riveted by this clever, unsettling adventure."
—Publishers Weekly

"A magical journey through the wilds of rural Iceland and into a kaleidoscopic terrain filled with secretly active military bases and muddied body parts that sully what began as an innocent expedition into the supernatural . . . An engrossing and creative story of the wonders of the unknown."
—Kirkus Reviews

"Cross-genre elements—including personalized, existential horror; noir threats; and the unsettling unknown—result in a disconcerting adventure whose dark humor prevails. Darkly comic and brimming with flawed characters, *Road Seven* examines the price of knowledge as the unknown becomes horrific."
—Foreword Reviews

ALSO BY KEITH ROSSON

The Mercy of the Tide
Smoke City

To Robin,

for the belief,
and the joy,
and the last song
on that one record

CONTENTS

1

napalm grays

"I became used to gazing between the staggered limbs of trees, at looking beyond the branches and needles, at finding the shapes *inside* the shapes. That's where I knew I would find the creature, find the unknown, find whatever mysteries it held: there, between the trees, ensnared in the hidden spaces of the world."
—Mark Sandoval, *Seen Through the Trees*

1

It was a help wanted ad from a monster hunter.

The monster hunter, really, if such a term could ever be said out loud without at least a little wince, a self-conscious roll of the eyes. Its arrival came via a forwarded link from Ellis, who in the subject line wrote: *Aren't you into this guy?*

It was a spring evening and Brian sat in his room, enveloped in the encroaching night, cradled in his usual pain. A few moths flitted in mortal combat against his window screen, and Brian had the napalm grays going on, had that deep and familiar knife-throb in the skull. The Headache That Lived Forever. Still, Ellis's line made him smile. Brian heard him downstairs in the kitchen yelling to Robert over the music, cupboard doors slamming closed. They were making drinks—pregame warmups, Ellis called them— before the three of them went out to get stupid, or what passed for stupid these days. Brian was already thinking of ways to bail—his head, when it got like this, in this kind of slow, heated roil, like a halo of barbs being cinched tighter and tighter, alcohol was no good for it.

Down the hall in the bathroom, he dropped a trio of aspirin into his palm and chewed them while he gazed at his face in the mirror. Three would maybe take the edge off, turn the headache from a sharp blade scraping along the bowl of his skull to a dull one. That was about it; you could grow used to anything. He leaned close and gazed at the galaxy of burst blood vessels in one eye.

Back in his room, bass-heavy nü metal ghosting through the floorboards, Robert bellowed laughter in response to something Ellis said. Brian sat back down, looked at the screen of his laptop. His bare feet on the wood floor, the occasional draft from the window fluttering the curtains. The moths outside, insistent and hopeful. Here was spring in Portland: the scent of cut grass, the blat of a car alarm, the creak of a shifting, old, many-roomed house. Ellis's place he'd inherited from his parents; Brian had been his roommate since they were undergrads.

His desk was choked with stacks of accordion folders, mugs of pens.

Outdated anthro journals he kept telling himself he'd read someday. He clicked on the link Ellis had sent, and it took him to a cryptozoology website, and not one of the good ones. Not one of the ones that Brian sometimes cruised (with only the slightest tinge of embarrassment), ones that tended to mirror or replicate the "reputable" sciences. No, this one, menandmonsterz.com, had all the trappings of the technologically inept and socially unhinged: woefully pixilated photos, a dizzying array of fonts stacked and butting up against each other. There was a link, holy shit, to a Myspace page. *What If Leprechauns*, one headline blared in what was almost certainly Papyrus font, *Were Really Pre-Stone Age Hominids!?!* This, alongside a fan-art illustration of the Lucky Charms leprechaun leering and holding a stone ax in each hand. Beneath that, a banner ad for hair regeneration. The type of site, honestly, that made antiviral software programmers rich.

And yet, the next part snagged him:

> The Long Way Home *author, alien abductee, famed cryptozoologist, and renowned cultural anthropologist Mark Sandoval is on the hunt for a research assistant. And maybe it's YOU!*

He snorted at the "cultural anthropologist" part and scrolled down past the iconic cover of *The Long Way Home*, Sandoval's memoir about his alien abduction (the image was a tiny human figure enveloped in a cone of light from some unseen but brilliant overhanging light source, the same image they'd used for the movie) and then past Sandoval's Hollywood-quality headshot. It continued:

> *Mark Sandoval is looking for a research assistant to accompany him on a site visit outside of the US. Position is* confidential *and* time-sensitive. *Terms and compensation commensurate with experience. Visit marksandoval.com to apply.*

"Brian!" Ellis bellowed from downstairs. "Get your pregame drink on, dear heart! Let's do this shit!"

"We're making the most terrible drinks we can," warbled Robert.

Brian typed in the address to Sandoval's website, and it was a much nicer affair. Professional, clean, and surprisingly understated, considering the man claimed to have at one time literally traded punches with a chupacabra. And there was the ad—the same exact information, with a *Click to Apply* button at the bottom. Vague as hell. Had the air of haste to it, something quickly cobbled together. But he clicked on it, scratched his chin with his thumbnail. Pressed three fingers against his eyelid, felt the sick, familiar throb in the hidden meat behind his eye. He quickly typed in the various fields—name, email address, phone number—and confirmed that he did indeed have a valid passport. Then he uploaded his CV, which he had at the ready because this, of course, was not *remotely* the first time Brian Schutt had dicked around with the notion of ditching everything in regard to his future. No, this was not the first time at all.

To be fair, it was admittedly a decent resume for a thirty-year-old who was still doggy-paddling through his academic career, who had yet to submit his dissertation—that obnoxious, convoluted, soul-shattering paperweight that it was. As cowardly as he felt when he thought about it, and as one-dimensional and chickenshit as that stasis made him feel, he really *was* close to being done. And he'd worked on two published papers that he'd been given credit on and had gone on a number of digs with his professor, Dr. Don Whitmer (all of them in the States, true, save for the one on the shore of Iceland's Lake Holmavatn, hence the passport) and Whitmer was most certainly no slouch in the anthropology world, so hey. There was that. Academic doggy-paddling aside, he really didn't look too bad on paper. Though what the hell a guy like Mark Sandoval was actually looking for in a research assistant was anyone's guess. Imperviousness to silver bullets? Telepathy? Acting experience?

Someone clomped up the steps and knocked on his open door. Then Ellis was leaning in the doorway, holding something muddy and dark in a wineglass. Scowling, he took in the state of Brian's room. The unmade bed, the balled up socks on the floor. Dirty clothes lay in drifts, piled against the molding like windblown garbage. Papers were literally spilling out of the drawers of his desk.

"It smells like you jerked off and then died in here," he said.

"You're a charmer."

"And then jerked off again."

Brian's dissertation sat on top of his dresser, a mess of paper stacked three, four inches tall. On top of it rested an old Vietnam-era pineapple grenade long since robbed of its charge. Something he'd bought himself last year as a joke. Supposedly. When the irony of not finishing the thing yet had actually seemed a little ironic, and not weighted and terrible.

Ellis offered him the wineglass and Brian said, "I don't know, man. My head's killing me."

Ellis frowned. "Drink it."

As if he were psychic or the room was bugged, Robert yelled, "Drink it!" from downstairs, drawing out the last word until it ended in a series of yips and howls.

Brian took a sip, smacked his lips. Took another drink. Squinted up at Ellis. And then it hit him. "Jesus. What's *in* this?"

Ellis ticked them off with his fingers. "Coke, whiskey, vodka. Instant coffee, cocoa."

"Ah, God. Barf."

"Oh! Nutritional yeast. Some cherry liqueur Robert got from a work party two Christmases ago. Onion powder."

"Ellis, no."

"We're pregaming, remember? Robert calls it an Arkansas Dust Cloud, but if I told you why, you'd probably throw up for real." His face brightened when he saw what was on Brian's laptop. "Hey, you went to the thing! The website."

Brian was a little embarrassed. "Yeah. I'm applying."

"You are? I was just *kidding*! I just thought you liked that movie. You're actually applying?" Ellis got louder the more he drank, more bombastic, and Brian assumed by the way he slapped his hand against his chest in shock that this probably wasn't his first Dust Cloud.

"Yeah. I mean, why not?"

"Because you live *here*," Ellis said, sitting down on Brian's bed and taking the wineglass from him. He drank a third of it and didn't flinch. A rind of dark flakes clung to the inside of the glass. "You live *here*, young man, and you're the only person I could ever cohabitate with and not ultimately throat punch to death."

"Besides Robert," Brian offered.

"Psssh," Ellis said, waving a hand. "Neither of us are in any rush there, believe me."

"Well, it says it's a site visit, so it's not like I'd be gone long anyway."

Ellis nodded, swirled the contents of the wineglass. "Seriously though, this room. Fetid does not begin to describe it."

"Listen, you mind if I finish this?" Brian said, pointing at his computer.

"Drink the fucking thing," Robert yelled from downstairs.

"He thinks he's too good for it," Ellis yelled back.

Sometimes, when Brian laughed and his headache was particularly bad, he saw white stars populate the corners of his vision. It happened now, and he winced a little and said, "Just let me finish this and we can head out."

Ellis had a moment of concern—they'd lived together long enough. He knew what one of Brian's bad nights looked like. "I'm just kidding you—if you need to stay in, don't worry about it."

"No, I'll just finish this. I'm good."

"That is so funny," Ellis said, standing up and smoothing his shirt. "Robert sent that to me as a joke. You're really applying?" He walked out, made as if to slam Brian's bedroom door and then, grinning, gently closed it instead.

There really wasn't much else to do. Under the *Availability* field he typed in "Immediately." The last field threw him for a minute. He sat there, tapping out a little rhythm on the lip of his desk. Bass throbbed downstairs, a new song, dance music that made wavering ripples among the various mugs of coffee sitting on his desk.

Why does cryptozoology interest you?

Blessed with the casual honesty afforded those who didn't really give much of a shit one way or the other, he typed, "Because I want to believe in the unknown. In the idea of something beyond, something atypical. Even if I know there's nothing out there in the dark, nothing under the bed, I still wish the possibility was there."

· · ·

They cabbed to a bar underneath the Morrison Bridge. As Ellis and Robert chatted with the driver, Brian thumbed through his phone. It was the usual confluence of the brutal and the mundane: A pop star wore a midriff-revealing top to showcase her new baby bump. A girl in a Seattle middle school accidentally shot herself in the thigh with the handgun she'd smuggled to class in her backpack. White nationalists convened on a small town in Alabama for a "Whites Only Commerce Day," urging business owners to turn away people of color. Bedlam and violence ensued, leaving one dead. A bubonic plague outbreak in China, five confirmed cases. In a small town in Idaho, a dog saved a child's cat from a tree. There was a video clip of the dog scaling the tree and picking the mewling cat up by the scruff of its neck. Brian watched, numbed.

Get me, he thought, *the hell out of here.*

· · ·

The place was called Drill. It was dark and hangar-like, its long walls festooned with repurposed slats of rusted steel spattered with useless rivets. A glossy cement floor. Dim and crowded, it stood next door to a French-fusion restaurant called the White Bird, and on the opposite side was a rundown, cobwebbed CPA office, some last remnant of old Portland hanging on like some vestigial tail. Their bartender had a handlebar mustache and a tattoo of a sparrow on his throat. Ellis's drink came with a charred pinecone snared into the lip of the glass, and the price of their three drinks combined equaled more than what Brian spent on groceries in a week.

A homeless encampment was clustered around the bridge column outside their window, a small satellite city of shopping carts and tarps and battered tents ringed around it. He saw the occasional flutter of flashlights or cell phone screens casting wan illuminations on the pavement. Here, he thought, was capitalism distilled: the old Portland had been vanquished, decimated, and in this bar was the new city rising from the ashes, a recalcitrant phoenix that flexed its wings and built code and drove hybrids and staunchly ignored the poor. A wealthy, tech-savvy phoenix that shat neck tattoos and charred artisanal pinecones. He felt momentarily buoyed by self-righteousness, and then he remembered where he was and what he was doing—slowly flagellating his way around a PhD and drinking a twelve-dollar IPA that someone else had bought for him—and felt indescribably old instead.

The bridge's column seemed to have become some kind of memorial. A few wilted bouquets, some illegible chalking of a name across the rippled cement. A scattering of tea candles. Headache or not—and tonight's headache, it turned out, had laughed at the aspirin, had given the aspirin a wedgie and shoved it in some random locker—he felt a true lurch in his heart, some tug of sorrow.

"How's the dad these days?" Ellis asked, waggling his eyebrows, pulling Brian from what passed for his reveries. "Any news?" Ellis and Robert took an unabashed pleasure in the travails of Brian's folks. Telling them the newest, insane events as they unfolded were pretty much the only good thing about the shitshow that was his family.

Tonight there wasn't much new to report, and Brian shrugged. "Not really. But I'm going to hang out with my mom and Brooke tomorrow, so I'm sure I'll get all caught up on the madness."

"I mean, is he a hippie? Is it like a love-in thing?"

"No, not my dad. No way. I think it's more about, uh, the nudity itself. Like the act of being nude. It's freeing qualities or whatever."

"Your poor mother," Robert said, and Brian had to agree. His poor mother. "Hey, Ellis said you applied to the Sandoval thing." They nearly had to yell at each other to be heard over the hair-metal thundering over the speakers.

"If by 'applied' you mean 'fired off a quickly and haphazardly answered series of questions,' then yeah, I totally applied."

Robert nodded, sipped his cocktail. "He's the *Long Way Home* guy, right?"

"Yeah."

"But he also did a Bigfoot book, right? That's why I sent that link to you."

Brian's curse: you study historical mythical creatures as an academic, your friends assume you believe the Loch Ness Monster is not only real, but is just misunderstood.

"Yeah," Brian said. "He's done a Bigfoot book, one about haunted highways, chupacabras. It's not really science, you know what I mean?"

Robert said, "Man, I loved *The Long Way Home*—"

"Because it had Brad Pitt back when he was still bangable," Ellis barked.

"The thing that Sandoval does that's so brilliant," Brian said, "is that he never finds irrevocable proof, you know? He never does. Just enough to *maybe* color your opinion that what he's seen *might* be real. It's sleight-of-hand stuff. Really, it's a hell of a brand he's built." And with the snooty, off-putting tone of *the academic*, the pedantic tone that he swore he'd never use and found himself using fairly often, even as his own career stalled, he said, "Mark Sandoval's more pop culturist than anthropologist, actually."

Shoot me now, he thought. *I have become what I despise. The transformation to ivory tower dickhead is complete.*

"That's true," Ellis offered, "but anyone who's been a guest on *Coast to Coast*? They can pretty much be put in the *Most Likely a Nutjob* file."

"But wasn't he on Oprah, too?" Robert said.

Ellis scoffed. "Yeah, back when you were in tighty-whities. You go on *Coast to Coast* with guys talking about werewolves and additional dimensions and endless holes—"

Robert lifted his fist. "I'll show you an endless hole." Brian burst out laughing, steeling himself against those white stars in his head.

He swirled his beer. "So this is four years of dating, huh? You guys have something really special. It's admirable. It warms me. Truly."

"Bite me," said Robert. "But seriously, you really applied?"

· · ·

They drank more and Brian's headache began to really settle in. It'd been this way for years, since he was a teenager. He'd missed his senior prom, splayed out on the couch in his living room with a washcloth over his eyes, his friends going to the dance and the ensuing parties without him, his mother high-stepping through the room like a cartoon character, afraid of making a sound. It really did feel like someone was continually scooping out the meat of his head like a curled rind of sherbet. Crazy how pain could become commonplace, like its own appendage. As familiar as a shirt you wore.

At one point, he wasn't surprised when he looked down—Robert had by then ordered them another outrageously expensive round of drinks, and auto-tuned country music was now chugging out of the bar's sound system at a bone-rattling level—and saw that his hand was shaking on the tabletop.

That was it. Covering the mouth of his new beer with that same hand, Brian shook his head and mouthed, *Sorry.*

"What?" Ellis yelled, his hand cupped to his ear.

He motioned at the speakers, his own ear, the beer again. Shrugged. Ellis nodded, gave him a thumbs-up. Robert waved goodbye. The headaches were nothing new to them. The napalm grays had bowed him out plenty of times before.

He pushed through the doors out into a dark, quiet night. The line of cars parked in front of the bar were laced in illumination from a street-light. To his right was the encampment, painted in shadows. Tarps and tents and mounds of belongings tied tight to shopping carts with bungee cords, with hanks of rope. Huddled shapes in the darkness; dark slabs of men on bedrolls, a woman sitting cross-legged next to a shapeless body beneath a sleeping bag. The city kept shuffling them from place to place, these people. They'd be here for a while, then the police would come through and evacuate the area and they would have to take their things to somewhere new. This, constantly, all over the city. All over the world. It all seemed intrinsically broken, this grand divide. Contain people until they spilled out, and then move them along to somewhere else. Whatever answer he had seemed half-formed, based more on some conflated sense of justice than anything else.

It was a beautiful night, wind-kissed and cool from the Willamette. It seemed impossible then, as he walked home, not to number and cata-log the balancing acts he had going in his life, as if something so scenic demanded it. There was the yawning chasm of pointlessness that was his academic career, and the fear all twisted up around that. Fear of failing, fear of succeeding. He had a fractured, confusing dissertation that was good as a blunt force weapon and little else. And there was his father, the nude absconder. His mother's life seemed powered solely on the jet fuel of her anger, still, these months later, an anger banked in the coals of her heartbreak and sharp sense of betrayal. Romance in Brian's own life wasn't even a topic of consideration—he was a sad, pear-shaped man who had grown accustomed by now to his own self-contempt. Just the general, seizing lethargy involved in trying to move throughout the day seemed obstacle enough. *I'm just a big ol' turkey,* he thought, *basting in the hate-glaze,* and just thinking it—this wretched attempt at fey irony—made him shudder with embarrassment. Enough.

He walked. Only a few blocks away from other homeless encampments lay the city's new jarring landscape: box condos, boutiques, kombucha bars, aesthetically chilling squares of studio apartments topped with rooftop gardens and dog-bathing stations. More envoys of nineteen-dollar cocktails. He'd grown up with these streets and trod a familiar path home even as everything looked so different.

Ellis's house was a century old: two stories and a basement, a leaning fence holding in a backyard full of blackberry brambles and tufted grass that both of them loathed to take care of. Going up to his room, the pulse of his headache had grown thunderous and red with each footstep, and at one point he had to put his hand against the wall to steady himself. He'd tried allergy meds, acupuncture, sinus remedies, all of it. All of the things he could manage on the threadbare insurance that the college offered. His mother had taken him to an herbalist once, and a woman at a party had claimed to be a phrenologist and mysteriously told him he was cursed with a "maelstrom in the sphenoid" after deliciously massaging his scalp. At times aspirin seemed to work fine. Other times, like tonight, the pain seemed poised to eat him whole.

In his room, he sat on his bed and cast another glance at the papers on his dresser. Any buzz from his two beers was gone. It felt as if someone had driven a luxury car into the back of his head at high velocity and parked it there. He splayed his hand in front of his face and watched the fingers tremble. Willing them to stop did nothing.

In front of the bathroom mirror, he shook three more aspirin in his hand like dice, chewed them to pulp, stared again into his red-threaded eyes. He had class tomorrow, teaching a Primate Biomechanics class. He dropped another pair of aspirin in his palm, tossed them in. Pictured blood worn so thin that it jetted hose-like from a paper cut, spurting from a dozen minute perforations on his body.

Back in his room he crawled into bed and cracked open his laptop.

There were a pair of emails waiting for him. One from his sister with *Dinner at Mom's tomorrow* in the subject line. The message just read *Bring the wine Mom likes*, a textbook example of the brusqueness that Brooke wielded like a club.

And then his heart rose from the depths of its thinned, overworked blood, did a lazy flip-flop in its cage when he saw the second message. It was from Mark Sandoval. The subject line simply said *Interview.*

Mr. Schutt,

Thanks for your interest in the Research Assistant position. From what I gather, you live in Portland? I'm impressed with your experience, particularly that you've studied with Don Whitmer. He and I go way back, actually. Great guy, hell of a teacher.

Any chance you're available for an interview? Sooner rather than later? The position needs to be filled immediately. Maybe we could meet up in Don's office?

Thanks,
Mark

• • •

The next day, after what turned out to be an astonishingly little amount of work—a few texts and a single explanatory phone call to Don Whitmer—Brian found himself introduced to Mark Sandoval in his mentor's office. Brian walked in on legs sea-drunk with nervousness; he'd just plowed through his Primate Biomechanics class and the following discussion group, and it wasn't until he was standing in the hallway outside Whitmer's office that his legs truly took on that terrified thrum. Since that final text from Dr. Whitmer—*Sure Bri you can meet him here*—had come through earlier this morning, his headache had dissipated. It was just a pale ghost now, its fingers occasionally feathering his skull, trilling a little ache here and there, and thank God for that. Meanwhile, his guts roiled. He'd worn a tie. His only sport coat. Tucked his shirt into a pair of slacks that pinched his belly fat like a bully.

Dr. Whitmer earlier that month had begun Brian's process of formally dropping out from the doctorate program. What he was doing wasn't that odd—lots of PhD students dropped out, enough so that there was a common parlance for it. Brian was pulling an ADB—"All But Dissertation." Whitmer, he knew, was trying hard not to take it personally. It left them in an odd kind of twilight regarding their relationship; Brian's life at the school was winding down, but he had still TAed for Whitmer as a grad student, still graded his papers and taught his lesson plans. Brian still considered Whitmer his friend. He still looked forward to their discussions, their time together; he would miss the hell out of the warmth and wry, understated kindness of the old man.

He knocked and Whitmer through the door told him to come in.

The office was windowless and small with barely enough room for his desk, a dented filing cabinet, and a beautiful oak bookcase that spanned most of one wall and housed his books and a number of relics from his fieldwork. A pair of dark leather chairs faced his desk, their back rails cracked and worn. Anthropology was as fact-based as anything else, Whitmer was fond of saying, and thusly was couched resolutely in the three-armed embrace of theory, investigation, and review. But as a field of study? Anthro would never, *ever* be financially akin to, say, engineering or drug development. It would never bring in the same type of money for the school. Whitmer's office was a clear reflection of that. It was the apex of the man's career, this room, and it would be his death-boat, his Viking funeral: he would die here, in this office. Figuratively if not literally. This was his final destination, as good as it got for Don Whitmer, and why should Brian be so presumptuous to think that he'd fare differently, or even as well? The fact that Whitmer seemed perfectly content with his life served only to scare the living shit out of Brian.

The two men stood when he entered. Everyone shook hands. Whitmer's hands were rough, calloused—the worn hands of decades of fieldwork, the hands of a man who still taught dig classes to kids at the Y twice a month. Well versed in chisel and brush and aching knees bent beneath a sun somewhere. Brian had always felt fiercely sentimental toward Don Whitmer, who was old as God, and who held a deep reserve of workmanship inside him that bordered on manic and belied his age and frame. On the Lake Holvamatn dig last year, the old man had transformed into an outright beast, running the excavation site until well past dark, oftentimes needing Brian or another student to remind him to eat and sleep. He'd be retiring within the next few years, and Brian felt as tender towards him as a grandparent. His face was leather-tan, seamed as a map, and today he badly needed to clean his glasses. Sandoval's hands, meanwhile, were smooth, cool. Writer's hands. Hands like his own.

Brian sat down in the vacant chair, the waistline of his slacks once more cutting painfully into his gut. He was sitting next to Mark Sandoval. He was sitting next to a purported alien abductee, a famed cryptozoologist, a *New York Times* bestselling author. It was a curious type of celebrity the man held, and a weird moment. Sandoval was wearing a gray calfskin jacket over an off-blue dress shirt, brown jeans and boots. Leaning back with his hands laced over his stomach, he managed to effortlessly convey, with his slightly disheveled haircut and going-gray stubble, exactly what he was: a fit, reasonably handsome multimillionaire just over the hillside of fifty. Given Sandoval's tertiary proximity to the anthropology field—even if only as a punch line, someone to be derided by actual academics and scientists—and his status as a famous person, B-list or otherwise, Brian felt both mildly starstruck and a little annoyed at being starstruck.

"We were just catching up," Whitmer said. "Mark was a student of mine back in Seattle."

"Long time ago," Sandoval said. He sounded almost boyish, certainly younger than he looked.

"Oh, indeed," Whitmer said with a little chuckle.

"Wait a minute," Brian said. His face brightened with sudden understanding. "Don, you're not . . . Are *you* Morgan Freeman? In the movie?"

Whitmer nodded, a curious mixture of humility and—what was that? Contrition? Shame? "Guilty as charged," he said.

Sandoval burst into laughter. "How often you get that question, Don?"

He nodded again. "It does happen sometimes."

"Wow," said Brian. "Really? *Wow.* How did I not know this? How am I just now finding this out?"

"Don's a humble sort," Sandoval said.

"It's not my story to tell."

"So you're the professor in Seattle? Before Mark"—he turned to Sandoval—"before you disappeared?"

"He was indeed," Sandoval said. "So when I read your CV and saw Don's name, I thought it'd be nice to touch base again. Don and I haven't seen each other in . . ."

"Years," Whitmer offered.

"That's right."

The moment stretched out, both men's faces unreadable. Brian felt like a bit actor in their drama, something weird unfolding between them. Something he wasn't privy to, something separate from him. And then Sandoval turned to him, that strange mask that he'd worn against Whitmer packed away. He loosed a gleaming smile that showed significant assistance from some top-notch orthodontists and said, "So! I hear you're dropping out."

Whitmer laughed, not sounding happy at all. "You'll find, Brian, that Mark gets right to the point."

"Why waste time?" Sandoval said. "Everyone's busy."

"Well," Brian said, suddenly having a hard time looking at Whitmer. "Just turns out academia isn't for me."

"Too bad you couldn't have made that discovery before student loans, am I right?"

A wan smile. "I hear you."

"Wasn't for me either," Sandoval said. "We're actually on pretty close parallels in a number of ways, aren't we, Don?"

"Well," Whitmer said, "there're definitely some similarities. Certainly." You'd have had to be an idiot not to catch the caution in his voice. Walking a tightrope of propriety. "You're both brilliant students, devoted to your particular fields—ah, I know what you think about your capabilities, Brian, but please allow me my opinions—and both of you are profoundly gifted in areas that are integral to our studies." He only mildly sounded like he was choking down something bad.

Sandoval looked at Brian and shrugged, raised his eyebrows. *Hey, that's pretty good.*

On the corner of Whitmer's desk sat an age-browned bird skull, the curve of its brainpan wrapped in a chorus of colored twine. Some talisman gifted to him on some long-ago dig. He said, "And I'm glad to see, Mark, that you've made such a name for yourself. As unorthodox and difficult a route as it may have been. Truly, I'm happy for you." He reached over and minutely adjusted the skull. "You've made your own way in the world, and you should be proud of that."

"Yeah," Sandoval said, steepling his hands over his stomach again. "It took some work. No lie. And thank you, Don. There were some dark clouds on the horizon there for a while, as I'm sure you remember."

"I do."

"I still can't believe you're the professor," said Brian.

And then Sandoval suddenly hunched forward in his chair and gripped the armrests, like he was about to stand up. It was such a quick movement, like someone spying a rat in a corner of the room. "Listen, Don. Would you excuse us, please?"

"Oh!" Whitmer frowned, adjusted his glasses. "Uh, certainly. Brian, if you'd care to stop back in after your interview, uh, we can touch base about how Biomechanics went today—"

And then Sandoval did stand up. He hooked his thumb over his shoulder and, smiling apologetically, said, "Actually, Don, I was hoping you could give us a minute."

"I'm sorry?"

Sandoval peered at the old man and said, "Would you mind stepping outside for a minute?"

Whitmer's gaze pinballed between the two of them. Brian, mortified, felt knifed by a profound sense of loyalty coupled with the distinct feeling that all of this would have played out in some similar way whether he'd been in the room or not. There was that sense of history between them, some kind of weird, subdued dick-swinging thing going on, academic or otherwise. Whitmer finally sucked his teeth and said, in a bright, clipped tone positively *snapping* with rage, "You know, I'd be happy to step out in the hall, Mark. Have a cup of coffee in the cafeteria, maybe?"

"Sure," Sandoval said. "Yeah, why don't you do that?"

Whitmer touched his glasses with his blunted, calloused fingers as he rose from his chair, which wheezed like an asthmatic.

Brian sat rooted to his own chair.

And then Whitmer winked at Brian, exempted him from his awkwardness just like that, and briefly placed a warm, liver-spotted hand on his shoulder as he shuffled out. The door clicked shut behind him and the room howled and jumped with his vacancy, with the strangeness of what had just happened. The man had just been kicked out of his own office! His professor! Brian felt the urge to go after the old man, to apologize. It felt nearly as intimate, what he'd just witnessed, and personal as sex, or a fistfight.

And then Sandoval walked around the desk and sat down in Don Whitmer's chair.

• • •

The summer he'd turned sixteen, Brian left a party and went to catch the bus at an unfamiliar stop. It'd been a quiet, windless night. The heat had been like a blanket you were forced to wear outside. Grass felt almost synthetic in its dryness.

There was a guy at the bus stop that night. A few years older, not that much bigger. He wore a baseball cap backward and a voluminous T-shirt. Acne had studded his cheeks. He was yelling at his girlfriend, who sat there on the little bus bench while the guy stood over her and berated her. Brian, dismayed, had rounded the corner and slowed as the guy called her every kind of name, some that Brian hadn't even heard up to that point. She sat there in a black hoodie with her hand jittering a little as she took long drags of her cigarette. Her nails were ragged and red-rimmed with old blood—one of those details that just get snagged in your head and promise to stay. He thought about walking past them, waiting at the bus stop four or five blocks down, but he was drunk and already a little lost and he thought for a moment that he might be brave. Her mascara was messed up, her eyes glittering with tears, and the guy leaned over her and called her these terrible things while Brian stood there a few feet away, staring at the weeds rising through the slab of sidewalk at his feet, and his heart clanged like a kick drum in the cage of his ribs.

Finally Brian offered a weak "Hey" and the guy stepped over to Brian fast, reaching behind his head to adjust the brim of his hat. (In the decades that followed, when Brian relived it, he knew that that was the moment he should have punched the kid, when his hands were raised behind his head like that.)

"The fuck are you looking at?" the guy said, and mock-punched him, his fist stopping inches in front of Brian's face.

And Brian had flinched, hard, and he'd turned and walked away, his face hot with shame and fear. He'd walked home—three or four miles—so that he wouldn't risk seeing them on the bus.

It was just one of those things that stuck with him, those moments of cowardice that would ride his skull to his deathbed.

Sometimes, usually at night, he got stuck in memories like that. Snared in them. Peeling back years of his life like a kid lifting rotten logs, looking for the dark, scurrying life hidden underneath it.

• • •

Sandoval leaned back—the poor chair groaned again—and laced his arms behind his head. His shirt cuffs pulled up and Brian saw, finally, the lattice-work of scars that began at his wrists. A scuffed boot peeked out from the behind the desktop as he crossed his legs. The fruity tang of spent alcohol hung close in the room.

"So yeah, thanks for coming out, Brian." Sandoval waved a hand at the door. "I was just hoping for some privacy, that's what that was all about. This is a sizably important matter, and the walls have ears, you know?"

"Sure," Brian said. Not believing a word of that. "Totally."

"Don and I have a long history."

"It seems like it," he said.

"So, okay. Long story short: before you came in, Don told me that you're one of the most promising anthro students he's had in years. That you're making a huge mistake, torpedoing your doctorate like this."

"He's a great guy."

"He also thinks your dissertation is 'fearsomely good,' and that's a direct quote."

Inwardly, Brian winced. "He's supported me a lot."

"See, that carries a lot of weight with me, though. Don's input. He and I have our differences, but he doesn't casually fling things around like that. Compliments. Accolades."

Brian decided right then: Sandoval was weird as hell. Sandoval made him nervous. Sandoval owned that booze-stink and thrummed with the kind of odd, unnerving energy that probably made light bulbs pop when he walked underneath them.

The man's books were a far cry from what even a layman would consider genuine cultural anthropology. Brian kept thinking back to the intimate, painful abduction and probe scenes in *The Long Way Home*; they seemed impossible to reconcile with the odd and charismatic man seated before him. Before leaving for class, Brian had quickly skimmed through a dog-eared copy of *Seen Through the Trees*, found amid a stack of discarded anthro texts in his closet. It had only reinforced Brian's understanding that Sandoval's work was leaps away, academically, from Don Whitmer's three-armed embrace. Light on investigation, big on personality. They were memoirs of a sort, really, Sandoval's books. Sugar-heavy entertainment housed in the flimsy, balsa-wood construction of pseudoscience. When you got down to it, they were mostly about Sandoval himself.

But Brian's future yawned wide and unknown, didn't it? School had mostly been paid for—he was beyond lucky in that way—but he'd still accrued some debt. And he had no real plan. He'd be paying off the interest of these wasted years—or dodging loan people—until brittle turds were tumbling out of his pajama leg in an old folks' home somewhere.

"Thanks," he said, and even managed to smile. "I've worked hard on it."

Sandoval tilted his head back and held up a single finger, as if about to make some proclamation. In a booming, oratory voice, he said, "*They Built a Pyre and Alit Every Beautiful Thing: Death Practices of Nordic Chieftains of the Preagricultural Straits of Northern Europe.*" Brian could see the wrinkles at his throat, white against his tan. A few more pale scars poked out of the collar of his shirt. Outside the door, someone's shoes squeaked as they walked down the hall.

"I'm not entirely sold on the title yet," Brian said.

"It's a mouthful."

"Ha, yes."

"Don let me read the first few chapters. I won't lie, man, it's impressive work."

A slurry of emotions belted through him at the thought of Mark Sandoval reading his dissertation. Excitement, fear, a strange stutter of anger toward Whitmer at such an overreach. But also, yes, a kind of fierce, blooming pride. "Again, thank you. I appreciate it. How'd you remember all that?"

"Oh, just one of those things. Dates, names." Sandoval tapped a silver temple. "Just got a mind for it. So it's done? Your dissertation? Please tell me you're not dropping out with the thing done."

"No." *Don't even get into it,* Brian thought. *Please. For all that is good and holy.* "It's still a mess."

"Edits, then."

"Always edits."

"So, ABD," Sandoval said. "You're sure."

"Yeah."

"It's a big move, man. And so close to finishing."

"I'm just sick of it," Brian said. He looked around the room. "This just isn't for me, you know?"

Sandoval leaned forward and smacked his boots on the floor. He turned the bird skull around so the tiny caves of its sockets faced Brian. "Do you speak Danish?"

Brian's hand wavered in the air like a boat in rough water. "A little."

"Icelandic?"

"A bit more. It's a tough language."

"That's what I hear. But you've been to Iceland before."

Brian hooked his thumb at the door. "I went on a dig with Don last year. Lake Holvamatn."

"Okay. Good. And you know your Norse mythology. Your monsters."

"Yes. That I can say for sure. I know the history of monsters like the back of my hand." In a moment that surprised them both, he leaned back in his chair and belted out in a terrible Southern accent, "Son, I say, I can tell you about every *gottdamn* ghost haunting, every *gottdamn* Viking burial mound from Krakow to Spitsbergen," and then shut his mouth so abruptly his jaw clacked shut.

But Sandoval loved it. He barked a single gunshot of laughter—"Ha!"— and some of the tension and strangeness seemed to ease from the room. "That's good," he said. "I like that. But seriously, it's good to know that you've got, you know, boots on the ground experience. When it comes to research and investigative, uh, *expectations* and all that, Don and I probably have a different set of protocols." He did this thing then where he kind of waved his hand in front of his face. Dismissively, or as if he was maybe wafting away the lurid stench of Whitmer's belief in maintaining site integrity or cross-cataloging inventory. "We care about different things."

"It won't be like a traditional dig, is what you're saying."

Sandoval dipped his chin down, touched his nose, then pointed at Brian. "Exactly. But again, it's good to know that you've got experience in the field. So, have you read my work?"

For the first time, he got a sense of the man doing something other than performing the part of Rich Eccentric Guy Pulling Weird-Ass Power Plays. For just a second, there and gone, Brian saw a great number of things at play on the man's face: bravado, worry, a naked want to be liked. All of it buried eyeblink-fast in the quicksand of supposed disinterest, a languid coolness that slipped immediately back over him like a mask. Mark Sandoval was a good liar, but not a perfect one.

Brian said, "You know, I have read a few of them. *The Long Way Home*, definitely."

Sandoval said, "Sure," like it was a given.

"*The Ghost in the Dirt.* I just revisited *Seen Through the Trees* today, actually."

Sandoval smiled. "Brushing up for the interview, huh?"

He nodded. "Exactly."

Sandoval leaned back and laced his hands behind his head again. Once more, there were the scars. On one wrist Brian saw a circle connected to a triangle by a right angle. The other arm: a square, a series of dashes, a hexagon. These welted and alabaster scars. Some cosmic roadmap, Sandoval's memoir suggested, some unknowable catalog number. Possibly even some warning or prophecy. His abductors would eventually be back, Sandoval's book implied, and answers would be forthcoming.

"Here's the deal," Sandoval said. "I've got a book that's past due and an outraged editor that's currently spelunking up my asshole, demanding pages. And my publisher's legal department is over *his* shoulder, muttering about suing me for my advance. And something just fell into my lap. A sighting." There was the definite sugar-stink of booze in the room now.

"Okay."

"So I weaseled an extension, Brian, but they're all frothing. *Frothing.* And litigious. And wanting pages. So this'll be blitzkrieg-fast: a few days of prep and then three to four weeks on-site. I need an assistant handling the day-to-day stuff for me before we leave, booking flights and all that, and then I need an absolute beast when we make it into the field. Relentless in pursuing the vital but no-fun shitwork that comes with the job."

"Yeah."

"Transcribing notes. Equipment maintenance that borders on the religious. Site integrity. I can see that last one surprises you. I'm not a total shithead, Brian—"

"I wasn't—"

"I'm not a total shithead, and I know what it takes to run a site. And another big part of this—and something that your background will be helpful with—will be talking to the locals, picking their brains about sightings or local mythology. Getting a *flavor* of the place. Anecdotes. Details. *Rumors.* I need to catch the *tone* of the place, okay? Half the time it's the guy that you randomly talk to on the street that busts things wide open, that leads you in the right direction."

"Definitely. I can do all that," said Brian. "No problem."

"I'll be doing a lot of the work on-site, a lot of the writing. So when I'm doing that, you're doing other shit. Checking gear, checking cameras. Reviewing footage. Doing interviews, keeping supplies stocked. Cross-checking physical evidence, as far-fetched as that might seem to you now. Biggest takeaway is we always have to be advancing the narrative, especially with my editor howling for blood like he is."

"I hear you."

"It's about the work, is what I'm saying."

Ah, finally! A fierce (but internal) eye roll from Brian. *The work,* he thought. Mark Sandoval was lecturing him on *the work!* The man who had penned a massively successful, magnificently vapid supermarket book about his supposed alien abduction! About fighting something in a darkened jungle that was almost assuredly a chupacabra! He claimed—*the man who was insisting it was about the work!*—to have nearly lured a fucking Wendigo from an ice cave in the Yukon! With a rash of rotten bacon!

The work. Sure.

Brian realized in that moment that if anyone from the anthropology department actually recognized Mark Sandoval, author of *The Long Way Home,* in Dr. Whitmer's office today, it would probably cost Don a smirk or two among his colleagues at the next faculty party. Some ribbing, surely, even as the poor guy worked his way toward retirement. *The* fucking *work* indeed.

And yet: Brad Pitt. Oscar nomination. Oprah.

Bullshit or not, played out quasicelebrity or not, Mark Sandoval still made millions.

"I totally understand," Brian said.

"Do you?"

"Yeah. I have a pretty good handle on what a traditional dig entails, those duties. And I'll be honest: it'd be pretty thrilling to branch out, use that skill set to do something new. Something a little outside of the norm. I'm ready for a challenge. You do something long enough, you invest enough time and money and effort into something and find that it's not for you—that it's actually pretty far from what you want, that its rigidity is pretty much the exact opposite of what you have vied for since, like, ever—and you suddenly find yourself very willing to take on things that might be a little outside of your wheelhouse." He was babbling, but Sandoval was nodding intently. They were having a moment.

"Your passport's current?"

"It is."

"Good. Let me ask you something, Brian. Do you believe in this stuff? I know you answered on your questionnaire, but seriously. Flat out. No lie." Sandoval broke the silence before he could answer. "I mean, you've studied monsters in a *historical* sense. Right? You know about them, how they were used as kind of . . . surrogates for people's fears or concerns. How they reinforced a society's value system, its ideologies. I get all that. But do you actually, you know, *believe* in any of this stuff? That the thing under the bed is real? The ghost on the lonely stretch of road?"

Without hesitation, Brian said, "Nope. I don't. Sorry."

Sandoval shrugged. "There's no wrong answer."

"I mean, I *want* to believe in that stuff. Aliens, ghosts. Loch Ness. I do. It would make the world a larger place. But if history has shown us anything, it's that the monster outside the window is usually just a branch tapping against the glass. That they were just a way to keep the children of the village from sneaking out at night. I mean, it's usually the dude next to you that you have to worry about, right?"

Sandoval nodded. "That's fair. I appreciate that. That's honest."

He stood up and held out that soft writer's hand, and Brian stood up and shook it. Sandoval thanked him for coming in, and he was a little surprised at how crestfallen it felt to be dismissed. That familiar stutter of smallness walked through him, that feeling he'd felt a hundred times before, whenever he went in for an interview or assembled a fellowship package, whenever he'd written the essay, filled out the paperwork, piecemealed the CV together and sent it off, only to receive the stark, impersonal email, the curt phone call in return. It was a feeling that had grown large and malevolent in recent months as his dissertation took on such dumb, crushing weight.

What was the best way to get in touch, Sandoval asked him. Email? Sure thing, Brian told him, knowing he wouldn't hear back. Sandoval said that he had some more interviews to wade through and that he'd be in touch in the next few days. "I know it's less than ideal, but please be ready to go. Pack up, have that passport ready. If I call, we've got to move. I should be able to let you know in the next day or two. Either way, yes or no."

"Okay," said Brian. "Can I ask one more question?"

"Of course."

"Where would we be going? Iceland?"

"Close," Sandoval said. Man, the booze sweat was strong now. "Hvíldarland."

"Hvíldarland," Brian said, drawing out the word. "Heard of it. Never been."

"Me neither. It's like Iceland's dirty-faced little cousin, from what I hear. Used as an ammo dump during World War II, seems like it's been slowly atrophying ever since. I'll be in touch, Brian. It was great talking to you."

• • •

That evening, Brooke picked him up in her little black two-seater, and they took the freeway through a no man's land of rough-edged suburbia, where office parks and mini-malls stood scattershot amid dollar stores and auto repair shops. Some punk band on the stereo railed about annihilation and Brooke mouthed along with the words, charms and skulls and a tiny magic 8-ball wobbling from the rearview mirror. He took it down and shook it, read through its catalog of doubts. *Don't count on it. Reply hazy, try again.* Once they got off the freeway, she drove fast, wending through blocks of residential homes that looked eerily alike, zooming past the sodium-lit windows of Plaid Pantry, 7-Eleven, Circle K, around SUVs with bass throbbing from open windows and rust-rimed sedans sagging from their deadened shocks. Past abandoned lots, weeds snarled in fence links like reaching fingers. Brooke finally turned the music down as they were about to pull into the entrance to Sunny Meadows—the apartment complex where their mother now lived—when she glanced over at him, rolled her eyes, and kept driving.

"You forgot, didn't you?"

"Oh shit," Brian said. "The wine."

"Yep."

"Sorry."

"Dude, you had one thing to do."

"Hey," Brian said, "I'm a busy guy."

Brooke laughed. "Oh, so you're eating Hot Pockets and masturbating full-time now, huh?"

"Oh, Brooke. Wow. Incredible. The comedy stylings of Brooke Schutt, everyone. Besides, it's not like Mom is short on wine these days anyway, you know what I mean?"

Brooke glared out the windshield. "Do you know what kind of an asshole you sound like?"

"One that forgot a bottle of wine? Jesus, it was an accident, Brooke. Sorry."

The parking lot of the Fred Meyer was half-full, forlorn shopping carts cast off here and there. Brooke got out and hoisted her purse over her shoulder, and for just a moment he saw the pockmarks at her temples, the old acne scars there like some ghost of Christmas past, rattling the chains of the history he shared with her. He softened, remembering her as a teenager with toothpaste on her zits, IMing her friends about how hideous she was, a kid prone to crying jags and a nameless fury long before their parents' relationship went south. They walked toward the pneumatic doors, Brooke in the lead (Brooke always in the lead), and Brian felt guilt clang inside him, remembering how close they'd been when they were younger. Closer, anyway. She'd always been tougher than him, had always held this staunch reserve inside her, but this thing with their parents had cemented the differences between them even more—she'd grown harder still, more resolute, and he'd been the one to become softer, gun-shy, rooted to one spot.

To her back, he said, "Brooke, seriously. I'm really sorry I forgot." She ignored him, her footsteps on the asphalt brittle and pronounced, like she was trying to stab the ground to death. Even when she wasn't working, she got plenty of comments from guys—such was the state of the world—and a rundown Fred Meyer parking lot on a weeknight evening was apparently no exception: a potbellied dude in cargo shorts exited the store, a 24-pack of Michelob Light in his arms. He lifted his lip at her and said, "Looking *fine* tonight, goddamn."

Still walking, Brooke lifted an arm and flipped him off. "Go die."

The guy stopped and turned, his face darkening. To her back, he said, "The fuck did you say to me?"

Brooke kept walking and the guy caught Brian's eye, his box of beers hanging by the knuckles of one hand. "You need to check your bitch."

"That's my sister," he said, and surprisingly, a stutter of shame walked across the man's face.

"Damn," he said. "I'm sorry, man."

Brian shrugged, turned and walked backward. "What if she wasn't, though?" Even this exchange was something he could only do because he was with Brooke—he at least knew that about himself.

The guy walked off, flapping a hand over his shoulder, cube of Michelob slapping against his thigh, flip-flops *pap papp*ing their way through the rows of parked cars.

In the wine section, Brooke grabbed two bottles of white—brands more expensive than he'd have chosen—and started to stalk off again. A little more plaintively than he wanted to sound, he said, "Hey!" and she finally turned around to face him.

"What is with you?" he said.

Brooke flicked her bangs out of her eyes, a habit she'd had since they were little kids. Cords leapt in her neck. "With me? Are you serious?"

"Yeah, with you."

She started to speak and stopped, turned to look at the shelves beside them, the long aisles of tiered bottles. When she faced him again, he couldn't tell if it was fury or tears that were about to brim over, but he'd clearly placed a dubious value on forgetting a bottle of eight-dollar white for his mom.

"Do you have a fucking clue what's going on?" she said. "Like, at all? In your life?"

He reared back, frowning. "Hey, easy."

"No, I'm serious. I love you, Bri, but you are just screwing up, hardcore. You're just treading water; you can't even remember to get a bottle of wine for Mom, who's, like, hanging on by her fingernails. To just let her know you're thinking of her. The most basic things."

A stitch of anger ran through him, heated and quick. "Right," he said. "Cool, Brooke. The air must be thin up there, on that high horse of yours."

She rolled her eyes as a small woman with a shellacked helmet of hair scooted past them, one wheel of her cart squeaking loudly. Of *course* he was treading water! They all knew it! She didn't have to say it!

"This is a conversation we've had before," she said.

"What, you lecturing me about how to live my life? You're right, we have."

"Oh, so this is living?" She gestured at him like a host on a game show. "In school for the rest of your life? Afraid to graduate?"

"I'm not afraid to graduate, Jesus. Besides, at least I'm not a thirty-one-year-old *bartender.*"

"What is wrong with— You know what, never mind." Brooke rolled her eyes again and started to walk off toward the registers.

This was, of course, a pointless barb to fling her way, but it was the best he could do. Unfortunately, it was also one that he used on her with unsurprising frequency. He could be Don Whitmer's age, decorated, with a PhD in anthro and the head of his department, and he'd still lose every argument to Brooke, who tended bar at the Oak and Fiddle five nights a week and was taking business classes at the community college. She was just quicker than him, and always had been.

Brian sighed. "Hold on," he said, and walked up and gently took the bottles from her. "Sorry," he said quietly. "I love you, too. I know Mom's having a tough time." Brooke nodded, flicked her bangs away with a finger.

This, for the most part, was what passed for conciliation among the Schutts.

• • •

Sunny Meadows: dozens of buildings winding a drunken, circuitous path around a field of dead and beaten grass, a jungle gym, a single basketball hoop on a swatch of buckled blacktop. Nearby was a pool, its bottom painted an impossible blue, though this time of year it lay covered with a tarp. Brooke never got lost, always found their mother's apartment amid the hundreds of apartments just like it. Even now, at night, when every building took on an eerie similarity, she drove with a confidence and surety that Brian lacked in, well, everything. Like some homing radar activated, he assumed, by her unfettered confidence and moral superiority.

She pulled into a visitor parking spot and turned the stereo down; some rockabilly guy crooning about the hot sweats faded to background noise. "So," she said, "when Mom talks about Dad tonight, try not to be a jerk."

He frowned. "Okay. Cool. When Mom looks at your outfit, try not to buckle under her obvious disappointment in you."

"You have got to expand your repertoire. You have, like, two jokes and they both suck."

"I'm just saying, I think your suspicion is unwarranted. I'm always nice to Mom."

"Ha," she said.

"I am. I don't need a lesson in how to talk to Mom."

"Just don't be a dumbass."

"You're the dumbass." He was thirty years old and they still fell into this easy cadence. "By the way, how do you do that?"

They stepped out into a night that smelled of cut grass, motor oil, honeysuckle. Brooke eyed him over the roof of the car. She'd put on a hoodie, and beneath it, her bright pink bangs hung over one eye. "Do what?"

"You always find Mom's place with no problem. This place is like a maze. I'm expecting, like, a minotaur to jump out and bite me in the ass."

"Brian, she lives in apartment 341-B. It's not like she moves around from building to building. It's the same apartment every time."

Cassie was surprised to see them. She opened the door and spent a moment staring at her children as if she was trying to place where she'd seen them before. She held a hand at her throat (Brian noted the light liver spots there with a mixture of quiet sorrow and a fierce bloom of almost animalistic loyalty) and then her mouth opened and a sound came out—"Ohhhhh!"—that was half frustration, half recrimination. Brian could see moving boxes stacked against the wall behind their father's recliner.

Brooke smiled and leaned against the doorframe. "You forgot, right?"

She ushered them in. "Oh, hush. I thought it was tomorrow, is all."

Kisses, hugs, and the three of them stood in the kitchen and gathered stock of the available ingredients for a makeshift dinner. "Man," Brian said, presenting the bottles of wine to his mother, "we should have brought stuff. We were just at the store."

It was a grim affair. There was the wine and an unopened bag of Avocado Oil Sea Salt potato chips. Rooting through her purse, Brooke laid out three protein bars and half a roll of Fruit Punch Life Savers. Cassie laughed and ripped open the chips while her children peered in her refrigerator. It was desolate: a line of condiments rescued from the old house, a half-empty container of white rice dried brittle as gravel. A bag of salad mix in the crisper that had turned to black slurry. Brian shut the fridge door and saw his mother sitting at the kitchen island, drinking wine from a pickle jar. Nine months since she'd moved into the new place and she still had yet to really unpack. She wiggled her eyebrows at him over the rim. His mother was in stasis, and how could he, of all people, get mad at her for that?

Brooke stood on her tiptoes and peered into a cupboard. "Don't you believe in food, Mom? Where's your food?"

"I work sixty hours a week, friendo. Who the heck has time to go shopping?"

"But you make food for a living."

"Exactly," Cassie said, and as if that answered something, lifted her pickle jar again.

On top of the fridge, Brian found two spotted bananas in a cardboard box of cookware, their stems poking from between the black handles of pots and pans bristling from the top. "How did these land here, Mom? Did you throw them from over there? Was it like a boomerang-type situation?"

"I just put them there. I set them there. What's with the interrogation?"

"They're, like, super mushy."

"I brought them from work a while back."

"Ah, bananas," Brian said. "Bananas and half a thing of rice and some chips. Taking good care of yourself, Mom."

When Cassie wasn't looking, Brooke fired him a look. He shrugged, opened his palms.

Consensus was quickly reached: they would go out to eat. They passed through the jumble of their mother's apartment. Outside, Cassie fished through her purse and locked the door and there was something about it, about seeing his mom grown a little smaller, a little more hunched and shriveled and way more sad since the divorce, locking the door to this apartment. Locking a door that was one among hundreds—her door right next to that door right next to that door—that hurt him in a way he couldn't really describe. The seamed flesh at her neck as she dropped her keys inside that horrible macramé purse the size of a duffel bag, the blue veins worming over the rigid bones of her hand—it tightened his throat a little. Watching your parent navigate the topography of heartbreak, especially as they aged . . . It sucked. Brooke was right.

They walked to a pizza place across the street from the complex. With the grammatically unfortunate name of Piece A' Pizza, it was bracketed by a mail supply store and a nail salon, and the whole thing could've been the site of a toxic spill for the lack of cars out front.

There were no other customers inside. They had to walk through a trellis wrapped in fake ivy to place their order, and their cashier was a sullen teenage girl wearing a hat shaped like a slice of pizza. She took their order, managing impressively to seethe with a blazing hatred and contempt—for them all, for the job, for the classic rock playing overhead at a nearly subliminal level—all without saying a word. She even managed to seethe against the hat. It was all there. Brian, watching her stab the register with her fingers, felt a curious lift. He almost wanted to high five her.

Brooke paid for dinner. She almost always paid, really; Brian buying the wine had been an anomaly clearly born of guilt. Tending bar, and with the capitalist urges of a Trappist monk and a frugality and work ethic that bordered on relentless, Brooke made a hell of a lot more money than he did. People meeting them together for the first time were always confused: with her full-color tattoo sleeves that bled up onto her neck, her knuckle tattoos and piercings, hair always dyed or bleached and in some varying state of intended dishevelment, Brooke had always been the one that vibed as the screwup between them. The disaster. But she was sober, resolutely single, taking her business admin classes, and focused (if not entirely myopic) on getting a nest egg together to invest in Portland's housing market before the city became untenable. She had her shit together. Brian, meanwhile, had that pasty academic look down pat; the patchy beard over a constellation of chin zits, unwashed hair, the gut mounded around his long sleeve button-up or his ironic T-shirt, his sagging backpack. He was a thirty-year-old man wearing a backpack! He looked the straighter of the two, but also usually looked like he'd just come from feverishly masturbating behind some book carrel somewhere. So, yeah. Looks be damned, whose life was in shambles, and whose wasn't?

"Thanks for the pizza," he said, and for once she didn't say anything snide back.

The booth squeaked along his haunches as he sat down and scooted over. Brooke sat down next to him. Cassie got in the other side of the booth, swirling her wineglass around.

"How's that pizza-wine treating you, Mom?" Brooke asked.

Cassie smiled. "Oh, stop."

Traffic chugged along outside the window. He thought half-heartedly about bringing up the interview with Sandoval—if only to tell his mom about how weird it was to see Don Whitmer removed from his own desk, kind of emasculated like that, since she pretty much thought the man walked on water and was the only thing that stood between Brian and destitution—but there'd be so much additional stuff to unpack alongside it. Specifically, why he was interviewing for such a thing to begin with, in the middle of the school year. He'd spoken to Brooke about his ABD plans but had sworn her to secrecy. So far she'd relented, even as she'd gone slack-jawed at his idiocy. Besides, by that evening, the whole interview thing had taken on the quality of an uneasy dream. Not necessarily bad, but a little off. Strange. He wasn't even quite sure how to frame it to himself, much less talk about it.

Cassie, as if testing her motherly mind-reading skills, set her wineglass down and said, "So, Bri. How's school?"

"Good," he lied. "Hung out with Don Whitmer today, went over some stuff. Things are good." Under the table, Brooke clacked his ankle with her boot. He smiled at her and kicked her back.

"That man," Cassie said. "Give him my best."

"Will do."

"How's the dissertation coming, hon?"

"Yeah, Brian," said Brooke, "how's the dissertation?"

"It's fine," he managed. "Slow. But I'm pushing through. It'll happen."

"Any idea when you'll submit it?" His mother took another sip of wine. When he was in grad school, she had been very into this idea of him *defending* his thesis, as if there had been chain mail involved, or a gunfight, rather than Brian sitting in front of a bunch of his teachers answering the inevitable softballs they'd tossed his way.

"Well, I still have to finish it first. Then there's the review. It's all still a ways away." He buried his face in his cup of soda. His mother cast a glance at Brooke, then back at him, and before he could wonder if she knew more than he thought she knew, or suspected more than he thought she suspected, they moved on. Brooke told them about a housing seminar she went to, how quickly prices were rising even further out of town, deep south and north. Cassie regaled her children with an admittedly pretty funny story (in a Cassie kind of way) about one of the women she contracted catering stuff out to who came down with a sneezing fit while on the phone with a client. When his sister and mother started talking about his father, he drifted. They were a family navigating their collective waters as best they could. His sister and mother, his fractured thirds—they loved each other. He knew it. And yet there was a sense—wasn't there?—that they were all kind of strangers to each other in vastly important but unspecified ways. And that was really kind of terrible, wasn't it? That chasm? Theirs was a fierce, stodgy, complicated love, awkward and entwined with so many other things. A love crafted, perhaps, from obligation, from their shared history. And worse, he felt obligated to defend his father in some small indefinable way. The intractable weight of blood, of family. And that in and of itself pissed him off more than anything.

Get me, he thought again, *the hell out of here.*

The girl with the pizza-slice hat came and slid their pizza onto the table, departing without a word.

"She is not happy here," Cassie noted, watching as the girl walked away.

"I love it," Brian said. "She'll destroy us all."

"So," his mother said, picking up a thread from some earlier point in the conversation he'd drifted from, "you'll love this. It's part of a 'clothing-optional personal recreation facility,' apparently. That's what they're calling it."

A tendril of cheese hung gelatinous and steaming from Brooke's plate to the pizza tin. She leaned forward, twirled it around her finger, slurped it up. "What does that even mean? That doesn't sound like anything. That's like a bunch of different words grabbed out of a hat."

"Oh, it's all tax related," Cassie said. She pulled a slice onto her plate, considered it for a moment and picked up her wine glass again. "It's all a big tax write-off for the whole sad-ass lot of them." She paused. "The fuckers." Brook and Brian shared a quick side-eyed look, there and gone. This was a new thing with their mom, the swearing.

"Asshole," Brooke said.

"You got that right," said their mother. Brian ate his pizza.

The divorce had opened new, untold avenues of hurt inside their mom. That much was obvious. Granted, their dad had left in a spectacularly shitty fashion, but in spite of the Houdini-like speed with which he had essentially vanished from their lives, it was still a slow pull of a Band-Aid when it came to discovering how much it hurt. They were all still feeling it, still exploring its boundaries. Brian still found himself vacillating between relief and resentment at the man's absence.

The previous fall, their father had left with Traci, a twenty-four-year-old nutritional supplement saleswoman who worked at his gym. This was immediately after Cassie had found a message window open on his computer that spelled out the long-running affair between the two, complete with a bevy of graphic sexual requests via his father and lots of emojis and some pretty smart puns, if Brooke was to be believed, about both Tantric sex and nutritional health from Traci. Brian had no interest in reading the offending message thread; he got his information from his sister and mother. Though as far as he knew, his mother still carried a folded, worn printout of the exchange in her purse, stapled in the corner like the world's crappiest school assignment.

Once he'd been called out on the affair, his dad hadn't denied it. Instead, he'd quickly and secretly cashed in a bunch of his stocks and his 401k and then absconded with Traci to live in what amounted to a high-end nudist colony outside Scottsdale, Arizona. His mother, working her sixty hours a week at a catering business she co-owned, suddenly found herself bereft of a husband, unable to make house payments on her own, her life pretty much upended. She hired a PI to look into the nudist colony. She and his father promptly began savaging each other in the court system. From what Brian could discern, his father's new digs sounded somewhat like Sunny Meadows, except with gates and a guard and clearance lanyards and—this is the part that hollowed his mom out, he could see it—a "clothing-free" option. Not to mention the twenty-four-year-old nutritionist.

There were rumors in nearby taverns, the PI had reported in his weekly summary, that wife-swapping abounded in the complex, that there was some kind of weird polyamory thing going on. Brooke—since she could stomach the details of their parent's marriage unraveling in a way that he couldn't—had seen the photos the PI had sent. Traci was, by all accounts, the youngest member in the complex by at least few decades.

"They do yoga in the morning," Brooke once told him. "Like, the whole compound, or facility, or whatever it is. Thirty or forty people doing the downward dog on the tennis courts. Naked. Their little yoga mats. Teats hanging all pendulous."

"Oh my God, Brooke. Stop."

"That private investigator has pictures."

"Gross."

"Red knees. Knobby elbows. Big old lady-bush gone all gray and wiry."

He said, "You are so full of shit."

"Traci's had a boob job, Brian. I can tell. She's got a tattoo on her lower back."

"Like a tramp stamp? The private investigator took pictures of Traci's tramp stamp? Isn't that illegal?"

"It says 'No Regerts,' Brian. Misspelled. *In cursive.*"

"You are so lying."

"Dad's old gray balls, swinging in the breeze. You can see his bald spot, too."

"You're telling me you've seen a picture of Dad's balls. While he does yoga. Naked."

"Hell yes, I have. It made me sick."

"I don't believe it."

"Well, whether or not you believe it doesn't change the fact that it's seared into my retinas for the rest of my life. It doesn't change the fact that he can go to hell."

So now, over pizza, Cassie regaled them with updates. It could be distilled down to this, really: court, court, more court. Their father flew back and forth when necessary, Scottsdale to Portland and back. But mostly it was lawyers lobbing legalities at each other. Their father was resolute in his arrogance, his belief in a lack of wrongdoing—this in and of itself was not that much of a surprise to anyone. It was his defining quality. That and his distance. He'd always been a workaholic, and ultimately kind of a shithead when forced into proximity of his family for long stretches. Like they were his kryptonite; the longer he was near them, the more irritable he got. It was his second marriage; his first wife lived in Maryland somewhere. They'd only been married a year, when Dad had been in college. Still, this affair, and the savagery of his contempt for their mother, had surprised them all.

After dinner, the three of them walked back to Sunny Meadows. Soon even this stretch of land would be one vast metropolis. The weedy hills beyond the apartment complex would also be leveled and filled with more boxes of people. It felt inevitable, given the velocity of the world now. They walked, and he watched his sister slip her hand into his mother's hand. In that moment he felt both apart from and feverishly touched with love for them.

Back at Cassie's apartment, they watched television. Their father had taken little more than a change of clothes with him to the nudist colony, as weird as that was, and the flatscreen was just too big for the new living room. The edge of it actually jutted out into the hallway that led to the rest of the apartment; you had to be careful not to knock into it. Brooke laid on the couch with her feet in their mother's lap; Brian sprawled out across his father's recliner. He unpacked his own pickle jar from a box in the kitchen, and he and his mom tackled the second bottle of wine together.

They got stuck on some old show that Brian vaguely remembered from high school, long canceled and relegated to the darkest corners of random odd-channel syndication. What was it called again? The star of the show was an anthropomorphic plate of outrageously flirtatious lasagna living among a human family, each of whom endlessly struggled with their love lives. That was, like, the whole premise: this horny plate of lasagna trying to bang this family that tried to bang everyone else. So weird. The teenaged children, a brother and sister, one in college, the other in high school, plowed through romantic partners like they were visiting a buffet table; the mother was continually exhausted from the father's brutish, joke-heavy, ceaseless advances. All the while the lasagna, moored to the kitchen table and seemingly desperate to copulate with a human of any gender or orientation, oozed lascivious remarks and sexual innuendo. It was never explained why or how lasagna-human relations were desired or, really, possible. Or even why they perpetually left that particular plate of lasagna on the table, or how it had gained sentience. The show had aired for only a season or two and had been canceled years ago. The lasagna itself was essentially a hand puppet slathered in cheese and meat, flaps of calcified pasta jittering as it spoke in a cynical, cigarette-ravaged rasp.

"This is fucking weird," Brooke said from the couch.

"Brian used to love this show," Cassie said.

"I did not."

Brooke snorted. "This seems like something Brian would like. You could relate, right?"

"You did, honey. When you were in high school," Cassie said. "It was always on when you were in high school." She was getting a little buzzed.

"Well, can we change it now? I can assure you the allure is lost on me these days."

Cassie flipped through the channels. Golf. News. Golf news. A woman shoving a plug of hamburger into an apparatus that pushed it out the other end in pink strings. Tanks rolling down some dusty, rubble-strewn road, impossible to tell if it was a film or a newsreel. The viral video of that dog leaping from the tree, the cat safely in its jaws. And there, wonder of wonders, was the film adaptation of *The Long Way Home*. They watched as a young Brad Pitt abruptly hitchhiked away from his small Seattle apartment, away from his dissolute marriage, his failed academic career. (Lolled across the recliner, Brian felt a flush of embarrassment rise to his cheeks at what seemed the brazen similarities to his own life.) The film eventually cut to some lonely stretch of wooded road, some interminable point beyond the city. Brad looked, honestly, pretty fucking Hollywood-handsome compared to some of the mutants that Brian knew and had gone to school with, himself included. Even in his dumb canvas jacket and worn cardigan, his five o'clock shadow, the guy seemed just too pretty to pull off being the frazzled, broken academic-on-a-soul-search type.

Yet the Schutts were enrapt, and Brian thought again of saying something about his interview with Mark Sandoval that day, but it was still too big of a jigsaw puzzle to unpack. In the film, Pitt smoked a joint with a trucker and got dropped off at a diner. He poured syrup on his hash browns with mournful eyes. Sparks flew between him and the waitress—again, Jennifer Garner looked like a million bucks considering she was snared in the graveyard shift at a diner in the ass-end of nowhere—before he paid his bill and wandered away into the night, only to step off into the brush a short while later, reasonably high, to take a piss. And then came the cone of light, the paralysis, the terror. The abduction, the paralyzed limbs. The probe that snaked its way through a tear duct, and the gossamer-thin ones that entered beneath his fingernails, the one writhing down his throat. The off-camera implication that the asshole, the urethra were also invaded. Pitt screaming and bucking beneath the white light. No aliens around at all, just that halo, those invasive threads. It was, Brian remembered, pretty close to what Sandoval had written in the book. It had landed Pitt an Oscar nomination.

"Ooooh, my Brad," their mother cooed, "not down the wiener, Brad, I'm so sorry," and Brooke let out a bright peal of laughter like a little kid.

Even Brian did. A pure and unplanned moment, an oddly sweet one given the wretchedness of the scene before them, and for a moment that odd collection of rooms warmed toward a home; the place became more than an odd repository of their mother's ghosts. He felt for a moment like they were people forming scar tissue together, healing together.

By the end of the movie Cassie was asleep, her chin tucked down, pickle jar nestled in her lap. Brooke walked her into her bedroom and tucked her in and they left. "Goodnight, babies," he heard her say from her bedroom as they stepped out into a night grown cool and rich with the sound of crickets. The wine had left him with another headache.

Brooke jammed on the heater of her little compact Hyundai. She pulled out of the complex and the first thing she said was, "I think we should disown the fucker."

"Who? Dad?"

"No, Rodney Dangerfield. Yes, Dad."

"I don't think it works like that."

"I'm just saying. It's kicking Mom's ass. She can't even afford that PI. I'm helping pay for him."

He was surprised. "You are?"

She nodded grimly. "What else does she have going on for her? I hope she takes him for every dime. I hope Traci loses her frigging saline bags in the settlement."

"I don't think Traci will have to actually give up anything, will she?"

She scowled at him, incredulous. "You do get that Mom's just putting on a good show for us, right?"

"I don't know. It's Mom."

"It's Mom?"

"Brooke, she just seemed happy to have us there. We got to have dinner, watch a movie. We got to hang out with her. She seemed fine to me. She seemed like Mom, you know?"

"Your whole life ripped out like that after someone's dumb enough to leave a chat box open." She bit her lower lip, changed lanes. "Just no fucking loyalty, you know? Dad can take his downward dog and stick it up his ass."

She dropped him off in front of his house. The night was cool, idyllic. He stepped out and leaned down at the open car door. "Thanks for the ride."

She gazed out the windshield with her hands wrapped around the wheel. "Listen. Just try thinking of some people besides yourself, Brian. Just try it out, see how it feels."

He pulled back a little. "Wait, what?"

"I'm just saying. Mom's going through a lot."

"Brooke. We're all going through a lot. We've all got stuff going on. This constant hard-ass thing you have going on, it's tiring."

"She's our mom. That's all I'm saying."

"I know that. And I'm saying I don't need a guilt trip, okay? I fail to see what horrible thing I did tonight."

"Mom needs us to stick up for her."

"I did stick up for her!"

"Not enough."

"Why? Because I didn't call Dad an asshole with you guys? I didn't join in the group assassination? Seriously, Brooke. Because I ate pizza instead of talking endless shit about Dad?"

"Whatever."

"Yeah, whatever."

He shut the passenger door, probably too hard, and Brooke drove off in a flare of red taillights. And just like that, that good feeling that he'd felt in his mom's apartment, like they were all coming together into something unbroken, that was gone. He stood in front of his house feeling like he'd stumbled further back than when he'd started.

2

So he turned around. Walked away from the house. Strode down those ever-familiar streets, his head blurred with anger. *Maybe Mom just wants to be listened to, Brooke. Maybe she doesn't need you to roll in and be her avenging white knight.* What did she want him to do, build an effigy of their father and light it up in the Piece A' Pizza parking lot? Loose some daddy-hurt howl and kick it in its flaming balls? Christ.

Walking, walking, he stepped over a Rorschach of vomit in front of a shuttered boutique where headless mannequins stood draped wraithlike in the window. He stepped over a smeared slice of pizza with a boot print in it. A man in front of the Saturn Hotel was talking to himself, waving his hand at his head as if besieged by gnats. He saw ECHO LUVS B in big looping letters on a wall, the ghost of old piss snarling in the air around him. A jukebox throbbed through the open doorway of a bar when someone stepped outside to smoke, and the laughter from inside sounded like it came from a different world.

He turned south, hooked around the corner, and the block went from bright to dark just like that. Streetlights stood moored at the corners, but there was nothing in between but an expanse of neon-scattered dark, traffic at his back and up ahead of him.

And there was a car stopped in the middle of the street, with the dark shapes of men clustered around it.

He heard someone titter and dread coiled fast in his guts; someone slapped the car's hood, and as if in response, the headlights flared to life, illuminating the street. Brian saw four guys standing around a white four-door Toyota with a sagging bumper. One of them slapped the hood again, his face ghoulish and undercut by the headlights, and Brian heard someone say, very clearly, "Knock him back to Coonbekistan," everyone loosing a chorus of laughter. Sour spit flooded Brian's mouth as he slowed his walk, heart seized in a panic.

He was soft, man. He'd always been soft. Soft-muscled, soft-*boned*. Ran a thirteen-minute mile in high school, dicking around, afraid to try. Saw himself as a sausage-casing of a man swaddled in academia and ironic T-shirts that seemed forever bunched too tight around his gut. Saw himself in pants that cut continually into his waist as he ran to catch busses that inevitably pulled away from him, exhaust clouding at his knees. Knife-thin lips and a double chin he tried unsuccessfully to hide behind a wan beard. Beleaguered with constant headaches that no washcloth or painkiller or darkened room could fix. Afraid of women and conflict both. Afraid, simultaneously, of succeeding and failing. Afraid all around! Of everything! Fathered by a distant, litigious, beleaguered nudist. Sibling to the fiercest person he knew, who managed to talk to him simultaneously with pity and utter contempt. *That* was who he was. That'd always been him. It was fine. It was his world.

But what it meant was that he was soft, he was a body-pillow of a man, and yet here he was and there were four of these guys. One of him, four of them. They'd said what they'd said, and he was soft, but that thing at the bus stop when he was sixteen, that guy at the bus stop: it was something that still kept him up nights sometimes, still had the ability to galvanize him with shame all these years later.

His throat seemed to close up a little, his legs already thrumming with adrenaline, when one of them stepped back and took a little bouncing step and kicked the passenger door. It buckled inward with an awful metallic *pong.* Then the driver opened his door and stepped out, yelling. Older guy, brown-skinned, a tight cap of white hair, white mustache. A grandfather. Slacks and a blue T-shirt. He was yelling in Arabic, pointing over the roof of the car at all of them. How old were these guys? Midtwenties? They looked like anyone. They looked like random assholes. Two had fashy haircuts, the consummate tonsorial decision of the white nationalist, but the other two were bearded and sloppy-looking dudes like him. They all had this casual air about them, like they were on their way to Drill to pick up on women and had just randomly decided to harass this old man on the way there. Fear rooted Brian to the ground, squared his feet to earth. He took his phone out of his pocket and started filming.

The driver slammed the door shut and stepped into the headlights himself, still pointing, still yelling. He started toward the guy who had kicked the door when another one of them blocked his way with a hand on his chest, kind of leaned his face into the man's field of view. "You're in the wrong country, Habib. You're not welcome. The fuck out of here."

Another said, "No Muslims allowed, my man. You're not welcome. Go home. *Go home.*"

The one who kicked the door—or the one next to him? They were all roving around, sharks in the water—said, "Head back to the cave. Take your people back to the dunes." It was almost jovial, which made it all the more terrifying. Brian's legs were trembling so hard he pictured how those newborn foals came fresh out of the womb, tumbling out and testing gravity on the wobbling stilts of their legs, flung hard into the world and trying to get their shit together fast.

The driver stepped back and cleared his throat and said, "Fuck you" very clearly. He kept his chin high. There was a moment of silence and then someone kicked one of the headlights in with a boot heel, this plastic-sounding crunch, and oh fuck, someone punched the old man in the face. He sagged against the hood, his hands curling over his head.

"Hey," Brian called out sharply. The word tumbled out of his mouth, surprising him as much as anyone. They all turned. Everything was jittery and grainy on his phone, the near-lightless night.

"Hey, drop that bitch," someone said. "Drop that fat little bitch."

Almost happily, one of them said, "He's filming us? Holy shit."

Everything took on the cadence of a whirlwind. Brian, saturated with nerves, asshole puckered in animal terror, took a step back as two of the guys strode up to him. He kept filming. A Ford Explorer drove down the street, threading its way past the Toyota. It didn't stop. The other two guys had the old man against the hood and they were hitting him. Brian could hear his grunts, could see their fists arcing above the lights and coming back down, fast and vicious. The two in front of Brian were grinning, standing in the gutter, bouncing on their toes and looking up at him.

"So," said Brian, his throat clicking and impossibly dry, his phone held out before the pair of them, "just out harassing brown guys, huh?"

"Oh, he's filming. He thinks he's a journalist," said one.

"He thinks he's antifa," said the other.

"*I see what you're doing over there,*" Brian yelled.

The old man had sagged to the ground by now. No one was doing shit about it. The world, the whole loud world was just right over there, right down the street where the light was, with the cars and the noise and the people. Here, there were just these young, emboldened boys and the man curled against the bumper of his car, his arms wrapped around his head.

He told himself to hit them, hit them back for the old man, but he knew he didn't have it in him.

The guy on Brian's left reached out, tried to snag his phone. Brian turned, kept filming. Someone grabbed his collar, fingernails raking his neck, and the rest happened fast.

The first few punches to his mouth blurred his sense of gravity—he was standing and then he was adrift—and then he felt the scrape of cement beneath his palms. He was down, covering his face, curling up. Kicking out until someone grabbed his leg and he turtled. The two of them worked hard above him, panting, but a lot of the punches glanced off, hit his shoulders, bounced off the hard bark of his head. At one point it felt like his ear was nearly torn off, that flare of pain almost the exact opposite of his headaches: a sudden searing heat, like a match being lit. He bellowed. A punch to his cheek bounced his head against the pavement, and after that things took on a loose, watery quality; something slightly painful was happening, but in another room somewhere.

He lay there some indeterminable amount of time. The clarity of cement against his cheek the only irrefutable thing. That and the heat in his ear. Things swelled inside him, thrummed symphonically, and next the world imploded, grew leached of its color. fell to something pinhole small, and then was gone.

• • •

Hands next. Hands on him.

Hands *touching* him, and he scrabbled to fight back and barked like a dog through that napalm throb inside his head, through the grasping fog of the napalm grays, and there was a black man in latex gloves above him, in latex gloves and a blue shirt, and he was saying, "Hold on, man. You're injured. Hold on. Don't move." His voice was calm, sonorous, patient, and Brian crab-walked away from him until he hit a wall, the grit of pavement beneath his palms. Knowledge in his head like being born again: a vast empty chamber, just the pain and the stuttering, fractured memory of the men hurting him. And then the paramedic was reaching down, reaching toward him with those gloved hands.

Once again the night dimmed and grew dark.

• • •

The susurration of a vehicle, the sway. The wail of an ambulance somewhere. Shit. It was here, that sound. Inside here.

He was inside the ambulance. Strapped in.

Brian's first thought: *No way in hell I can afford this.*

He could see the frosted delineation of the ambulance's six-pointed star in the vehicle's window, and the ghostly, muffled wail of the siren cocooned around them. Antiseptic smell. He tried to move his head, but they had his neck locked in something. One eye was tightening shut. Everything inside him felt hot and shattered.

"Relax, my friend," said the EMT. He had a little gold nametag pinned above his left pocket that said *Hamms*, like the beer, and Brian noted with a kind of detached wonderment the minute spattering of blood across the man's shirtfront. Nearly ink black on the blue fabric. "Looks like you got in a tussle, yeah?" he said. Still that calm, deep voice.

"These guys." Brian's voice sounded funny. Slurry.

"Yeah? Gonna shine this in your eyes for a sec. Just look straight ahead." He bounced a penlight from one of Brian's pupils to the other. "You got jumped by some guys?"

"They were messing with this old guy in his car. Four guys." The napalm throbbed; he wanted to close both eyes, sleep forever.

"Yeah?" Hamms pushed against the bottom of Brian's foot with his fingertips. "Can you feel that?"

"Yeah."

He pulled on Brian's ankle. "That?"

"Yes. They kicked his . . . his . . ."

Hamms smiled. "Ass?"

"No, what's the word. Lamplight. Not lamplight, the thing in front of your car." All of a sudden the words were right behind some doorway, obscured but almost visible. Answers spied through gauze. He could picture it but couldn't find the sounds to match it.

"A headlight?"

Brian nodded. "The headlight. They kicked his headlight in. Kicked his door. Kicked his ass, too, I guess. Bad."

"What's your name, my friend?"

Brian told him.

"Someone called 911 on you, Brian. It was just you lying there when we rolled up."

Brian closed his eyes. "He was like a Muslim guy. Or they thought he was. These white nationalist guys. Nazis."

"Well, it was just you when we got there. Somebody got you real good, though." They hit a pothole and Hamms swayed a little above him. Brian heard the crinkle of the paper crisply wrapped over his gurney.

"Is my ear still on?"

Hamms peered down, nodded. "Probably need some stitches though." Brian caught a trace of something, his aftershave or deodorant. Cinnamon, maybe.

"There's no way my insurance covers this. I'm so fucked. This is like a million dollars, right? I can't even really feel anything."

"I'm thinking you're in shock, bud. We'll get you checked out just to be sure. You took some hits. Better safe than sorry."

"Oh shit. My phone. Did you grab my phone?"

Hamms winced. "Sorry. Didn't see a phone."

Brian closed his eyes and Hamms urged him to keep them open. He asked Brian the year. The month. The day. Brian named them all. Kept thinking of the febrile crunch of the headlight, the way that man had curled up so small against the bumper of his car, so childlike. And had it really only been an hour ago, the argument with Brooke? Less? It felt like it had happened in another life. He'd just had pizza with his mother! Served by a morose high-schooler in a pizza-slice hat! His dissertation was growing a fur of dust in his bedroom. This was some other world, this ambulance, some dark, errant fork in the road.

It was time for the IV, and Hamms effortlessly connected the needle with the bag of saline solution next to Brian's head and then connected both to his arm. "Gonna be a pinch." He kept asking questions. Who the President was. Vice President. What city they were in. County.

When they arrived at the hospital, Brian tried to stand but Hamms insisted he be pushed into the ER while still on the gurney. He pushed him through the emergency entrance and down a hall, left him flush against a wall by the nurse's station, bid him goodbye with a wink and a pat on the arm. Brian lay there, immobile. He could see the lobby of the emergency room and felt embarrassed to be lying down. Each person in the emergency room sat in their little orbit of anguish or discomfort. A disheveled, assumedly homeless man sat in one of the plastic bucket seats with a black garbage bag tied around his sleeveless bicep, muttering furiously at the muted television screen in the corner of the room, as if it had personally wronged him. Blood lay in dried rusty threads down his forearm to his palm. A bent and white-haired couple, small and wizened, sat huddled next to each other, the woman's hand curled around the man's arm as she silently wept and pressed a tissue to her nose. A little boy sat with his mother, who nursed a cup of soda nearly as big as her head. She stared at her phone while the boy, with a galaxy of dried snot around his nostrils, chanted, "Fart. *Butt.* Fart. *Butt*," and kicked his heels against his chair legs with each word. Brian turned his head and stared up at the ceiling.

"Fart. *Butt.* Fart. *Butthole.*"

Without looking up from her phone, the mother said, "Joel, shush it."

"Fart, fart, *butthole.* Fart, fart, *butthole.*"

"Shush it now, for reals."

A nurse came by. Ponytailed, grim, ageless, and entirely well versed—he could tell by the way she looked down at him, both there and not there—at stemming the tide of her little pocket of chaos. She said, "Can you write?"

"Sure," Brian said, and she handed him a clipboard and a pen. He thought about calling Brooke, thought about basking in that sweet moment where she'd feel terrible about the way she'd spoken to him, when he told her he had an IV drip, that he was bloodied and shoved against a wall in the ER. But he decided against it; feeling bad wasn't really part of Brooke's lexicon. Besides, oh yeah, no phone.

"Fart. *Butt.* Fart. *Butt.* Fart *up* a butthole, fart *up around* it."

"Joel! You shush it now! Don't make momma smack you."

He put Ellis as his emergency contact, his phone number rising phantom-like in Brian's mind. Under *Symptoms You Are Currently Experiencing,* he started with *Face smashed in by Nazis,* then crossed it out and wrote *Face trauma.* He thought of other symptoms as well, considered writing them down: *torpor, lack of motivation, heart-seizing flurries of encroaching mortality, saber-sharp insecurity, a wickedly diminished desire to fuck. Overweight. Afraid.* He put *Consistent headache for years* instead. The nurse came by and smiled this time when she took his clipboard. "A doctor will be by in just a minute," she said. "We'll get you all taken care of."

"Fart. *Mouth.* Fart. *Mouth.* Fartmouth! Mouthfart!"

"That is *it,* mister man!"

There was a moment of silence, a harsh, ragged intake of breath, and then the little boy's yowls filled the room. Brian lay there and listened as little Joel was reminded—as they all were—how it was that life really worked.

3

He was eventually wheeled into a kind of large staging area, a long room sectioned off with a series of standing blue curtains where all the people on gurneys apparently went before they were sent to their final destination—to surgery, a hospital room, some other realm. His gurney was slotted into a space by another nurse who then left him alone, the curtain pulled mostly shut. The open wedge showed an occasional staff member zipping by, or, once, an owlish old man with a walker who caught Brian's eye and scowled at him through the fabric as if Brian was personally responsible for his woes. He caught an eyeful of the man's leathery, drooping ass through the back of his hospital gown before the old man was intercepted and lead back to his own bed.

When Dr. Bajeer entered his little cloister and introduced himself, it was clear that here was a man who had never doubted himself, at least not while working the ER floor. A man much more accustomed to Brooke's way of being, her laser focus, her unwavering confidence. He was a short, calm man, and he frowned at Brian's chart as if he could discern the fate of the world from it. He looked to be Brian's age, give or take, though he had a severe demarcation of white hair right above his ears, little racing stripes. After what seemed like a long time but probably was not, the doctor looked up at him, seemed to finally take in his battered face, the blood on his shirt.

"Mr. Schutt, how are we feeling?"

"Um. We're not feeling so hot."

Dr. Bajeer nodded, offered the quickest ghost of a smile. "I understand, yes. What I would like, with your permission, is to ask you some questions."

"I've been getting a lot of that."

"Yes. We want to see if there's, ah, any brain trauma, you know?"

"Sure."

The same cavalcade of questions: *What year, month, day was it?*
Did he know where he was?
Could he follow Dr. Bajeer's finger?
Could he hear in each ear?

Could he feel Dr. Bajeer tug on his finger?
Did he have sensations in both sides of his face?
Could he shrug his shoulders?

"Is it okay if I do that?" said Brian. He lifted his arm, gestured at the neck brace he was locked into.

"Sure," said Dr. Bajeer.

Brian shrugged.

"Okay," Dr. Bajeer said, clicking his pen a few times, scribbling a note. "Now just some questions. This is called a Mini-Mental Status Examination. It's just to check on, like I said, head trauma, possible brain injury. And then we can get a nurse in here and get you stitched up, looks like you need a few in your lip there."

"And my ear."

"And your ear, okay. You ready?"

"Sure," Brian said. Compliant as dough, growing tired. What other choice did he have?

Could he name these two objects Dr. Bajeer was holding? This wristwatch and this pen?

He could.

Could he repeat the phrase No ifs, ands, or buts?

He could. "I don't know if this is super important," he said.

Could he count backward by sevens from one hundred?

"One hundred," Brian said. "Ninety-three." He stopped. "Eighty-something. I don't know. I couldn't do that on a good day, probably." Knowing even as he said it that it was a lie. He thought of the ambulance ride. Saying the word *lamplight* when he meant *headlight.*

Another wry, patient smile from Dr. Bajeer, the scratching of his pen on Brian's chart.

"I've got a concussion, don't I? Shit."

Could he make up a sentence? It can be about anything, but it must contain a noun and a verb. Tell me which word is the noun and which is the verb, please.

Brian, truly no slouch in the sentence-designing department, given his long-running tenure as an academic man-baby, opened his mouth to speak: *I bet the Nazis beat the shit out of that old man and he drove away.* But then he got hung up on the words *noun* and *verb.* One, he remembered from childhood incantations, was a person, place or thing. The other showed movement of some kind, action.

But he couldn't remember which was which. It was right there, maddeningly out of reach.

Headlight. Lamplight.

"Are you having problems with this one, Mr. Schutt? It's perfectly fine. There's no way to answer incorrectly."

Brian let out a little snort of derisive laughter. "It's just . . . I can't remember which one is which. Noun and verb. You know? This is a trip."

Dr. Bajeer nodded.

Dr. Bajeer's pen scribbled like mad.

Dr. Bajeer looked down at Brian on his gurney, moored there upon the crinkling, blood-spotted paper. Someone a few curtains over, maybe the old man, lowed. It sounded very much like a cow mooing. It was a mournful and terrible sound, so strange and out of place, and something tightened in Brian's throat. He grinned, honestly scared now, and said, "*That* man is outstanding in his field. Get it? Out standing in his field? That's a little, uh, a little bovine joke for you, Doctor."

"Mr. Schutt, can you tell me," said Dr. Bajeer, pen wedded to his clipboard again, "how long you've been having headaches?"

• • •

So it was a doughnut, and you went through the hole. That was the CT scan.

They had taken his neck brace off. He felt very tired: the jagged edge of adrenaline had given way to a bone-deep fatigue as the circular apparatus hummed around his head. His headache throbbed. His ear throbbed. His face hummed with pain. He felt like a blood bag jammed through with bone shards and brought resentfully to life. The purpose of the CT scan, a nurse had informed him, was to take quadrilateral scans of his brain. A schematic of his brain in four sections. To note any issues, any possible swelling, trauma. He was steeping in a slow broth of unease even as he felt his eyes drooping.

"Oh, we don't want you to sleep, sir, that won't help us," he was gently admonished.

He thought briefly of the paltry insurance he got as a contracted employee at the university, and the ungodly amount of debt he was racking up for all of this. Dear Christ, he'd accepted a ride in the ambulance! He was getting a CT scan! His headache pulsed in its old familiar housing, its old familiar way: this was one of the precise ones, with that single isolated spot radiating an ache that throbbed darkly all throughout the rest of his skull. He thought about rising up, could picture it happening. He would rise like some embattled Hollywood film star, pulling the electrodes from his skin in a brazen rebuttal of death. But he, like the old man who may or may not have started mooing like a cow earlier, was now in an open-backed hospital gown, his clothes lying in a stack on the chair in the corner.

"A noun is a person, place or thing," he said as the white tube slowly began enveloping him. "A verb indicates an action or occurrence."

"Sir," the nurse said, "please just sit still, okay? This won't take long."

• • •

And then he was back in his little curtained slot, leaning against his gurney and thumbing through a magazine article about breast pump dos and don'ts. The old cow-man was gone, or sleeping, or perhaps had died, having mooed his last moo. Then Dr. Bajeer walked in with his clipboard.

"Mr. Schutt," he said, and walked up to him, close enough that Brian could see the pores on the man's nose. This close, Dr. Bajeer was a riot of scents: wintergreen chewing gum, cologne, something antiseptic. "Why don't you have a seat, please."

Brian looked around their little open-ended stall. Their little intimate stretch of space. "Here?" he said, pointing at his gurney, blood-dotted and wrinkled. "Or the chair?"

"Uh, actually," said Dr. Bajeer, turning on the computer in the corner of the room, gazing up at the wall-mounted screen as it flashed to life, and then walking over and shutting the curtain, "on the gurney's fine. So you can see the pictures here."

The doctor spent a minute logging into the system, clicking buttons, opened files.

Eventually, images unfolded, bloomed to dark life on the screen.

"So I have news," said Dr. Bajeer. "It's not good, unfortunately. All told, Mr. Schutt, I'm sorry but it's not good at all."

• • •

He was riven then with medical terms. The doctor clicked his pen against various points of the overhead screen, an image of Brian's brain. Looking him in the eye, Dr. Bajeer spoke clearly, emphatically, and a litany of half-understood words dropped like stones from his mouth. Ice crept from the floor, up Brian's legs, rooting him to the ground.

Shards of sentences drifted through the maelstrom. Hung in the air like arrows in midflight: *Astrocytoma. Stage III, possibly Stage IV. We won't know for sure until we perform a biopsy. But it's severe.*

How was this man so calm? Delivering this news?

What, Brian asked, or someone with Brian's voice asked for him, was the difference between Stage III and Stage IV.

That was something that Brian should discuss with his neuro team. But Dr. Bajeer could provide him with literature in the meantime.

Again, Dr. Bajeer circled the whitened area of his brain—his brain!—that denoted the location of the tumor, this collusion of traitorous cells inside his skull. Brian heard his own voice again, a voice murky and distant, asking if it was terminal. A brain tumor like this, if it was terminal or not.

The doctor paused. "I can't give you a prognosis until we get a biopsy. But as I said, it's very serious."

"And this", Brian said from that far away swampland, "would explain my headaches?"

Dr. Bajeer nodded. "Yes. We call this cerebral edema, brain-swelling. You're experiencing a lot of intracranial pressure as the tumor grows. In a way, you're fortunate that you came in this evening." Brian managed to laugh at that, though it again was a dry, clicking sound, like he'd tried dining on a handful of sand.

"I don't feel lucky."

Again, Dr. Bajeer nodded, grave and unsmiling. "I understand. But there are things that can be done. I would like you to strongly consider, Mr. Schutt, allowing me to contact a neurologist. He or she would begin the process of assessing your options with you. I can contact one immediately, after I leave this room. We can begin arranging a biopsy, your pathology report. We could do this now. I would suggest it."

His brain! This interloper in his brain! He pictured a fist knocking against the yellow bowl of his skull, finally punching its way out, like a zombie bursting through the soil of a grave. He nodded at the doctor.

"Very good. I'll be back in a moment, Mr. Schutt. I'll have the staff place some calls. Now's the time to make some calls of your own. I'm not sure when you'll be leaving, if a neuro team is available. They will want to perform a biopsy and possibly remove the tumor immediately. You should contact your family." He gestured at Brian's face. "Meanwhile, I'll get someone in here to stitch up your lip, take a look at your ear." Dr. Bajeer nodded grimly one more time, then clapped Brian's shoulder, squeezing with surprising strength. He walked around the blue curtain and Brian heard the whish of the pneumatic door opening and closing. In moments, the doctor had both explained so much—the headaches, the missing words—and also utterly demolished the footholds and foundations of Brian's life. Just like that.

A fucking *brain tumor.*

As if resurrected by the news, he heard the old man moo again. A zombie cow-man, woeful and lost, something resuscitated and drawn grudgingly back down mortality's ugly hallway.

Brian looked at the screen where the CT results still glowed. That pale, asymmetrical blemish in the curved egg of his brain. The old man lowed again, anguished.

Brian scooped up his blood-spattered clothes and walked around the curtain, bare feet slapping on the floor. He found a bathroom less than a dozen feet away. He stormed inside and locked it, leaning against the door on a pair of legs now seemingly carved from ice. A toilet, a sink, a wastebasket. An empty steel cupboard for leaving piss specimens. He got dressed.

There was some surety that this was the wrong thing to do. That this was, truly, absolutely, the *wrongest* thing to do. But he did it: he bundled his gown in a ball and put it in the wastebasket by the toilet and walked out into the room of blue curtains. He strode past the old man on his gurney. He walked through the *whoosh*ing doors, out through the emergency room, and into the night.

He stepped out of the hospital unfixed, terrified, woefully damaged, and strangely exultant.

• • •

The house was silent, dark, Ellis's snores audible as soon as Brian crept in the door. He felt like a stranger tiptoeing through the place. It felt like someone else's home now. The dumb, naive Brian that had lived before this one.

In the bathroom he spilled a loose handful of aspirin into his palm without turning on the light, chewed them to pulp. Fuck his liver, right? Who cared? What was the point of worrying about *that* particular issue when his brain was steering the whole operation into an early grave?

In his room, on his laptop, there was a message from Mark Sandoval.

Brian,

Appreciated the meeting today. Pardon the hackneyed seafaring lingo, but I liked the cut of your jib. I think you'd do well.

The position's yours if you want it. Call me.

—M

2

how in the hell do they grow pumpkins in hvíldarland?

"It was the same answer down every road we traveled. Every highway apparition, every back roads haint, every shimmering blacktop spirit seemed to signify the same thing: wherever you went, you took yourself along with you."
—**Mark Sandoval**, *Night Roads*

1

They met at the airport, and Sandoval bought their tickets with cash.

It was a quick hop from Portland International to SeaTac, then an eight-hour flight to Reykjavík, Iceland. Sandoval, in the roughly forty-eight hours since Brian had officially accepted his offer of employment, had proven to be generous with credit card and money roll both. He'd also named a small weekly stipend as well as a commission to be issued at the end of the project that was so generous that Brian had actually stammered, "Sorry, what's that?" after Sandoval had named it.

This was his first time flying business class. Something inside Sandoval seemed to loosen when they finally rose off the tarmac; he pressed his head against the seat and in his slow exhalation seemed to breathe some kind of silent thanks. He was sloughing something off. Yet Brian—Brian already had a mantra down, this tic he couldn't get rid of; he'd been hijacked, down at the cellular level, after all. He couldn't stop thinking about it.

Stage III, Stage IV.

I can't believe I just bolted.

I ran. I ran away. Jesus.

Across the aisle, Sandoval immediately started packing the booze away. Brian was reminded of that sugary-sweet stink in Don Whitmer's office, the fug of the man's obvious hangover, the two Bloody Marys he'd put down in the airport bar before their flight. He leaned back in his own massive seat and watched Sandoval upend a pair of miniature vodka bottles into his plastic cup.

Midway over the Atlantic, the flight attendant simply left the cart next to Sandoval so he could withdraw drinks at will. The privileges of international business class. At some point, he brandished his cell phone and winked at Brian yet again. "You've seen the footage, right? That the woman sent in?" The obvious slur in his voice, the drooping lids. Brian had already seen the Hauksdóttir footage a number of times at Sandoval's West Hills home the day before. Still, provided he didn't fall down dead in the interim—oh, how easy it was to joke like that, as if it weren't actually possible—he and Sandoval still had a month of traveling together to get through. Diplomacy mattered.

Brian said, "What the hell, let's take a look," and Sandoval handed him his phone.

· · ·

The video: a jittering, pixilated shot of dusk wheeling toward night. Just a hint of steely blue behind the cragged mountains in the background. The camera quickly dropped to churned earth, then rose again to show rows of white tubes in the foreground, their skin milky and translucent, alien-looking.

"Greenhouses, right?"

"Yeah," Sandoval said. "She's growing fucking pumpkins out there, you believe it?"

"How in the hell are they growing pumpkins in Iceland? At all, much less in March?"

"It's not Iceland, remember?" said Sandoval. "It's Hvíldarland."

Onscreen: for a moment, a long series of moments, nothing. A wavering facade of gray-to-black pixels, more soil, those long white tubes like miniature airplane hangars. The film quality, digital or not, sucked.

And then the form began to uncoil itself slowly out of a patchwork of those gray shifting pixels.

The bad quality, to Brian, made it more suspect than not. Easier to manipulate. But whoever was wielding the camera had stopped moving at least, and the shape continued to unspool slowly out of the stilled gloom, muted whites and grays that his eyes kept trying to decipher. Then, like a key fitting a lock, the image registered: a horse had walked around the corner of one of the greenhouses, its mane hanging in silken silver strands. The image wobbled, washed across the greenhouse and calmed again, the camera taking in the shape of the animal in its entirety: the head, the muscled neck, the rolling curve of the shoulders. There were the rippling haunches, the tail a silken silver as well. The camera jittered and zoomed in as the animal dipped its head to the ground and then rose once more.

There was the black eye, the lips, the square teeth.

And yes, there, okay: the horn above the eyes, atop the ridge of the skull. It was a scalloped horn, the color of pale cream.

Suddenly the animal heard something, saw something, got spooked, and simply turned and trotted away with a quiet, supple strength into the surrounding darkness. Swallowed back into the gloom in seconds.

Okay, so.

Sure.

A unicorn.

A unicorn on a pumpkin farm.

A unicorn on a pumpkin farm in a small, beleaguered, mostly forgotten island in the Atlantic.

It was like a shitty *Mad Lib*.

Sandoval peered over at him, leaning across his armrest like a proud, expectant father.

"CGI?" Brain said. He handed the phone back.

Sandoval frowned. "Pshh. Please."

"Or maybe they attached it somehow. Surgically," Brian offered.

"The horn?"

"Yeah."

It took a while for Sandoval to answer. He lifted his red cup and swirled it, gazing into its contents. He set it back down on his tray and leaned forward, his elbows on his knees. Staring at the milky gray screen mounted in the seatback in front of him, he finally spoke. "It's good you're dubious."

"Well, I mean . . . This is why we're going, right? To investigate?"

"You've heard of Lazarus species, right?"

Brian nodded. "Sure. Species thought to be extinct that get—"

"Rediscovered. Right. Storm petrels, Omura's whale. On and on. Creatures assumed gone forever, only to be found again. Happens more than you'd think. Even now, where the undocumented world has atrophied like hell."

"So you're saying the unicorn is a rediscovered species? Come on, Mark."

Sandoval pulled back the curtain on the drinks cart again and selected another tiny bottle of vodka. "I'm saying it's good that you're doubtful. Especially when we find the thing and you have to eat those bitter, bitter words." He winked, upending the bottle into his cup.

"Okay." Brian smiled. "Sure thing."

"Seriously though. Just make sure that your doubt doesn't blind you to something that's right in front of your face."

• • •

Dawn broke like a dropped plate: impolite, quick, the day yanked from darkness and suddenly suffused with light. In the Reykjavík airport, they met the charter pilot their host had arranged to fly them to Hvíldarland. He introduced himself, with a heavy Icelandic accent, as Orvar. He stuck the cardboard sign he was holding—SANDOVAL in block letters—under his armpit and high-fived Brian after taking in the state of his face. "Someone parties hard, yeah? Shit, man." Thin and pale, he wore a bleach-spotted *Hammer Time* T-shirt and a strap around his glasses, the lenses of which, Brian noted with more than a little unease, seemed significantly thick for a pilot. Encroaching on legally blind territory, actually. He also had a number of shitty stick-and-poke tattoos scattered on his arms. But Orvar walked through the airport with an offhanded confidence, his ID on a lanyard around his neck. All of their luggage had made it through, and Sandoval fussily inspected all the gear on the floor of Baggage Claim again before he allowed Brian and Orvar to load it onto a trolley.

They pushed everything out onto the tarmac where a small Cessna waited. A brisk wind came off the ocean—the airport was perched practically right next to it—and Brian stood with his hands in his pockets and his shoulders hunched as Sandoval packed the plane, Orvar talking at his back the whole time. He was a big fan of Sandoval's books, he said, and kept asking, in his heavily accented English, what Sandoval thought "getting the bone up with a vampire chick" would be like. Sandoval, even drunk as he was, managed to decline answering.

Seemingly moments later, the plane rose into the sky, the engines blatting like a lawnmower, the sea, gray and implacable, suddenly below them.

Hvíldarland, Sandoval had informed him earlier, was a sovereign island country just thirty miles across at its longest point. A population of less than thirty thousand people. The southern half housed the island's capital and largest city, Kjálkabein, where over half of the country lived. Hvíldarlanders were a populace screwed over resoundingly by overfishing, and the country had yet to make the leap to tourism. As a result, they were struggling. Meanwhile, the majority of the island was uninhabitable and unpopulated. At its midrange was a valley flanked by a number of outlying hamlets and villages, all of them branching off from the main road that ran north to south through the majority of the country. The road itself was called, inexplicably, *Vegurrin Sjö*, or Road Seven. Beyond that valley lay expanses of moss-covered hills and volcanic ranges, small saltwater fjords, steppes, nearly the entire country ringed in those merciless mountains or rock-strewn spits of beach. The pictures he'd looked up had shown a beautiful patchwork from above: greens and grays, those tiny clusters of townships radiating from Road Seven like spokes from a broken wheel. He'd been surprised to see that he could even find the Hauksdóttir farm on Google Earth, its long driveway like a brachial offshoot from the main road, a long row of greenhouses on each side of the driveway, orderly as church pews. North of Road Seven and the farm lay a forest, impenetrable and dense from above, and then what had looked, at least online, like a blackened swath of burned woods. The northernmost tip of the island had featured a scattering of buildings that may have been hangars or warehouses, all of it ringed in a fence that lined the sea. Some kind of installation, but a small one, with the air of abandonment about it.

"Here we go," Orvar said, and then spoke Icelandic into his headset, clearing something with whatever passed for traffic control at the Kjálk-abein airport. The plane dipped down.

2

The airport consisted of a single stunted runway with a pair of open-ended hangars tacked on the end. There were a few other scattered outbuildings beyond, equipment or storage sheds, that appeared so dilapidated that cardboard had been taped over a number of windowpanes. Salt hung in the air like brine. The terminal itself was the size of a decent fast food restaurant and smelled, once they entered, like a machine shop. Fluorescents buzzed overhead and broken-down cardboard boxes lay stacked behind an empty information desk. *Somewhere between "business casual" and "abandoned due to zombie outbreak,"* Brian thought. In the middle of the room were two long rows of pastel bucket chairs lined against each other, populated by only a few people staring down at their phones or into open paperbacks. One woman was knitting. Two men in dark uniforms stood laughing in a doorway marked *Employees Only* in English and Icelandic.

"Not exactly a hub of commerce," Sandoval noted.

Orvar helped them bring their gear inside and Sandoval tipped him, a sheaf of US bills passing from one palm to the other. Orvar bowed and thanked him, called him "my good bro." There seemed absolutely no trace of irony to it.

"Hey, Orvar," Sandoval said. He gestured at the two men in the doorway. "Before you go, do we talk to those guys about renting a car? Or getting a taxi?"

Orvar squinted one eye. "You want a taxi?"

He walked over, clapped one of the two men on the shoulder, slapped palms with the other one. Brian and Sandoval stood there, bags of gear hanging off their frames, gathered around their feet like boulders. When Orvar sauntered back, he clucked his tongue and said, "No good, bro."

"What's no good?"

"Well, we have no rental place here at the airport, yeah?"

"What? Do you have one in town? In, uh, Kjálkabein?" Brian felt like he mangled the word.

Orvar shrugged. "Not really. I mean, people don't really come here, man."

Sandoval turned and looked at Brian, the look on his face obvious enough—*you were in charge of this.*

Orvar clucked. "And the other bummer is this: our taxi guy is sick. Strep throat."

Sandoval turned back to him. "Wait. Thirty thousand people live on this island. And you have one taxi in the entire country."

"Yeah."

"And the driver's sick?"

"With strep throat, yeah. But look! I don't have to fly back for another few hours. I'll give you a ride."

"Jesus Christ."

"It's cool, man. No problem. Where are you guys staying?"

This, at least, Brian had had the wherewithal to take care of before they left. He retrieved the printed reservation from his bag and shook it open. "It's uh, the Natura Haf Hotel?" Again he felt like he brutalized the accent.

Orvar winced, sucked air through this teeth. "Ah, that shithole? That's too bad. That place got shut down last year for bedbugs. They just opened up again."

"Yeah, right. It was four hundred dollars a night, per person. Bedbugs."

"I'm telling you, man. They were shut down for four months last year. But listen, I'll take you to the best place in Hvíldarland. One hundred percent. My uncle runs it. Right down the road. Cheaper, too, and you won't get eaten alive."

Part of Brian was relieved—at least Orvar had become transparent. At least his grift was obvious. He cast a glance at Sandoval, who shrugged and adjusted one of the bags on his shoulder. "I don't give a shit," he said. "Wherever it is, let's get going." Beads of sweat dotted the man's forehead. Brian figured he was sobering up and unhappy about it.

Orvar shot the devil horns at the uniformed men as they walked out into the nearly empty parking lot. The minivan he stopped beside had once been red but was now faded to the jolly pink of a reasonably healthy lung. Great washes of rust crept down toward the wheel wells. *Like weeping tumors,* Brian thought, and something chilled and knife-edged wormed down his spine—things like that just kept coming now, unbidden and haunting. He got in the back with their bags and the minivan began bouncing along a series of potholes as they made their way toward town. Orvar put in a cassette of Paul Simon's *Graceland,* cranking it to a volume that nearly hummed in Brian's ribcage, and the airport shrank and disappeared in the back window.

3

If you knew a little pop culture, you knew Mark Sandoval's story.

You'd at least heard of him, or one of his books, even if you hadn't actually read one. (But chances were that if *you* hadn't read one, and you were in, say, an average-sized sedan, someone you were with probably had.) His was a name that came up as an answer during somewhat nerdy subsections of trivia night. Sandoval rested in the back part of the mind, a celebrity tumbled earthward, Icarus-style: famous, but with nowhere near the fervor of his earlier fame.

The story went:

When he was in his late twenties, Sandoval was assistant anthropology professor at a small but respected liberal arts university in Seattle. (He never named names in his book, hence the shock when Brian discovered that Don Whitmer had been involved). One morning he didn't show up for a class he was scheduled to teach. Just skipped it. The head of the department (again, Don Whitmer, played by an earnest and affable Morgan Freeman in the film) was understandably frustrated. Pissed, even. This was not, after all, a new occurrence, Sandoval dipping out on his responsibilities. After multiple offers of a sympathetic ear from the school's dean and more than one warning from Whitmer as to his tenuous footing regarding his employment, Sandoval and Whitmer had a meeting and Sandoval was removed from his position. It was something that probably could have been contested if he'd been of mind to do it. But long story short: he'd lost his job. He was fucking up big time.

Thing was, after that meeting? Sandoval just disappeared.

He was gone for thirty-four days.

Just vanished. Puff-of-smoke kind of shit. In *The Long Walk Home*, he wrote that his wife, who had admittedly left him just days before, grew frantic at his disappearance. His friends and colleagues were mystified. He was not, they say, depressed or in debt. He partied, sure, but not to excess. His position on campus, had he been able to keep it together, seemed almost assuredly tenure-track. (Again, this was via *The Long Walk Home*, and all of it strained through the colander of Sandoval's heavy-handed and admittedly one-sided prose.) The police briefly talked to the wife but ultimately came to believe it was probably a kidnapping that, as the days continued to pass with no ransom demand issued, had possibly turned fatal. There were simply no leads to follow.

And then, thirty-four days after his disappearance from Seattle, Sandoval was discovered by an off-duty policeman in a phone booth in Middleton, Delaware, nearly three thousand miles away. Wearing only a pair of soiled boxer shorts, Sandoval sat curled and sobbing on the booth's metal floor, rocking himself like a child. He was emaciated and dehydrated and initially appeared to have difficulty regaining speech. Not a heavy man to begin with, he'd lost over forty pounds since his disappearance.

Most notably, nearly the entirety of his body was now covered in a series of raised scars (circles, squares, trapezoids, octagons sutured together by an interconnected series of lines.) Only his face, hands and feet were spared. Though his language capabilities eventually returned, he purported to have no memory of the previous weeks. The scars, how he got them, and what they may or may not represent were, he claimed, a mystery.

Sandoval returned to Seattle as a strange dichotomy: both pariah and minor celebrity. Eventually he seemed to recover entirely. He was not evasive about what happened, but said he simply didn't know. Claims by his wife that he had issues with drugs were fervently rebuffed. He did not return to his position at the university.

Within a year of his return to Seattle he'd written a memoir. It was sold to a major New York publisher after an extensive bidding war (rumors at the time placed his advance in the mid-seven-figure range). The bulk of the material was purportedly penned from memories unearthed after claiming to have undergone months of regressive hypnotherapy, though repeated media requests to name the therapist (titled only "Dr. X" in the book) were never answered.

And Mark Sandoval became famous. His memoir, *The Long Way Home*, became hugely popular. It became one of those books that was purchased by people that don't often like to read, a book that stayed for years on supermarket shelves. A book that was gifted to people who were impossible to shop for.

And it was in this book that Sandoval claimed, as evidenced through his scars and his numerous regressive-hypnosis sessions, to have been abducted by aliens.

Brian remembered being a kid and watching the unending *Saturday Night Live* skits at that time, in which an alien was always bugging one of the cast members—arms and legs done up in pink makeup suspiciously like

Sandoval's scarring—about inconsistencies in that "dumb story you wrote about me." (His mother had found these skits hilarious.) Sandoval cowrote the screenplay for the film adaptation. Brad Pitt nabbed an Oscar nomination for his portrayal of a frightened, weeping Mark Sandoval, wandering Middleton streets with a brutal, unknown lexicon strung along his body.

Five books followed over the next couple decades, "nonfiction exposés." All of them farting around between memoir and monster hunt. They were all well received, at least in terms of sales, though none were ever as successful as *The Long Way Home.* He remembered seeing Sandoval on *Oprah*: Sandoval had worn a leather jacket and a terrible goatee-mustache combo that was woefully, painfully indicative of the times. He'd looked like the sleazy older guy who'd try to pick up girls in a head shop.

Oprah, holding up a hardcover copy of the book, had touched Sandoval's knee with her other hand and said, "Now really, Mark. Aliens? We're supposed to believe that *aliens* came down and took you onto their ship? Did these things to you? These strange and confusing and sometimes hurtful things? I think some part of us wants to believe that there's more than just us out there, but the things you write here . . . I mean, *really?*"

And Sandoval, without missing a beat, tucked his thumb under his chin and put his finger against his nose. *Thinker in repose.* (It was a gesture Brian would become intimately familiar with years later; it seemed one of the few natural, uncultivated things about the man.) Sandoval had nodded sagely, waited a beat and said, "You know, Oprah, sometimes? In matters of faith—and *you* know this better than most—just because we don't understand it, doesn't mean we can't handle it. Or that it shouldn't happen."

"What do you mean by that?"

"*I* believe . . . Well, I'm of the opinion that there's a grand plan. Okay? And it's one that we're not always privy to. We can't always encapsulate it into our understanding. But we still do our part, our tiny part, even if we can't see the big picture at the time."

"So things happen for a reason."

"Exactly. Even if we don't know what that reason is at the time."

Oprah had seemed grudgingly accepting of that answer, if not exactly satisfied. She'd eyed him almost suspiciously. "That's certainly a gracious way of looking at what happened to you, Mark."

And Sandoval had smiled, a smile that disintegrated the foolishness of that goatee, the gelled hair. A smile that dissipated that huckster sheen of his. He leaned back, and viewers could see the scars peeking out of his sleeves.

"Well," Sandoval had said, "I have been around the block a few times, after all."

Cue the audience's gentle laughter.

4

Orvar shuttled them through Kjálkabein, past rows of stolid concrete buildings with their brightly-painted colors and slanted roofs. A downtown consisting of two- and three-story buildings that could have held families or shops or safety bunkers, if it weren't for the occasional OPEN signs in various windows to delineate them. The "best hotel in the city," it turned out, was named the Hotel Magnificence, and it was a boxy three-story affair with a white-tiled roof and a lime-colored facade, tucked behind a narrow strip of lawn and flanked by a parking lot. The name of the hotel had been done in white script on a black awning over the double doors.

"The clerk is my Uncle Viktor," said Orvar as they pulled their bags out of his van. "He'll hook you up."

Sandoval tipped him again, and Brian cursed under his breath. "You better not be screwing us, Orvar."

"I'm saving your ass from bedbugs, bro. That's what I'm doing." They watched, squinting against the wind, as the van pulled out of the parking lot. Orvar honked twice and rounded the corner.

The lobby of the hotel was large and dim. The wall sconces threw a buttery light up toward the ceiling, with little of it going elsewhere. The carpet at their feet was a woven pageantry of images: squadrons of dragons attacking castles, embattlements, a line of men pouring oil from a balustrade down upon an invading army, all the soldier's faces drawn back in horror, every one of them, attacker and recipient both.

"Hey, check this out," Sandoval murmured, toeing a trio of unicorns on the carpet, forelegs curling in toward their bellies as they reared back on hind legs, eyes wild and merciless, nearby soldiers cowering in fear, running away. Malevolent, vengeful things. "You believe in signs, Brian?"

If that's a sign, he thought, *we're screwed.* Before he could answer, a man opened the office door behind the counter and cried "Hello!" Brian and Sandoval both started.

"Orvar sent us," Sandoval said.

The man rolled his eyes, his hands clutched in front of his chest. "Oh, that boy," he said. "Such a good boy. My nephew."

"You're Viktor?" said Brian.

"Hello! Yes!" Viktor cried again as they walked up to the counter. Handshakes all around. Viktor expressed zero concern over the state of Brian's face.

They were in luck, he informed them. There were vacancies. He typed two-fingered and assigned them their rooms via an ancient, chirring desktop. The only commonality shared in his and Orvar's bloodline appeared to be their paleness and the stick-like thinness of their limbs. A few sad thatches of black hair made the joyless trek across Viktor's mostly bare dome, and as if to counteract it, his mustache was a fierce, coal-black thing, something a cartoon villain would wear as a disguise. He looked like he'd slept in his suit, and he dropped their keys twice before managing to hand them over. Sandoval paid with his credit card again, seemingly unconcerned with their lost deposits at the other hotel.

Viktor informed them there was no elevator, so they trekked with their gear up three flights of stairs that smelled of mildew and carpet cleaner and then parted ways, their rooms next to each other.

Brian's door opened reluctantly, as if it had at one time been swollen and water-logged. It was a small room, with a single window and enough space for nightstands to bracket the bed. A wardrobe stood against one wall, and a doorway led to a cramped, tiled bathroom. Rust stains around the bathroom faucet, a dryer-scorched comforter on the single bed. A chiaroscuro of dead insects darkened the bowl of the overhead light fixture. Brian's loneliness flared; his first keen understanding at just how far he'd distanced himself from everyone who could help him, and he hurriedly shut the overhead light off, tears suddenly threatening to loose themselves and spill over into something significant and consequential.

Dropping his bags in the corner, peeling off his shoes and socks, he tucked himself in beneath fusty sheets and laid a forearm over his eyes. It was only afternoon, or at least *felt* that way, but he napped, falling into a weird, jet-lagged sleep populated by odd and frightening monster mash-ups: Bigfoot, red penis erect, gleefully rode old eight-legged Sleipner, who bellowed and hurled uprooted trees like javelins into the heart of a shadowed city. A kraken wielded its tentacles, stuffing dozens of bare-breasted sirens into its pink maw like they were screaming, red-haired fish sticks. A werewolf gripped the rear legs of a Pegasus and smashed it against the walls of a great banquet hall again and again until the body hanging from its paws was limp and broken, wings torn, great red freshets of blood slicking the floor.

He woke bathed in sweat and in his half-sleep swore he could hear Sandoval crying out in his own room next door. Heart thundering, he wondered if he'd imagined it. If it was just the last jagged remnants of his own dream, the final vestige of invented beasts echoing in his head.

• • •

He took a shower and headed to the lobby where he found a carafe of coffee at a side table and a half-dozen pastries on a tray, their glazes cracked as the vellum of a medieval manuscript. Brian helped himself to two. It was late afternoon in Kjálkabein, the light strange and watery in its dilution through the front windows. He sat in a leather-bound chair against the wall, his head still sleep-fuzzed. He ate his doughnuts and stared at the inherent violence of the unicorn tapestry at his feet.

Pulling his laptop from his bag, he connected to the hotel's Wi-Fi and fired off a message to Ellis:

Elllllis,

I got the job! Holy shit. Mark Sandoval and I are off gallivanting around at the edge of the Arctic (for real!) It's crazy. I'm gonna be out of town for the next few weeks, so the house is yours. I lost my phone (it's a long story), but you can get in touch with me here. Mark Sandoval's a trip. But the guy's giving me a nice stipend (I'll put my rent in PayPal this month if that's cool), and there's gonna be a serious commission at the end of it all, so hey. Think I should ask for price points on the book?

Anyway, I signed a nondisclosure agreement, so I can't get too specific, but, dude. This is some wild shit.

—B

He scrolled through news and social media and waited for his boss. It was all repetitive, brutal, sharp as a stab wound: Neo-Nazi recruiting posters had been found wheatpasted around a number of college campuses in Idaho in what looked like a coordinated effort. In Portland, information on an as-yet unnamed suspect was being sought by police in a hit-and-run beneath the Morrison Bridge, which explained the chalk-and-candle vigil he'd seen. The owner of the cat-rescuing dog in Idaho turned out to owe over twenty thousand dollars in child support, and now some people were conflicted about liking the dog and others were mad about people being conflicted.

His fingers hovered over the keys. The words *astrocytoma, edema, stages of brain tumor* just sat there at his fingertips. It was a decision, to begin mapping out the thing sharing this interior space within him. He just had to type the words to begin the process of discovery. He just had to start.

Instead he logged in to his university account—he still had it, after all—and scoured articles about unicorns in various databases. Historical, mythological. It was a quick refresher on a notedly limited amount of information: Ctesias returned to Greece from Persia in the fourth century and wrote of a blue-eyed unicorn with a tricolored horn. Caesar claimed in *The Conquest of Gaul* that they lived in the Hercynian Forest of Germany, and that the top of the horn was branched out like a tree limb. There was the story of Risharinga, the unicorn man from *The Mahabharata*. The sixteenth-century, multi-panel Franco-Flemish tapestry, *The Hunt of the Unicorn,* artist unknown. But by 1580, physicians like Ambroise Paré were mostly calling bullshit on the idea of unicorns as a whole, and attributing previously sacred, magic-laden horns—that royalty had once paid big bucks for—to those of narwhals and rhinos.

All told, it was slim pickings from a historical perspective.

Sandoval eventually came down, hungover and bleary-eyed but still sharp enough in his sport coat and gray jeans. He poured himself a cup of coffee and gazed down at the pastries. "These any good?"

"I mean, yeah," Brian said. "Doughnuts."

Sandoval picked one up with a napkin. He sat down next to Brian and chewed for a while. Brian closed his laptop.

"Well, I feel like shit," Sandoval announced.

"You celebrated on the plane, for sure."

"That's one way of phrasing it." Sandoval crossed his legs, leaned back.

"Hey," Brian said, "can I ask you something?"

"Shoot."

"Why did we even get a hotel room? If we're going to spend a month out at this farm? Why bother?"

Sandoval balled up his napkin and held up a finger while he chewed. "More than once," he said, "I've flown out to a site only to find that it's a scam, right? Or just some easily explained phenomena. Like, okay . . . it didn't make it in the book, but when I was working on *Night Roads,* I flew out to Georgia, this stretch of back road a few hours outside of Augusta. Looking for a specter that drivers said was haunting the area." He sipped his coffee and winced. "Turned out that it was actually two brothers with a pair of flashlights and a garbage bag on a string. Just kids screwing around. We might get to this farm and have to turn right back."

"Makes sense."

"I mean, I hope we don't."

"And I had an idea about our little horned friend in the pumpkin patch."

"Shoot."

"Horn buds," Brian said.

Sandoval leaned back again, his tongue working a molar as he thought. "I've heard this before. Refresh me."

"Every horned animal's born with these horn buds on the sides of its skull, right? So this doctor, this guy named Franklin Dove, he just transplanted the horn buds of this bull calf from the sides of the skull over to the center. This was in the 1930s. Just to check it out. And he was right, the buds fused together, and boom. Bull's got a single horn in the center of his head. He'd use it to push up fence wire and stuff. Easy as that." Brian flipped open his laptop, showed Sandoval the grainy black-and-white photo, that horn dark as a witch's claw rising out of the bull's head.

"Dr. Dove's bull, right. Did that video look like a bull to you?"

"No," Brian admitted. "But it might've been a reindeer."

Sandoval slowly reared back and frowned at him. "Interesting. Like someone went amateur scientist on a reindeer? Fused its rack into a singular horn?"

He reminded Sandoval about Julius Caesar's take on the unicorn, the horn fanned out like a tree branch. "Or it's just an anomaly," he said. "Just a poor, fucked up reindeer."

"Interesting," Sandoval said again.

And then Viktor appeared from behind his office door like some balding, mustachioed wraith. "Good afternoon, friends!"

While Viktor booted up his ancient computer, they walked to the counter and Sandoval asked him how far it would be to the Hauksdóttir farm.

"Oh, far," said Viktor without looking up from the computer.

"Like ten miles?" asked Brian. "Twenty?"

"Eh, miles," Viktor said. He put his hand out, dipped it back and forth. "I'm not sure."

Brian exhaled. "How far in kilometers?"

"Far," Viktor said again.

Sandoval turned to grin at Brian. "Jesus, this guy."

Brian said, "Can we walk it?"

"You could. But it would be not fun. It would not be a good time."

"And you have one taxi."

Finally Viktor looked up from his keyboard. "Daniel Danielson, yes. It's a minivan, his wife's. But he has—"

"Strep throat," Brian and Sandoval said together.

"Já. Yes."

Sandoval turned to Brian. "We'll just hit a café or something, offer someone cash to drive us out there. This is ridiculous."

"You're the boss," Brian said. He pushed off from the counter.

Viktor ran a hand over his skull and then held up a cadaverous finger. "There *is* an alternative to this, you know. Absolutely! You know about borrow and return, yeah? Like a, ah, a leasing arrangement?"

Sandoval looked him over. "Like a car, you mean? Like us renting a car from you?"

Viktor held his thumb and forefinger an inch apart. "A *little* bit like that, yes. Mostly. But not quite."

5

They gathered enough gear to set up a meager perimeter around the site that night, should it prove to be worth their while, and consolidated the rest of the stuff, clothes and instruments, into Sandoval's room. If the trip wasn't a bust, Brian would come back to the Hotel Magnificence and get the rest of it tomorrow.

"It's a beautiful way to travel the country, really," said Viktor, the three of them once more standing at the front desk. Through the lobby windows, the afternoon sun was a brindled, hazy coin through the clouds. Brian had to admire Viktor's hard sell, his willingness to brazenly toss the truth aside: the mist outside was so heavy he could hardly see beyond the parking lot.

"It's a fucking insult, is what it is," said Sandoval.

There was another exchange of cash ("I think this will be a great experience for you, traveling like this, seeing this place like hardly even any *Hvíldarlander* does!" said Viktor, slipping Sandoval's dollars somewhere beneath the counter) and they took leave with his hand-drawn map in Brian's pocket.

"Fucking scam artists," Sandoval muttered.

Each man wheeled a child's bicycle through the lobby doors.

They rode down Kjálkabein's dew-damp, misted streets and quickly found the main road, *Vegurrin Sjö*, Road Seven, that bisected the island. Brian waved at the pedestrians they passed. The mist painted everything metallic and ghostly. Sandoval rode up ahead in his four-hundred-dollar jeans, his sport coat, astride a ten-year-old's rainbow-colored bicycle. Pedaling furiously with his elbows jutting straight out. Something seemed to open up inside Brian at the sight of it, some joy. In spite of everything, look at where he was! What he was doing! On a tiny island in the Nordic Sea, riding a child's bicycle alongside his woefully hungover boss as they prepared *to hunt down a unicorn*. It was insane! Didn't the fact that he was here seem as unlikely as the thing coiled and multiplying inside his head? As impossible? Couldn't the wonderment of one cancel out the other? He decided in that moment that the entire world was salvageable.

That somehow everything would be fine. If he could stay moored in this moment exactly, he would be safe.

And then Sandoval spat over his shoulder, "Where did he even get these things?"

"The bikes? Maybe some guest's kids forgot them or something."

"Shit, they're probably Viktor's kids'."

"Guy's sketchy," Brian said.

"Hell yes, he is."

Kjálkabein soon gave way to the outskirts, rows of single-story buildings, and further still to scattered industrial outbuildings heavy with the look of disuse. Fields followed beyond that, dotted with a few farmsteads of sheep and horses, the occasional animal lifting its head to eye them as they passed, and then there was just the coal-black pavement of Road Seven and the quiet wonders that lay on each side of it. The mist had burned off a little by then, and beside the road were moss-furred lava beds, and glacial-hued lakes, and rising, stone-scattered escarpments that led to the mountains beyond. If it wasn't freezing, it was close to it, everything ice-rimed, the color of the grass muted with frost. Brian's elbows clacked against his knees as he pedaled. He saw a trio of reindeer up on a hillside—reindeer!—and was about to point them out when Sandoval slowed so they could pedal side by side. Sweat dripped off the man's chin, darkened his shirt collar.

He said, "Things like the rental car? I really need you to step up, Brian. This bullshit should not have happened."

"I just—I figured they'd have taxis. You know? Car rental places. They didn't have any online options through the airline, but I just figured."

"Yeah, well. You should have looked into it. You should have made sure."

How to be recalcitrant on a purple bicycle, your knees practically knocking against your own throat? "You're totally right, Mark. Sorry."

Sandoval nodded grimly. His point made, he once more pedaled ahead.

Rippled, lichen-covered lava beds now spanned in both directions, a vibrant green upon the black. They could occasionally see puffing tendrils of steam ghosting from the ground. "Those are the geothermals," Brian called out. "That's probably how it's warm enough to grow the pumpkins."

Grasslands, green fields studded with boulders. Fields dotted with wild horses, goats. Occasionally they passed one of the offshoots from the main road and could see the little villages tucked into the hillsides beyond, brightly painted and snug. Traffic was sparse but steady; there were few houses directly situated on Road Seven. An occasional porch-bound dog barked in their wake and at one point a mottled gray and white mutt launched itself from the yard where it lay and Sandoval swerved, rode into the ditch and fell. The dog was chained and loosed volleys of high, hoarse barks, the chain pulled wire-taut as the animal rose on its rear legs. Sandoval staggered up from the ditch, cursing, and stood on the shoulder, his hands on his knees.

"You okay?"

Sandoval waved him off and launched a thin gruel of vomit onto the buckled shoulder. A woman came out onto the porch and put her hand above her eyes as a visor. Sandoval spit and wiped his mouth and got on his bicycle again. The woman called to the dog, and it barked twice more and trotted back to the porch, the chain hissing in its wake.

• • •

On his map, Viktor had drawn what looked like a pair of testicles next to the road, and Brian immediately spotted their real-life equivalent as they crested a rise—two shoulder-high boulders, painted white and resting beside a rutted driveway. Even if they'd missed them, he could see in the distance the two rows of greenhouses and, further back, the farmhouse itself. It stood out strikingly against all the flatness, this leveled land among the encroaching forest and the crags of mountains beyond. Brian followed Sandoval down the driveway, smelling churned earth, manure, ocean. Sandoval's tires kicked up little globs of ice-choked mud as they pedaled along.

The house was a white clapboard thing two stories tall, with a turreted roof. A porch spanned the entire ground floor. The house was incongruous with any architecture in Hvíldarland he'd seen up to then, and he realized with dismay that it was going to be a pure screaming pain in the ass to catch anything substantial on film there. The property was big, much bigger than the video had implied, and they just didn't have enough gear. Even with the stuff back at the hotel, they'd need a half-dozen more cameras, easily, and with an equally large expanse of flatland at the back of the house, it just wasn't going to work. A nightmare.

By the time they made their way to the house itself, a woman was standing on the porch with her hands on her hips. A child poked out shyly from behind each leg. Sandoval, gasping, staggered off of his bicycle with an apologetic wave of his hand. Brian, more than a little winded himself, at least managed to use his bike's kickstand before unwrapping himself from the origami of their bags. The air had a bite, even with the sun out.

Brian walked up onto the porch, his hand held out. Behind him, he heard Sandoval retch in the yard, just once. The woman's eyes passed over his face—there were clearly a number of questions she wanted to ask—but finally looked over Brian's shoulder, frowning. "Is Mr. Sandoval okay?"

"Oh," Brian said, "yeah. He ate something bad on the plane. He's fine. I'm Brian, Mr. Sandoval's research assistant." This all came easily, smoothly.

"Karla Hauksdóttir." Her umber hair was threaded with gray, pulled back in a ponytail. She had a deep notch in her chin, smart as a tap from an ax. A narrow, worn face, a face marked with time and labor. Blue eyes like the deep starburst of cold inside an iceberg, eyes fanned in crow's-feet. She wore jeans and a long-sleeved, embroidered blouse at least a generation out of fashion and pale from washing. Her work-roughened handshake reminded him of Don Whitmer all over again. She peered over Brian's shoulder again.

"Mr. Sandoval, do you need some water?" She looked at Brian. "And do you need anything? I mean, for your face."

"I'm good, thank you," Brian said, and after another moment Sandoval walked up the steps. He let out a chalky little laugh and said, "I knew I should've gone with the vegetarian dish. Goodness."

"Ah, I'm sorry."

Sandoval held out his palms. "No, I'm sorry. *Mortified* is more the appropriate term. So embarrassing."

They all stood there, the moment painfully drawn out—*Hey, we're just here for the unicorn, lady*—until Karla said, "Well. Ah, these are my children, Gunnar and Liza."

"Hey," Brian said. He waved, awkwardly, something a magician would do during a card trick, his insecurity suddenly blooming fiercely. When judged by adults, Brian had long tucked himself away amid his meager armament—sarcasm, contempt, mocking self-aggrandizement, the relative breadth of his academic accomplishments—it all worked well enough. But when it came to the mercilessness of kids, their frank judgment, their perceptiveness, all that stuff suddenly found itself packed away. Kids made him nervous.

But Gunnar peeked out from behind Karla's leg and lifted a dirty little hand in response while Liza's gaze—both of the children had the chilled blue eyes of their mother—kept ricocheting between the two men. They were maybe ten and seven years old, the boy older, both with hair blond as corn silk. They stood on the porch in faded shorts and T-shirts, bedecked in the day's filth. Liza in particular looked like she had earlier in the day, perhaps, sipped from a trough of chocolate milk. It had to be in the forties, but there they were, seemingly impervious to the cold.

Liza said in English, "Why did that man throw up in the grass, mamma?"

Karla dipped her head down to quash her smile and tucked a lock of hair behind Liza's ear. "He ate some bad food, Li-li."

Gunnar pointed and said to Brian, "Why are you riding a girl bike?"

"Hush," Karla said. She hid her smile behind knit brows and wrapped her arm around the boy.

Brian tried not to laugh. "That's a really good question," he said, and Gunnar beamed. "It's kind of a long story."

"I'm so sorry we're late," said Sandoval, pushing ahead. "As your son's pointed out, we've, uh, had some transportation issues."

"It's okay. At least you made it, right?" Karla tilted her head and offered a smile, dreamy and wistful, in a way that made Brian wonder if she might have partaken in a bit of a joint or something before their arrival.

But whatever. They'd made it.

They'd arrived.

They were in Hvíldarland, looking for a unicorn.

• • •

Sandoval started in with Karla about the layout of the farm, asking where she had seen the unicorn—he called it "the sighting in question"—and Karla took Liza with her to the far end of the porch to point out the location.

"Why didn't you drive here in a car?" Gunnar was leaning back against one of the porch columns, looking up at him with his arms crossed. He was wearing a heavy metal T-shirt, black and too big for him, the design flaking and indecipherable.

"We couldn't find one."

"Oh." This seemed to satisfy the boy. "We have trucks. We have a farm truck over there and my mom has her little white truck. My dad has a four runner. He lets me drive it." His Icelandic accent was slight compared to his mother's.

"That's cool." Brian gestured at the bike on its kickstand. "I'm actually just borrowing that."

Sandoval wasted no time: at the end of the porch, he handed Karla Hauksdóttir a sheaf of paper and began going over the contract she'd need to sign before they could legally start their investigation. He marveled at Sandoval's faith in himself as A Brand. He had, after all, just dry-heaved on the woman's lawn moments before. If Brian had an ounce of the man's fearlessness, he'd already be submitting his dissertation to publishers.

No, scratch that.

A little fearlessness and he'd be in the hospital, under the knife right now. They'd be pulling that tumor out with a pair of salad tongs. If he had even an ounce of bravery inside him.

He sat down on the steps and peered up at Gunnar. Felt the worn, rough-hewn wood beneath his palms. "How are you not freezing, by the way?"

The kid shrugged. "It's not really cold anymore. It was a while back. In January it was really cold."

"What kind of stuff do you guys do around here? For fun."

Gunnar shoved his hands in the pockets of his shorts, kicked the toe of his shoe against the chipped paint of the porch. "We ride bikes. Go around the farm. Mamma pays us money to pick bugs off the pumpkins sometimes. I have a racetrack around the corner of the house that I made."

"That's cool."

"And we're starting a band."

"That's awesome. What kind of music is it?" Look at this—here was Brian, suddenly chatting with a ten-year-old.

"It's metal."

Bian smiled. "Nice. My sister loves metal."

"Liza's going to play drums, my mom's playing bass. I'm going to sing." He peered down at Brian through the sweep of his hair. Shrewd, a little shy. Trying not to let his eagerness show. "You can play guitar if you want." Trying to make it sound offhand.

"Ah, you know, I can't really play guitar, unfortunately. I played the trumpet in school but I was really bad at it."

Gunnar nodded. "Maybe you can learn guitar," he said quietly. He kicked the floorboard again with the toe of his shoe.

"Yeah, maybe. It's a definite possibility. What kind of metal are you into? Like, black metal? Hair-metal? Nu-metal? There's all different kinds, right? That's what my sister says, anyway."

"I see you know your stuff," Gunnar said like a wizened eighty-year-old man, and Brian suddenly laughed again for how strange his life had become in the past seventy-two hours, tumor and all. "I mostly like American heavy metal from the '80s and '90s, with some thrash thrown in," said Gunnar, with all the precision of someone who'd had it memorized for some time.

"His father gave him some cassette tapes when he was little," Karla said from her spot at the end of the porch.

"Oh yeah?" Brian smiled. "That's cool. I'd like to hear more about that sometime."

This was prompt enough, apparently: Gunnar immediately dropped to his knees. It was only then that Brian realized the kid had sharpied big black gauntlets on each wrist. Sharpied warrior bracelets, something sandwiched between *Mad Max* and an '80s Sunset Boulevard guitarist. The boy burst into a passably snarling falsetto, an invisible microphone clutched in one dirty little fist in front of his face.

"Na na na na na na!
I've got you, got you in my sights!
Na na na na na na!
I don't know if it's wrong, wrong or right!
Na na na na na na!
But I'm gonna give you, give you
a love bite!"

"Gunnar, please," Karla said, laughing with a hand over her mouth. Liza grinned and wrapped her arms around her mother's leg, rubbing her face against Karla's thigh.

The boy stood up, casually brushed his knees. A showman.

"That was pretty good," Brian said.

Gunnar flicked his bangs out of his eyes. "That was the song 'Love Bites' by the band Steel Viper."

"Yeah, I haven't heard them, I guess."

"It came out in 1988, off the album *Chain the Viper.* It's a really good album. I can show you the cover later."

"You remember all that stuff?"

"Yeah. I listen to them a lot. There's a really good solo later on in the song. So you're going to live here, right?"

"Gunnar," Karla said. "They just got here."

Gunnar looked from Brian to his mother and back. Quieter, he said, "But you are, right?"

6

The front door opened into a large living room. Plants and toys lined the deep-set windowsills, and through an archway was a dining room where a chorus of mismatched velveteen chairs circled a long glass-topped table. Karla suggested they put their bags there for now. Their footfalls were loud on the wood floor. There was a stairwell off to one side, and the stairs leading to the second floor were dotted with plastic horses and a red bucket. Through another archway lay the kitchen. The kids' art hung on every wall in every room, as far as Brian could tell, and was bracketed amid framed, age-yellowed portraits of dour, unsmiling men and women. Standing, sitting, people clustered in dooryards or in front of unadorned, simple churches. Dozens of small frames on each wall. It could have come across as oppressive, but to Brian it felt quietly celebratory, reverent. He liked the house immediately.

They dropped their bags and headed back into the living room where the children, already unconcerned with them, lay splayed out on the couch. Amid the highbacked chairs and heavy, tied-back curtains, the plasma screen on the wall seemed the room's one concession to modernity.

Brian was not particularly surprised to see the lasagna show unfolding silently on the screen.

Sandoval spoke politely to Karla about the surrounding area, any neighbors she might have. Recon masked as small talk, Karla gesturing at the window as she spoke. Onscreen, the oldest daughter leaned into the open refrigerator, and the quavering, glistening lasagna—what the *fuck* was this show called?—scooted closer to her across the tabletop. Predatory and quivering, the means of the lasagna's locomotion was unclear. It strained forward, and just as it was about to make contact with the young woman's ass, noodle-to-denim, she straightened up and exited the kitchen. The lasagna trembled.

Brian pointed at the television and said, "Karla, do you happen to know the name of this show? I watched it as a kid but I can't remember."

She turned to the screen, and stared at it for a moment, frowning. "I'm sorry, I don't. I don't think I've seen it before." A string of Icelandic flashed at the bottom of the screen as the lasagna soliloquized on its plate, now alone in the kitchen. Breaking the fourth wall, addressing the camera, gruel slathered and quivering below a pair of googly eyes. Karla said, "It seems strange. It's probably not great for the children, actually."

Liza took her fingers from her mouth. "I want to keep watching it," she said.

"You can't even read what it's saying yet, Li-li," said Gunnar.

"I can too."

"Do you mind," Karla said, turning off the television, "if we do this in the kitchen? I'd like to go over these papers, but the children's dinner is on the stove."

"Mamma! I was watching!"

"Come color in the kitchen, Li-li."

Karla led them to the kitchen in the rear of the house, Liza hanging her head and stomping her way along, Gunnar behind them all, trumpeting loudly through an invisible air horn. The kitchen was careworn and clean. There was an old, burn-marred wooden island in the center, and through a large window above the sink there was a gorgeous view of the northern woods. Jars and cans and plastic baggies of herbs lay inside stacked cabinets with their doors removed. A cast iron pot sat quietly bubbling on an old four-burner stove. Next to the back door sat a round-edged Frigidaire festooned in magnets, more photographs of the children. Trinkets and drawings. The house resounded with the sense of sturdy, long-used things valued and cared for. The children took their seats at the island, drawing supplies already scattered there. Karla offered coffee in heavy ceramic mugs and Brian and Sandoval each took one gratefully.

"I really like your house," Brian said.

Karla lifted the lid on the pot. "Oh, thank you." She stirred the contents with a wooden spoon, divined the need for a pinch of something that lay in a baggie on the counter. "It's a family home. We've been here a long time."

"Those are pictures of your family, then? On the walls?"

"Yes, exactly. Farmers and fishermen, mostly. During the war, some sailors. My great-grandfather built the house." Sandoval cleared his throat, picked at a piece of lint on his jacket. He squared the pages of the contract where it sat on the counter. Impatient to begin. "We've lived here since then," she said, "my family, except for a little bit during the war."

"World War II?"

"Uh-huh."

"What happened then? Do you mind if I ask?"

Karla peered at Brian over her shoulder, assessing him. "Of course. It was . . ." She turned back to the stove and gestured with the spoon, roved it in a circle. "I don't know the English word. The British, when they came here, used the fields as storage. For their bombs, their shells and vehicles and things. Some officers lived in the house then."

"Wow. Really." He and Sandoval shared a look. Sandoval shrugged, nodded. *Context for the book, sure.*

"Then they left in . . . 1942? And the Americans took it over. They returned the house to my grandfather in 1944, because by then they had built the base at the end of *Vegurrin Sjö.*"

"Road Seven."

"Yes."

"Right there!" Liza said, pointing at the wall of the kitchen with a crayon. "*Vegurrin Sjö.*"

Brian walked to the kitchen window, raised his mug. He could see another rutted road like the driveway out front, a kind of mud-hewn back trail that led to the gray ribbon of the road that eventually disappeared through the mouth of the trees beyond. "There's a base up there?"

"Yes."

It took him a second. "There's a *US military* base on the island?" He was thinking of the haphazard scattering of buildings he'd looked at online. "Really."

"Yes." She clacked her spoon against the pot, covered it. "I mean, it's small. You don't really see the men very often. They hardly ever come into town, but sometimes. Sometimes you can see things are being delivered to them by helicopter."

"It looked like there'd been a forest fire around it."

"Oh, they burn the woods around the base all the time."

"Really," Brian said. He kept resisting the urge to eyeball Sandoval. *Are you hearing this?* "Why's that?"

Without hesitating, Karla said, "Because of the *álagablettur,* of course." She smiled as she said it, and turned to face them. She crossed her arms, this air about her of . . . antagonism? Of daring them to say something. He wracked his brain trying to recall the term, couldn't pull it from his slim Icelandic vocabulary.

"What was it again? The what?"

"The álagablettur," Liza piped up, looping big scrawls of blue crayon across her paper.

"It means the woods are haunted," Gunnar said. He was rededicating himself to his wrist gauntlets with a Sharpie.

Liza said, "There's ghosts out there."

Now he and Sandoval shared a look.

Karla said, "And you're not to go out there, are you?"

A chorus of two: "No, mamma."

"Anyway," she said, shedding the strangeness of the moment just like that, or at least moving past it, "I'm sure they just burn the woods so they can see the cars and things that come down the road." She stepped toward the sink, brightening. "Can I get you anything else? Water? More coffee? A beer?"

The meal took longer than planned, so the children were sent out to play during the last stretch of daylight. Karla Hauksdóttir retrieved her reading glasses and took a seat at the kitchen island next to Sandoval. Brian stood at the window, looked out at the dense copses of pine and birch, many of their trunks gnarled and bent as arthritic hands, everything growing dark in the gloaming. The children ran in the yard, Gunnar (he'd finally put a jacket on) trying to throw pinecones into a basket that Liza held, her squeals and laughter seeping through the glass.

"Will I need a lawyer for this?" Karla said.

Sandoval opened his mouth, shut it. He scratched at a spot next to his eye. "I'll be honest. It's a pretty boilerplate contract, Karla."

She waved her hand in the air. "I don't know what this means, boilerplate."

"It's a pretty standard contract."

"Ah."

"But if you wanted to get a lawyer involved, I certainly wouldn't say no. We want you to feel good about us being here."

"Of course."

"But my concern," said Sandoval, and here he spread out his hand atop the papers, tapped them with all five fingers. "My main concern is that we can't actually start our investigation until the contract's been signed. My publisher is very clear about that. No photos, no filming, no interviews, nothing. Technically we're not even supposed to have our gear here."

"I see," Karla said, nodding. She flipped a page, peered at it over the tops of her glasses.

"And we've only got a limited amount of time, so. . ." He let it hang there. Smart. Mercenary, but smart: Put the onus on her. Unspoken, but claxon-loud in the room: You *called* us, *remember?*

He took a pen from inside his jacket, showed her the places she needed to sign and date, set the pen down. Outside, Gunnar threw a pinecone high in the air and it bounced off the top of Liza's head and into the basket she held. For a moment it looked like she might cry and then she began shrieking with laughter, her eyes wide white O's.

Karla signed, and Sandoval rolled the contract up into a tube and mock-bowed, thanking her. He went to secret it away in one of his bags. "I guess that's it then," she said, and it was impossible to read the tone there; she could've been resigned, or concerned, or quietly grateful. She rose, took off her glasses and folded their stems and put them on the counter. A loaf of rye bread was removed from a covered basket on the counter and she handed Brian a knife, handle first, and asked him to cut it up. She stepped out the kitchen door onto the porch to call the children. The sound of the ocean filled the room faint as a whisper through the doorway. It was another world here.

Sandoval came back in from the dining room. "Did you see how big those fields were?" Brian offered quietly as he sawed through the bread. "This place is way too big, man."

Sandoval rinsed his mug out in the sink. "We'll just have to move them every twenty-four hours. Saturate the area."

"You think that's gonna work?"

"We'll map it out. We'll come up with something."

"Those greenhouses, man. So much for line of sight, you know what I mean?"

"We'll figure it out, Brian."

They ate in the dining room. The last gasp of twilight limned the mountains that stood beyond, snowcapped and serrated as monster jaws. Occasionally, very occasionally, the headlights of cars could be traced making their way down the road. Brian was incredulous to find that Gunnar had made the bread they were eating.

"Metal fan *and* a baking genius? Impressive."

"Thanks," said Gunnar, frowning into his bowl, red-cheeked and thrilled.

"And this stew is delicious," said Sandoval. He'd salted it so much that Liza had stared.

"Reindeer," said Gunnar. "It's expensive."

Karla looked at him.

"It is, though," Gunnar said. "It's a treat, right? Mamma said it's because we have people visiting." Karla tucked a lock of hair behind her ear and sighed, smiling a little.

After dinner, Liza and Gunnar moved a pair of the island stools over to the kitchen sink and began doing the dishes. Gunnar washing, Liza drying. Brian watched as the children held a glass baking tray in their four little hands, stacking it into the dish drainer together. Sandoval went outside to begin scouting the area—he said this without a trace of irony or embarrassment—and Brian and Karla brought the rest of the dishes in from the dining room.

"Those are awesome kids you have."

Karla stacked silverware onto a plate, gazed in at them where they sat

on their stools. "They've been through a lot. I'm glad they have each other."
There was another indecipherable smile.

• • •

That evening Sandoval cornered him out on the porch. He took him around
the side of the house. It was full dark, the sky a shotgun-scatter of stars,
a night fanged with chill. He leaned in close and said quietly, "There's no
fucking *reception* here."

"No? You sure?"

"It's spotty, apparently." Sandoval scrubbed his hand down his face
once, savagely. "Karla just has a landline."

"I don't even have a phone at this point," Brian said.

"Yeah, well, it's a pain in *my* ass, okay? No internet, no phone? Again,
Brian, I can't stress how important this kind of thing is. Knowing this stuff."

"Okay," he said. "We just didn't have a lot of jump time between me
getting hired and me getting on the plane. You know what I mean? I get
that it's part of my job, but there just wasn't a lot of time."

Sandoval looked out at the woods. He sucked at his teeth, and the light
from the window sectioned his face in clear, delineated planes. He cursed
once and then nodded. "No, you're right. I'm sorry."

"Hey, it's fine. Believe me."

"It makes things a little complicated, though. I guess we have to go
into Kjálkabein to send emails. I can make calls via the landline here, but
that's expensive as hell. It just means a lot more back and forth than I was
thinking."

"Well hey," Brian said, "look at this way. If you wanted a space free of
distractions, we just got dealt a royal flush. Right? No one can bother us
out here."

And it was there and gone again: the dawning on Sandoval's face. Fast,
but not poker-player fast.

Fast but noticeable.

It was relief. A look of pure, unbridled relief on Sandoval's face.

• • •

Karla offered once more to let them sleep downstairs. "It gets very cold at
night. The wind's bad." She jabbed her hand out toward Sandoval's chest,
like she was stabbing him with her fingers. "It cuts."

"It's okay. We don't want to miss anything," he said, hoisting a bag over
his shoulder. "But thank you."

They pitched their tents in the yard where the cold glare from the porch light threw long shadows on the ground. They were new, expensive tents that Sandoval had bought, weatherproof and oddly alien in their shape. Brian's headache had snarled and coughed to life, then settled to a hum. It was impossible now not to think of it as something alive, separate. His breath hung in tatters as he assembled his tent.

Gunnar and Liza sat huddled on the top step of the porch, bathed and fresh-faced in their pajamas and heavy socks and puffy thermal jackets. They plied the men with questions as they worked.

Gunnar: "Have you seen those tents that unfold all by themselves, right when you open them up? *Vroop!*"

Liza: "Do you snore when you're sleeping? Gunnar snores."

Gunnar: "I do not. Hey, Brian, where did you get your sleeping bag?"

Liza: "What's the biggest pumpkin you ever saw?"

Gunnar: "Do you like snow better, or the ocean?"

Liza: "What's the most candy you ever ate?"

Gunnar: "Do you know the Dokken song 'Breaking the Chains'? It's famous."

Liza: "Do you know how to play the guitar? Brian, do you? We're having a band."

"He doesn't, Li-li," Gunnar answered. "I already asked him."

Eventually Karla came out, ushered them upstairs. The single video camera and three motion-activated digital cameras they'd brought were all cued in to Sandoval's laptop. His tent would be their headquarters, in a sense, this little bubble of fabric and polyester the nexus of their life for the coming weeks. The house would sit like an appendage, Brian imagined, gargantuan and seldom utilized.

The unicorn, Karla had said after dinner (and she'd said it so straight-faced and sincerely that Brian, his stomach sinking, realized that she *believed* her story, if nothing else, with utter conviction—how had he not thought of this before?) had seemed to favor the outer edges of the fields. That was where the video had been filmed. Well beyond the greenhouses, in the area skirting the woods. They'd directed the eyes of their equipment there, though Brian was confident they'd need two dozen more cameras and a series of floodlights connected to heat and motion sensors. At least. Yet here they were. Playing games in the dirt. Sleeping in ice-grass.

They were the guest of a woman who remained utterly convinced she'd seen a unicorn. This was no giggling, self-conscious claim of a child seeing an ernicee while drifting off to sleep, its wings aglow. No sailor's booze-mad, red-faced proclamation of a magyr swimming along the bow of his ship, flexing its webbed hands as moss hung in serpentine trails from its breasts. This was a mother, a business owner, in a house, with a job and children—who insisted sober and straight-faced that she had witnessed the impossible.

His earlier jubilance was quashed, sloughed off by his headache. What rose in its place was a quiet flurry of doubt, insistent as heartburn. What in the hell was he *doing* out here? He checked the batteries on the cameras once more, checked the sight lines, checked that everything was running clean on Sandoval's laptop.

The two of them bid each other goodnight, and Brian lay in his sleeping bag, both tired and not. In spite of his doubt, he felt the strange calm that came with having the next month or so of his life planned out, as ridiculous as it was. An alarm would sound on Sandoval's laptop if any of the cameras were activated. They'd made it. They were here. Tomorrow he would return to the Hotel Magnificence and get the rest of their gear, and they'd begin their work in earnest.

The dome of fabric above him was a blank, featureless sky. His thoughts churned: he wondered about Sandoval, his mother, these little kids. Brooke. His father. Traci and her possibly fake boobs and Brooke's unyielding desire for the woman's ruination. He thought of Don Whitmer's clear disappointment in him, and how he hadn't even been able to apologize to the man before he left.

After a while Brian unzipped his tent and put his jacket on and crawled out. Stretching, he turned and saw the dim shape of Karla Hauksdóttir sitting on the porch steps. He let out a little bark of surprise and then raised his hand in greeting. She raised hers in return, and the motion detector turned the porch light on with a loud click. A tendril of smoke purled above her head.

She was wrapped in a man's coat, the collar edged in fur, and Brian sat down on the step below hers. The world beyond was a scrim of darkness spattered with stars, a slivered moon. The weak gleam of the greenhouses. They watched a single car thread its way along the road and disappear.

Karla said, "Couldn't sleep?"

He shrugged. "Jet lag, I guess. How about you?"

"This is my only time to relax, really. After the kids are in bed, before I check on the crops in the morning."

"Got it."

"There's some coffee left, if you'd like that. If you want to stay up and wait to see if something will happen."

For a moment he was confused, thought it was an offhanded attempt at hitting on him, and then he blushed at his own foolishness. "Does it come out often?"

She smoked, and he waited for her answer.

"No," she finally said, ruefully. "Just the once. Just that one time."

"Okay."

"I keep hoping it will appear again since I emailed Mr. Sandoval, but it hasn't. Which is a little embarrassing to me."

"It's okay." *He'll find a story either way,* Brian thought. "Have you ever thought about trying to trap it? Setting a trap out there?" he asked.

"No," she said stiffly. "I haven't thought of that." It was clear she was bothered by the idea, that he'd made a mistake by suggesting it.

They listened to the wind sloughing through the woods, listened to it moan and curl around the corner of the house, ripple the fabric of the tents in the yard. Sandoval's snore, light and pinched, served as the cross-note. Karla lit another cigarette. "You know, there's a word they have across the way."

"Across the way?" He turned to look at her again.

"Iceland," she said. She lifted her chin then tucked her face back in the folds of the coat's collar. "The important people across the way." Impossible to miss the sarcasm.

"Ah. Gotcha."

She stretched her legs out in front of her, thunked her boots on the step next to him. Sandoval's snoring halted, picked back up. Quieter, almost a whisper, she said, "So, they call this word *ástandiö.*" Brian turned to her, braced his back along the railing. Beneath the porch light, she waved her hand in a circle, drew errant scribbles of smoke. "It means, like, *the condition.* Or *the situation we have to deal with right now.* Okay? It was a term they used during the war."

"This was World War II again?"

She nodded. "It was a word they used because of all the British soldiers that went there—to Reykjavík mostly—and all the Icelandic girls that fell in love with them. And had babies! It was a real situation. So, ástandiö." Her laugh was stilted, with little love in it. "People were unhappy. By 1942 there were probably as many British as Icelandic men over there, okay?"

"Sure," Brian said. "How do you know all this?"

She pulled her head back to look at him. She was frowning. "These are the stories we tell to each other. This is our history. You don't have stories you tell with your family? Passed down?" Brian thought of his angry, distant father doing a wobbly downward dog at a sun-blasted nudist colony outside of Scottsdale, arms trembling, his balls mashing his yoga mat. He suppressed a shudder.

"Not really," he said.

Again the waving hand, the curls of smoke. "Well, this is our history.

Our stories. So. In Iceland, the people were unhappy. All these British men. Boys. These pregnant girls. But the funny thing is, the thing that's interesting to me, is that there was no ástandiö in Hvíldarland during the war. None. Do you know why?"

Was she angry? Is that what he heard? Was it anger at him, or anger at the past?

"No."

"There was no ástandiö here because we were so grateful! This has always been a poor little place. Hard ground, lava rocks, moss. So hard to grow things here. Before the war, there was no little airport in Kjálkabein. Kjálkabein itself was much smaller. We had the hot springs. The woods. Little groups of houses here and there. And this place, the farm. We relied on trade with Iceland. Wool, timber, what little we could grow. Fishing. Then the war came. And the British took over my grandfather's house." She pointed off to the side of the house, away from Road Seven. "Over there you can still see the pieces of a building they took down. The children will play and find little things here and there. A key, an old American cigarette pack. Bullets. One time a rusted bayonet."

"Wow."

Karla shrugged, lifted her cigarette hand dismissively. She took a drag and the bright orange glow lit her face for a moment. "It was wartime. The Germans had invaded Norway and Denmark. Iceland asked us—the one time they *asked* us anything, really—to remain neutral, like them. We had no defense force. We said yes. They said we would be rewarded for our loyalty. My mother was very young at the time, younger than Liza is now. She'd never seen a gun before. Never seen an airplane. There were less than twenty officers here at the farm, then they all moved to the base up north. Three hundred men here total? There was no point to it, and still we were grateful. It was like they were put here just so the Germans could not take it. My grandfather thought we were safer with them here, that we would be protected. Is this boring you?"

"No. I should be writing it down, actually."

"Oh, you're kind." She smoked. "Everyone was placed on rations. They had even less than before because they had to report their crops to the British, who took some. Blackout conditions at night. Not that that was hard."

He decided that Karla seemed still wounded by the story, tethered to it.

"So what happened after the war? The British left, right?"

Karla smiled at the wordplay. It took Brian a moment to get it. "Oh, I mean—"

"No, that's funny." She leaned over and stubbed her cigarette out on her boot, holding her ponytail against her neck with her free hand. She put her cigarette butt in a nearby coffee can. "The British thanked us for our service and reminded us Iceland would reward us politically in the years to come. Then the Americans came and stayed at the house while they built their base up north."

"Did you ever get paid back?"

"By the end of the war, Iceland had money. They were becoming a republic. We should have celebrated: no one in Hvíldarland was made to fight the Nazis. We were safe. We were still poor, but we were our own people again. Mostly."

"So they didn't pay you back."

"In the past eighty years? They've helped us sometimes. Food, aid. But they do it like an older child to a younger one, you know? As if they were giving us a great gift. As if we should be so grateful. It did not help our relations over the years."

"Your English is really impressive, Karla. My Icelandic is terrible."

"Well, we learn it in school. And my ex-husband is from Idaho."

They sat, looked out at the darkness, the way the land seemed lighter than the sky. For lack of anything else to say, Brian asked where they'd met.

"He was stationed at the base."

"Oh."

"I had a flat tire on *Vegurrin Sjö* once and he stopped his big military vehicle and changed it." She turned shy at the memory; he could sense her burrowing into her big coat, into the memory itself.

"Pretty smooth," said Brian.

"Oh, but I knew how to change a tire," she said, smiling.

He laughed. "Nice."

"A few months later he came to my house and knocked on the door. My mother was still alive then, and he asked us both to dinner in Kjálkabein. He was done with the army."

"He's still in the picture?"

"Oh yes. You'll meet him. We share the children. He's a veterinarian now."

"Wow. I'd love to talk to him about the base. What they do there."

She shrugged, pulled an invisible shred of tobacco from her lips. "He said they did boring things with satellites. Weather satellites, data collection. Mostly, he said, they stood around."

Brian pointed a finger at her, squinted one eye shut. "That's right, stood around and burned back the álagablettur. Kept back the bad spirits."

She looked away from him, looked out at the fields. After a moment she said, "You laugh, but some people believe it. *I* do. Many Icelanders and Hvíldarlanders do."

"Okay."

"You're a scientist."

"I'm an anthropologist," he said, wanting to curl up at the lie, at the grand act of conceit that saying such a thing required. A lazy, petulant, privileged dropout was what he was.

"I don't know what this means."

"I study cultures. Societies. How they develop."

"I see."

He said, "And a lot of times, the old monsters help us. They show us what people cared about. What they were afraid of, what they valued. You want to learn about a society, learn the stories they told their children when it got dark out."

"Well, I tell my children that those woods are full of ghosts." She drew out the last word, light and airy. She fluttered her fingers. And then she turned hard, unsmiling. "I tell them that, and I tell them to stay away."

"So you believe in ghosts. And you think you saw a unicorn."

"I did see a unicorn, Brian."

"We thought, Mr. Sandoval and I, that it might be a reindeer that someone had . . . operated on."

She said nothing.

"Or ponies. A horse."

Karla shrugged. "I know what I saw. It was a unicorn."

"Is everyone in Hvíldarland this open-minded?"

He couldn't tell if he'd upset her. She picked up her cigarettes and he thought she would rise and leave and then she set them back down on the steps. "I grew up on the stories as a child. The *huldufólk*. The *einhyrningur*. The álagablettur. We all did, people my age. In school, outside of school. I don't think much of it, really. But I also don't let the children play in the woods. When the British were here on the farm, they were building a big gun on the edge of the sea over there"—she pointed to the east—"that they dismantled when they left. But they were carrying a bunch of the shells through the woods, a group of soldiers, when a single shell exploded. And then *boom boom boom*, like a chain, all the shells blew up. My grandfather said that eight men died. The only British casualties in Hvíldarland during all of the war. And now it's said that they haunt the woods around here, these men. Bad-spirited and angry, lost."

"Pissed off at dying in such a dumb way."

She picked up on his tone. "You don't have to believe anything, Brian. You can study the culture all you want, and believe none of it." He winced at the cutting tone of it. "But I don't let the children play in the woods. You can call it an álagablettur or common sense, it doesn't matter to me."

"I didn't mean to upset you."

She shrugged again and now she did hoist herself up with one hand on the banister. "Who's upset? I will say, though, you are in a funny business. Not believing in fantastic things but hunting for them."

Brian stood up as well, his knees popping like bubble wrap. "You know, people keep telling me that. Like wanting proof is some inconvenience."

"Oh, it's not a bad thing," Karla said. "But what happens if it's right in front of you and you refuse to see it? Have a good night, Brian. Welcome to Hvíldarland."

7

The wind ran strident hands along his tent and finally woke him. His little world filled with the dim light of morning. He lay there, his eyes closed, and did this new thing, this thing that he'd begun after Dr. Bajeer had shown him his CT scans, both a lifetime and a number of days ago: He lay there and kind of tested the interior of his head. Tried to picture the tumor, tried to locate the malignancy growing there, like a man feeling a room in the dark. But he felt nothing. Or rather he felt the same. He couldn't find it inside himself.

Bleary-eyed and needing to piss, he unzipped his tent and stepped out into a fog that curled along the rising slopes of the mountains, obscured the trunks of the trees. The field lay threaded with tendrils of ground fog. It stilled him. If unicorns were going to be galloping around, he recognized that it would indeed be in a place like this. His talk with Karla the night previous—had she really insisted that the woods were haunted with the ghosts of dead British soldiers?—seemed distant, jarring, too intimate. A conversation he would've had while drunk. He took the long walk to one of the greenhouses. Stepping around the corner, he pissed into the grass.

He was sitting on the porch, nervous about going into the house alone that first time, not wanting to be too presumptuous, when Sandoval crawled out of his own tent. He was squinting, his hair flattened on one side. "Morning," he said. He was wearing a T-shirt and shorts, and for the first time Brian saw clearly the scars that stood out in raised relief against his tan. Like someone had laid out a chemistry assignment all over his arms, his legs. These wending striations of hexagons, circles, squares. All connected. Like a map leading nowhere, circling in on itself.

"Hey," Brian said, trying not to stare.

After Sandoval dressed they went inside the house; Brian speed-checked the feed of their camera, which of course showed nothing at all save for the moon's wan illumination moving from one side of the screen to the other. The motion sensors hadn't been activated at all.

Sandoval frowned down at his monitor, a coffee cup in one hand. "That sucks."

"Well, first night."

He nodded. "How'd you sleep?"

Brian thought of telling him about the conversation with Karla, her insistence on the veracity of the álagablettur. And then she walked by on her way to the bathroom, offering them a shy smile. "Good," he said. "How about you?"

"Man," Sandoval said, uncurling his arms above his head. "I don't really feel much when it comes to jet lag, but damn if I didn't have some crazy dreams." Brian thought of his own dreams back at the hotel, the cavalcade of old beasts that had hung their hooks in the netting of his sleep.

The children were silent, hunched over bowls of oatmeal at the kitchen island, their hair sleep-knotted and wild. Karla washed dishes at the sink. Sandoval, standing next to the kids in a white T-shirt and jeans, thumbed through the contract, as well as an itinerary that Brian had tentatively drawn up for the next few weeks. Neither Liza nor Gunnar could take their eyes off Sandoval as they wordlessly scooped oatmeal into their mouths. Gunnar cast one last look at his sister, rich but wordless, the salient dialogue of siblings, and then plunged forth. "Mr. Sandoval?"

"Yeah, buddy," Sandoval said without looking up.

"Did it hurt to get all those lines on you?"

Sandoval put the papers down on the counter. He smiled at the children. "I don't actually remember, bud."

Liza squinted at him, still half-asleep. "Was your mom mad when you got them?"

Karla Hauksdóttir laughed down at the frenzy of suds on her hands and Sandoval smiled as well. "No, she wasn't mad. I was a grown-up."

Stirring her spoon around in her bowl, Liza considered this. "But you didn't have to *pay* for them, did you?"

And all the adults laughed then, laughed loud, and Liza blushed and ducked her head toward her breakfast, clearly pleased.

"No, honey," Sandoval said, "they didn't cost me any money."

• • •

At the intersection where the driveway met Road Seven, next to the white rocks, a small white school bus opened its doors and the children climbed aboard. Karla was already at work in the greenhouses with her crew of three or four local men, and Brian and Sandoval watched all of the morning's activity from the porch. When the little school bus had finally crested the rise, heading off to the school in Kjálkabein, Sandoval set his coffee cup on the porch railing and appraised him. "So I don't want to have to tell you the obvious."

"You don't have to," Brian said.

"Yeah, you say that."

"I mean it."

"I think it might just be in my nature," Sandoval said with a lopsided grin. "Just the kind of guy I am. A perfectionist. A control freak."

"Well, if you have to do it, go ahead."

"Okay. Whatever you do, Brian, don't lose that contract."

"I won't, boss." He was feeling good; for the next few hours, he had a purpose, clear and direct. Much of the previous night's uncertainty had dissipated with the morning light.

"I'm not kidding. Lose a leg before you lose that thing."

"There's the love I was looking for, Mark."

"If you can't fax it to my publisher, just scan it and email it to me. I'll head into town and email it tomorrow."

They watched each other. Sandoval's look wasn't cold, not like the look he'd given Brian the day before, but it was still mercenary enough. Sandoval was wondering, Brian knew, if he should just go himself. But he could also see the restlessness at work inside the man: Sandoval was jittery, squinting, pacing the porch. Smoking cigarettes like a beast. He wanted to get started. He wanted to find this thing. It was possible the man truly was powered by belief.

Finally Sandoval nodded, seemingly satisfied, and picked up his coffee cup again. "Alright. I'll start checking the perimeter of the farm. We'll come up with some kind of mapping system when you get back. We've got to get the most out of the camera spacing, like you said, so we're not pissing in the wind for a month, hoping for something in one spot when it could be two feet away. And I want to start talking to people this afternoon. Laying the groundwork, getting our faces out there."

"Got it."

"And keep a lookout for a car, yeah? Someone's got to have a car for sale on this island. Christ."

"Will do."

And that was it. Brian, loosed upon the world with a pair of empty duffel bags crisscrossed over his shoulder and the signed contract folded in the inside pocket of his jacket. He notched the soles of his shoes in the pedals of his little bicycle and set off down the driveway, heading down the long road to Kjálkabein.

• • •

The dog that had chased Sandoval was not on its porch today. He saw two, three, four little villages in their radial spokes off of the main road, little stacks of buildings painted green and red and yellow and orange, nestled beneath the blue-gray eye of the mountains beyond. He thought his brain might crack open for the strangeness and beauty of it. He passed a corrugated shed with a dead pickup on cement blocks out front, the windows gone. He saw tire treads that weaved in and out along the muddy shoulder of Road Seven, and after a while he was in Kjálkabein.

• • •

The town was like some wonderful embattlement against the environment, he decided, against the drab featureless sky, the slate steel of the sea beyond. All the buildings color-saturated, like a refutation of the elements, the cutting wind, the inevitable long months of snow and ice and darkness. He saw things this time that he'd missed on the way to the farm when they'd used Viktor's crude map. He saw concrete medians thronged with flowers: clusters of humming yellow jonquils, thumbings of purple wildflowers. Hardy flowers. He saw women in heavy coats as they chatted with coffee cups in their hands and pushed strollers. He saw a man in a shiny tracksuit smoking a cigar and walking a little white dog. The wide smooth streets, the traffic, the sense of compartmentalized efficiency that had always seemed to him distinctly European, even in a small town like this.

He backtracked his way to the Hotel Magnificence, which was easier than he'd thought it would be. Wheeling his bike through the lobby, he was greeted by Viktor, who looked today even more malefic and pale in his black suit. He kept smiling at Brian and smoothing down his mustache, as if he were trying to smooth out the smile itself. "Good morning, my friend!"

"Hey, Viktor. You have a fax machine, don't you?"

"Já, of course."

Brian took the contract out of his jacket, careful to remove the paper clip. "Can you please fax this to the number right there, up top? It's important."

"International?"

"It's international, yeah."

Viktor let out a little chuff of air. The mustache-smoothing kicked up a notch. "It will cost a little more, I'm afraid."

"I understand. Can you charge it to Mr. Sandoval's account?"

"No problem, my friend. The bikes are working okay for you?"

Brian smiled, adjusted the duffel bags bandoliered across his chest. "It's been fun, actually. I don't know if Mr. Sandoval feels the same, but I'm having a blast."

They stood there in awkward silence as the fax machine made its requisite squawks and squeals, and then Viktor handed the contract back, made a little notation to Sandoval's account on his ancient computer.

Brian carefully put the contract back in his jacket. "Thanks. Also, I wanted to talk about renting or even buying a car, if there's any way we can make that happen."

"Okay, sure, sure."

"I'm gonna go grab the rest of our stuff. We'll be checking out today."

"Ah, you'll be staying at the Hauksdóttir farm. This is wonderful for you, I'm glad." Viktor's head bobbed like it was on a string, his grin manic. Brian decided that the kids at the farm were the least odd of the bunch he'd met so far.

He headed up the stairs to Sandoval's room. The lights in their dusty sconces cast the hallway in a buttery, dim incandescence. His shadow was a hulking, trembling shape on the carpet.

He unlocked the door and stepped into a room full of wreckage. The stink of piss was like a fist in his face.

• • •

The gear had been savaged. Everything had.

Their EVP recorders had been reduced to a nimbus of plastic shards on the carpet. Husks of cracked plastic on the unmade bed turned out to be the rest of their digital cameras; the tripods had been shattered and tossed in all four corners of the room. The clothes that Sandoval had left overnight—guy had brought a nice wardrobe considering he'd mostly be sleeping outside—had been torn from the closet rod and flung around the room. Shredded. A single jacket dangled from a lone hangar.

The smell of piss was acrid, sharp, practically animal-like. They'd pissed on the carpet, the bed. Sandoval's clothes. The gear. *One dehydrated motherfucker did this,* Brian thought, a hand cupping his nose. *Good lord.* Gingerly, his heart hammering in his chest, he tiptoed through the destruction.

He stepped into Sandoval's bathroom, a room as rust-stained and moored in sadness as his own had been. Shower, sink, commode. Tiny inset window high up on the wall. In the tub, floating beneath a skin of water, lay a mound of papers. A manuscript. Double-spaced, 12-point type. Legible save for blurred handwritten notes in the margins. His footsteps squeaked on the floor as he bent over to see the title in the upper corner of a page.

Monsters Americana.

Some impulse drove him to touch the water, to watch his fingers break the surface. He plunged his hand into the water and pulled the plug. With a morose gurgle the pages rippled like unsettled animals at the bottom of the tub.

Suddenly he turned, convinced that someone was behind him. Spiders scurried up his spine. He slammed the bathroom door against the wall, sure he'd find someone—the person who'd broken in, or some victim grown blue and cold, someone drowned in the tub and returned to life. Something worse. But there was nothing. The door slammed, reverberated, bounced back at him. He stopped it with his foot, his mouth chalk-dry.

He stepped out of the bathroom and picked up the phone on the nightstand, half expecting it to be dead, but the tone was there. He dialed downstairs. The smell of piss was truly wretched now.

Viktor, brightly: "Já, front desk."

Brian gave his name and room number in short clipped tones. He felt his panic give way in stitches, like fabric ripping, revealing the anger underneath. He found himself stepping toward it with something like relief. It took him a minute to figure out who the anger was for, and he was a little surprised to find that he actually was furious with the desk clerk of the Hotel Magnificence. "Viktor. You need to get up here, man."

"Ah, Mr. Schutt, what—" on the other end of the line, Viktor made a sound like he'd just ingested a pool ball—"what can I do for you, friend?"

"Viktor. Get up here. Right now."

8

Viktor stood in the doorway with the back of his hand pressed against his nose.

Salvaged, random pages of *Monster Americana* lay drying on top of the bed's comforter as Brian blotted them with a towel. "I'm just saying, you seem pretty unsurprised."

"What?"

"You and your nephew," Brian said, "are the only people that know we're here. And then this happens." Unable to look Viktor in the eye, he still managed to say, "It's a little fucking suspect, is all I'm saying."

Viktor stepped into the room. "What? *Us?* This is a joke? All of Kjálkabein knows you are here! The American monster hunter with the scars? The writer and his—" and here he scowled and waved his hand to indicate Brian, a gesture that could mean any great number of things. "You ride those bicycles down the whole island! All along the road. *Everybody* knows who you are!"

"Well, I think we better call the police then."

Viktor sighed and crossed his arms. He gently closed the door behind him. "You don't want to call the police, Mr. Schutt." Brian could see him start to raise his hand to his nose again, and then drop it at his side.

"I think I do, Viktor."

"Police here, they do nothing for you."

"I still need to call. This is screwed up. This is a crime."

"I can offer you a slight refund, okay, a *half* refund, but the police . . ." He dipped his head and his voice took on a low, conspiratorial tone. "They're very bad here. They will blame you for the robbery. They'll say, 'Why did you leave your room unattended all night and day?' They will want money to take your case."

"It wasn't a robbery, Viktor. They didn't take anything. They just destroyed shit. They destroyed a manuscript, Viktor. A *book.* Do you have any idea how much money Mark Sandoval makes on his books? We need to file a police report." As if in agreement, some last vestige of bathwater gurgled down the drain in the bathroom. Brian looked at Viktor and Viktor looked at the carpet as if deep in thought. He endlessly smoothed those few strands of hair on his scalp with the tips of his fingers.

When he looked up, he said, "I don't think you will be happy with this idea."

Brian set another wet sheaf of manuscript on the bed and toed a piece of camera that lay on the carpet like a deceased pet. "Call the cops, Viktor."

With a hiss of frustration, Viktor spun on a heel. "Fine. I will call from downstairs. Your life is your life. Squander it as you wish."

• • •

He was still blotting the manuscript on the bed, placing pages upside down and willing himself not to read them—Sandoval's unpublished manuscript felt as sacrosanct and private as his own dissertation—when someone knocked on the open door.

"Hello? Is this the right room? Ah, yes it is—the smell is quite strong, isn't it?"

Cops everywhere were universal. The same sense of reserve, of assessment, of contained willfulness. That same sense of bravado, of implied ownership of a room. Brian had seen enough footage of enough shootings of enough unarmed children to be distrustful of cops; it was only his standard default of politeness—particularly in the face of authority—that led him to walk over and shake the officer's hand, and he cursed himself as he did it. This one wore a dark uniform, the sleeves of her coat lined in black and white checkers, and it gave her an air of some clownish utility. Officer of Ska, Agent of Skanking. She was heavy-boned, tall, a copper ponytail hanging behind her cap. Interesting though: No gun. No bulletproof vest. A belt on her hips held cuffs, a flashlight and a short baton, a canister of what Brian assumed was mace or pepper spray. So different, this officer, from the images of militarized cops he was inundated with in the States. "Constable Jónsdóttir," she said. Her handshake was cool and dry.

"Brian Schutt."

"Ah. American?" He could see the cop searching his face, the scab on his lip, the shiner around his eye grown purple and green.

"Yep."

"Well," she said, looking away from him and eyeing the room, "this is quite the mess here, yes?"

"It is."

"Does this have anything to do with what happened to your face?"

"No," Brian said. He waved a hand on front of his features, a magician doing a trick. "This happened in the US. Before I came here."

"Okay." Jónsdóttir pulled a notebook and pen from her jacket. "So you weren't here when the break-in took place."

"No."

"The clerk says it was not your room?"

"My boss's. We'd moved everything here overnight. I came here today to get the rest of our stuff."

She examined the door, the doorframe. "No trouble with entry. Hmmm. They use actual keys here, not like the electronic key cards?"

"Right," said Brian.

Jónsdóttir straightened, her eyes roving the ceiling—Brian automatically looked up as well—and then to the window, the bed. She walked into the bathroom, came back out. "The clerk says they urinated on the clothes?"

"Yes. They urinated on everything."

She leaned down, lifted a shirtsleeve from a pile of clothes on the floor with the tip of her pen. Brian could see the knife lacerations in the fabric.

"Your clothes?"

"My boss's."

She clicked the pen a few times, frowned. Absently tapped the pen against the badge on her chest in some quick internal rhythm. "Okay. Let's get down to business then, Mr. Schutt. Let's start with what was stolen."

He paused. "Well, nothing."

"Hmm?"

"Nothing was stolen."

He told his story, what little there was. Jónsdóttir occasionally scribbled a note in her pad or grunted in affirmation. After spending a moment examining the bathroom, she came out and pointed at the lone unshredded jacket on its hanger. "So why would someone do this, Mr. Schutt? Destroy your things? Your equipment. This is expensive equipment, yes?"

"I don't know why, honestly. And it is, yeah. Expensive, I mean."

"Why did you bring all of this equipment here? This surveillance equipment, to Kjálkabein?"

"Oh! I'm sorry," Brian said, flustered. "I thought I'd mentioned that. I'm here with my boss, Mark Sandoval. He's a writer. He's working on a book. He, uh, he's the guy who wrote—"

Crouching down before the shattered insectile husk of an EVP recorder, once more touching it with the tip of her pen as if it were a corpse, the woman's face positively bloomed in recognition as she turned to stare at him. "*The Long Way Home?*" Jónsdóttir said. "*That* Mark Sandoval? In Hvíldarland?"

Sandoval's name always brought out interesting things in people. A weird miasma of fascination, contempt, admiration and mockery. Much of that was in play in the way the cop shut one eye and grinned at him. Brian was reminded again that Sandoval's celebrity was an unabashedly weird kind of celebrity.

"That one," Brian said. "Yeah."

Jónsdóttir stood. "I'm imagining you're here for the unicorn then."

"How did you— Yeah. We are."

"Out at the Hauksdóttir farm."

"It's a small country, I guess."

Jónsdóttir nodded. "It is that."

"That is why we're here, yeah. What do you think about it?"

"About what? The unicorn?"

"Yeah," Brian said.

"Ah," she said. "You know. As kids we're taught the stories." She smiled and it sloughed some of the hardness from her, pulled a veil of years away in one motion. "*Asmund and Signy. Hans. The Cat in the Cave.* You know, kid's tales."

Brian nodded, maybe a little too eagerly. "Yes! Invisible, Hans slays the ogress, cuts off her head."

Jónsdóttir nearly laughed. Not quite, but it was there. "Yes. It's a weird mix here, different than Iceland. We're more isolated. We are used to being alone. My friend's mother believes in trolls. Really believes in them. I think we all just want the world to be bigger than it is. More magnificent."

Brian tried to scope out a ring on her finger—that line about getting used to being alone reverberating inside him—and said, "But you heard about the unicorn."

"Karla Hauksdóttir called us. She sent our detective the video she made." Her look said it all—a kind of muted pity. Brian bristled, felt strangely protective of Karla, even though he doubted her as well. Their odd, lonely host, raising her children in that big, rambling house amid the fields.

"So . . . What about all this, then? What can we do?"

Jónsdóttir frowned. "I'm not too sure, Mr. Schutt, to be honest. We don't get a lot of vandalism like this. There are only five constables and a detective here."

"In Kjálkabein?"

"In the whole country," Jónsdóttir said, and smiled again. "Which is mostly Kjálkabein, it's true."

"Shit."

"Yes. Most of the time we deal with auto accidents, getting sheep out of the road. Folks having too much to drink, you know. I would say it's not a good sign, all this damage."

"I agree with you there," Brian said, looking at the warped, drying pages on the bedspread.

"Whoever did this decided to destroy these things rather than sell them. That seems significant. And the pissing, well. This seems to send a message. It makes you wonder."

"About what?"

"Well," and here she clicked her pen again, and squinted down at her notebook, "did the people who did this know that this was Mark Sandoval's room? Isn't that the whole point? Random vandals would be taking a bit of a risk, já?"

The title of a new Mark Sandoval book flitted through his head: *The Cops of Kjálkabein: Masters of Understatement.* "I hear you."

"I think it's strange that there is no forced entry, though perhaps it's simply a matter of picking the lock. I'd like to speak to the desk clerk after we're done here. You're welcome to come to the station and file a formal report. But without something stolen to look for, there's not much hope."

"Can't you, I don't know, dust for fingerprints or something? Get DNA from the, you know, urine?"

At last, it was a true smile that Jónsdóttir gave him, and it was a dazzling and pure thing to see. "Oh, I like that! 'DNA.' 'Dust for fingerprints.' Like in your *CSI: Miami.* But hundreds of people have been in this room. Do we run everyone's fingerprints?"

"Shit," Brian repeated.

"I'm sorry, Mr. Schutt. You've seen this country, yes? This isn't—"

"This isn't Iceland, I know. I've heard that."

"I was going to say this isn't *CSI: Miami,* but you're right. I pay for my own uniform. I wish I could help you more. I'm sorry."

· · ·

He put the remnants of *Monster Americana,* such as it was, in one of the duffel bags, and left everything else for Viktor to take care of. An act of petulance he felt was fair payment for the bullshit he'd said about the cops—Jónsdóttir hadn't been terribly helpful, but it was far from the shakedown Viktor had insinuated. Downstairs, he was spared a conversation with the man, who could be heard talking in hushed Icelandic with the cop. They quieted as he approached. He tossed the room keys on the counter, wordlessly took his purple and pink bike from behind the desk, and wheeled it outside.

The empty duffel bags slapped against his legs as he pedaled through town. Once again he was floored by the quiet, careworn beauty of the place. Kjálkabein was like a high-contrast photo in its searing, saturated colors: here was the steel gray wash of the sea spied between the slats of brightly-painted buildings, the wide-mouthed alleyways. Even the cars, boxy, rounded European models, were like bizarro versions of the vehicles he was familiar with: everything seemed suffused with a little magic, a murmur of strangeness. Jónsdóttir was right: Hvíldarland really wasn't Iceland, wasn't Reykjavík. It was scrappier, worn down, a little more busted up. Hvíldarland was the scabby-kneed little brother smoking cigarettes behind the school, and still it was beautiful. He slalomed along Road Seven, strangely aloft as he left the town behind.

Strangely, because Sandoval was clearly going to flip out. All of the equipment was gone. From a technical standpoint, they'd been unprepared for the size of the farm before this, and now what? They had virtually nothing.

The epiphany—if it could be called that, as it struck him with all the severity and grace of a punch to the forehead—arrived as he pedaled with a rippled, moss-furred lava bed on one side and a striated green and brown steppe on his other.

He stopped, veering onto the rocky shoulder and straddling his little bike, blinking at the pavement.

Christ, he was dumb.

Destroying their equipment wasn't supposed to *stop* them.

It was supposed to scare them. It was supposed to run them out of town.

This was classic noir shit: they'd been given a warning.

9

He jostled his way down the Hauksdóttir driveway and passed Karla, who waved with a gloved hand from the mouth of one of the greenhouses. The frame of his poor bike squeaked its way over the ruts. He found Sandoval behind the house, that stretch of land where the grass met the woods. Sandoval was crouched, attaching one of their motion cameras to its tripod. There was salt in the wind and Brian could hear the shirr of the pines beyond, a sound both intimate and woeful. It made him homesick as hell, and for a brief moment he wanted to tell Sandoval about his head, his poor ruined head and the thing resting inside it. He wanted Sandoval to tell him, fatherly and wise, appropriately somber, that it was okay to go home.

Sandoval heard him, or seemed to feel Brian's eyes at his back. When he turned, his hair whipped across his face. His face was wooden, his eyes were impossible to read. The camera, tiny as it was, hung loose in a fist at his chest. His face changed then, bloomed, like what Brian imagined would happen after the hypnotist told someone to wake up. Like he recognized Brian again. He blinked and noted the limp duffel bags hanging at his hips.

"Where's the stuff? You put it in the house?"

Brian paused—*This is where the whole thing shits the bed*, he thought—then told him. It didn't take long. Sandoval listened, nodding here and there. Just Brian's voice and the sound of the wind, the occasional clack of some forgotten shutter around the other side of the house. When he was done, Sandoval said, "That's it?" He dipped his chin toward the bags. "That's all of it?"

Brian nodded. "I saved the manuscript. Everything else is toast. I left the clothes."

"And they *pissed* on my clothes?"

"Yeah. And cut them with a knife."

"Jesus. Those jackets, too? Those jackets I brought?"

"Everything. I just left everything there."

Sandoval leaned over and spit. "Those were nice jackets," he said quietly.

"Yeah. A lot of nice gear, too. I'm sorry."

Lifting his head and squinting against the pale silver coin of the sun burning through the clouds, Sandoval said, "Oh, don't be sorry, Brian."

"You're not . . . I mean, you're not pissed? That was a lot of gear."

"Pissed?" Sandoval said. He came over and laid a warm hand on Brian's shoulder. "I'm ecstatic. I'm thrilled. Inside this battered shell of mine, Brian, I am jumping up and motherfucking *down*."

Brian felt that same sense of inertia, of disconnect, that had come with looking at his CT scans. "You are? What about your book?"

Sandoval shrugged. "That book sucked."

"What? But it's a, you know, *book*."

"Brian, I have copies, dude. Besides, you know what this means, right?"

Brian resisted the sudden urge to turn around, look at who might be coming down the driveway. "Yeah. That someone's threatening us."

"Exactly. It means we're on to something. That's what it means."

"I guess," said Brian. "Mostly it just feels like we've been warned, you know?"

"We *have* been warned!" Sandoval cried, jubilant. "Listen. This comes down to one thing: People are messing with us." He squeezed Brian's shoulder again and leaned in close, all silver stubble and lantern jaw and bloodshot eyes. "There is no hook in a story like people messing with you. Guaranteed. We're on the right track."

"I think Viktor had something to do with it. The room was trashed, but the lock wasn't broken."

"That little mustachioed dick-rabbit. It wouldn't surprise me. He just pockets some cash in exchange for a room key for ten minutes. Something like that, right?"

"Maybe. The cop was talking to him when I left. He didn't want me to get the cops involved."

Sandoval hooked his arm around Brian's neck. "Are you worried? You look worried."

"Yeah, I'm worried," Brian said, uncomfortable with their proximity. "It seems like a pretty clear message, Mark. A real obvious 'get the hell out of here' kind of thing."

"This is a *good thing*. I'm telling you. This is a significant development. Now I've got to go make some *very* expensive phone calls on Karla's phone and get some new gear shipped out here, quick. But I'm serious, Brian. This is the best news we've heard yet."

And there went Sandoval, practically humming as he jogged to the house. When he got onto the porch, he turned and called out, "Everyone loves a mystery."

10

"So you're saying there's no way they'll let us in?"

Karla washed her hands from a hose as they stood clustered around one of the greenhouses. It was the highest edge of afternoon in Hvíldarland, a time that they'd been assured didn't last long. "Night," Karla had told them, "comes very fast here." The bracken and brambles of the woods were already becoming cloaked in shadow, the treetops hung with the last of their dusty light.

"Of course not," she said. She turned the spigot off and flicked her hands free, a smear of dirt on her forehead, her hair pulled back. Brian saw through the semi-opaque skin of the greenhouse the globes of pumpkins stacked in their rows of soil, nestled there like strange, distended pearls. He smelled loam, earth, sea tang. The occasional cutting wind that brought with it the scent of pine. "It's a military base. It's not a community pool." She laughed at her own joke.

"How long will it take to get there?"

"It depends. Do you want me to drive you? It won't take long at all then."

"But what if we get in? Are you going to come in with us? Wait for us outside?"

She put her hands on her hips and turned north, squinting at the line of trees beyond, making it clear that she would do no such thing. "With your bicycles it's not a long trip, but the woods? The road?" And here she traded a glance with Brian, heavy with meaning—he remembered their talk the night before: her belief about the trees, the woods thronged with the weighted, furious souls of men gone a bad death.

She's not kidding, he thought. *She really fucking believes it. All of it.* It stirred dread inside him like someone raking a stick through a dying fire.

And then: *Of course she does. She sent you a video of a fucking unicorn. She believes every last word.*

It was like being adrift at sea and understanding that no one was around for miles. It was a chilling, heartbreaking realization: *You're on your own here. These two are believers. Brooke, Dad, Mom. Don Whitmer. Dr.*

Bajeer—not one of them is going to save you. Once more he had a fierce, almost violent yearning for his childhood, the simplicity of it. The desire to go home.

Sandoval's eyes roved between the two of them. "What?" he said. "What about the woods?"

"Nothing," said Brian. "If we're gonna go, we should go now, before it gets dark."

• • •

They pedaled north, Sandoval sticking a digital camera in his pocket at the last moment. Risky if it was confiscated, but what was the point otherwise? Soon enough they were past the Hauksdóttir property and around the bend in the road. The forest grew heavier, limbs leaning in toward their inky, wending line of pavement. Even with daylight still above their heads, the dense, bracing copses seemed to swallow almost all the day's illumination. Brian's head suddenly muttered in disagreement and he wobbled and righted himself.

As he looked around, he could understand how such a place became one of stories. How it could be considered enchanted. Two hundred years ago, even a hundred, almost the entirety of the island would have been considered the wretched, untamable wild. It would have needed to be corralled in some way, contained, beaten back. If only by tale. *We make up stories to define the world, and in defining it we conquer it,* he thought, *even if we have to pull monsters and spirits from the air.* The whir of their spokes in his ears, birds occasionally twittering in the branches, he rode his dumb little bike, always with the wind sloughing through the bows, pushing his hair back. He stared into the woods to the side of the road and, beyond a few yards, could see only darkness. The same thing behind him. Branches clacking like teeth in the wind, rhythmic like that. This was a place of myth, easily.

He could feel it, something charged in the air. Oddly, quietly electric. A hum in the bones, a feeling that made him almost want to hook his fingers under his ribcage, scratch the maddening itch that suddenly lived there.

"You feel that?" he asked Sandoval, who was leisurely pedaling beside him, ridiculous and rakish in his sports coat, knees skyward on his rainbow-colored bike.

"What?"

"I don't know, just this place." *Like there's a cloud of bees right behind my head? Like I'm sucking on glass shards?* "I'm getting an álagablettur kind of feeling, I'll be honest."

Sandoval grinned. "Yeah? What's that feel like?"

"Seriously? Like I'm chomping on tinfoil."

They pedaled.

"And my head hurts," he said. He wobbled once more and righted himself.

Threads of thin, gritty snow began to line the limbs of the pines, dust the ground. Were they rising in elevation? He exhaled deeply, saw skeins of fog purl in front of him. He tried imagining two centuries back, the wildness, *the wilderness,* and how the path below their feet—if there had been a path at all back then—would have been little more than a snaking thread of cracked, frozen mud. The forest would have invited such ideas as monsters and sprites. The forest would have bowed to the notion of unseen things, nearly insisted upon them. One could walk through a place like this in the brightest of days and then in a matter of steps watch as the canopy of trees overhead swallowed all the sunlight. From there it was not a stretch—no, not at all—to imagine the tickle of twined, misshapen fingers against the back of the neck, fingers light as silk, playful yet ready to seize. A chortle in the dark, a chorus of snapping limbs behind you. But when you turned back, those grasping fingers would simply be the many-nubbed spur of a branch, still and lifeless.

No. Not a stretch at all to imagine that.

They'd ridden long enough for Brian to wonder if the road had actually branched in two, if they had somehow missed a turnoff. It was dusk, and that dread was like a snake slowly coiling around his ribs now. Not cinching, not yet, but not far from it.

And then they crested a rise and saw a sign, and through the last of the trees lay a vast, blackened emptiness. The sign read:

CAMP CARROLL
JTF HVÍLDARLAND
Restricted Area
Authorized Military Personnel Only

Beyond the rusted sign lay charred land. The buildings stood beyond that, bracing the sea and wrapped in fencing. But first, that burned, dead ground dotted with the nubs of cut and charred stumps. The fingertips of buried giants failing to extricate themselves. The slash-burn had been new enough that Brian could still smell the char in his nose. Like the campfires of his youth, really, but different, too. Something rich and bitter to the stink. A burn recent enough that it seemed he should have been able to witness tendrils of smoke rising from the ground.

In front of them were maybe two dozen buildings of simple gray-painted brick and steel siding. Nothing more than two stories high. Some of the buildings were little more than windowless, dark boxes, and all of them were lashed with some array of antennae on their roofs. A line of Humvees were parked against one building. There was a hangar and small airstrip at the far end of the lot, an asphalt field scattered with yellow stencils. Lines of tar where the pavement had buckled and been repaired. A few halogens on rooftops lit the grounds in cold electric light, but there were great pockets of shadow as well.

At the top of the rise, Brian sidled up next to Sandoval. The compound beyond the burn was ringed in razor-wire fencing and a gate. Next to the gate sat a guard's booth, little more than an upright coffin. It all had an air of desolation about it, the whole place. No soldiers hustling from building to building. There was no gut-thumping rattle of choppers landing or taking off, no planes trundling along the runway. Coupled with the devastation on each side of them and that scorch-burn in his nostrils, the place gave Brian the fucking creeps.

It was going on full dark now.

Sandoval said quietly, "So this is here, just out in the middle of nowhere."

Brian thought of the vague, half-remembered podcasts Robert and Ellis sometimes listened to: hushed, feverish announcers murmuring about an armada of secret US bases tucked away in distant corners of the globe. Bases used for the detainment and torture of prisoners, the housing of warheads and chemical weapons, biological experiments. The place wasn't sprawling, but what was he expecting? Towers topped with machine guns? Dudes in hazmat suits clomping around like some kind of shitty sci-fi movie?

Brian said, "Karla called it, though. It's definitely a military base."

"Shit yeah, it is."

The breeze picked up. Ash snaked in gritty skeins across in the road.

Sandoval pushed off down the slope toward the base.

"Wait," Brian called and then, reluctantly, pushed off after him.

Almost immediately an amplified voice came over the loudspeakers moored along the fence-line. Brian almost toppled in surprise. It sounded like the voice of God: it was everywhere and nowhere: "*Stop.*" A young, almost boyish voice, insectile with amplification.

Brian's feet shirred up little clouds of powder as he stopped.

Sandoval kept coasting.

"*Stop.*"

Slowly, Sandoval's wheels drew lines in the deepening ash. With sudden, scrotum-tightening panic, Brian saw a soldier lean his torso out of the guard's booth, the dark, bristling arm of his rifle aimed at them.

"Mark," Brian called out. "Dude, stop."

Sandoval peered back at him over his shoulder; Brian saw a wedge of white eye and, there it was, a sneer. He winked and skidded the bike in a little pirouette. It clattered onto its side as Sandoval stood up and faced the base, his palms raised. Jesus.

Sandoval spoke loudly, overenunciating. "We were just hoping to check stuff out. Get a tour." He took a single tentative step forward. Behind him, Brian gently laid his bike down, put his own hands in the air. His heart was a stone rattling in his throat.

The kid's rifle didn't waver at all. "Sir, this is an American military installation." Without amplification, the kid sounded like he was practically Gunnar's age.

"I understand that," Sandoval said, walking toward the guard.

"All non-military personnel need approval from the camp's Commanding Officer, sir. You are not cleared, sir." Somehow, even through the fear of having a gun pointed at him, the youth and *Americanness* in the kid's voice gave Brian another odd, savage stab of homesickness.

"Well, hey," said Sandoval, still walking forward, his palms held up, "how about we get your CO out here and talk about it?"

The kid lifted his rifle, leaned back into his booth.

"Brian," said Sandoval without turning around, "get your ass up here."

"Stop," the kid said again, back on the loudspeaker, his voice edged now in something like real panic. Brian thought, *I don't want to die next to a mutant slash-burn, or whatever that is back there. Or shot down by some piss-scared kid firing at me from inside a steel coffin. Tumor or not, I don't.* He raised his arms higher, sweat trickling madly down his sides. He stayed put.

Sandoval was almost to the guard shack when a door slotted open from one of the buildings and a trio of armed men trotted out. All three of them were helmeted, beefed up with gear, clunky with body armor. They ran low to the ground, their gun barrels roving in tight circles before them.

It's just us, Brian wanted to say, his mouth glued shut with panic. *Mark's detoxing and I'm a dipshit with a brain tumor. Just chill, guys.*

At the fence, two of them turned and squatted, kept their rifles poised along the perimeter of the fence line. The third one stood up, his own weapon pointed at the buckled blacktop, his eyes bouncing between Sandoval and Brian and back. Sandoval walked up to the fence. The soldier lifted his chin toward Brian and called out, "Get your ass up here."

Brian reluctantly walked up next to Sandoval.

"The fuck're you guys doing here?" the man said through the fence. "No, keep your hands up."

Sandoval shrugged, put his hands back up. "We just came to check out the base."

"No. What're you doing *here?* In Hvíldarland. You tourists?" He grimaced. "What's with the bikes?"

"Lieutenant," said the kid from the guard booth, "these are those guys."

"What guys?" said the lieutenant. An eddy of ash curled around his boot.

"The American guys. The ones we got the memo about."

Sandoval's grin was genuine and ferocious. "You got a *memo* about us?"

The lieutenant shut his eyes for a second. "Jesus wept, Curtinson."

Curtinson cursed under his breath and stepped back into the booth. Brian made eye contact with him and the kid lifted his lip in a snarl, embarrassed and pissed.

The lieutenant shouldered his rifle, tapped the other two men on the back. They stood as well. "So you're the writer guy, dicking around on that farm."

"That's us," Sandoval said cheerfully. "Wow, this is great! Now that we've been introduced, can we get a tour? Fifteen minutes. Just real quick. Be great PR for you guys."

"Nah." The lieutenant leaned over and closed a nostril with his thumb and blew.

"Look, I've got a camera in my bag, you guys can have it until I leave. Or I can take pictures and you can check them before I take off. I'm all about transparency."

The lieutenant, undoubtedly younger than Brian and beating Sandoval by decades, did the other nostril and let out a tight-lipped little smile. He pulled a tin of chewing tobacco from his pocket and thocked it against his leg. "There's nothing here to tour, sir. We gather weather data. You can look it up on Wikipedia."

"Well then, what's the big deal? Right? Hell, give us *ten* minutes."

A little less bemused now, he nodded behind them and said, "Sir, that sign you passed is pretty serious. I suggest you guys go back to Kjálkabein or that farm or wherever you're staying. Be tourists. Get some pickled fish, go to a museum."

"Come on."

"I'm informing you now—if I see you here again, I'll have you detained and arrested."

"Perfect!" Sandoval cried. "A tour!"

The lieutenant scratched an eyebrow with a thumbnail then kept it there, a pained look on his face. "It could lead to extradition, sir. Being put on the no-fly list. A lot of legal headaches for you. So we're gonna wait here until you take off on your bikes. The woods can get a little tricky at night, so I'd hurry if I were you. And again, I'm informing you that you've been officially warned not to come back."

Sandoval was already walking backward, his hands thrust in his pockets. Even without seeing his face, Brian could tell he was smirking. "That's it? You don't want to know why we're here in Hvíldarland?"

The lieutenant pocketed a healthy wad of chew inside his lip. "No disrespect, sir, but I don't give a flying fuck."

That insouciance of Sandoval's? That could be so infuriating when you were on the receiving end of it? It was admittedly an amazing thing to watch the guy leer at four armed soldiers who only moments ago had been pointing guns at him. "We're looking for *unicorns,*" Sandoval purred, and hoisted his little bicycle up by a tasseled handlebar.

"Lucky you didn't get your ass sniped," Curtinson muttered from his booth.

Sandoval called out, "You haven't seen any unicorns around here, have you, Curtinson? Come on, man. Five minutes and we'll be out of your hair."

The lieutenant spat a thread of tobacco juice on the ground. He pointed a gloved finger at the two of them. "Sir, let me be clear: you've got a better chance of getting blown by a unicorn than you do of getting in here. Ride safe."

11

It had thrown him, the studied, measured speed with which the soldiers had poured from the building. Curtinson's metallic rasp over the loud-speaker. That fear, while guns traced over him. And before that, there'd been the forest itself. The unsettling nearness of it, the discomfiting way he'd felt on the road. Watched and unnerved and fogged with something.

Now they rode back toward the farm. The charred ground again gave way to heavy brush and then thicker forest. They coasted for a while on their tiny bicycles and neither spoke. Eventually—quicker than Brian remembered—the road leveled out and rose again, and trees once more braced them on each side, a wall of blurred darkness. The sky above was a thinned thumb of velveteen dusk. He pedaled and pedaled, breathing hard, his head down, and when he looked up, the leaning limbs of pine trees were suddenly close enough to touch with an outstretched hand. Had they been this close on the way there, the branches? Nearly brushing against his arms like this?

Sandoval was almost indecipherable in the gloom up ahead, visible only for the faint ghost of the white tassels on his handlebars.

They rode, and in increments—almost infinitesimal but not quite—the trees seemed to bend toward them. Brian's thoughts grew muddied, but the moment that he recognized it—*I'm fading here, I think something's happening*—he awakened again as if slapped. He wanted to close his eyes and then open them, as if to catch the trees like you might catch someone sneaking toward you in the night, but he was too afraid. As they rode, there were moments when he had to duck his head away from a leaning branch. Once when he looked up, the night was jeweled with a shocking number of stars, a dark sky ripped open and teeming with them. And then he wobbled again—his balance had been giving him trouble today, and he knew what that was all about, didn't he?—and a knotty branch seemed to reach forward and skate across his arm in a hot welt of pain. The world hung molasses-slow before him. He felt like he'd been doped somehow.

"Mark—"

"I know," Sandoval said in the darkness ahead, his voice calm and measured. "Keep going."

The whir of their spokes, Brian's own labored breath in his ears. Like when he'd been hit earlier—he was afraid now, but the fear was in another room somewhere. Distant.

He pedaled.

And then, in his ear, someone said his name.

Someone said his name, a chilled exhalation that stirred the hairs on his neck, that ran torrents of gooseflesh up and down his arms. It was breathy, a whisper so sorrowful and barbed with loss. He veered, cried out, and when he craned his neck back to see who'd spoken, of course it was just the winding ribbon of Road Seven in the dark. No one was there. Just the leaning trees twining their branches into the canopy above.

"Mark—"

His thoughts were lacquered and slow. He could hear the gritty contraction and expansion of his lungs in his ears, the febrile hissing of his tires against the road.

I think I'm dying. Stroke. Aneurysm. Something.

Again he heard his own name hushed in his ear. A longing and a sorrow in a single rustling breath. He looked over his shoulder again and saw the woods had enveloped themselves, the trees had devoured each other across the road, root and limb entwined to form a tunnel of pure dark behind him. The night sky had been swallowed. The trees had done this, formed a depthless black that rushed up behind him, in silence. Something malicious, something shed entirely of its sympathy.

Something reaching.

And when he turned back to face the road—his heart thundering, everything still so achingly slow—there was a tree in front of him.

The bark of the tree suddenly so close to his face that he could read its rough-hewn cracks and tributaries as easily as the whorled landscape of his own fingerprints.

The briefest sense, then, of flight, and the inevitable solidity.

• • •

He seemed destined to return to life with the dark, formless shapes of men standing over him.

"Just stay still," Sandoval said. "You're cool."

But it was too much like the attack, the ambulance, and he quickly sat up. The trees were trees again; they kept their distance, ten, fifteen feet from the road. No snarling crooked limbs. No whispering. The world hung before him as it had before. The gleaming shotgun-scatter of stars he'd seen before were replaced now by a night sky more reasonable, more realistic. He waved his hand in front of his face, red droplets spattering on his palm, and that languid, dream-like quality was gone. The world was the world again. His face hummed, his mouth hot and coppery.

"Ah," he said, "my mouth hurts really bad." What came out was slurred and insensible, a weepy drunk's last bed-laden proclamations before the abyss took him.

"Yeah, you probably shouldn't talk, Brian. You hit your face again."

"Ah. Ow."

"I think you lost a tooth. Wait. Yeah, here it is. You're bleeding quite a bit, bud. Damn."

Sandoval reached into his sport coat, and being Mark Sandoval, he had a dark blue square of folded handkerchief ready to go. Even in the weak moonlight Brian could see the monogram in white stitching. He gave Sandoval a look, one readable even through the mess of his face.

Sandoval grinned. "Give me a break. I've got a brand to uphold."

He put the handkerchief to Brian's mouth, and Brian took it with a shaking hand. "I saw the trees leaning in. Reaching for us."

"Yeah?" Sandoval said.

"Didn't you?"

"Just sit here for a minute."

"There was no moon. The trees covered the moon up. But also the sky exploded. Stars everywhere."

"Okay."

"Someone said my name."

"Sure."

"Don't patronize me," Brian said.

"I just . . . I didn't see anything like that, bud."

"Why'd you say 'I know,' then? When we were riding?"

"I thought you were gonna chew my ass about pressing those jarheads to let us in."

The sudden hole in his mouth: a front tooth, the ones around it wobbly and loose. Blood seeped from his lips as if straight from a tap. The hot animal taste of it threatening to make him sick.

"So you didn't see anything?"

"I was ahead of you. I heard you crash."

He took the handkerchief away from his mouth. "Someone said my name. Right in my ear." His breathing came in ragged hitches.

Sandoval nodded, squeezed his knee. "I'm not saying it didn't happen."

The process of rising was a complicated one, a series of levers and pulleys in a body suddenly gone jittery with adrenaline and panic. Finally he was standing and Sandoval wheeled his bike over to him. "Can you ride this thing?"

Brian nodded, and Sandoval gestured at the handkerchief. "Might as well just put that in your mouth, man. You're still gushing."

"You didn't feel the forest, like, closing in?" He looked down and saw the long, laddered scratch from the tree limb going down his arm, pink and stippled with blood. Spatters of blood on his shirtfront, coal-dark in the night. "I looked back, and . . ." He shrugged, unable to convey that sense of closing in, of *permanence* that he'd seen behind them.

"Nope. But if you say you did, I believe you." Sandoval's daredevil grin, those ridiculous white teeth. "I told you we were on the right track, buddy."

"You're the only person—ah shit, ouch—only person who could see this as good news."

"Let's go," Sandoval said, astride his own bike. "You got this."

Once more they rode. The woods were dark now but unwavering. The woods were polite. The woods kept their distance. After a while the trees began to thin; shards of moonlight began to shine through their trunks. By the time they left the forest and saw the Hauksdóttir house glowing pale as a cataract in the bowl of the valley, he'd almost convinced himself that it was an act of imagination, a panicked byproduct of having guns pointed at him. Maybe even because of the tumor, hell. Some odd vision borne of his own mind.

• • •

The driveway was packed. A silver BMW sat next to a jacked-up black 4x4—big tires, overhead lights, one side panel primer gray—and Karla's little two-door pickup. Brian and Sandoval slowed in that no man's land between the greenhouses and the house itself, stopping just beyond the reach of the porch light.

Brian fished the handkerchief from his mouth. "Karla believes in the álagablettur," he said. The Icelandic word came out strangled behind his split and swollen lips. His poor mouth. His poor face. God, everything from the neck up was on the slag heap. "Like she really believes in it." *Shit*, he thought. *Don't I? After what just happened? What did just happen?*

Sandoval lifted his chin toward the driveway. "Whose cars are those?"

Neither of them could answer that. "Then let's," Sandoval said, "keep what happened between us for now. Might be safer that way. Okay?"

"So I just wrecked, you mean."

"You just wrecked, exactly. The dumber we look, the better off we are."

"My mantra," Brian managed, earning a smile from Sandoval.

• • •

Gunnar marveled at the sight. "So much blood," he said from his spot at the kitchen island, enthralled at the trail of red spatters on the floor that Sandoval was wiping up with a wet rag.

It'd been madness when they entered the living room moments before. Everyone rising up, Liza crying out, this sea of faces turning to them—there'd been two other men in the room besides Karla and the children.

As a group they'd moved quickly to the kitchen then, a bevy of hands holding him up, drops of his blood pattering to the floor behind him. A chair was grabbed from the dining room and he sat in it, leaning forward and spitting red into the sink as everyone whirled industriously around the room. The children's father, Shane—dark hair to his shoulders, band T-shirt—leaned down in front of him, lifted Brian's chin toward the light.

Gunnar said, "It's like the front of *Kill 'Em All*, right, Dad?"

"That's right," Shane said. He'd splayed out a tackle box on the island behind him, a massive steel thing, dense with folding trays and compartments, and now he turned and rifled through it, a curtain of hair obscuring his face.

"So you're a doctor?" Brian said, which earned big laughs around the room from the adults.

"Vet," Shane said.

"Oh."

"But what *happened*?" asked Karla.

"It just got dark out there," said Sandoval. "Really fast."

"No night pollution," said the other new man. "A way deep dark out there, you bet." This one was heavyset, a gray head of hair that just hung over the shirt collar. Face as doughy as a rumpled towel, blue eyes lit with a kind of sad bemusement. *Hound-dog eyes*, Brian thought. The same eyes you'd see affixed to any number of old men eternally perched on bar stools or church pews.

"Oh, I'm sorry. So, yes, that's the children's father, Shane, and this is Vaughn," Karla offered. "A friend of the family."

"Hi there," said Sandoval, standing now and tossing the bloody rag in the sink beside Brian. He started washing his hands. "Mark Sandoval," he said over his shoulder. Brian, seated where he was, saw threads of blood lacing their way down the drain and turned his face away.

"Vaughn Keller. Good to meet you. And I'd shake your hand," Keller said, turning to Brian, "but damn if it doesn't look like you're right in the middle of the something."

All this activity. Karla reached into the sink and wrung out the bloody rag and opened the back door, tossed it out onto the porch. She took a clean washcloth from a cupboard and poured some alcohol on it from a bottle beside the tackle box. "I can use this, right?"

"Yeah, that's fine," Shane said. "Just get all the blood out of there." The leaning branches and darkness of the forest seemed a century ago, Hamms and Dr. Bajeer even longer. He'd had his ass handed to him by white supremacists and a tree in the span of four days.

Something inside him was stirred by Karla's touch. It wasn't sensual, wasn't remotely sexual—it was an unexpected flare of gratitude; this was the first time he'd been touched in a conciliatory way since Hamms, since the fight—if it could be called that—with the four men, and that had been a touch of stark utility. And what about before that? She gently dabbed his cuts with the alcohol-soaked washcloth, her fingers cupping his jaw. He resisted the urge to thank her through the sting of it. He found himself surprised at the urge to weep.

"You lost a tooth," she said.

Sandoval brightened and reached into his jeans. He set the tooth down on the counter with a flourish.

Gunnar and Liza squealed in delight, leaned over on their stools to get a better look.

"Shit," Shane said, impressed, nodding at Sandoval. "Nice work."

"Shit," Gunnar said.

"Gunnar," warned Karla.

"Sorry, mamma," Gunnar said. Liza hunched her head, clapping her hand over her mouth to hide her giggles.

Karla said, "Does that word show your light to the world, Gunnar?"

"Daddy said it."

"Daddy," said Karla, "can make all the *kúkur* words he wants, because he's big. Are you big yet?"

"No, mamma."

Shane leaned back, eyed Brian in frank appraisal. "You know what's coming next, right?"

• • •

Surgery loomed, inevitable and bloody, and the children were exiled to the living room. Gunnar kept trying to peek around the doorway until Karla barked something at him in Icelandic and he shuffled off. Moments later, a laugh track—punctuated with bursts of calliope music and Icelandic shouts—began churning from the living room.

Karla began threading a needle for sutures, and Shane in his blue latex gloves removed a few plastic-wrapped syringes, set them on the counter. He withdrew a vial and held it up, squinting at the ceiling light.

"God, I hope this works," he muttered, shaking his head.

Brian and Sandoval traded looks and Keller bellowed laughter from where he stood in the doorway, the sound phlegmy and raucous. He pounded a fist over his heart. "Guy's got one joke," he rattled, "and I laugh every goddamn time." Shane grinned and inserted the tip of the syringe into the vial's lid, jacking a minute amount of liquid in.

"How's this?" Karla said, and held up the needle and its thread.

"Perfect." This cadence between them. Shane took the needle gingerly between his fingers, laid it on a piece of gauze on the island. Some sad, quiet smile was at play on his face as he took it from her. The face of a guy walking through the hallways and rooms of an old love. Someone noting the requisite landmines and oases both. Brian didn't even know them and it was hard to miss. He wondered how long they'd been divorced.

"How's the pain?"

"Pretty bad," Brian admitted. He turned and spat in the sink again.

"I bet it does. This is just a little bit of lidocaine. It'll sting, and then your mouth'll be numb for a couple hours. Cool? And I can give you a pain reliever for the tooth until tomorrow."

Sandoval leaned against the back door, his arms crossed. He said, "So, Shane. Idaho, huh?"

It was only a minute pause, the way the syringe froze in transit as it traveled toward Brian's face. But it was there. Brian himself might've been the only person who saw it.

"Born and raised," Shane said.

"How'd a guy from Idaho corral a gig as a veterinarian in Hvíldarland? That's got to be a story."

The needle sank in the skin above Brian's lip. He let out a hiss of pain.

"Well, he was the other kind of vet first," said Keller. Heads turned. Keller rubbed his stubbly chin, pointed a finger at the darkness over Sandoval's shoulder. "Stationed up at Camp Carroll."

"Oh yeah?"

Shane withdrew the syringe, laid a wad of gauze over the injection site. "Yeah. Last two of my four years there. Then Karla and I hooked up." He set the syringe down behind him. "Had those two nerds in there." He tossed the square of gauze in the sink.

"You went to school here? Veterinarian school, I mean?"

"Nah, across the water. Akureryi, up north. Folks here don't care too much about diplomas and certificates. I do good work and they see me around town. That's mostly what matters."

From the television down the hall came the sound of shattering glass, a trashcan being knocked over, a car horn, followed by the children's laughter.

"Let's give that a second to work," Shane said to Brian, and leaned back, his gloved hands resting between his knees.

"What's Camp Carroll all about, anyway?"

Shane turned and grinned at Sandoval. "Karla told us you went up there. They weren't too hot on letting you in, were they?"

"Nope."

Brian went to touch his face and Karla *tsked* him, leaned over and gently pushed his hand down with her own cool fingers.

"That's good," Keller said. Lifted his bottle to his lips. "That's their job."

"The guys at Carroll didn't do this, did they?" Shane asked.

"He ran into a tree," Sandoval said.

"Looks like it," said Keller, and heaved another one of those phlegmy laughs. "Looks like the tree ran into him."

"I wasn't paying attention," Brian said.

Shane picked up the needle. "I'm about to stitch you up. Okay? You probably don't want to talk."

"Sorry."

Karla blurted out, "You found the álagablettur, didn't you? You did."

"Babe," Shane said wearily.

"Ah, again with the haunted woods, Karla," Keller said. He frowned at the beer bottle he held to his chest. "Come on, hon."

Sandoval said, "You're not a believer, I take it."

"Not," Keller said, "in the least. And I don't think the earth is flat either." He set his empty beer on the counter and leaned into the refrigerator, helping himself to another.

"You can believe what you want," Karla said stonily.

"And I sure as hell don't believe in unicorns, my dear."

Shane turned back on his stool and said, "Hey, Vaughn? There's no grand requirement that you *have* to be a dick, okay?"

Landmines abound, Brian thought.

"Well," Sandoval said, breaking the awkward pall that had suddenly fallen on the room, "all that aside, we didn't see any *alaga*-whatever. I mean, I still want to hear more about it, but it was just *dark* out there, you know? We couldn't see a damn thing. Next thing you know, boom. We're not used to this kind of dark in the States. At least not in the city. Like you said, Vaughn, light pollution." Even to Brian, he sounded believable.

Casual enough. And then he changed the subject, smooth as a sleight-of-hand artist, and asked if there was a dentist in town. Brian could feel the tension dissipate, thin as vapor.

Shane said, "Sure. Down in Kjálkabein. The one by the airport, right, Karla?"

"Yes, she's good. That's where we take the children."

Sandoval said, "Any chance we can get a ride tomorrow morning? I owe this guy some dental work."

"Of course."

For a moment, no one spoke. Just the faint murmur of the television down the hall. They heard Gunnar say, "Liza, *stooooop*, that's mine."

"Well, trust me," said Keller, frowning at the floor and drumming his fingers against his beer bottle. "There's nothing going on out at that base that's worth a shit."

"No disrespect," Sandoval said—and once more Brian was reminded that he was just one of those guys that could pull it off without sounding like a total asshole—"but how would you know?"

Shane gently pushed Brian's face to the side, his fingers splayed on Brian's cheekbone. He couldn't feel it at all. The needle broke through the skin of his lip with a distant sense of tugging. It wasn't pain exactly. Just a pressure.

"Hell," Shane said with a curious, unreadable smile, "Camp Carroll is practically Vaughn's home away from home. Isn't that right, Vaughn?"

12

Four days passed. Five.

A routine was established.

The morning after Shane stitched his lip, a visit to the dentist in Kjálk-abein yielded a bottle of pain pills. The dentist was trepidatious about implanting the tooth again once she discovered that Brian was sleeping outside in the elements. The decision to wait to get back to the States for a tooth to get grafted into his jaw wasn't a hard one. Who needed the agony of that while sleeping on a bedroll inside a tent? Sandoval agreed, of course. But a few days after the accident, Brian had begun to welcome the looks he got from locals, the double take his mashed face and missing tooth earned him. Rather than hindering things, it seemed to help with the interviews, made people more forthcoming. Locals wanted to talk to him about his injuries, compare battle wounds; there was an air of camaraderie about it. As rural as Hvíldarland was, as reliant upon the machinery of their bodies as the land and sea made people here, there was no shortage of folks with which to compare wounds. The pain pills both nauseated him and worked a little too well, so he took them at night. He would drift to sleep high, his body rootless and lost on some voluminous sea, mind swaddled in gentle, feathered arms. But they also left him brutally groggy in the morning, his sleep shot through with weird dreams.

Even without pain pills, the place seemed to have the same disorienting effect on Sandoval. One morning Brian unfolded himself from his tent and immediately saw Sandoval at the edge of the woods, standing with his back to the house. The ground was thatched, as always, in standing fog. Sandoval's hands hung limp at his sides. Brian called his name but Sandoval didn't turn. Brian crouched in the mouth of his tent and put his boots on, never taking his eyes off the man. He heard the faint Doppler of a passing car on the road. Sandoval never moved. Just stood there in his pajamas; sweatpants and a thermal shirt. No shoes. No socks. The ground rimed in frost.

Brian had called his name again, louder, and started walking toward him. Every low-budget horror movie played through his mind: he'd touch Sandoval's shoulder and the man would suddenly spin around, zombiefied, or with some kind of tendriled alien parasite seeping the life's-blood from his face, or he'd be cast in ice, some kind of frozen, lurching man-thing—

When he was halfway there, Sandoval did indeed turn slowly, his hair corkscrewed with sleep. He lifted a hand, wearily calling Brian's name in greeting.

Brian froze. "What the hell, dude?" His own voice seemed *loud* in the still morning, stanched in unease.

Sandoval had started walking toward him, but he walked stiffly, like he'd been stationary for a while in the chill.

"Boss, you okay? You freaked me out a bit there. I called your name."

"Long night," was all Sandoval said. "Sorry." And then, the only time it'd happened, he'd crawled back into his tent and slept for another hour while Brian drank coffee on the porch and waited for him to come out.

Little weird, really.

More than a little weird.

Meanwhile, Brian still played the game each morning before rising, spent a few minutes trying to isolate the tumor inside himself, trying to locate its specific mass in that bowl of bone behind his eyes. Taming the beast. When he traveled to Kjálkabein for whatever reason—to place the online order Sandoval had meticulously drawn up to replace their destroyed gear, to hunt down a half-remembered volume of local lore in a bookstore some fisherman had told him about—he never checked his own emails and staunchly avoided any search terms that would bring him closer to understanding what was happening to him. Ignorance was a reprieve, chickenshit or not.

The villages that sparked off Road Seven: a small grid of cobblestone streets, ancient boats and trucks moored in overgrown yards. Cinderblocks barely visible among weedy fields. Snarls of fallen chain link, or warped wooden fences leaning like teeth from a broken jaw. But the sunny, bright-ly-painted little homes lay tucked in amid all this, neat as rows of playing cards. And all around these little hamlets stood nature's insistence on a beautiful disorder: the rumpled lava beds, the pools of ice-blue water dotting massive fields of shattered stones. There were a dozen or more of these villages that fanned like spokes off the road.

His bad Icelandic, when he spoke to people in the villages on his own or translated for Sandoval, was met with polite, commiserating grimaces and responses in English. When he asked about unicorns he got nothing at all, confused shakes of the head as if they'd never even heard the word. Pressed about the álagablettur, he discovered that many Hvíldarlanders viewed Karla as an eccentric. "You're staying with that woman, the pumpkin farmer?" a man named Olafsson had asked him. A wiry red beard hung to Olafsson's navel, his crown pale and freckled as an eggshell. "She's an odd one, her. It's her people that've spread those rumors about the woods. My wife says, anyway. Because of those military folks that died on their land, yeah?" Sandoval had trekked across the road, deciding to try interviewing folks on his own, and Brian and Olafsson stood outside a garage on the outskirts of one of the villages. Olafsson and a handful of his friends appeared to be taking apart an ancient semi. Blocky chunks of motor lay on the oil-stained pavement around them. A few of the men had openly laughed at the bike Brian had leaned against the building, but then quieted once they saw the stitched-up turnbuckle of his face. "It's all bullshit, that whole story. Your United States, now. *That's* a crazy place," Olafsson said, his mouth curling with distaste. He spat on the pavement. "My wife and I went there one time. New York. Too many people. We don't have anything as bad as that here."

"So, uh, no *einhyrningsins* then," Brian said.

"Eh?" said Olafsson.

"So no unicorns here in Hvíldarland then."

Again, Olafsonn leaned and spat on the ground. "No nothing in Hvíldarland. But surely not any unicorns. Shit."

"Got moss," said yet another man, wiping his hands on a rag. "Got rocks. Sheep shit. Horses. Fish out there, sometimes, if you can handle the sea. Got wind, always. You see any unicorns? Look around you."

• • •

A week after their arrival in Hvíldarland, Brian woke to another morning awash in meager gray light. He'd taken his last pain pill the night before and the vestiges of his usual troubled sleep still haunted him. He had some dim memory of a man with the head of a unicorn stretching on a yoga mat in an arid desertscape, the dusty valley before him filling with a tide of dark blood. Remembered in another dream a pale hand bursting from the bone-cave of his own skull like a zombie writhing free of a grave, and how he'd suddenly felt light, free of some weight. Brian was relieved to be done with the pills. His face was slowly healing. The stitches, those weird, stiff interlopers, still bristled from his lip for a few more days.

He got out of his tent. Always the morning fog hanging in tatters on the ground, obscuring the mountains, turning the greenhouses vaporous and strange. Road Seven was nearly invisible. The occasional hum of a passing car was relayed to him in odd, muted tones. Gunnar and Liza ran along the length of the porch, jackets and boots on over their pajamas. *Clomp clomp clomp*, Liza whipping at Gunnar's legs with a woven belt as she squealed and laughed, her tangled morning-hair fanning out behind her.

Sandoval strolled out the front door with a pair of ceramic mugs. He walked down the steps, dodging the children as they made another circuit around the porch, and handed Brian a cup of coffee. It was as idyllic as something from a movie. He'd just gotten to the point where he could drink coffee again, and he took the mug with something approaching rapture.

A rhythm, a schedule. Most mornings, Sandoval would review the previous night's inevitably disappointing footage, then walk to the waypoints where they'd set up the camera and motion detectors, and move them to the next established position. Given the nature of the video Karla had sent him, Sandoval said he wanted to focus on the tree line. They were still waiting for their shipment of new gear to come in via General Delivery to the Kjálkabein post office; Sandoval didn't trust the mail carrier not to tamper with the stuff. The less people involved, he said, the better. Brian had thought for a moment of arguing, but then conceded he might actually have some kind of a point.

Brian's part of their morning routine: he looked for clues, such as they were. He looked for tracks in the earth, bite marks or horn rubbings along the trees, scat on the ground, any sign of visitation. He tried to keep his own doubts at bay, treat the place with the sanctity of any traditional site. But short of a flashing neon arrow that said *This here's proof of a unicorn, buddy,* he had no concrete idea what the hell he was looking for. Not a clue. That morning, he walked a few feet into the woods and pissed against a pine tree.

He heard Gunnar and Liza thunk down the porch steps, their laughter both closer and quieter amid the fog. Ghostly.

They were good questions, the ones Sandoval had asked him in Whitmer's office: *Do you believe in this stuff? Flat out. No lie.*

Brian zipped up, leaned a forearm against the tree in front of him, gazed deeper into those impenetrable woods. People with acne were once thought to be carriers of the bubonic plague; it was believed the sick could simply gaze upon the living and infect them that way. Through the eyes. But ignorance hadn't made the dead, stacked and tiered like cordwood, any less real.

Do you believe in this? In these things?

The forest was just a forest. The tree he'd run into had been just a tree. Nothing had conspired against him that night. Nothing chased them. Nothing had spoken in his ear. The only interlopers were the darkly dividing cells in his own brain, and the fear that went with that.

A bird called out, hidden among the tree's upper limbs. The soil beneath his feet was burnished with moss, flakes of dead bark. Sticks and loam. The building blocks of life and death down there in the churned earth.

Something happened out there, he thought.

Nothing happened out there.

He stepped from the trees just as Gunnar motioned to him from around the corner of one of the greenhouses.

"Hey, Brian! Brian, come look!"

Liza was squatting down, staring at something on the ground. Gunnar waved his hand in a *Come see* gesture. "Hurry!"

Brian turned, started walking toward them. Sandoval, a small figure out near the edge of the road, heard the commotion and started toward them as well. No one in any hurry.

"Poop!" Gunnar yelled. "Brian, look at this, we found poop!"

• • •

"This is a load of shit," Brian said, and drily laughed at his own joke. He and Sandoval and the children stood between a pair of greenhouses, the house obscured. The sun had begun to throw wicked little shards through the cotton batting of the clouds overhead, the fog just beginning to burn off. Sandoval was filming.

Liza giggled at Brian's bad word and scratched at a bug bite on her ankle with a stick she's picked up somewhere. Gunnar stood before the pile of shit with his arms folded, so jazzed and proud he was practically hopping up and down. Brian saw new Sharpie bracelets drawn on his wrists.

"You said shit," Liza informed him.

"I did. Sorry."

"Don't let doubt make you blind," Sandoval said, squinting into the camera's eyepiece as he roved around the poop, treating it with all the sudden piousness of someone rolling up on the Kennewick Man dig. "Remember, Brian? You remember when I said that? This is what I'm talking about. This is what we've been waiting for. *This.*" He lifted his face from the camera. He looked crazed, his eyes huge. "Seriously, you remember when I said that?"

"Sure, but this—"

"Well, this is something that's right in front of you." The back of his shirt rucked up as he crouched. The three of them saw the raised linework of his scars over the jutting knobs of his spine.

Brian gently tested the stitches on his lip with the pad of his thumb. "Poop," he said, mindful of the children. "Poop is what's in front of me, Mark. That's all it is. This is a joke or something."

"It's magical!" cried Liza, holding her stick aloft.

"It's not magical," said Brian.

Sandoval continued wheeling around the pile of shit, speaking into the camera's microphone. Gunnar and Liza were thus privy to such thoughtful missives as, "Note that amongst the potential unnatural or supernatural elements of the feces, there are also a number of more ordinary grass seeds and stringed, pale weeds—be sure to check for consistency in regard to standards of local flora."

"Those aren't supernatural elements, Mark."

"Shush. And also note the quality of *dryness* to the fecal matter—that'll need to be quantified as well. When did the subject stop here? How *old* was the fecal matter by time of discovery? Also note that if this particular section of the farm was under surveillance last night—admittedly unlikely, given our meager materials at the moment—why was the subject not visible? Explore possibilities of other camouflaging agents at work here."

"It's magical poop," cried Liza, waving her stick in the air again, and then blessing Brian with it, once on each shoulder, as if knighting him.

"Gunnar," Sandoval said, leaning in close with the camera, "can you move your feet, honey? Just a little bit."

It had to be a trick. Obviously. Someone was screwing with them again.

"Brian, go and get a dig shovel and some sampling sets from my kit. It's in my tent. No, it's in the dining room. The big bag."

Brian started walking. Behind him he heard Sandoval call out, "*This* is what they didn't want us to find. *This* is what they tried to steer us away from."

He grabbed the stuff and came back, finding Sandoval still crouched and wheeling with the camera, Gunnar beside him. The boy pointed and quietly said something, and Sandoval laughed loudly.

Brian set the dig blade at Sandoval's feet.

"Look at it," Sandoval purred.

"Oh, I'm looking at it," Brian said.

The four of them stood before a pile of glitter-dusted horse shit. Horse shit positively frosted, in fact, in a gleaming coruscation of granulated glitter that went from gold to topaz to a rich purple. It was a pile of glitter-coated horse turds that also happened to be studded with what looked to be a half-dozen jewels as big as Brian's thumbnail.

A pile of glittery turds rife with half-embedded emeralds and diamonds and rubies, turds that were by far the brightest thing out there in that gloomy morning.

As if something magical—oh, like a unicorn, maybe—had paused in its nightly ministrations and decided, then and there, to take a shit.

3

just perhaps maybe the slightest monkey

"I began to wonder if I was the lost one."
—**Mark Sandoval,** *See Me*

1

A week before he and the kid flew in a juddering twin-engine plane over the worn checkerboard tarmac of the Kjálkabein airport, Mark Sandoval had dinner with a blind date at the White Bird. It was a French-fusion place tucked below the Morrison Bridge, between a CPA's office with yellowed posters in the windows and a new bar that broadcast the grand assholishness of its clientele by the fact that its name, Drill, had actually been drilled into its brushed-steel facade. The White Bird was gloomy, housed in a room roughly the size and dimensions of a rail car, lit only by the candles on each table and a single hanging chandelier. Waiters in white coats and facial piercings prowled the narrow lanes between tables, speaking as low and intimately as physicians delivering grave news. The place had been a city staple for years and so was outrageously, notoriously overpriced; it was due only to Sandoval's fame, however diminished it might have been, that he was he able to get them a table without a reservation. The White Bird was not his first choice—it wouldn't have been his second choice, or third—but his date, having heard "absolutely *innncredible* things about it," had insisted on the place with a buoyant ferocity that did not bode well for a subsequent date. Still, he agreed to meet her there. He was lonely.

The date had been set up as a favor through Sandoval's lawyer and his lawyer's wife. His date, Viv, was blonde, fit, and brutally tanned, which seemed at odds with the fact that she was a dermatologist. Once they were seated, she'd scanned the menu like an MMA fighter looking for an opponent's weak spot. She had a wonderful freckled expanse of cleavage that fairly sang with erotic promise in the dim light of the chandelier. Sandoval had met her in the restaurant's tiny waiting area—he'd had trouble finding a parking spot for the Jag and was a few minutes late—and she'd risen from the little bench she'd been sitting at, still wrapped in her coat at that point, and offered her hand. "*You* must be Mark." Was it insouciance? Flirtation? They'd been seated at a window table while lust and loneliness flitted around Sandoval like warring devils on his shoulders.

Their emaciated, tattooed waiter took their wine order—Viv, with no apparent compunction regarding propriety, ordered a hundred-dollar bottle of 2010 pinot from a Willamette Valley winery Sandoval had heard good things about—and then departed quietly in his white coat, a ghost banished. Sandoval was surprised, both at the fact that she'd done so without consulting him and that he hadn't really minded.

"Guy looks about one bad shift away from giving plasma," he said.

"I think he's cute," said Viv. She took a sip of her water, her eyes roving about the room before settling on him. She was probably ten years his junior. Old enough, he knew, to own her own practice. His lawyer Tad, and Tad's wife Heidi, had both insisted it would be a good fit. "You'll just love her, Mark," Heidi had said. "She vacations in Mumbai every year over the winter and offers free medical advice there to the people, a Doctors Without Borders type thing. Beautiful, smart. You'll get *such* a kick out of her."

"And she's got a thing for the weird ones," Tad had offered.

The waiter came with the wine—he offered the sample taste to Viv as Sandoval looked on, smiling and bemused. The waiter went to pour him a sample and Sandoval held up a hand.

"Wonderful, thank you," Viv said, and the waiter set the bottle down and left just as vaporously, murmuring that he'd be back in a few minutes to take their order.

They sat with their wine for a moment while the restaurant breathed around them. A corona of half-decipherable talk and clinking silverware. The diffusion of neon in a nearby window turned all the raindrops dotting the glass a marvelous red. They made small talk for a few minutes—the difficulty in scheduling at her office, how they'd met Tad and Heidi, the weather. Sandoval helped himself to the wine. It really was very good.

"So, Mumbai," he said. He willed himself not to look at her chest.

Viv, midsip, nodded and set her glass down. "Right! Yes. Heidi must have told you."

"She did, yeah. Said you do great things there."

"Heidi's wonderful, isn't she?"

Sandoval, who did not much care about Heidi Hemphill one way or the other, especially since he was generally in her vicinity only when he and Tad were having a meeting or lunch that could be written off as tax-deductible, said, "Oh, she's a hoot. She's great."

"Did you know she macramés?"

"No," Sandoval said. "I didn't know anyone macramés anymore."

"Oh, they're hideous," said Viv. "But darling, really. She works so hard on them!"

"So you head there for the winter? Mumbai?"

"Yep, I have a few friends who run a clinic there. I go and help out."

"Indians?" said Sandoval.

"I'm sorry?"

"Are they actually from India, or, you know, Americans? Your friends, I mean." He tapped at his forehead where a *bindi* would be.

He watched Viv hold her glass and decide whether or not she should be offended. It was a calculable thing. "Well, one of the doctors on staff is British," she said stiffly, "and they have local interns. The couple I know are from Virginia."

"Got it."

She tilted her head, appraised him; the smile had turned brittle. He saw that she'd decided to be offended. "Does that lessen the impact of the work, do you think? The importance of it?"

Sandoval poured more wine. He felt heat on his face, blood creeping up his cheeks. His scars, when he got tense or angry, itched terribly, and he resisted the urge to rub his back against his chair like a bear against a tree trunk. Ten minutes in and he'd already pissed her off. Christ. She filled out the dress though, and his loneliness sang out alongside his idiocy, a single note in harmony. He said, "Not importance, no. But it does come across a bit as the great white saviors coming in to help the wretched brown people, doesn't it?" He couldn't help himself.

They were saved by the waiter, who came to take their order and remained dutifully oblivious to Sandoval's flushed face and Viv's obvious anger. She ordered the salmon and tomato salad, oozing a deadly cheer as she did, refusing to look at Sandoval. He ordered the duck breast—now *there* was the power of suggestion, good lord—with gorgonzola and artichoke. He momentarily quelled the urge to order another bottle of wine and then decided *fuck it* and went ahead. The waiter left and Viv attacked a piece of bread that lay in the basket between them.

"Listen, I'm sorry," Sandoval said. "That was shitty of me. It's shitty to knock someone's altruism like that."

"Oh, it's fine," Viv said, buttering her bread with short, precise strokes. "It's nothing new."

"No, please. It's not like I'm out there doing anything charitable, abroad or otherwise. It's guilt, is what it is. Guilt and nervousness are the leading causes of men talking out of their asses more than anything, I guarantee it."

Viv relaxed a bit. "Well, I don't know if *that's* true."

"For this guy it is. Tell me more about it, please."

And she did. She talked about the clinic, the ceaseless tide of children there that needed help, the poverty and malnourishment, the anguished parents, the orphans who weren't lucky enough to have parents. The sense of hopelessness she often felt in spite of the good work the clinic did. "So much of it is like putting a finger in a dam and watching two more leaks sprout right next to it."

Finger, leak, sprout. Sandoval nodded, asked questions, distracted. Still trying not to look at Viv's freckled chest. She was pouring her soul out here, or at least talking real with him. Honestly, openness. When was the last time that had happened? And what was he doing? The wine came, another pinot, along with their plates.

"And what about you?" Viv asked, wineglass held by its bulb between her tented fingers. The wine seemed to be doing good things for her as well. A bumpy beginning, but they seemed on better footing.

And then: "Heidi told me you're a writer? Which I think is *fascinating*, but beyond that I don't really know anything about it. What kind of stuff do you write? Is that a terrible question?" Sandoval's fork hovered in the air over his duck.

His hopes had been sputtering and misfiring but still rising like some sci-fi rocket. Now they immediately plummeted. *She didn't know.* Heidi Hemphill hadn't told her? Had just told her he was some *writer?* Shit. "Um," Sandoval said, drawing it out, managing to smile and frown at the same time. He held up one finger and poured another glass of wine.

"What?" Viv laughed. "You looked *pained,* Mark."

"I'm just trying to figure out how to answer your question."

"Oh, it can't be that bad. You're published, right?"

"Oh yeah."

"Do you write under a pseudonym? Self-help books? Don't tell me its *erotica?*"

"I'm a little hesitant, to tell you the truth."

She set her glass down and leaned forward, grinning. "Oh my God. It *is* erotica, isn't it?"

"No, no. Sorry."

"Pop psychology! Young adult! Ooooh, this is fun."

Sandoval and his work. His books. The first one had formed him, and thusly had always been his armor. But if *The Long Way Home* (and what it signified, and what had happened to him to instigate the book itself) was a buoy, it was also the anchor around his neck. His sword and hair shirt both. The books after that were not so integral to him, so enmeshed with his personality, his coda, his guilt, who he was. But *The Long Way Home* had been written years ago, by a different man. What band wanted to get up on stage and play songs that were twenty years old? But bands did it all the time. Everyone did it, one way or another. *Monsters Americana,* his supposed Next Great Book, the one he'd been working on for so long now, was frozen, mired and immobile. Unwieldy. The only book that had truly terrified him. But *The Long Way Home* was the one that had built the myth of Mark Sandoval. And you couldn't fuck with the myth.

Without the myth, what was left of him? His regret? His scars? His willingness to discard people like trash?

"I wrote *The Long Way Home*," he said, frowning at his plate.

There was a moment of processing—he could practically see her working out the equation, all the tumblers falling into place. Viv's face brightened in vague recognition and then shifted as she searched her data banks for the story. It happened often enough.

"Mark," she said slowly, drawing his name out. "I know this name. Mark . . ."

"Mark Sandoval. Yeah."

"That was the book about the aliens," she said cheerfully, her voice rising on the last word. Her dismay obvious. "Right?"

"It was," Sandoval said.

"Wow," Viv said, and Sandoval snorted and poured another glass.

"I'm sorry," he said, "I thought Heidi told you."

"No!" Viv said, still smiling, eyes darting over each of Sandoval's shoulders. "I mean, it's fascinating! What a story. Wow, what an experience. No, Heidi just told me you were a writer. So, goodness. Abducted by aliens. Wow," she said, trilling a high, nervous little laugh. "That must have been something." She looked around the room like he was holding her hostage and she was trying to find someone to slip a panicked note to. "I loved the movie," she blurted.

He drained his glass, set it down and spun it lightly between his fingers by the stem. He heard the warble of a cell phone a few tables over. He said, "There's something freakish about it, right? Shameful." He frowned at his glass. When would he learn? The world became smaller the older he got, not the other way around. He vowed to have a word with Heidi. Many words.

"I mean, either it happened," he said, annoyed at the slur in his words, "and it's stunning and historically significant. Globally important. Or it didn't happen, and it's an elaborate joke, a sham. One or the other, right, Viv?"

Sandoval unbuttoned his sleeve, started rolling it up.

He held up his forearm between them. The candlelight jittered and wavered along the underside of his arm, the scarred rhombuses and trapezoids and circles.

"Which is it, Viv? Am I a test subject or a fucking liar?"

Viv's facade gave way. With her mouth in a tightly knitted line, she took her wallet from her handbag, removed a credit card. She gave him a smile so rich with pity that Sandoval felt a paroxysm of hate toward her—real hate, as raw and luxurious as it was scalding. He resisted the urge to squeeze the tender globe of his wineglass, squeeze its shards into his palm, render the whole fucking thing a red-pulped mess.

"I should probably go," she said. "It was nice meeting you, Mark."

"You too. You can put your card away. I'm gonna go ahead and order another bottle."

She didn't argue. The sound of her heels marked her exit, a sound quickly lost in the crowd.

Moments later the waiter appeared at his side. "Finished?" he asked, motioning at Viv's plate.

"Ah, just getting started, actually." He had the plates sent away and ordered another bottle, carefully buttoning his sleeve again.

2

A few hours later he found himself at the bar next door. One of those hip-shit joints full of reclaimed steel buttresses and type trays inset into the walls, a place where the servers wore fedoras and had handlebar mustaches and sleeve tattoos. *Drill.* He ordered a cocktail and the bartender served it to him with a charred pinecone kind of rammed onto the lip of the glass. Sandoval sat down on a barstool and scratched his nose and looked at his cell phone for a minute.

He sent Viv a text message. A terrible, mean-spirited message. He realized only after he sent it that it was full of typos.

It was a weeknight and the place was dim and mostly quiet. A few couples sat at tiny tables along the wall, leaning close together. Everyone seemed very beautiful, enmeshed in their private lives. He set his pinecone on his napkin, and then lifted it, smelled it. It smelled like alcohol and a forest fire. How, he wondered, did they char the pinecones? A blowtorch? On a stove? He watched the bartender make drinks, and when his cocktail was finished, he put up a hand. The bartender came over, a blue sparrow on his throat, and raised his eyebrows.

"Another one, please," Sandoval said, concentrating on his posture, his words. He'd lost track of the amount of wine he'd drank at the White Bird.

The bartender seemed to think about it but took the bill Sandoval pushed across the bar. A minute later his drink appeared, with another burnt pinecone that he smelled and once more set carefully on a napkin. He nodded in time to the music piping softly through the speakers. The wine and cocktails sang in his blood, heavy, heavy. He gazed at the deep gloss of the bar, the lacquer liquid and gleaming in the light. Someone at a little table in the back had a laugh that ran along his nerves like a broken bottle down a silk sheet.

He texted another terrible thing to Viv, something lewd and cruel and shitty, his heart like a cinder inside his chest, beneath his ribbons of scars. No, he thought. Actually, *his heart was like a blackened pinecone.* Ha. That was it. He sipped his drink and his teeth knocked against the glass. Viv's text said she would call the police if he sent her a message again. Everything roiled inside him, outside him, he felt like destroying the bar and sliding down to the floor and weeping, and grabbing the bartender by the neck and holding onto him like a brother and also ramming his face into the gleaming bar top.

He drained his new drink, the dregs burning the back of his throat. He set his glass down loud on the bar, loud enough to be heard over the Appalachian hillbilly shit they were now playing over the speakers. Loud enough to turn some heads, and to send the bartender toward him with a look on his face that said *No more.*

Sandoval picked up his burnt pinecones and, *boom boom,* threw them at the bartender. He staggered out.

He could hear the rain when he stepped outside, see it in silver strings falling from the dark belly of the bridge he stood beneath. He tried to remember where he'd parked the Jag while his hands absently roved his pockets for his keys. Laden with a chorus of fury inside him, a nameless kind, the kind that did no one any good, the kind that had never done anyone any good in man's long love affair with fury; it was the kind that just heaved around inside you like a tornado. His hands were black with ash from handling those stupid fucking pinecones. He thought of holding them under the falling water but instead ran them down his face, pulling his jaw down into a rictus.

3

Forty minutes later he was bloody and lurching around his living room in his boxer shorts, hyperventilating and holding a reddened dishrag to his face.

Much of his sprawling four-bedroom West Hills home was comprised of windows, and he spent a few frantic minutes trying to drunkenly free himself of his bloody clothes while yanking down all the blinds on the ground floor. The whole goddamn *house* seemed to be made of windows right then, and he ripped a number of blind cords in his haste, his heart a bumbling slurry of booze and panic.

After the blinds were drawn, he made a greyhound in the kitchen and sat down on the couch in his underwear, willing his heart to slow. His watch read 1:13 a.m. Seemingly every light in the place burned. He dialed Tad Hemphill and left a message, his voice shaky and cracking. The greyhound, instead of calming him, turned him slower, turned the panic into an even more resolute, fanged and beastly thing. Nausea boiled inside him. The dishrag pressed to his nose stank of his own blood.

His laptop sat on the curio next to the fireplace, and when he heard the *ping* of an incoming message, he walked over to it, his head tilted back, under some drunken assumption that it was possibly Tad getting back to him. He barked his shin on the Michael Amini cocktail table, three thousand dollars' worth of fucking uselessness and brutally sharp angles. He cursed into the dishrag, pain singing an aria up his shin, and hopped on one leg, nearly staggering onto the glass top of the table. Tad Hemphill, he of the cotton-white pompadour and hairy ears and ceaseless supply of anti-Semitic lawyer jokes. Tad! Golf buddy of judges, deadly litigator, husband of pleasant, well-intentioned, oblivious Heidi Who Macraméd. Goddamn if he didn't need Tad Hemphill tonight like a kid needed his mother. The Jag had a silver spiderweb of glass running in a crazed line up the windshield, a divot in the hood. Blood undoubtedly dripping from the undercarriage onto the garage floor, a forensic wet dream of DNA, even as he himself sat there bleeding on the couch.

He gingerly took the rag away from his face: a Missoni Home cotton towel sent to oblivion. That shit was not cheap, either. He let out a sputtering, slobbery gasp, and knuckled a single tear away. Tad hadn't called him back; it was an email he'd gotten. Peering down, he didn't recognize the sender's name on the screen. Something with umlauts. His vision trembled and he gazed down at the fire engine–red of his blood on the rag. He spun around and stormed back into the kitchen, heaved a torrent of wine-dark gruel into the sink. His guts like God's hand inside them, squeezing. He tried to free himself from the briar-tangle of his thoughts, to simplify them.

The Jag was parked in the garage.

The garage door was shut.

It was locked from the inside. There were no windows in there. It was a cement cube.

It was contained.

It was *contained.*

He dropped the bloody dishtowel in the sink, his reflection a pale ghost in the window above the faucet. If the cops came in right now—what would they see? A drunk? A celebrity? An alien abductee? Not a killer, not for sure. He was still in good shape for a guy in his fifties, pecs not sagging the way most men his age invariably let them. He still had his hair. His gut was reasonably flat, especially considering how much he drank. This—the reminder of his drinking—was enough to tangle him in the briars again and he had to close his eyes, breathe. Feel his feet on the cold tile. The kitchen reeked of alcohol and bile.

He heard his phone ring and he raced back into the living room, cursing again as he bounced off the doorframe.

"What's up, buddy?" Tad cried, his voice reedy with booze and exuberance. Sandoval could hear the heartbeat-thump of music in the background. "How'd the date go?" Lower, he said, "You dip your wick? Vivian is a *particularly* good-looking woman, is she not?"

Sandoval choked out, "Tad, I'm fucked. I'm totally fucked." He could feel himself starting to unravel, like the fear had been held together with twine and cloth and was starting to come unwound now that he could confess. He tumbled toward the unraveling almost gratefully.

"Hold on," Tad said.

"I'm so fucked."

Sharply, Tad said, "Mark, shut your mouth. Hold on a second." Sandoval sat down on the couch.

The disco-thump of background music vanished. "Okay. I'm back. Talk to me slow and steady. Where are you at?"

"I'm at home."

"You by yourself?"

"Yeah."

"You sure?"

"*Yeah.*"

"Okay," Tad said. "What's up? Go slow."

Sandoval let out a slow, shaky breath. "I hit somebody."

A pause, the moment drawn drum-tight. "Who, *Viv?*"

He leaned back and laid a forearm over his eyes. "No, Christ. With my car."

Tad gave a pained little exhale, like someone out of shape doing a sit-up. "Okay. Question still stands. Viv? Pedestrian? Another car?"

Sandoval pressed his face against the crook of his arm and then sat up, reached for the greyhound glass that held a last few ice cubes, a dredge of pink water at the bottom. He rose and walked to the kitchen. He opened the blind above the sink, and the night beyond the window was intractable, distant; he took some odd measure of comfort that the world was moving on without him in spite of what he'd done. The great and grinding wheels of life would continue to chew everyone up. "Some guy," he said.

"*Some guy?*"

"I hit a guy with my car, Tad, and then I drove off. Some bum. He came out of nowhere. He was laying in the street."

"A literal bum? Or, like, 'You lousy bum?'"

"*A fucking homeless guy*, Tad, alright?"

"Christ on a chariot," Tad hissed. "Clearly you've been drinking."

"Clearly."

A beat, two. "That complicates things, Mark. Significantly. I won't lie to you. Jesus wept."

"I hit my face on the steering wheel. I'm covered in blood. The windshield's all cracked. The hood."

"Did you run him over?"

"I don't know. He kind of bounced off."

A pause. "Was there, like, a *thump thump?* Did the wheels go over him?"

"Fuck, *I don't know*, Tad! Does it matter?"

"Sweet lord, everything matters, my boy. Start from the beginning."

He made another greyhound, so much vodka in the glass that this time there was only the palest wash of watercolor-pink among the ice cubes. He pressed the phone hard against his ear and found the story coming easily enough now that he'd started. He was in a rush to be free of it. He told Tad Hemphill about the terrible date with Viv, going to the hipster bar, even the bit about the pinecones—Tad actually snorted with laughter at that, and surely he'd be okay if his lawyer was laughing, right? Surely?—and then how he'd finally found the Jag. How he'd sped up along the rain-slicked streets, mostly empty at that hour, and he'd only looked away for a second—he'd thought he'd felt his phone vibrate in his jacket and he'd had an absurd, ludicrous thought that it might be Viv reaching out to him—and then the terrible percussion had transmitted itself through the hood, the windshield, thrummed up into his hands, into his face as he bounced off the steering wheel. It was only when he talked about leaving the man in the street and seeing that brutal arrangement of limbs on the gleaming pavement that Tad interrupted him.

"Anybody follow you?"

"I don't know. It was down in the industrial section, southeast. I didn't see any other cars. I'd hardly even been driving, only a few blocks."

"A few blocks from where you got into your car?"

"Yeah."

"Were there a bunch of guys there, hanging out? Other hobos?"

"Hobos? I don't know, Tad," Sandoval said helplessly. "I just . . . I took off. I didn't wait to see who took out a magnifying glass and wrote my fucking license plate down. You know?"

"Alright." Sandoval heard him breathe. "This is the deal, Mark. Have a seat." Sandoval was still at the sink, looking at his reflection. A man holding an empty glass, blood-smeared and ashen, nearly nude, succumbing inevitably to age and mortality. Strange latticed scars spanning his body, a few drops of blood buried in his gray whorls of chest hair. He wondered where Tad was—in a coatroom at a party somewhere? Sweating and drunk in a club bathroom? He had trouble picturing portly Tad Hemphill in anything but a five-thousand-dollar Italian suit with a drop of Alfredo sauce on his tie.

Tad said, "Are you listening to me?"

"I'm listening."

"But are you *hearing* me, Mark?"

"I'm right here, man. I'm with you."

"Because this might be the most important bit of lawyerly advice I will ever give you. I can't *technically* advise you to cover anything up, and I can't *technically* assist you in hiding evidence. But you should know that you have the right to keep your mouth shut if anyone asks you about this. If someone does that, I would strongly urge you to just *shut the fuck up.* If anyone asks you about this, call me. If anyone asks where you were tonight, you zip it and call me exactly one second later, okay? If anyone knocks on your door, don't answer, and call me. If it's the cops and it sounds like they're going to break in, ask them if they have a warrant, then run upstairs and call me. Okay?"

"Okay," Sandoval said.

"What's the pattern you're picking up here, Mark? What are the common threads?"

"Shut up."

"Good."

"And call you."

"Excellent. Shut up and call me," Tad said.

It was undeniable, the relief that flooded through him, the net that Tad was throwing his way. He imagined Tad Hemphill standing next to a chest-high stack of greatcoats and furs on some four-poster bed at a garish, droll lawyer party out in Lake Oswego somewhere. He felt his terror quieting. He felt suffused with a grand, encompassing love for the man.

Talking to Tad, he knew immediately that he could live with this act in the long run. Live with its knowledge. That he could still manage to flourish in some way. That he was one of those people who could diminish and quell a memory staunchly enough to move beyond it, to still live something resembling a life.

Hadn't he done it before?

Christ, look at him! His entire life was a testament to that, if nothing else. He raised an arm and ghost-Sandoval raised an arm in the window, both of them covered in their raised glyphs and symbols and lines, their drink in a curled fist. He could survive this.

"Do you understand, Mark? Are you with me?"

"I hear you," Sandoval said.

"That's the life preserver I'm throwing your way. That's my piece of advice: call me if anyone contacts you."

"Thank you, Tad."

"Just play it cool. Be patient. It was the Jag, right?"

"Yeah."

"Is it in the garage?"

"Yeah."

"And the hood's parked away from the garage windows?"

"There's no windows down there."

"Okay," Tad said. "Okay." He coughed, cleared his throat. It was a stentorian, old man–sound that went on for a while. "And Mark?"

"Yeah."

"How's the book coming?"

"The book?" He felt sucker-punched, pulled out of their shared narrative.

"The book you're writing. The monster one. *Monsters of America* or whatever."

Sandoval bristled. "Well honestly, the book's not going too good, Tad," he said archly. "Why?"

"Well, because now might be a good time to head out of town. Maybe it's time to tackle some research for a while. In Uganda or something. Do you understand me?"

He did.

4

He dozed fitfully that night, his sleep scattershot with half-lit dreams: the bus trip, the rest stop, the cold light in the clearing. He awoke ash-mouthed and dumped out four aspirin from the jumbo bottle on his nightstand, chewed them to bitter pulp, a body on automatic. He lay there splayed like a dead starfish on silk sheets, an idiot organism reduced to the simple machinery of pumping heart and lungs. Eventually a stutter-quick flashflood of images and textures came to him—Viv's freckled chest, a blackened pinecone on the glossed bar top, the silver crack in the windshield. The car's halted velocity juddering up into his hands. The black-on-black silhouette of a sprawled body in the rearview mirror.

He rose up, padded to the bathroom, glanced briefly at the chalky flakes of blood still rimming his nostrils, the pinecone ash still ribboning his cheeks like some goth chorus girl, and heaved into the toilet.

Showering, he tested the edges of his panic like a man defining the walls of a darkened room. Evaporated was last night's brash notion that he'd be fine, that he could live with himself. Hadn't he seen the man move in the Jag's rearview mirror? Maybe even start to rise, simply dazed and shaken? Some part of him seized on it, tried to reshape the moment to fit the desire, even as he knew it was bullshit. Whistle past the graveyard, liar. You know he wasn't moving.

He stood dripping in his bedroom. He cracked the blinds that looked out onto the hills, the city below. Wind shuddered the tops of the trees. He shaved, dotting the occasional cut with a spot of toilet paper. He dressed in slacks, a button-up, a three-hundred-dollar Robert Talbott tie, its pale pink offsetting the blue of his shirt. Hands shaking the entire time. Waiting all the while for the knock at the door. Cops in riot gear, plastic shields and beanbag shotguns, his door splintered to shards by that big handheld iron they used. But no, that insidious, calculating, mercenary part of him insisted: he was rich and white. They'd come to the door and knock. Even with a warrant, they'd knock first.

He took his laptop, padded into the kitchen. It was afternoon by now.

Wary of a search warrant that would get his computer confiscated—even hungover he was still thinking—he checked the local news sites but didn't type anything specific in a search engine. Checked local Twitter sites. Facebook. Nothing. No mention. If anything, the panic intensified, grew barbs. Sandoval's guilt was like a nameless shape writhing in a canvas bag.

He checked his email, saw a message from his editor. He didn't click on it—he knew the refrain: *How is the book coming along? Getting to the point where you can send anything to us?* The unspoken thread, rising increasingly toward the surface these days: *You know we paid you a lot of money for this book, right, Mark? You know you've sucked at our teat for years now without giving us any blood in return, right, Mark? You know I'm trying to keep my bosses from suing you for breach of contract, right? Mark?*

The other message was from someone with an email handle of *khauksdottir.* He vaguely remembered the mad jumble across the room, barking his shin on the coffee table. (It was blue this morning.) He marveled for a moment at the juxtaposition: he was torn between running for his life and taking the Range Rover down to Powell's and spending another unsuccessful afternoon dicking around in the café with the swollen, unwieldy shitstorm that *Monsters Americana* had become.

He broke his own brand-new rule and googled *countries with no extradition to US.* Short of Algeria—hadn't Burroughs lived in Algeria for a while?—they all sounded like terrible places to live. He bounced back to his email window and clicked on the *khauksdottir* message. It was as brief as it was odd:

Mr. Sandoval,

I am a fan of your books. I apologize for my English, I don't often have need to use it when I write. I live on a small island called Hvíldarland, near Iceland. My children and I live on a small farm on the north end of the country. I was a witness to something sneaking onto our farm at night recently. This is the video I took.

This is not a hoax, I promise you. Perhaps you would be interested in hearing more? Please feel free to contact me if so. I believe you are the best person to contact.

I look forward to hearing from you.

Sincerely,
Karla Hauksdóttir

He watched the attached video.

Watched it again.

A third time.

A plan began to unfold then. *Now might be a good time to head out of town.*

He sent Karla Hauksdóttir an email. Why yes, he was definitely intrigued by the footage, would she be available to talk soon? Ideas tumbled, tumbled into place. Always with that remembrance of the juddering steering wheel beneath his palms.

He took the Range Rover out, double-checked to make sure the garage was locked, drove down the winding road into the city. Ordered a latte from the café in Powell's. As always, he felt enveloped by the susurration of voices and movement around him. He fired off an email to his agent and his editor, and included the Hauksdóttir video. Said he was willing to return the entire advance for *Monsters Americana* if he didn't turn in a manuscript for this idea in six months. He stepped outside onto the sidewalk, legs too caffeine-choked to sit anymore, Burnside traffic slow and ceaseless next to him.

He left voicemails for both men. The same message for both: "Call me. I'm dead fucking serious about this. This is a moneymaker. This is a gift from me to you. You send me out there and I write this thing and we're talking two million copies sold, *boom.* Merchandising lines, tie-ins, everything. I give you *this* book in six months or I sell my house and give you your money back. It's a win-win. *Call me.*"

He went into the parking garage, got in the Range Rover. His phone pinged: a message from Karla Hauksdóttir. Her phone number, times she was available to talk.

He tapped out an email to Dani, told her he was sending her monthly payment early and not to give him any grief about it because he'd be out of the country. His thumbs were a blur over the screen. He was cooking, sweating out his hangover.

And now it was *hope* galloping in his chest. Terror getting booted down the stairs, further and further down.

Sandoval drove back out onto the street with the triphammer of *maybe, maybe* yodeling in his blood, this animal, insistent aria. A light rain began falling again, couples holding hands on the sidewalks. His phone chirped. It was his agent. He put it on speaker, tossed it on the passenger seat.

"You have got," his agent said, "to be fucking kidding me. A *new* book? A *unicorn* book? Jesus Christ, Mark. These guys want your blood at this point."

"I'm not kidding you," Sandoval said. He grinned with those perfect teeth, caught himself in the mirror for a second. "I'm not kidding about any of it. This is gold."

His agent didn't say a word for two blocks. Sandoval sweated, drove, willed him to say yes.

Finally his agent let out an embattled sigh and said, "Shit. Let me make some calls."

5

The last time he'd seen Don Whitmer, all those years ago, the man had been sitting behind his desk then, too. They'd both been a hell of a lot younger, and Whitmer had winced and said, "You can't float on charisma, Mark. We need you here."

And a young Mark Sandoval had said in return, "I hear you, Don." Young, dewy-eyed, lost, practically dripping with sincerity. And maybe, okay, just a tiny little bit dope sick. "I'm sorry."

Just like a tiny little fingernail's worth of a little bit, though.

Whitmer shook his head, looked over Sandoval's shoulder. "You say that, but you've said that before. You're just not putting in the hours. Your class load is suffering."

"Okay."

"You're not here when you need to be here, Mark."

It was December 16th, 1994. Seattle. They were seated in Don Whitmer's generously sized office inside Washington College of the Arts, and sleet was turning yesterday's snow to a gray, obscene mud in the gutters outside. It was the day the perfect storm touched down in Mark Sandoval's life. The catalyst for all that would happen to him afterward.

Seriously, it was crazy how shit went down sometimes.

Don Whitmer in 1994 was a different man. A thin man with an astonishing network of veins tracing his arms, Whitmer back then had fairly writhed with a kind of wire-bound vitality; he almost literally thrummed like a power line and seemed nearly incapable of staying still. He had been Sandoval's professor, and was now Sandoval's boss. And Don was unhappy. In '94, he still had a full head of curly hair and wore large square eyeglasses that continually caught the overhead lights, frequently turning the lenses into white, unreadable cubes. Even then, with half of his face obscured by those glasses, those sometimes-white lenses, he'd vibed his discontent at Sandoval hard.

WCA was a small liberal arts campus that through catastrophic mismanagement would go bankrupt in five years (of course neither of them knew that at the time, and Sandoval wouldn't have given a shit anyway) but on that particular Friday, Whitmer's office was cavernous and studded with dark leather chairs and large potted plants in the corners. Sandoval felt the hammer coming down and resisted the urge to gnaw on the shredded meat that had been his fingernails.

Whitmer's desk was massive, polished to a gleam, populated only with an *In/Out* tray for paperwork, a blotter, and a single thread-wrapped bird skull, the bones of which had taken on the fine yellowed quality of an old newspaper. Whitmer was the chair of the WCA Anthropology Department, and this was a suddenly-not-inconsequential thing to be, given the recent generosity of a particularly benevolent donor (and a colleague of Whitmer's) who had died and surprised everyone by leaving his entire and not inconsiderable fortune to the anthro department. The school suddenly found itself in a windfall, and the dean saw stars and hearts whenever Whitmer walked by.

None of this bode particularly well for Mark Sandoval, who was at that moment pretty well immersed in the *sitches,* which his cute pet name ("sick" + "itches" = "sitches") for being maybe just a little dope sick and wanting to scratch at his *very* minute scabs, which were the byproduct that came from being a *mostly* social and very intermittent IV dope user, which was not, admittedly, a particularly creative or smart thing to be in Seattle in 1994, given the number of his ex-friends and acquaintances that were sliding or nearly sliding from this mortal coil with alarming regularity via OD, bad dope, holdups, etc. But all told, his *sitches* and cramps aside, Sandoval also felt pretty bad for Don Whitmer. He'd put Don in a shitty position, and Don really was a good guy, and a solid anthropologist, and even now, as he was axing Sandoval from the department (because that was clearly what was going to go down), the man's eminent fucking *reasonableness* and *kindness* were the things that sang out the most.

He'd bucked Sandoval up countless times, thrown him bones (pun intended) academically again and again: research credits on papers, hustling up funding for him to come along on site digs—Death Valley, Arizona's Gila River, even a battery of hill forts in Gloucestershire—and had gone so far as defending him from other department heads in regard to his growing fuckups. It was a small school, and Sandoval had, yes, been screwing up massively as of late, and it was also true that he himself hardly understood Whitmer's fierce loyalty, even as he recognized it as such. But even he could see that the man had finally hit a wall. Enough was enough.

Whitmer said, "You've got to show up. That was a final yesterday." Outside, ugly spats of sleet made halos of the lights that lined the pathway outside the Sciences building. Barely afternoon and the world already going dark.

"I am *so* sorry, Don. I—I don't know what to say. I'm mortified. Seriously."

Whitmer adjusted his little bird skull, then leaned his chin into a palm and just sat there looking at Sandoval, who was clamping down pretty hard on his knees in order to not worry the scabs in the crooks of his arms. Whitmer said, "Mark, I'm just . . . How is the school supposed to address this issue? How am I?"

"Like I said, Don, I'm mortified. I could blame the power company, but that doesn't matter in the long run, does it? This is a recurring theme, and I understand that. I have no excuse."

Whitmer puffed out his cheeks, slowly exhaled. His lenses caught the light again. "That's right," he said wearily. "A power surge, wasn't that it?"

"Like I said, I had my alarm set for six forty-five. But my apartment building's a hundred, hundred and ten years old. Fuses are constantly blowing. The whole place is held together with chicken wire and rats, you know? I woke up to the clock flashing 12:00, over and over again."

He kept wanting to rattle off a catalog of all the ways he'd get his shit together, *starting right now,* if he just got one more shot. All these things that he couldn't *actually* say: he and Marnie would get off the dope, he'd pay Dieter back for the package he'd been floated, he'd grade his papers, he'd *show up to the fucking classes he was supposed to teach—*

"Mark," Whitmer said, and in just that one word, any last foolhardy vestige of hope disappeared, vaporous as a squirrel fart. That one word, his name, had the finality of the guillotine. Whitmer opened a drawer in his desk and pulled out a manila folder. He licked his thumb and leafed through a few pages. Gazing at Sandoval over the tops of those big square glasses, he said, "You mind if I read you something?"

"Sure."

And Whitmer held the paper before him, squinting, and listed the dates in which Sandoval had been "absent, tardy, negligent or unprofessional in regard to his assistant professorship" under Whitmer's tutelage for the past fifteen months. Some of them were from Whitmer's own records, but others, he was dismayed to hear, were from other professors or even, in more than a few cases, his students. Whitmer droned on and on, and then flipped a page and kept going. Sandoval chanced a surreptitious scratch of his arms while the man was busy reading; the relief was simultaneously delicious and gone before it started.

Whitmer finished reading and set the folder down. Dope sick or not, Sandoval felt the hot flush of shame on his cheeks. He scowled at a cigarette burn in the dirty canvas of his shoe.

The silence stretched out. Whitmer looked at him, cleared his throat, expectant.

Sandoval finally lifted his gaze, angry. Whitmer saw it and Sandoval was surprised to see the old man level a finger at him.

"Listen to me, Mark. You were a fantastic student, and I was thrilled to offer you this position. But this . . . If it was anyone else, you'd have been out on your can a long time ago."

"Okay," Sandoval said, and shrugged. In lieu of scratching, he ran a palm over his stubble.

Whitmer took off his glasses, set them on his desk. There was a dark purple indentation on the bridge of his nose. "That was a *final exam*, Mark, and you weren't there. You understand, as an assistant professor, that the fact that you missed handing out a final exam to thirty-one of your students the day before their winter break begins is a significant event, right? That this has caused significant hardship for people other than yourself?"

"Don, come on. Of course I do."

"Carlisle wants you gone, Mark." Whitmer put his glasses back on. And that was that, wasn't it? WCA was not a big school, and if the dean wanted you gone, you were gone. Sure, Sandoval could request hearings, submit letters of appeal, but if the deck was stacked—and they had plenty of his missteps on record, apparently, and Whitmer had clearly stepped away from his corner—he was done.

It was a strange feeling, the bottom dropping out of everything. It wasn't *bad*, per se, just strange. The *sitches* were bad, but this, this just felt like . . . falling. His anger was gone. What had taken its place was a particular hollowness. The wind changed outside and sleet ticked against the window.

"I'm really sorry, Mark," Whitmer said, and Sandoval believed him. He was a good guy, had always been a good guy. His belief in Whitmer's inherent goodness would years later sour to a kind of miasma of resentment; he would come to consider the old man a prig, too adherent to propriety, academically stifled and stifling in return. But right then, on that dark and sleet-battered Friday afternoon on Capitol Hill, it felt almost like a father admonishing his son. "You're a hell of a researcher, Mark, and a terrific writer. You have years of site studies and books and papers and professorship inside you, if you want it. But that's the thing."

"I have to want it," Sandoval murmured.

"You have to want it. And I'm just not sure if you're there yet."

"I don't know if I'll ever be there."

Whitmer nodded. "And that's okay too," he said softly.

"So I'm just kicked out? There's no process in place?"

"We've been sending you letters, Mark. I know Carlisle's sent you at least two, three letters about putting you on probation, not to mention the phone calls." Softly, he said, "Are you not opening your mail?"

"Honestly, I'm not spending a lot of time at home."

"Okay."

"Marital troubles."

"I understand. I'm sorry to hear it."

And that was it. Don Whitmer wrapped Sandoval's clammy hand in his warm, work-roughened ones, and bid him what was essentially goodbye. He walked down the halls, down those brightly lit, right-angled corridors that did their staunch duty in keeping the outside world at bay, in stopping the elements from gaining entrance, in halting the disparate combinations of things that could encroach and cause chaos. His last time there. Gone were the last tenets of orderliness and normality. He was fired.

He was screwed.

Wind, like someone's furious searching hand, ran along his body when he stepped outside. His guts chortled, cramps tightening him up. Sleet smacked loud against his jacket. The red taillights of cars along Denny Avenue flared in the darkness.

It was evening now, and it hit him once he got outside: Sick for sure. itching, cramps, cold sweats.

He stopped at a payphone with crude swastikas scratched into the glass and dumped in a handful of change. It was night in DC; she might already be at the club, just starting her shift. Missing her had its own pulse, its own backbeat.

Three rings and her answering machine.

There was a Thai place across the street and he talked as he watched all the people inside. "Well, I just got booted from school, Dani. You believe it? I appear to have hit a rut, yeah?" His laugh sounded like someone stepping on a branch. "Listen, I really miss you. Marnie's at home, so don't worry about calling. Guarantee she'll throw me out the door when she finds out about this." He dipped his head against the scarred glass. "Anyway, yeah, I miss you. I wish you were here. I'll give you a call when I can."

He considered scoring, heading down Broadway or into Cal Anderson Park, but then thought of Marnie hearing the news about losing his job and seeing him smoothed out on top of that and decided it'd be better to face the music first. She could always tell if he was pinned at all, even a little bit. So, okay. He'd tell Marnie, get it over with, *then* go score. Or maybe bring some *to* Marnie and then tell her?

Or just kick, he thought. *Just knock it off. Christ.*

They lived in a one-bedroom not far from school, a ground-level apartment with a nice lobby and a big picture window that faced the street. Spent needles and dog shit dotted the shrubbery in front of the place; homeless men would frequently thread their way through the shrubs to knock on their window to ask for money or, in one case, to hand Marnie a pocket bible and inquire about her soul.

When he came into the apartment after the chill of the walk, the smell hit him. The place *stank*. Dirty laundry, the reek of dishes sitting too long in fetid water. Garbage can mounded high and rotting under the sink. His coat dripping with sleet, he flicked the light in the front hall and nothing happened. He walked into the kitchen and flicked that switch. Nothing. The clock on the stove was black as everything else.

"Goddamn it."

He considered copping again—Marnie clearly wasn't home, and what was the point of staying here if they'd shut the power off? But then another flurry of cramps seized him, and he flicked his lighter and walked like a blind man to the bathroom, his free hand pressed to his guts. He lit a bunch of Marnie's hippie candles on the back of the toilet tank and took a grueling, watery shit. When he was done, he blew out most of the candles and took a few into the living room where he could at least watch the street and wonder where the fuck Marnie was and try not to think about scoring. Somehow it seemed unfair that she should be gone now when he had this news to unload. They'd been married five years; she'd been on a full ride to Cornish for painting when they'd met. She'd managed to graduate, barely, after Sandoval had eventually gotten her turned on to coke and then snorting heroin. She'd graduated to popping by the time she got her diploma, and yeah, he felt bad about it. God. Of course he did. He carried the candles—the scents of pine trees and sugar cookies ghosting in his wake—and set them down on the coffee table. Outside, the sleet had turned to rain, and the frying-oil sound of it in the shrubbery was comforting.

He sat down in his green chair by the window. He felt something under his ass and reached down. Yet another bill, he figured, but in the scant candlelight, he saw her handwriting. She'd written on the back of the electricity bill, and that was some irony, right?

He squinted, leaning close in the candlelight.

Mark

I'm so done. Finally.

You can keep everything. I don't care anymore. You're a train wreck, and an addict, and a thief and a liar, and I'm stepping off this train

*before you take me with you. Go fuck yourself, and I mean that
sincerely.*

—M

Then he noticed that all of Marnie's paintings—crude, menacing, heavy-
stroked things, canvasses of bright, neon-colored women being mauled
by wolf-men hybrids, dog-men, cat-men, cartoonish things, backgrounds
that consisted mostly of triangles and circles and fierce drips of primary
colors—were gone from their familiar spots on the walls. *A train wreck?*
A thief and a liar? A drug addict?

They had split and gotten back together a dozen times. She spent more
time at friends' places than she did at the apartment these days. Even spent
a few months at her mom's place once. Never left a note, though. Never
taken her stuff before.

He was sick in his guts. He walked the small apartment holding the
sugar cookie candle. It did not entirely cover up the odor of the terrible
things he had done to the bathroom, just kind of merged the two scents
together in a way that was somehow more horrific. He kept wanting to try
the light switches. He kept scratching his arms. He kept sniffling his runny
nose and palming the sweat from his face.

"I need to get clean," he said to a spot on the wall where a painting had
once hung. The candle's flame trembled. Shadows writhed. "I feel like that
would definitely alleviate certain issues."

He lit a few more candles and brought them one by one into the bedroom. He sat on the unmade bed and spent an hour or so going through
Marnie's things, seeing what he could sell or trade. *If he decided to.* There
wasn't much; some clothes, some shit jewelry. But the bookshelves were
full of Marnie's art books from school. They would fetch at least some
cash. This was his life then: he'd become reduced to this simplicity, to an
engine of need.

He was pulling books from the bookcase with his sugar cookie candle
next to him when there was a knock at the front door. It was a *confident*
knock, a knock that reverberated throughout the small apartment. Sandoval
froze. He was a statue, breathless and still. The world became so quiet he
was sure he could hear the candlewick hissing, the flame devouring oxygen,
his eyeballs rolling in the lubricated beds of their sockets.

Only two people in the world would knock on his door like that.

"Open it up or we're gonna knock it down," Dieter said, already sounding bored.

Sandoval tiptoed into the living room, goose-stepping toward the picture window, and saw Julian standing there with his hand cupped against the glass, staring in at him.

"Mark," he said through the glass, "quit messing around. I can see your candle, numbnuts."

Sandoval stared directly at Julian through the glass and blew out the candle.

Julian smiled. "You little fucker."

He was wearing a trench coat—Julian always wore a trench coat, it was part of the evil-villain shtick he cultivated—and in a whirl of fabric he stormed off through the shrubs, presumably to the front door of the apartment building to assist Dieter in smashing the door in. Sandoval tiptoed to the window and gently slid it open, the tang of night air glorious after the apocalyptic potpourri of his fusty, soiled, closed-in apartment. Mist kissed his face like a lover.

He gently set his feet down on the spongy ground and started speed-walking down the sidewalk and Julian stepped out from behind a dumpster and punched him in the ear. Sandoval stumbled to his knees. The pain was galvanizing, gigantic, and he let out a breathless little scream while staggering and clutching at his ear with both hands.

"You dummy," Julian said, cinching a hand around Sandoval's bicep and hoisting him up. They marched back to the shrubbery in front of his building, and Julian escorted him back through the open window. Back into his stinking, lightless, Marnie-free apartment. *At least she's not here to see this bullshit,* he thought. Maybe if he yelled, someone would call the police. It was still Capitol Hill, after all. Sure, the bushes were gleaming with spent rigs, but this was still a nice neighborhood. He stood in the darkened living room while Julian pushed himself in, then shut the window.

"Stay put," he said, and walked past Sandoval and opened the front door.

"The lights don't work," Julian said to Dieter in the hallway.

Dieter said, "You know a junkie that pays their bills?"

They walked into the living room, looked around. Dieter's nose curled. "It smells like shit in here."

"Got any more candles?" Julian asked.

"In the bedroom," Sandoval said, still cupping his ear. The side of his skull felt hugely swollen, like someone was trying to park a car in his head. Fear had cinched his asshole up like a bag with a drawstring, as if he'd never need to visit the bathroom again.

Dieter told him to shut the blinds and he did.

He told Sandoval to sit in his green chair, and Sandoval sat in his green chair. Julian brought candles back and forth from the bedroom and the bathroom until all the candles were alight on the coffee table. The room trembled with a greasy, uneasy light. All those buoyant scents—peppermint, watermelon, apple, cookie dough, vanilla—fogged together to make something wretched.

Julian said, "Now it smells like fairyland *and* diarrhea. Great."

"Why isn't your power on?" Dieter asked, his arms folded across his chest.

"I don't know," Sandoval said.

"Where's your wife?"

"I don't know."

"The fuck do you know," said Julian.

"She left me."

Dieter said, "Yeah, right. College man like you? The Professor?"

Sandoval held out the note to Julian. His mouth moved with the words as he read it. Julian handed the note to Dieter. Dieter had a ponytail and a linebacker's build that he packed into a leather jacket too small for him. His hands were dainty things, tiny, the knuckles dimpled. He held the electricity bill between his thumbs and forefingers.

"That sucks, man," he said.

"I know."

He flipped the note over. "And you owe like a hundred and eighty bucks to the power company."

Sandoval sighed, checked his fingers to see if his ear was bleeding. It was, a little.

Julian gazed down at him with something that was almost respect. "You *are* having a bad day."

"Okay," Dieter said. "So." The two of them crowded Sandoval in his green chair by the window, the candles backlighting them. Julian, besides his gangly scarecrow body folded into that trench coat, had his wiry red beard done up in a pair of rubber bands. A kind of casual cruelty, an offhanded willingness to do great and brutal harm, exuded from both men like bad cologne.

"I mean, you know why we're here," Dieter said.

"And clearly I don't have it," Sandoval said, gesturing at the walls, the candles, the darkness.

Julian punched him in the thigh. It was surprisingly effective: pain sang along Sandoval's nerves, great and generous bolts of pain shooting down to his ankle. He huffed and grabbed his leg and leaned over the arm of the chair. A pair of brass knuckles caught the light on Julian's hand.

"Whoo. Break your cocksucking leg if I do that again," Julian crowed, happy about it.

"You understand," said Dieter, "how an economy works, yeah? How goods and services are traded under the expectation of monetary reimbursement?

The implied exchange? The good faith? It's like the cornerstone of society, that expectation." Dieter had once told him that he'd taken a year of business classes at UW Seattle before the heroin business proved too profitable. "This is a reasonable expectation we have for you."

Sandoval sat up, his hands laced around his thigh, breathing hard through his nose.

Dieter sighed, stuffed his little hands in his leather jacket. "Mark, get serious. You're into us for six grand. That's money *owed*. That's a package of dope you were supposed to flip for us. Instead, you and your wife either shot it into your arms or, I don't know, spent it on paints for her shitty artwork—"

Sandoval gasped and said, "Don't talk about my wife's artwork."

"Whoa, did she take her paintings?" Julian suddenly said, looking around. "Damn. She took her paintings."

"—and it's money that *we* had to front for you. Me and him. I don't like carrying your debts. It's unjust."

"What do you want me to do? Pull six grand out of my ass? I lost my job today."

"For reals?" said Julian, tugging on one of his beard-thatches. "Man, you are really in the shit." He crouched down, his forearms on his knees, trench coat pooling behind him. Sandoval could see candle flames reflected in his eyes, running bright along the ridge of the brass knuckles. That stupid, stupid beard done up in rubber bands.

"Listen," Julian said quietly. "This isn't a new spot for us, Mark. You're nothing we haven't seen before. But look"—and here he took the knuckles off, dropped them into his coat pocket—"we're giving you a break. See? We're willing to work with you, but you gotta work with us, man. Make an effort. I mean, Jesus."

Sandoval thought of Don Whitmer saying *You can't float on charisma, Mark.* Saying that he was a hell of a researcher and writer. He thought of Dani, her willful scars, her tattoos, her litheness. The way she lit him up. How she was over at the other end of the country. He thought of Marnie, sweet and shy and idealistic and now, thanks to him, carrying around a sizable monkey of her own, sweet skinny Marnie, his wife with smears of paint on her tights, thumbs poking out of her sweater cuffs, her little crooked front tooth, their love lost and pissed on, squandered, his infidelities, his selfishness, his habits. All of these people he'd either infringed upon or brazenly, repeatedly disappointed—because what else did he do? What other avenue was there for guys like Mark Sandoval to walk down? He was who he was. He found himself suddenly weighted down with hatred for these men before him while simultaneously suffocating under a coffin-sized brick of self-loathing. He and Dieter and Julian might as well move in together, might as well get matching tattoos: they were triplets from the same wretched shit-pile. They were the same.

Sandoval leaned forward and gazed into Julian's hooded, soul-dead eyes. Very slowly and clearly he said, "Don't you have some other errands to run, Julian? For people a lot smarter than you? Huh? You dumb little sandwich-boy shit-rat lackey fuck." It was the best he could come up with.

Julian shrugged. "Okey doke."

The beating was quick. A flurry of arms in the half-dark, arms with missiles and boulders and bombs attached to the ends of them. Sandoval and Julian and Dieter all gasping, grunting with effort in that little corner of the room, the violence as intimate as sex. Sandoval tried to curl up on the chair and protect his face and they grabbed at his hands and fell on top of him, balancing with one hand against the wall, against the back of the chair. Starbursts of pain and the bright animal acknowledgment of being *hurt*, of a body infringing upon his body, the feel of skin split and blood running wet down his face, pain where there had been no pain before, rings and fingernails scratching down forearms and cheeks, lips pulped, the sounds so *personal*, the sea of candle flames shuddering on the table nearby, Sandoval by the end of it loosing spluttering, childish sobs, begging them to stop, spit and blood hanging in great loose strings from his face, strings that trembled and caught the light and then finally broke under their own weight, pattering to the carpet, his shirt, the chair.

They leaned before him with their bloody scraped hands on their knees, panting like they'd done wind sprints.

Dieter stood up and retied his ponytail. "We'll be back in a week," he said, still breathing heavy. He ran his hand under his nose, left a streak of Sandoval's blood there. "Seven days, payment in full."

Julian said, "And don't call me that again, Mark. I'm not dumb, and I'm not a rat."

Gasping, weeping, Sandoval bled in his chair.

Dieter turned at the front door and appraised him. "And if you don't have the money? Mark, you listening to me? Nod if you're listening. Okay. If you don't have the money next week, Mark, me and him will saw your head off and throw it into the Sound. Okay? Hand to God, man. Your debt is my debt and that's no good for me. It's time for you to get serious."

6

The widening gazes of his fellow pedestrians, a taxi driver's moon face at a stoplight asking if he needed help, Sandoval waving him away and staggering on. He'd left the apartment in a hurry, shoved shit in a backpack. His jacket was ruined, bloodied, and he'd grabbed one of Marnie's windbreakers from the bedroom, the dark one with the inside pockets. Blood kept falling on it and he kept wiping it off.

He walked downtown, and inside Cooper's, the line of regulars sat curled over their glasses as if they'd atrophied there, men gone too long without sun. Ropes of neon gleamed on the bar top from the signs on the walls, some shitkicker music on the jukebox. He turned heads as he walked to the ATM at the far wall by the bathrooms. Murmurings, quiet hoots of commiserate laughter. He pulled out three hundred dollars, the most he could withdraw at once, and tucked it into his wallet.

At the Greyhound station he got more hoots from the smokers gathered outside the doors. He hoisted his backpack over his shoulder and zipped up his jacket and walked into the bathroom. Paper towels spilled from the dented garbage can, tiles wet with piss and God knew what else. A scratched, unbreakable mirror warped the ruination of his face.

Someone in a closed stall let out a pinched, tremulous fart and then laughed. At the sink, Sandoval wetted paper towels and gingerly dabbed at his lips, cleaned the blood from his nose, from the oozing cuts around his eyes. Watery pink dimes of blood fell to the countertop. The man in the stall farted again and giggled, "Eee-eee-eee!" Sandoval's adrenaline was souring. He was shaky and sick again. He wanted to cry. Marnie's windbreaker was dark enough to hide the blood.

People clustered at their gates. They sat disconsolately in the orange bucket seats, plugging quarters into tiny televisions mounted on the armrests. A mother sat with three sleeping children lined up in the seats next to her. They went from biggest to smallest like little nesting dolls. The mother looked at him and quickly looked away.

He waited in line, ignoring the furtive glances he got from other people waiting their turn, and when it was his turn, the ticket agent's eyes grew big and she said, "Just a minute," and walked into a back room. A moment later she returned with another agent who wiped his mouth with a napkin and threw it in the trash. The man looked him up and down. "Help you?"

"I'd like to buy a ticket."

"I can't make you out, man."

"I just want to buy a ticket," said Sandoval, enunciating.

The woman said, "Honey, an ambulance is what you need. You need a hospital, is what."

"It's worse than it looks," Sandoval said, and took out his wallet. "How much is a one-way to DC going to set me back?" He thought of smiling, then worried his lip would split open again. His hands were cold, racked with tremors.

The man had a hawk-like nose and sleepy, bloodshot eyes. He had creases in his shirt like he'd slept in it. He shrugged and said, "Man wants to go to DC, Sharise, who are we to say?"

"I don't even know if the driver's gonna let him on, a face like that."

"Money talks," the man said, and asked Sandoval when he wanted to leave.

"Yesterday," Sandoval said. *A lifetime ago,* he thought.

The man nodded, tapped at his keyboard. "That's about what I figured."

The woman walked back into the office, shaking her head. The man took Sandoval's money and in return gave him a sheaf of tickets stapled together, pointed to the spots on his tickets that showed layovers, boarding passes. Four and a half days on the Grey Dog, Seattle to DC.

Sandoval pocketed his change, adjusted his backpack. "Is there a gift shop, anything like that?"

"A gift shop?" The man lifted his chin, motioning behind Sandoval. "Got a little kiosk back there, coffee and shit, but it closes at ten. What you need?"

"I was just hoping for some aspirin or something."

"You good with your tickets, you see how all the layovers and things are gonna work?"

"Yeah, thank you."

"Okay, hold on." He walked into the back office and came out a moment later, placing a travel-size bottle of aspirin and a few Band-Aids on the counter. "You still bleeding from your eyebrow there, just so you know. Better cover that up or the driver probably won't let you on."

"Thank you," Sandoval said. His vision swam with sudden tears. "Thanks a lot."

"Blood on your shirt there, too. Yeesh. Zip up your jacket, man. Yeah. You got it."

Through the wreckage of his mouth, Sandoval slurred, "I appreciate it," and cracked open the bottle of aspirin.

"Man, you not the first guy to get stomped in his life, you know? Four, five years ago, I got jumped by a bunch of good old boys in a bar in Bremerton. There for my brother's wedding." His laugh was musical, generous. "Bunch of rednecks from the naval base. Boy. I didn't look as bad as you do, but I wasn't far off. Bus leaves in ninety minutes. Good luck to you."

Sandoval wanted to shake his hand, wanted to lean over the counter and hug him, wanted to be his friend and work at the Seattle Greyhound terminal alongside him, dispensing aspirin and life-saving acts of kindness, but instead he swallowed down his tears and took his Band-Aids and aspirin and walked back into the bathroom. The giggler had vacated. He put a pair of Band-Aids on his eyebrows, and one on his cheek where someone's knuckles had laddered up the bone and scraped the skin raw and oozing red. He still looked horrible—worse, now that some discoloration was starting to come into play—but he was no longer a walking open wound.

He ate some aspirin and when he went to put the bottle in the inner pocket of the windbreaker, he felt things in there. He took them out.

Jesus. A joint—a fat, misshapen joint—and half a pack of Juicy Fruit gum.

In a bucket chair, he fed a few quarters into a television and gazed numbly into the little green-tinged screen. A Christmas tree leaned disconsolately in a corner of the terminal, its lights burned out, the linoleum beneath the tree dusted with dead needles. When the bus arrived and he stood in line waiting to board, there was some distant part of him that expected Dieter and Julian to walk into the station, as if they'd known he would run. But a larger and more significant part of him was simply fatigued beyond words. Poor Marnie. Had she gone to her mom's in Reno? Was she still in town? Sandoval imagined Dieter and Julian striding into the station and him just dropping to his knees, just begging them to finally end it for him.

The bus was quiet and dark, almost full. He kept his head down and the driver didn't look twice at him. Sandoval shuffled down the aisle and near the back, after shoving his backpack in the overhead compartment, sat down next to a black man with shoulder-length dreads and an olive-green field jacket. The guy wore a knit tam and his eyes opened in sleepy irritation when Sandoval slumped next to him. He seemed wholly unimpressed with Sandoval's face, but maybe it was just too dark to see.

"Cool if I sit down?"

"You already are, man," the guy said, and closed his eyes again.

A few minutes later they were off. Sandoval listened to the sound of rain on the roof and watched the city lights slowly peel and curve across the glass.

7

Oh, kicking the monkey on the Dog. It was a *small* monkey he had, sure. Of course. But still: it was straight misery. A case of blind acceptance. The wheels of the Dog churned *slow*. Time crawled. There was just so much of it.

Time for one's broken face to swell like something independent from the rest of one's body, to pulse symphonically with one's heartbeat, as if the pain was being directed by the world's most uncreative conductor: *POOM poom POOM poom POOM.* Pain for miles, hours. Time to sweat, to cramp, to keep a straight face through it all—he wasn't one of those dopeheads that needed three days and a mattress to kick; his *sitches* were light. He'd be damned if people on the fucking Greyhound would get to look down their noses at him.

But *time.* Time was a killer.

He envied those passengers with their Walkmans and Discmans, their horseshoe-shaped neck pillows, their books. He sat in the dark of the bus as it rolled stolidly through the night, this steel tube packed with the scent of body odor and unwashed feet and cigarettes and the hope of *going somewhere else.* The night peeled away to show darker night, then later to the constellations of far-flung towns glowing in the distance of the freeway, of old ruined agricultural buildings lurking in the blackness, buildings long shed of their usefulness. Gas stations and truck stops simmering under sodium-lights, billboards ticking past endlessly. There was nothing to do but think and quietly kick and try to leap from his skin and feel his dumb animal heartbeat pulse in his face.

Daylight arrived on the horizon like someone filling in a pencil sketch. Softly, everything in muted bands of gray. Only the highway's yellow lines and the other cars sang with any color, and even those seemed leached out. A dim, dark, morose morning, and yet if it wasn't explicitly hope that Sandoval was feeling, it was something similar. A lightening. They were in Idaho by now and he was feeling a little better. He'd made it out of the city.

Try cutting my head off when I'm staring at the Washington Monument, you assholes. Try teleporting. Come get me.

Come try it.

• • •

"Shit, man," Nathaniel said quietly, gazing out the window, "a guy wasn't depressed before, he's depressed now."

"I love it," Sandoval said, and it was true, he did. "We live here for a reason, right? Bring on the gloom, I say."

Nathaniel shrugged, tilted his bag of trail mix, chewed. "I guess, man. Shit bums me out." He'd surprised Sandoval by waking up at dawn and taking in his seatmate's wrecked face with little more than a comment hoping that Sandoval had gotten a few swings in.

They talked, tentatively at first, and then more animatedly as the folks around them awoke, as the morning brightened. Morning on the Dog: as close to a metamorphosis as it got. People yawned, stretched in the aisle. Began the slow ceremony of destroying the toilet in the back of the bus, the ministrations of too many doing too ungodly much in too small a space. Still, he felt better. He'd spent a decent amount of the previous night composing rich, detailed fantasies in which he'd walked out of his apartment, blood-swathed, with Dieter and Julian begging for their lives behind him, the two of them professing fealty and unending buckets of dope for their right to continue breathing. It'd helped pass the time.

The bus stopped in the early morning at a gas station called The Pump'n Pig. Atop the roadside sign sat a bubblegum-pink pig holding a giant gas pump. The pig was joyful, laughing, inexplicably wearing black dress shoes and a bow tie. A statue fifteen, twenty feet tall, weather-worn and spattered in years of calcified bird shit. It seemed a testament to Sandoval that anything was possible. It was a *sign*, this gas station pig, this Idahoan nudist, this grand, stupid gesture to gaudiness and excess. Sandoval walked past the gas pumps into the convenience store and shopped and waited his turn in line. He bought himself cigarettes, a bottle of juice, a box of crackers. He got a handful of quarters.

He and Nathaniel stood and smoked under the awning of the store, the pig before them a dazzling hot pink beneath that gray sky. Nathaniel rolled his cigarettes poorly, frequently spitting and pulling shreds of tobacco from his tongue. Sandoval offered him a Marlboro and he took it. The other riders mostly gave Sandoval the side-eye. He tapped some aspirin into his palm, swallowed them down with his orange juice.

"That's a platinum-level beating though," Nathaniel said when he saw Sandoval probe his swollen eye. "Dude know martial arts or some shit?"

"It was a couple guys."

"I hear you." Nathaniel nodded, spat again, examined one of his dreads and tossed it over his shoulder. "What I'm thinking, I'm thinking you put your wick somewhere it did not belong."

Sandoval laughed, which hurt.

"Am I right?"

"No," Sandoval said. "You're giving me way too much credit."

The bus driver walked out of the store and yelled, "Ten minutes." He lit a smoke himself, milling around and kicking at gravel in front of the bus. The sun came out through a dark bed of clouds.

"Catch you back on the bus," Sandoval said, and walked over to the payphone in front of the store. Dumped quarters into the slot. The thunk of the coins felt definitive; he just knew Dani would be home, and she was.

"Hey, it's me," he said.

"Shit," she said. He smiled into the receiver, felt his scabs tug. "You got *fired?* Jesus, Mark. I thought you were getting clean." They'd always been like this—eschewing formality, falling into a quick familiarity that not even Marnie could match. He and Dani had met when she moved to Seattle two years before. She stripped while working on her piercing and body mod apprenticeship at a shop in Belltown, and he'd met her after a random visit to her work; he could count on one hand the times he'd gone to a strip club. She'd talked to him, he'd bought a dance, it'd gone from there. It'd been a sustained, fevered affair, one that he'd done a piss-poor job of hiding. It had undoubtedly compounded the complications of his marriage, helped it toxify. Eventually it reached the point where Marnie would do dope with him as a way to keep him home. Their love gone that rancid, that terrible. Six months ago a friend of Dani's had offered her a slot in her shop in DC and Dani had taken it. So now he called, pined for her, left messages.

"I've got it nailed down," he said. "It's fine."

"Yeah, right."

He leaned his forehead against the steel case of the payphone. She was right: he was in deep. He'd played the *I'm getting clean, I promise* song so many times she could mouth the words along with him. Before she'd gone to DC she said, "It's getting away from you. I love you, Mark, but you're in it deep."

"That's not the half of it," he said to her now. "Things are crazy."

"Oh God. What happened?"

"You sure you want to hear it?"

"Oh, fuck off. Of course I do."

He let it all go in a rush. He was surprised not at his honesty with Dani, but at the fact that he was truth-telling to her in ways he hadn't even done with himself during all those previous hours on the bus. All through the dark night before, he'd been deflecting blame, ignoring it, and here he told Dani that it was his fault that Marnie left, of course it was, that he'd gotten her hooked—the thing latched on her back not as fierce and long-fingered as the one on his own, but surely nothing to sneeze at, either. His wife! He'd done that to her! How the world had slipped away from him, how everything had at first been soft-edged, how he could see why people liked the stuff when he started smoking it, and *definitely* when he got up the guts to shoot it, but she had been right, Dani had been right. There was no corralling it: it was a faucet that was either cinched tight or going full force. He was in trouble. He doubted that Julian would really kill him over a six-thousand-dollar debt, but who could say? He told her about Marnie leaving, about Don Whitmer, the beating, pulling money out of the ATM, buying a bus ticket. The operator came on and he fed more quarters into the payphone.

"Wait," she said, "*where* are you going?"

He paused, turned and scrutinized the horizon. God, that pig. That beautiful, hideous, ridiculous pig. He wanted it to wrap him up in its hot pink arms, he wanted to fight battles with it. The two ugliest things alive, he and that pig, strolling down the backbone of the world together. He didn't have to say where he was going. His silence was his answer.

"Wait, you're coming *here*? Mark."

"You don't want me to come?"

"Well, are you straight or not? Are you off dope?"

"I will be."

"*Mark*—"

"Seriously, Dani, I just got the *shit* beat out of me. That guy, Deiter? You met him once at the Comet. Dude with the ponytail, the baby hands? He said he'd cut my head off. Okay? Said he'd cut my head off and throw it in Puget Sound."

"Christ," she said. "You're not really selling me here."

"I'm saying I'm motivated. I'm scared shitless. I can kick. I feel good right now, actually."

"You can kick, huh? You can kick. Where have I heard this?"

Sandoval kept his mouth shut.

"What, you're gonna live with me? I live in a house with four other people, Mark. I work forty hours a week at the shop and pick up shifts at the club. I can't just be like, 'Hey, my dope sick sometimes-boyfriend's gonna stay with us, cool? Oh, and he's married and owes money to drug dealers.'"

"I'm not dope sick," he said, sounding like the churlish, dope sick infant that he was.

The driver climbed on board and tooted the horn.

"I need you," he said.

"Oh, Mark," Dani said. "I'm really mad at you right now."

"I love you," he said.

"What're you gonna do for money here? How're you gonna *live?*"

"It'll work out," he said quietly, knowing that she would let him stay. "I just need a little time to get things straight. I'll be clean by the time I get there—"

"In three days or whatever."

"—and I'll tackle the money thing as soon as I roll into town. Promise. I'll get us set up. I'm a wine man from here on out. Wine and espressos, swear to Christ."

Dani growled in frustration, and Sandoval leaned his forehead against the ridge of the phone box and smiled, felt the scabs pull again. "I gotta go, baby. I'll call you when I make it into town. Three days."

He felt something like a slow, unfolding explosion inside the bomb shelter of his ribcage: who else would do this for him? Who else would love him like this? Who else, really, had yet to be run through by the sword of his selfishness? She was all he had left. His last island.

"Three days," she said, and hung up. Sandoval ran for the bus, his feet clapping against the pavement.

• • •

He was studying English at UW Seattle, Nathaniel was. Heading home to DC for the holidays, and they rode through that deathly time of day on the Dog, that endless, loveless stretch between 3 and 6 p.m., where time stumbled and dragged and then stopped entirely. Sandoval was crestfallen to feel the *sitches* start to sink their fangs in him again after his earlier reprieve: the cramps, the feeling his joints were comprised of molten glass chunks. A film of sweat that felt oily and yellow on the skin. He felt like something plastic being melted under a magnifying glass. They were in Montana by then, and it should have been beautiful, but all Sandoval saw was sagging barns and barren fields, sun-bleached billboards, homes with leaning stands of trash piled against their side walls. Roadkill beyond count. The back-of-the-bussers had been loudly discussing breast sizes for some time—which sorts were ideal, the varying pros and cons of "little bitty ones" versus "tig ol' bitties"—to the point where Sandoval was gripping his knees with his hands and preparing mentally and spiritually to go back there and clock the first dipshit he laid eyes on.

Nathaniel took his headphones off and turned to him. He leaned over and said quietly, "Can I ask you something?"

"Sure," said Sandoval, grateful for the distraction. He palmed sweat from his face, felt the pastiche of Band-Aids under his palm as he did.

"Are you kicking right now?"

He looked at Nathaniel and saw the kid—and he was a kid, truly—was free of judgment. Sandoval opened his mouth to deny it and then blurted, "Christ, is it that obvious?"

"You're just looking a little peaked, man."

Sandoval looked at the seats around them and then nodded. "A little bit, yeah."

Nathaniel nodded. "Dope? Or booze? Probably dope, right?"

Sandoval's eyes cut across the aisle. "Shhh. Come on."

"Shit, nobody cares, man. On the *bus*? You just gotta relax."

"Relax? With the fucking idiot brigade back there? I wish."

Nathaniel smiled, adjusted his tam. "Get you some earplugs, Mark."

"Get a cattle prod. Stun gun."

Nathaniel cracked the lid on his half-empty Coke cup and poured in a generous dollop of vodka from a pint of Smirnoff that he'd tucked into his jacket. "Shit, I coulda given you this before, man. Sorry. Hold out your juice bottle there."

And so, yes, he was feeling much better when they wheeled into a rest stop outside Bozeman an hour or so later. Night had fallen, and it looked like every rest stop ever built on any stretch of sad and desolate and windblown highway—a pair of squat cement outbuildings flanking a small visitors center full of vending machines, a thin scrub of trees beyond.

It was bitterly cold out, the grass gritty with frost, a hard skin of old snow riming the pavement in thin gray washes. The few riders that got off the bus to smoke and hit the restrooms cinched their coats tight against their throats and hustled. "This one's a pee and flee," the bus driver barked before closing the bus door against the chill, earning him a few guffaws. "Five minutes." Overhead hung a gleaming scythe of a moon, the night flung with nickel stars.

They pissed with the other passengers and then hurried behind the back of the men's bathrooms to huff one more cigarette out of the knifing wind. Sandoval patted the pockets of Marnie's windbreaker and remembered the joint he'd found in the inside pocket. He pulled it out with the zeal of a magician pulling a rabbit from his hat. Nathaniel laughed silently, cigarette smoke curling from his mouth; they were drunk.

"You wanna?"

"Hell yeah, I wanna," Nathaniel said. "Make it quick though, driver's not waiting long, man."

"We're fine." Sandoval mouthed the words around the joint. His lighter kept sparking and dying. Nathaniel cupped his hands around the flame. Success! Sandoval took a few quick puffs, got the cherry going.

Both the taste and scent hit him immediately: chemical, acrid, manufactured. He licked his lips, frowning.

"Ah, goddamn," Nathaniel said, his nose curling in distaste. "It's wet."

"Wet?" Sandoval said. He held the joint between his fingers, stared down at it.

"Shit, yeah. Weed with PCP or some shit mixed in. Embalming fluid. You smell that?"

"Yeah," he said, and then, lamely: "This is my wife's."

"Your wife's?"

"My wife's coat. I found it in her coat." Marnie was, what—smoking PCP now? Was it just a thing she had been given and forgotten about? Had someone given it to both of them, at some party?

"You don't want that shit, Mark." Nathaniel said softly. He cupped his hands, blew into them. "For real."

Sandoval sagged against the wall, rolled the back of his skull against the brick. Thought of Marnie and the maelstrom of emotions that came with her, the bomb-blast realization of this new facet of her. His wife smoked PCP! He felt destructive, ruinous.

"I'm gonna smoke it," he said. "Why not?"

"That shit drives people crazy, dude. You'll be jumping off an overpass, thinking you can grow wings and buttfuck a car or something. My brother's friend tried to do that. Dude from Woodridge, he tried to fuck a car. Not even kidding."

"I'll just have a *bit*," said Sandoval, squinting and holding up the joint.

"Dumb," Nathaniel said. "Real fucking dumb, man." And then he pushed off from wall and said something about getting back on the bus. The wind was so strong Sandoval could hear the snapping fabric of Nathaniel's jacket as he rounded the corner. Then he was gone. God, it really was acrid. Like smoking the inside of a wall, or if you ground up a calculator and smoked that. Sandoval being Sandoval, he marveled for a moment, there against the cement wall of a men's bathroom in a rest stop somewhere in eastern Montana, at just how *bad* it really did taste, as he gazed down at it in his hand. And then came the thought of Marnie again and his self-pity flared and he huffed more, sparks from the cherry whipping through the dark.

He walked back into the cavernous echo chamber of the men's bathroom some indecipherable amount of time later. He may have heard the bus's horn toot once, though it could have been an air horn from a truck on the freeway. He ran the cherry against the wall, put the rest of the joint in his pocket.

Inside the bathroom: a dented mirror above a pair of sinks. Drawings of crude and woefully improbable biology. Two tissue-clotted urinals, a drain in the floor. A pair of empty stalls.

He shuffled into the stall of the less brutalized toilet and latched the door behind him. Perching on the back of the tank, his feet on the lid, he lit the joint again, and was soon ensconced in a bitter cloud of smoke that marijuana was only the faintest participant in. Sandoval sat folded on the toilet tank like a troll, occasionally coughing. He realized that somewhere in the past few minutes he'd resigned himself to not getting on the bus. That the bus was probably gone. Hadn't he heard it leave? The passage of time was taking on a malleable, taffy-like quality. His limbs felt as if they were belted to the floor with invisible anchors. His breathing had grown tinny in his ears, bright and crackling like a blown speaker. He gazed at the hand cupping the tiny remnant of the joint as it hung over the toilet bowl, and he felt his entire body being pulled toward the floor.

Overhead, the lights flickered with a sizzle and snap, then suddenly glowed brighter. *Hospital lighting,* he thought, spit gone electric in his mouth. *Kill-floor lighting.*

He rose, the rasp of his boots on the cement nearly infinite in their sonic variants. Dropping the joint in the bowl, his hand seemed miles away, an appendage spied through a tunnel, a convex distortion, and when he laughed, it sounded distant, mud-clotted, horrible. "I haven't smoked pot in a long time," he said through the invisible netting wrapped around his head. The words reverberated, like physical things that roved and bounced within the stall.

He leaned over with his hands on his knees and retched. Two, three gut-heaving yowls. A bowling ball full of warmed blood, that was what his skull had become. He spat and missed the toilet. The saliva fell to the cement with a sound like someone clapping their hands in an empty gymnasium. *Maybe the bus is still waiting for me,* he thought. *Maybe I didn't miss it. Maybe I should go out there.*

Fear's dirty fingernails wormed their way inside him, lifting and testing. *I just want to sit on the bus now,* he thought, leaning his head against the filthy stall wall.

I shouldn't have done this, he thought. *I should have listened.*

It was the last thought of any real cohesion for some time.

• • •

And what happened next?

What happened next really was the ten-million-dollar question, wasn't it? And ten million was being conservative, when you considered the advance he'd gotten for *The Long Way Home*, the years of significant royalties, the translations, the options and profit points on the movie, the advances for the other books he would later write, the generous fees for speaking engagements, the write-offs, even the emasculating acts of his later years in which he'd slump hungover in his little booth, signing books and promo glossies at sci-fi and comic conventions, diminished as his star would later become. But yeah, ten million was on the slim side, and all of it—the whole thing, his whole blessed, magical, fucked up life after that point—hinged on what had really happened in that dark cement box of a bathroom in Bumfuck Nowhere, Montana, after he smoked that joint. What had happened there, and what happened in the scraggly snow-dusted copses of scrub pines and blackberry bramble out behind the rest stop, and in the mostly empty parking lot, and later in the deep, dark woods.

He remembered staggering around the bathroom for a while, just feeling the kettle drum of his nerves jangling, alternating between outright panic and a feverish euphoria that quickly sputtered out and was very different from a heroin high. He walked to the sinks and gazed slack-jawed at his face in the dented mirror covered in half-peeled stickers and marker scrawls. He spent some time examining the whitened vistas of his eyeballs, trying to discern patterns in the red silken threads of veins buried there.

His heartbeat sang in his sour mouth. He gripped the counter and sneered.

Marnie, he decided, was *wrong* for leaving him. Don Whitmer had lost a valuable employee. He would eat stew from the bowls of Dieter and Julian's skulls. He tapped a fingernail against his canine and marveled at the sound of it. He spent a lifetime spitting in the sink, trying to get rid of the chemicals abrading his gums, his tongue.

And honestly, maybe he was the one that broke the light above the mirror. Maybe he did. But at some point—days, minutes later—he noticed that the only light in the room was the single bulb on the ceiling, flickering in its steel cage. His limbs continued to weigh him down and he slowly began to sink toward the floor, an ice sculpture melting. He grinned and watched himself in the mirror.

And then something skittered behind him and he stood up, his hands slapping at the wet countertop.

But there was nothing there.

Just the entrance door, the dented garbage can with its a grim tide of paper towels ringing its base. His breath was ragged, his blood so loud he thought he might be able to hear it moving inside him; he gazed down at his hands again and became lost within the parchment-fine skin, the blued veins.

When he looked back up, he saw a little man standing behind him in the mirror.

Sandoval screamed, childlike and breathy. The man—for lack of another word—was maybe four feet tall, as khaki-colored as a pair of pants, mouthless and nude. As smooth as a thing culled from wax. Thin-limbed and bald, it tilted its head almost inquisitively. While the eyes themselves were as black and lightless as any sea-bottom, the flesh ringing the eyes writhed with movement. These circles of roiling, putty-colored flesh. Sandoval breathlessly screamed and hoisted himself up on the counter, his ass soaked in sink water, and the little man ran away on hind legs suddenly grown multi-jointed, its legs hooking backward like an insect. Fast, so fast, but somewhat hobbling, too. Watching the thing move made his eyes itch. He screamed again.

The little man ran into the far stall, the one Sandoval had just smoked in. The door clapped shut and slowly drifted halfway open.

Sandoval crouched on top of the counter, piss now warming his thighs.

A hand with too many knuckles reached out over the top of the stall door and slammed it closed. *Bang.* Then opened it and slammed it closed again. *Bang.* The bright sound of metal against metal. *Bang.*

Oh, long, knuckled fingers.

Too many knuckles.

Bang. Bang. Bang.

Then the hand pushed the door open and the little man's waxen head peered at him around the edge of the doorway.

The flesh where a mouth would be began to grow thin. Translucent, the skin of bubblegum. The coils of flesh around its eyes squirmed. The skin of its mouth finally tore open to expose the black cave of its mouth and the light bulb on the ceiling exploded with a febrile *pop!* The room was flung into darkness.

Sandoval screamed and hopped to the floor. He slammed against the door, found the door handle and flung it open and staggered outside.

The world was frozen and blue.

The parking lot was scoured in a watery cobalt illumination, as if God had put a scrim over the moon. A pair of big rigs sat hulking in the gloom at the far end of the lot. He heard a bang inside the bathroom, something metallic buckling and scraping across the cement floor, and hot piss again sluiced its way through his jeans and then turned icy. He stumbled toward the parking lot because his lizard brain told him that beyond the parking lot was the inevitable human river of the highway. Cars and their headlights and their drivers. *People.* He stumbled toward the ineffable tide of life out there beyond the parking lot, there on the highway, he could hear it, hear it like his own blood in his head, like his own heart, the highway, of course, that's what he wanted, he wanted to be among them, people, he didn't understand how he could've ever *not* wanted to be among them—

His foot hooked over his other ankle and he fell.

He shredded his palms, the back of his hands a cold blue, and when he looked up at the sky, it was not pinpricked with stars or scudded with a veil of clouds but was instead lit now with a disc of light. That disc of dark blue light. A light so large that it seemed to block all else out, to span from treetop to treetop on each side of the lot, and where had it been only seconds ago? And then the blue became white, white as chalk, as fresh paper, a light so bright that as he put his hand up to cover his eyes—and he was truly screaming now, yes, definitely, something integral cracking inside his throat—he could see the delicate framework of his bones beneath the skin, the black latticework of his own bones laddered below the pale flesh.

• • •

In the blackness, something feathered his cheeks. He scrabbled up, hands slapping at his face, but with the terror came familiar scents—pine, dead leaves, earth—and a bitter, numbing, ferocious cold.

He'd been covered, or covered himself, in a mounded layer of pine branches, the needles brushing his face. Dawn was the thinnest wash of color among the trees. His hands and feet were frozen, disconnected things. Sandoval's eyes were mostly gummed shut, and he wiped at them and saw that he lay among a thick stand of scrub pine and was flanked all around by a dark wall of brambles. He curled over into himself again, seized up with cold, shoved his hands between his thighs. Wind sloughed through the treetops and he pulled more branches over his body like some kind of burial mound, his teeth chattering.

Eventually, a cold morning light purled through the filigree of trees, and he rose and started walking. With little thought as to direction or solution, he put one foot in front of the other, a kind of chemical sludge coating the back of his throat. His bones ached with exhaustion. He staggered through the underbrush, hands jammed in his armpits, careening off trees and hardly flinching when branches scraped across his face, jabbed him in the ribs. He barely put his hands out in time to break his fall when he hooked a shoe over a dead tree limb. He stared at his scraped palms—they were bleeding freely—and stood up with a grunt and half-furious sob and continued on. Woods and woods and woods.

Once he walked into the remains of a rotted fence still hung with sagging barbwire and simply pushed the fencepost over. Some of the trees were dusted with old snow that tumbled like sugar when he caromed into them. It was hard to separate what sound was the wind and what was the highway; he considered the possibility he was walking in a large circle. Or perhaps he'd simply gone mad. Maybe he was still in the bathroom, the little waxen man terrifying enough that Sandoval's mind had simply gone somewhere else. Perhaps the withdrawal and booze and PCP had driven him over some irrevocable edge. It seemed impossible that a day and a half had passed since Seattle and Julian and Dieter.

Some time later he saw a building. A long sort of warehouse, pale green with a corrugated white roof. He walked to the tree line and came to another fence, and he cupped his hands with the sleeves of his jacket and stepped under the wire. The ground went from soft pine needles to dead, almost white grass gone hoary with frost. Leaning against the building were nail-shot pieces of lumber, a stack of bald tires, a blue metal door riddled with bullet holes. He walked around the side of the building and there was a small white truck with a canopy, the gray sky reflecting off the windshield. He saw a small cross hanging from the rearview mirror, beaded seat covers and an empty gun rack. Beyond the truck lay a two-lane road.

The wind had quieted. The day was still; his footfalls on the gravel seemed shockingly loud. When he came to the rear of the truck something lunged at him from the open canopy and Sandoval lashed out. He let out a clotted, guttural scream and his hand connected with something hard. A dog. He'd struck it in the head. A spotted, sallow mutt with yellow teeth, it yelped and retreated further into the canopy near the cab of the truck. Sandoval stood there and started crying. The dog's tail began to wag and it approached him again with its head tucked down and for a while Sandoval petted it. Then he started walking the shoulder of the road where the asphalt met the gravel and the dead weeds. No one ever came out of the warehouse.

For a long time the road was empty. He stopped crying. His nose began to run and he wiped it with the sleeve of Marnie's jacket. When a few cars began to appear, he stepped further into the weeds to let them pass. Farmland and forest, and he saw on the horizon a blue hazy mountain whose top was obscured by distance and weather. Closer were fields gone pale with cold and sometimes the skeletal remains of old buildings fallen to misuse.

Walking warmed him. The chemical taste in his mouth was terrible and he continually spat in the grass. Then he remembered the gum in his pocket. Chewing it, the taste flooded his mouth.

Eventually a black truck, a big one, passed him and then slowed and pulled onto the shoulder ahead. He paused, his heart pinballing in his chest with a sudden terror—the image of the waxen man's mouth opening through its sheen of flesh—and then he walked up to the passenger side. The man had rolled the window down. He was Latino, young, with a little black goatee over a double chin, his hair close-cropped. "Need a ride?"

"You bet," Sandoval said. His voice was glottal, rusted.

"I'm just going to town," the man said.

"Okay," Sandoval said, and hoisted himself in.

He had never felt a warmth in his life like the heater that blew on his legs, his hands. The man lifted a plastic bottle from between his thighs and spat tobacco juice into it. It didn't take long for Sandoval's scent to fill the cab, and the man rolled down his window halfway but didn't say anything about it. "You work over at Western there?" he asked.

"What's that?"

The man lifted his chin toward the rearview mirror. "You work over at Western Meats? The plant? My friend, he works the stunner there."

"No," Sandoval said.

"Bettencourt Ranch?"

"Not me." He looked down at his palms, the filth caked in his pants. "I'm just passing through."

"That sounds about right, I guess," the man said, and then spit more tobacco juice into his bottle.

They came to a small town and the man surprised him by not dropping him off immediately at the nearest curb but instead took him to a small grocery store and pulled into the parking lot. Sandoval's smell was significantly pronounced by then and he felt bad for the man. With a grimace the driver rose up and dug into his back pocket and took out his wallet. He held out some folded bills between two fingers. Sandoval was about to reject it but then realized his own wallet was gone. Abandoned somewhere, lost. He took the money and said, "I lost my wallet."

"Okay."

"I mean, I really did," Sandoval said.

"I believe you. Straight up, man."

Sandoval looked down at the money. Two twenties and a ten. He felt himself threatening to come undone again. "How am I going to pay you back?"

When he smiled, the man's teeth were small and white inside his little goatee. "You just get yourself fixed up, man. They got groceries in there, some shirts and sweatpants and stuff. It's all cheap crap, but it's clean."

"Thank you," Sandoval said. He'd run out of room inside himself to say or do anything more. He stepped out to a sunny, heatless day and shut the passenger door.

• • •

He bought a turkey sandwich and an oily basket of French fries from the small deli. Sneering through the panic that seized him in the tiny cement bathroom, he threw his soiled pants and boxers in the garbage can, put on both pairs of sweatpants that he'd bought. He drank cold water from the bathroom faucet, hunched over and gasping until his stomach ached, and then willed himself to look in the mirror. Of course nothing resided there, no small figure against the doorway. Just his own face peering back, haunted and worn and still a little crazed. He washed his hands carefully. Back in the store he bought a bag of chocolate chip cookies and got ten dollars in quarters. The cold knifed through the sweatpants as he found a pair of payphones outside. Dani was home.

"Hey," he said. The question was, what was real and what wasn't? What was true and what wasn't? "I need you to come get me. Okay? Something happened."

"Oh, Jesus," she said, irritation and worry in equal measure.

"Something bad, Dani. Please."

"Where are you?"

Sandoval asked her to hold on. He put the receiver on top of the phone and ran quickly into the store.

He had to ask the clerk what town he was in.

• • •

The clerk called the deacon at the Presbyterian church down the street, who gave Sandoval a bed in the church's basement for the two nights it took for Dani to drive to Saber Valley, Montana to pick him up, seething and furious, in her roommate's VW Vanagon. In that time, doing odd jobs for the deacon and sleeping on a cot in the pitch-black supply closet, a great and ceaseless slideshow of memories had begun—and not stopped—playing in his mind. It was an endless procession, but with it came a willingness, an ability to see that something truly amazing had happened to him. This, if nothing else, was the root of what made him *him*: this unflinching resilience. To view hardship—and grave errors—as opportunities. The darkness helped, laying there in the basement closet, daring something to happen. Daring the darkness to form some mouthless golem.

Dani pulled into the church parking lot in the brittle light of afternoon and was greeted by a skinny, bruised, strung-out-looking Sandoval, a Sandoval who wore a pair of hand-me-down denim cords and held a sagging plastic bag full of canned soup and folded sweatpants. He gave the deacon and the deacon's wife a hug. During his two nights in the dark, he had concocted a plan.

"What in the fuck," Dani hissed when they got into the van.

"Baby, please," Sandoval said. He set the bag down on the floorboards and hoisted a shoe onto the dashboard of the Vanagon, which was littered with bundles of the roommate's sage. "I have this figured out. I'll tell you everything, let's just get going back on the road, okay?"

"I'm fucking exhausted, Mark. I've driven for two days to get here—"

"Dani," he said, scrubbing his face, feeling the answers leap inside him like some young colt testing the give of a fence. The solution was right there. The solution quelled all, quashed the cavalcade of regret about Marnie, about school, about Julian and his threat of beheading. "I'll drive if you want. I'll drive the whole way to DC. But let's just get started, okay?"

Dani sighed. "Jesus. You are such an asshole." She looked amazing. "I thought you were going to get clean."

"I am clean."

She laughed.

"I am. And listen, I have a plan."

"Oh, perfect." She held out a hand game-show style, showcasing Sandoval where he sat in the passenger seat. He saw that she'd pierced both of her wrists. "Your plans," she said, "got you wearing someone else's pants outside of a church in Dog Dick, Montana, holding a sack of Campbell's Chicken Noodle soup. You can't even ride the Greyhound without fucking up. Don't tell me your *plans*, Mark."

And Sandoval *laughed*. He was that free. He was that sure.

"This one's different," he said, and set the sack of soup cans behind his seat so he could stretch his legs. "Seriously. You know why?"

"No, you ass. Why?"

"Because this one's going to make us rich."

4

ghosts of the álagablettur

"I asked Alfredo, who had spent a significant amount of time in the house on Montavilla Street as a young boy, who had long been witness to its ever-changing list of horrors, if he'd ever been afraid while inside the rooms, inside the mansion with the red door. 'Oh no, *senor*,' said Alfredo, 'they meant me no harm in there.' He touched the crucifix that lay at his throat and drew hard on his cigarette, gazing out at the dusky streets of Mexico City below us. 'Sad and lonely is different than evil and bad, *si*?'"
—**Mark Sandoval, *The House With the Red Door***

1

Sandoval wore long sleeves to hide his scars. He drank a Coke, hunched low to the table. This was his attempt at being clandestine, though it still felt to me like everyone knew who we were. How could they not? Our singularity—or at least our *Americanness*—probably flared like neon whenever we went into town. The stupid bikes didn't help.

I ordered some dark stout called *Svartur Hundur.* Black Dog. My Icelandic was improving, if nothing else. I figured if I was going to be riddled with headaches anyway, and since I'd sent myself to another country in a potentially lethal case of problem avoidance, then screw it. I'd already run away from home like some petulant kid; I might as well get a little buzzed. Sandoval had been reluctant to come out, immersed as he was in his apparent goal of losing his mind, but he'd finally capitulated.

It was our first night away from the farm since the "magical" shit had been discovered ten days before. Usually by now I'd be asleep in my tent and Sandoval would be skulking the fields with his night vision goggles, petitioning unseen things to speak to him. It felt weird, being nighttime like it was, sitting in a place with people in it that weren't the Hauksdóttirs.

The place was a coffee shop that doubled as a bar at night. I hadn't even caught the name of the place, but there was a coffee cup painted on the window outside, and a neon sign for an Icelandic beer hummed in the steamy window. The front of the place was a weathered, splintered pastiche of shingles painted an ebullient orange. Strings of hanging Christmas lights hung from the ceiling, candles wavered on tabletops. Handsome, fair-haired clusters of people leaned toward each other, yelling over their own din. Bicycles leaned in a row out front. Karla had told us it was her favorite place to drink (her face had taken on the wistful look of a mother remembering the heady days when she could go out drinking with impunity) and had drawn us a map, signaling our destination with an ink drawing of a foamy mug of beer.

Two weeks since we'd arrived and this was all I knew for sure:

One, Sandoval had charmingly but resolutely lost his mind.

And two, the tumor seemed static. Not better, but not worse. (I knew this wasn't true, but it was what I'd decided.) I'd had no bouts of inertia since leaving Camp Carroll. The headaches were sometimes bad, sometimes more manageable. Every morning I lay in my tent and tried to feel it inside me, tried to feel the cells multiplying, and I kept thinking: *If I hadn't been told, I'd have never known. Nothing would've been different at all.*

I'd avoided doing a web search on any of the terms.

Fear stilled my hands from doing that, every day.

"It'd be just the way of the world," Sandoval said now, spinning his Coke can, "that something happens while we're gone. That'd be just perfect."

"Dude, a couple drinks," I said. "Then we'll head back. You have to slough stuff off a bit, man. Chill."

"This is work," Sandoval said, eyeing me. "We have a job. There's an active search going on."

Except we didn't have an active search. We had Karla's blurred footage and a pile of bedazzled horse turds that Sandoval had spent a small fortune on sending to a lab in Atlanta, Georgia, to get tested. We had his slow-burn tumble into the land of mania.

His sobriety seemed to have sharpened the whole thing into an obsession for him. Gone was the drunk, leering guy I remembered from the airport, the hotel. A pile of scat had undone him. He'd tipped over the edge. He managed maybe three hours of sleep a night, as far as I could tell, and spent the rest of the time walking through the woods in the dark with his goggles on, one hand holding an EVP recorder, the other pushing branches away. I could sometimes hear him talking out there when the wind blew in the right direction. *I'm not here to hurt you.* Even then his voice was thin and ghostly; he'd gone deeper and deeper into the woods around the Hauksdóttir house as time progressed.

Sometimes I'd just find him standing there in a copse of trees, his face still and almost rapturous.

I'd asked Karla a few days before: "Are the woods around here the álagablettur?"

She'd been shrewd with her answer. "I don't know what you mean."

"I mean, when Sandoval goes out there at night," and I'd motioned out the windows of the kitchen, "is he in danger?"

"No more than anyone else."

She'd seen the look on my face and softened. "There might be things out there that he would see. But they can't hurt him. The real danger is north. The woods up north near the base."

Part of me wanted to fall into this rapture, too, just so we were all on the same page.

I resisted the urge to email Ellis and say, *My boss has been sent adrift by a pile of horseshit with junk jewelry packed inside it. You believe that? He's not a pop culturist or an anthropologist.*

He's just unhinged.

But I had yet to email Ellis, of course. Or Don Whitmer. Or my sister, or my mother. I hadn't checked my emails in days.

What could I have said? If I told them a little, I'd have to tell them everything.

Now I leaned back in my chair and said, "Look, Mark. We're here. Let's just enjoy it."

Sandoval shrugged, sipped his Coke. Still hunched over like what I imagined a new convict would look like at his first trip to the prison cafeteria. Guarded, suspicious. He'd lost a significant amount of weight and his beard was coming in. Half the time I'd have dinner with Karla and the kids and Sandoval would beg off, deciding to walk the perimeter instead. It really was a beautiful, rich landscape, that farm and forest, and it was filled with absolutely nothing that Sandoval needed. Yet still he walked along it every night.

"Remind me to check the eastern cameras before we crash, I think I need to nudge one of them a bit."

"Try to enjoy yourself."

"I am, Brian. This is me enjoying myself."

I drained my glass. I was still unused to the empty slot in my mouth where that tooth had been.

"I'm gonna grab another. You want one?"

"Seriously, Brian. One more and we're out of here, okay? We need to move those cameras."

It wasn't the first time that I'd mused on the fact that he really had become a ghost hunter. Someone so adamant at chasing shadows. I'd told him about the soldiers who'd died on the property, and that too had emboldened him. I'd listen to him play back his EVP recordings in his tent, his own voice forlorn as it asked if anyone was there, if they had anything to say, if they wanted to let him know anything.

And those long swaths of utter silence between his questions.

Some mornings I woke up embarrassed to be where I was. Hunting a unicorn? Paid off by some deluded rich guy to be his yes man? Those mornings I woke to a fine crust of new snow on the ground outside my tent, convinced entirely that Sandoval had grown damaged in some intrinsic way.

He'd insisted that we weren't leaving any time soon. We'd run our full tenure in Hvíldarland.

I'd made a mistake.

I walked to the bar and leaned over the empty seat between two men. I set my glass down on the bar top, tried to catch the bartender's eye. One of the men half-turned to me, lifted his lip in a sneer. The type of guy that was pretty common in Kjálkabein: stocky and red-faced, with big, work-roughened hands and a heavy, formless jacket. Nose squashed as a root vegetable. Worked the docks in Kjálkabein, maybe, or busted ass at one of the automotive shops scattered along Road Seven. Catch a guy like this in the right mood and he could be friendly and generous with his time. This wasn't the right mood.

"Vandamál?" Problem?

"No, sorry," I answered in English. "I just wanted to order a beer."

He said something over me to the man next to him—Icelandic and clipped, something lost in the din—and his friend muttered something back without looking at us. The first guy turned back to me and said in English, "Why don't you back up, okay? Before you piss me off."

I stepped back. "Like I said, sorry."

"You fucking Americans. You come in here." He gestured at my glass with a reddened hand. "Do this shit, when my friend and I were having a conversation."

I held up my hands. "Hey, sorry to bother you."

I started to turn, head back to our table to gather my coat, when a hand fell on my arm. My heart leapt—the grip was strong—and then a voice rattled behind me: "What's up, my man?"

Vaughn Keller stood there, a knit cap jammed on his head, snow turning to droplets on the purple scarf wrapped around his throat. He looked at me and the two men and took his hand from my shoulder.

He threw a sheaf of króna on the bar between them. A big enough amount to widen their eyes. "My friends, get yourselves a few rounds."

Keller herded me back to our table with a hand on my elbow. He leaned in close; his breath stank of cigar smoke and booze. "What was that about? What're you pissing off the locals for?"

"I didn't do anything."

Keller laughed. "Oh yeah?"

"Seriously. I was just trying to order a drink."

"You just got one of those faces, huh?"

"I guess so."

Sandoval frowned when the two of us came up to the table. "Vaughn, right? What brings you here tonight?"

"Honestly, I was running some errands in town and saw a certain pair of children's bikes outside. I just had to come in and say hi."

Sandoval shook his Coke can, set it down. "I thought you were getting another drink, Brian."

"We should probably go, actually," I said. "It's getting kinda late."

Keller grinned and clapped me on the shoulder. "I would be honored," he said, "to give you two gentlemen a ride."

• • •

The evening snow scoured our jackets like sand. Fine granules of it glossed the streetlights, softened their coronas of light into something angelic. Keller led us to his BMW.

We put the bikes in the trunk. I sat in the backseat. Keller turned the heater on, unpeeling his scarf from his neck like someone doing a magic trick. Something from my parents' era—Bob Seger?—drifted low from the speakers. Cologne and cigar did battle with that indefinable new car smell.

We took off. The car was practically silent. "Almost didn't recognize you, Brian," Keller said over his shoulder. "You're all healed up."

"Yeah, I'll be entering the Prince Kjálkabein pageant any day now."

"Decided not to fix the tooth?"

"Dentist didn't really want to do it," I said. "We're sleeping outside. It's cold, dirty. She was willing, kind of, but I just figured it was easier to wait 'til I made it home."

Driving those dark roads, Sandoval and Keller's silhouettes limned in the dark, I couldn't help but think of all the car rides I'd taken with my family as a kid. My father silent behind the wheel, fiddling with the radio stations as he drove. Brooke and I constantly getting into fights, until my mother—who had never been remotely religious—would finally bark, "God give me *strength!* Not one more word or else! This is my last nerve!" And then, unified by our mom's outburst, Brooke and I would sit companionable and quiet the rest of the way home. It brought to mind that way I'd felt enveloped by the darkness, the quiet. Ensconced in it, safe.

The three of us stayed steeped in our own silence until Sandoval, being who he was, couldn't help but throw a feeler out there. "How long you been at the base, Vaughn?"

"Oh, hell. Years now. I'm a terminal fobbit."

"A what?" I asked.

"Fobbit. Someone who stays at a base, doesn't go to the front lines. No risk, no danger."

"Ah."

"I stay in the back and tap keys on a computer."

Sandoval said, "Never seen combat?"

"God, no. I'm not military. I have a Masters in Statistics. I'm part of a civilian crew that does data analytics, weather stuff."

"You live on the base?"

Keller shrugged. "I mean, I've got a *room* at the base, but it's not much to look at. I keep an apartment in town."

"They let you do that?"

"Sure. Like I said, civilian."

Sandoval said, "Listen, you sure you won't help us check the place out?"

Keller's wet death-rattle of a laugh that turned into a coughing fit. "I got no pull there, guys. Sorry."

"Well, I had to ask."

"Sure. But listen, Mark. Brian. Can I be square with you?"

Sandoval looked at him. "Yeah."

"Here's the thing," Keller said as he pulled off onto the shoulder of Road Seven. unfettered darkness all around us. "I like Shane. And I care about Karla Hauksdóttir and those kids. I've known this family for years, and I want to be kind when speaking about Karla. But the whole thing with the horseshit, guys? The jewels? It's all over the island. You guys are . . . Well, whatever credibility you might have had when you got here, that's been expended. People are laughing at you."

"Well, Jesus, Vaughn. There's no shortage of people who've laughed at me," Sandoval said. This was said matter-of-factly, kindly.

"Someone's playing you. You know that, right?"

"Could be," Sandoval said. It was impossible to miss that smugness, that surety. The righteousness of a religious convert.

Keller glanced at me over the seat. "I implore you to reason with this guy," he said drily.

"If I could have," I said, "I'd have done it already." Sandoval laughed.

Keller sighed and started the car. After a few minutes, we passed the white rocks and started our way up the driveway. The house loomed large, windows frosted with incandescence. He held out a hand at the scene before us. "Look at this. You guys are out here sleeping in tents. Walking around in the woods, freezing your dicks off. For what?"

We pulled to a stop next to Karla's truck. I could see into the dining room, all those long-dead Hauksdóttirs in their tin frames on the walls.

Sandoval cracked the door open. *"God himself must needs be traduced, if there is no unicorn in the world,"* he intoned in a pretty terrible British accent, one foot on the ground.

"Shakespeare never slept on the ground in Hvíldarland. You're letting all the cold air in."

"It's not Shakespeare," Sandoval said. "It's from a guy named Edward

Topsell. Religious guy. Compiled a bestiary in the early 1600s, and that's what he said about unicorns. Essentially, God himself must be blamed if there are no unicorns."

"Bold shit."

"Indeed." Sandoval and I stepped out.

Keller leaned over the passenger seat to stare up at us. "Listen, you know what's happened since the 1600s, right?"

Sandoval grinned, pulled his collar up. "What's that?"

"About four hundred years of us collectively pulling our heads out of our asses. Science is your friend, bud."

"Thanks for the ride, Vaughn."

• • •

Later that night, the four of us ate dinner while Sandoval strode the black fields. Looking for his unicorn. Listening for a whisper of those dead British soldiers. A telltale hot spot among the trees, a gravelly, mournful response to the questions *Are you there? Can you hear me?* on his EVP recorder. Looking and listening. For anything. Something to anchor him here. A ghost. A unicorn. Anything. He had a book to write, after all. It was the only reason I could figure why he was so reluctant to leave the island, why he kept trying: it was hard to make something, and even harder to make something from nothing.

• • •

That night, I decided to scout along the tree line myself. Some way of trying to align myself with Sandoval. Some last vestige of hope that my allegiance would make it easier for him to listen to me. I put on the second pair of NVGs, spent a few minutes adjusting them, and when I was done, the field was awash in a cold blue light. It was slightly grainy, nothing like the hot, bright-green images I'd seen in films. The sky suddenly hung incandescent with stars and I was momentarily chilled; it reminded me of the sky I'd seen as I pedaled back from the base, before I'd had my run-in with the tree.

I walked easily through the woods now, snarled as they were. I turned back and the house shone bright, each window a rectangle of white light. I listened for Sandoval, expecting to come across his lighted form. But there was nothing. Nothing alive, anyway. Nothing with four legs, or two. Just the cutting wind, the trees, the ceaseless call of the sea over the mountains.

I walked deeper into the woods. It was nothing like how I remembered the álagablettur, that crushing sense of closeness.

I turned, walked further away from the house. I heard the soft crackle of twigs underfoot and made my way around a large tree trunk. In the goggles, it was the bleached blue of Karla Hauksdóttir's eyes.

And something stood in front of me. Its eyes gleamed.

I made a strangled chuffing sound and stepped back; I had the briefest moment to think, *It's real the woods are real,* as panic and jubilation both rocketed through me, and the thing turned and trotted away, its mane feathered in the wind.

Fucking miniature horse trotting through the trees in the middle of the night.

I stalked out of the woods and peeled off the NVGs, tossed them in my tent. Heartbeat knocking in my throat. Sandoval was sitting in a chair on the porch, writing in his journal. His breath plumed from his mouth. "Hey," he called out, "you tried the goggles! See anything?"

"Nope," I said, crawling into my tent and zipping it closed. Fury and terror warbled my words. "Not a thing."

2

Our routine—post-Bejewelled Turd Discovery—deepened. It had shaped up like this:

After waking, I'd spend those first few minutes trying to gauge the depth and severity of the tumor, then wander bleary-eyed and cold into the house to wash up. Some mornings the headache wouldn't even be there, which was almost more worrisome. Like an intruder somewhere inside your darkened house. Karla had insisted that we make ourselves at home, but Sandoval and I both had a sense of propriety that bordered on aloof. We stuck to quietly recharging our gear and making coffee in the morning, using the bathroom, taking dinner with the family. That was about it. Otherwise we were outside.

Occasionally we'd get hit with a dusting of snow and Sandoval would take his laptop or his notebook into the dining room and write at the Hauksdóttirs' big glass-topped table, but usually he worked on the porch or in his tent. I made coffee, did some dishes or took a shower while the house came alive around me. If the kids weren't staying at Shane's, I helped a bit there. They were hilarious in the morning, struck monosyllabic with sleep, flattened hair and pillow lines in their faces. Staring off into some middle distance as they ate the cereal and toast I put in front of them. Karla seemed grateful for the help. It was a weird rhythm to fall into, curiously domestic, but I liked it. I liked these people, like Karla's willingness to embrace the odd, kooky angles of herself, and it all helped me ignore how I'd pretty much cut off contact with my own family. I knew it was temporary, I knew it was a mirage, but it felt like this brief hiccup of normalcy. I savored it.

I'd go outside after the kids had gone to school and Karla's work crew had arrived. They'd all head out to the greenhouses, and there would be Sandoval on the porch, scribbling in his notebook in his fingerless gloves and North Face jacket, hood cinched tight.

Trying to get Sandoval to eat something would produce middling results, and in late morning he'd either keep writing or head into the woods or to one of the hamlets radiating off of Road Seven. We steered clear of Camp

Carroll and the álagablettur, everything north of the house, and I liked that just fine. He kept insisting that would be the endgame—the base or the álagablettur, but he also insisted we had to "exhaust all the other possibilities first."

Part of Sandoval's blooming paranoia had to do with the internet, with communication. He'd sent the unicorn shit off to a lab in Atlanta and worried that his email could get hacked. That if the results came back positive—"And they will," he assured me daily—and someone found out about it, we'd be screwed out of one of the greatest discoveries in history. So he wanted the results to be sent to me.

"Why wouldn't *my* email get hacked?" I asked.

He shrugged. "No one knows who you are. No one cares about you."

Mark Sandoval, that envoy of delicacy. But he had a point.

So the best part of my day, hands down, was pedaling into Kjálkabein on my little bicycle to check the email address I'd set up to receive the news. I'd ride to a coffee shop not far from the Hotel Magnificence, take refuge in the comfort of brewed coffee, of people talking quietly, of rain beading the windows. Reveling a little in the normalcy of it, the routine. There were a great number of things I was afraid to do while I was there, of course: check my personal email, reach out to my friends and loved ones, enter the term *Stage III astrocytoma* into even the lamest of search engines. I would hold tight to that sense of normalcy until it killed me.

I was heading back out of town after another fruitless visit and was pedaling along that stretch of Road Seven where everything went sagging and industrial when someone honked behind me. A blat like a clown car.

I veered onto the shoulder and waved them on, still pedaling. The horn sounded again—*bluuunk!*—and I turned and saw a little blue Peugeot puttering along behind me, swaths of paint in different hues like someone had taken spray cans to it. The driver honked again, and an arm came out of the driver's window, motioning me over. The size of that arm did not dispel in me the notion of a clown car—it was a massive appendage, poking out of the little blue vehicle like that.

Both of the men in the car wore black balaclavas tucked into their collars.

I thought about pedaling as fast as I could down that straight stretch of road, but the ridiculousness of it stopped me. It was broad daylight! We were on a highway! The main road! I halted, my scalp tightening, my body flooded with that loose, watery feeling that was becoming so familiar, that feeling that screamed *run*. I felt the space where my tooth had been, the little knot of scar tissue on my lip.

The car rose on its shocks when the two men stepped out. The passenger was tall, thin, the driver short and muscled. Warped, funhouse versions of each other. Both wore gloves, cargo pants tucked into combat boots. Those masks. Only the pale skin around their eyes showed, their lips.

The skinny one held a wooden fish bat in one fist.

I rode the bike into the field, had some vision born of decades of bad cinema—as if my feet would be a blur on the pedals, as if the men would grow to distant, frustrated specks behind me as I rocketed toward the tree line.

I made it ten, fifteen feet, until my front wheel hit a lava rock embedded in the earth. I toppled over the handlebars, rolled, got a face full of gritty loam between my molars. Someone grabbed a fistful of hair and yanked me up to my knees.

My arm was hoisted behind my back and I was frog-marched back to the car. "Help," I yelled, and across the road, a sheep bleated as if in response. The men laughed. The one holding my arm smacked my forehead against the lip of the roof when he pushed me in the backseat.

Not another car anywhere.

They sat in the front—the shocks sank again—and turned to me, each putting an arm over their seat.

"Let me start off by saying kiss my ass," I said, my voice cracking at least twice in the process, and the driver, almost casually, punched me in the eye. My head bounced off the seat behind me. It was so close in there, he hardly had room to extend his arm. It still hurt.

"Shit," I said.

He said, "You need to get out of my country, man." It was spoken in a bad Hvíldarlandic accent, like an American shooting for a bad punchline.

This was to be my hell, then—to be beaten repeatedly, while my assailants said the same dumb shit over and over again.

"Get out," said the passenger. "Go home, don't come back." This was said in a heavy Russian accent, and he made a shooing motion towards me like he was being harried by flies. Everything on them looked brand new. Gloves, masks. Even their teeth were white and beautiful.

The tall one reached over and gently tapped the fish bat against my ear, twice. Action films once more ran dizzyingly through my head—I could take the bat, break his arm, hoist my legs over the seat and choke the other one out. I had to piss. I felt like I might have already pissed when I had fallen in the field. There was still grit in my teeth.

A car drove by, an old white pickup stacked high with caged chickens. It kept on going, had no interest in the drama that was unfolding in this little square of a car. I looked out into the field and saw my little bike out there, its color forlorn and strange amid the desolation. "You're wasting your time," the driver said. "There's no such thing as an *einhyrningur*, okay?" The other one pressed the roughened tip of the bat against my forehead.

"I don't know what you're talking about. I don't even know what that is."

The passenger pushed the bat against my forehead until I was looking up at the roof of the car, and then the driver leaned over the seat and gripped my testicles and squeezed. That dark roiling ache exploded up into my guts. I bellowed and tried to curl over but the passenger kept the bat against my forehead so instead I raised my legs up, tried to curl into a ball that way.

"Forget about the fucking unicorn," he said, pronouncing it like *eyooni-corn*. He pushed the bat against my forehead once more and then took it away. "Nobody wants you here. Go home."

In between gasps, I said, "You're the guys that trashed our stuff. At the hotel."

"Maybe," said the driver. "Or maybe all of Hvíldarland wants you gone. Maybe wherever you go, someone's watching you. Maybe time ran out for you a while back."

"Go home," said the passenger. "We're not asking again, *tovarishch.*" Languorous and slow, a single eye winked beneath the mask.

They turned around in their seats then. Dismissive like that, like I wasn't worth worrying about. The passenger tapped the bat against the glass of his windshield. "Get out of the car now," he said, and the Russian accent here was gone, a facade cast aside. This was spoken with just a flat, almost droll kind of menace. Boredom, even.

I stepped out onto the shoulder of Road Seven. The driver let out another honk as they turned around and sped away. I walked, hunched over and aching, toward my bike.

• • •

I found Sandoval at the edge of the woods, threading a tripwire along a line of trees with a spool of sewing thread. I watched him, crouched, testing the buoyancy of the line with his fingertips. Somewhere I heard a little bell jingle. I knew that it would either be buried beneath the sound of the wind or alert whoever had tripped it, and I thought, *This was the man who'd written half a dozen books? Whose body has purportedly been scarred by extraterrestrials? This was our supposed envoy, our spokesman?*

"That's not gonna work," I said, setting my bike down. "Whoever trips it will hear it first, then they'll run."

It was like watching someone wake up. The way his features drew away from that dulled, sleeping look into someone *here*. And it took an unnerving length of time, the two of us just standing there. But then he grinned, pushed a lock of hair out of his eyes, and it was Sandoval again. "That's okay," he said. "We'll get 'em on video first. I'm thinking we should start putting the cameras in the woods. Maybe leave the EVP on overnight."

"The hell is happening to you, Mark?"

"What do you mean? Nothing."

"You're . . . What was that, right there?"

"I am absolutely fine."

"Listen." I exhaled. "I, uh—I just got jumped by two men in masks. On the road."

Sandoval nodded, looked at the woods again like he couldn't wait to get back to it.

"One of them had a bat. They said no one wanted us here. They told us to leave."

He spat on the ground, nodded again. "Walk with me, Brian."

We made our way to the house and sat down on the porch. Sandoval lit a cigarette, saw that the wind was blowing the smoke my way, and switched sides with me. He stared out at the driveway and Road Seven beyond, scratched his chin with the hand holding the smoke. "You know I've been walking around with an EVP recorder out there." He tilted his chin at the trees. "Just talking. Asking questions."

"I know."

"Haven't gotten anything yet. I keep trying. But part of me . . . I don't know, part of me just likes walking around out there. You know why?"

"No, man," I said, weary. Tired of all of it. "Why?"

He leaned in close. "Because I'm a little afraid to," he said. "I think of those poor British bastards all the time. Poor guys thinking they lucked into the safest spot in all of the war, and then getting blown up by their own ordnance. That's dark. That's a dark turn."

"How in the hell is a ghost going to activate a *tripwire,* Mark? Or ring a bell? What're you looking for out here? Ghosts or unicorns? What the hell are we *doing* here?"

"You think I'm falling down the rabbit hole."

"I never said that." *Classic Brian Schutt. Pure chickenshit.* Brooke would have laughed her ass off. Here I was, obviously alluding to something, and then buckling like rice paper when I got called on to say it plainly.

"Give me a break, Brian. It doesn't take a genius to see that you're phoning it in. Scale of one to ten, how many shits do you give about any of this? How invested are you?"

Now the anger came, the righteousness. Still adrenaline-shook, I embraced it. "I just got jumped by two men in masks. I'd say I'm invested."

"You remember when we talked in Don's office? The interview?"

"Sure."

"And I asked you if you believed in any of this stuff. And you said you wanted to."

"Yeah."

"Did Don Whitmer ever mention me?" Sandoval asked.

I was confused by the curve ball in conversation. "No. I didn't even know you knew each other until that email you sent. When you said we should meet at his office."

"I rode out of that part of my life like I was on a bullet train, okay? I was in a bad way. And I had to make certain choices after that. Don, I hadn't seen him in years, since he threw me out on my ass. Justifiably." He ashed his cigarette. "I wanted to rub it in his face."

"Why?"

Sandoval winced, rubbed an eye with his thumb. "You know, success. The fact I'd done something. That I'd made it in spite of him. Fifty-one years old and in a dick-swinging contest with a man who tried his best to help me out. Pathetic, right?"

"Listen, Mark. No offense, but what does this have to do with what just happened to me out there?"

He ground his smoke under his boot, stretched back and put the butt in the coffee can behind us. "You saw the evidence. I mean, you literally held some of it in your hands. My question is, what will it take for you to believe?"

I couldn't help but feel a trill of pleasure run through me, that dark little ripple of joy people took when committing acts of pure meanness. It was my turn to lean toward him now. I hissed, "That was a pile of horse shit. With some junk jewels and glitter sprinkled on it. That was somebody screwing with you, Mark."

"Nah," he said. "You're not seeing the whole picture."

"I'm done," I said. "I'm leaving."

He waved a hand at the woods and said, "I see the lights out there sometimes. At night. These floating lights."

I went cold. All-over cold. "What're you talking about?"

"It's their souls, Brian."

We sat there.

I said, "You see lights in the woods. At night."

"Yeah." He stood up. His knees popped.

"Why don't you film them?"

"They don't show up. Not on motion sensors. Infrared, digital. Nothing."

"But *you* can see them."

He said, "Who trashed my room, Brian? Ruined my manuscript? Busted up the equipment? Who threatened you?"

"Nationalist assholes? Xenophobes? Somebody who thinks we're grifters?"

"Keep trying."

"It doesn't *matter*, Mark."

"It does. It's actually one of the very few things that matter. Who calls to me out here?"

"Jesus Christ," I said. "Are you hearing yourself?"

"The tests will come back, Brian. When they do, it's gonna blow the lid off of everything we've ever thought of these animals. Of the world. Historically. Culturally. Genetically. *Spiritually.*"

I laughed, a sound that came out strangled and afraid. I *was* afraid. "The kids and I are making band shirts when they get home from school. I'm gonna do that, and then I'm gonna have dinner with this family and pack up my stuff. I'll be heading to Kjálkabein in the morning and catching a flight to Reykjavík." I stood up. "It's been real, Mark."

"I need this," Sandoval said.

"I'm sorry I didn't turn out to be the right guy for the job. Things got out of hand."

"You have plane fare? Enough to get home?"

"I'll figure it out," I said.

"Listen. Brian, listen to me. We'll move things ahead. We'll go the álagablettur tomorrow, and then we'll go to the base."

"That's just *stupid*, man. I just told you someone jumped me!"

"What if Shane can get us in? To the base. Someone to act as a, a guide."

"Mark, *no one wants us here.*"

He pointed a finger at me, bared his teeth at me in this wolfish grin. "Why? Think about *why.* If there's an answer to all of this? It's either in the woods or at the base. That's all that's left."

"Mark."

He said, "I know that stipend I'm giving you won't be enough to get you plane fare back to the States. There's no way."

"Fuck you."

"Do tomorrow—the álagablettur and the base—and I'll buy you out. Give you your commission early. We'll call it even." He started walking backward, hands in his pockets. Heading back to the trees, to his bells and threads and floating lights. *Who calls to me out here?* That grin, laconic as it was skeletal.

I said, "You've lost it."

"I need this, Brian. I need *you.* I'm sorry, but I do."

3

Sandoval was already in the dining room when I trudged into the house the next morning. It was sleeting outside and the rest of the house was still silent and sleep-heavy. He was writing in his notebook, a cup of coffee at his side. I decided right then that I'd call my parents today, both of them, and Brooke and Ellis, too. I still didn't know if I'd take Sandoval's deal—I mean, I *knew* I'd take it, but that early in the morning, I told myself I reserved the right to change my mind. But calling them today, when I knew I was heading home, it gave me some breathing room. It ceased to be an open-ended abandonment of everything. My sojourn to Hvíldarland could become less a crazed bridge-burning of my life and more just an odd trip coming to an end, now that there was an endpoint. Everyone—especially Brooke and my mom—would be furious with my silence, but it was a lot easier to frame stuff like that when you could say, *Anyway, sorry I didn't call, but I'll be home tomorrow.*

Like some cheap-shit, worrisome harbinger, my head hurt like hell that morning.

I poured a cup of coffee and gazed out the front door at the grim weather, then put on my coat, hoisting my bag over my shoulder.

"Going somewhere?" Sandoval asked from the table.

I stepped out on the porch, felt the bite of the morning. Got on my stupid little bicycle. My knees clacked against the handlebars all the way to Kjálkabein, rain spitting against my coat.

• • •

It was a mustard-colored, rectangular three-story building on the town's southeastern end. Unlovely and utilitarian, *Lögreglan* in foot-high letters above the glass double doors.

The desk clerk took my name, eyed my ID for a minute and then got on the phone. He hung up and gave me a room number down the hall.

I found Constable Jónsdóttir hunched over a Tupperware container of soup in the Kjálkabein Police break room. The room overlooked the rear parking lot and the police motor pool. Dumpsters, chain-link fencing, a line of four or five squad cars parked at an angle, sleek as sharks. The room held a few couches, a pair of tables, a microwave, refrigerator and sink. A vending machine sat in one corner. It looked like any number of teacher's lounges I'd been in.

Jónsdóttir laid her spoon down on one napkin and dabbed at her mouth with another. We were alone. She seemed wholly unsurprised that I'd dropped by. "Mr . . . Scott, was it?"

"Schutt."

"Right, Mr. Schutt. Your face is looking better. How are the Hauksdóttirs?"

"They're good."

"I told my husband you were here." She looked down at her soup for a moment, bashful. "He was hoping we might drive out to the farm and visit Mr. Sandoval. He has some books he was hoping to have autographed."

"Listen," I said, "I'm leaving the country, but I wanted to let you know. Two guys in masks jumped me on Road Seven yesterday. They told me that Mr. Sandoval and I had to get out of the country. You know, *or else.*"

Jónsdóttir stood up, carefully put the lid on her soup container. Something her husband had made her, I hoped, before she hit the cold, brutal streets of Kjálkabein, where sheep wandered brazenly into the city limits, and guys got into bar scuffles over whose dad had once pulled up a torpedo in a fish net. Maybe that wasn't fair, but my head hurt like a monster that morning, and I was afraid and frustrated and angry.

"Let me go get some forms and I can take your statement. But you're leaving the country today?"

"Tomorrow, probably."

"Nothing official can be done if you aren't here to press charges. You understand? If we find anything, I mean."

"I understand. I'm not willing to wait around. I'd still like to make a statement."

"Of course," Jónsdóttir said. She put her soup in the refrigerator, balled up her napkins and threw them in the trash. "I'll be right back with the forms."

• • •

The fields lay furrowed with water, the sound of the rain soothing as it fell from the eaves of the house. I'd ridden home through it, and now was warming up in the living room. Thumbing through channels, looking for that loathsome lasagna, knowing it was there somewhere. It'd become some kind of talisman to me. Gruesome but telling, like Roman haruspex divining bird entrails. But, you know, with more dick jokes. The lasagna never left, moored forever on that goddamned table.

Karla was upstairs showering. The zippering and clomping and clicking of various pieces of equipment told me that Sandoval was in the dining room, prepping our gear for the trip. We were just waiting for Shane to show up. The children, their yellow slickers glowing in the fey afternoon gloom, their fingers fat and useless with heavy gloves, were playing outside. Polar bears, those children. Impervious to cold.

A gelatinous blur on the screen: there it was.

"What I mean is, you and me could make some beautiful music together," the lasagna said in English, Icelandic subtitles across the bottom of the screen.

An exchange student? A pen pal of the daughter? A girlfriend? She had on a beret and a fringed sweater befitting the era. She was doing the dishes, her back to the leering lasagna. She said in a French accent, "Sorry, I do not date dinner foods!"

The laugh track went *big* on that.

The lasagna said, "Where you from, darlin'?"

"Nice," she said.

"Nice?" he said.

"No, Nice," she said.

"That's what I mean. *Nice.*"

Laugh track subdued.

I was losing my mind. My skull was a detonation.

"You asshole," I whispered, jamming my head into the back of the couch. "You viscid, mucilaginous asshole." A half-dozen ibuprofen roiled my guts, had barely taken the serrated knife-edge off of the ache.

I walked to the foot of the stairs. "Hey, Karla?" Even raising my voice squeezed the membrane of my skull.

"Yes?" Her voice drifted from around the corner of the stairwell.

"Can I make some calls? I can leave you cash now, or PayPal you the money later."

"Yes, that's fine."

I heard Gunnar and Liza clomp up the front steps. They ran through the house, found me in the kitchen staring at the phone. "Brian," Liza shrieked, "come play with us! Be the monster again! Come outside!"

And I almost did. Nearly took it as a sign, brushed aside the phone calls, put on my heavy coat, went to play with these kids that I'd come to care about. But I'd be heading home after our trip to the base later tonight. If

I didn't do this now, I never would. So I said, "I'm sorry, Liza. I've got to make some calls first. But if I've got time afterward I will, okay?"

Gunnar nodded, the responsible one. "That's fair, Li-li."

• • •

I was the only one of us who had actually talked to my father since he'd abandoned us for Traci and the nudist colony. It wasn't out of any profound sense of loyalty on my part; he'd called me once to complain about my mother's lawyers, maybe a month after he'd left, and I, eternally afraid of conflict, had stood and listened. This had always been the inherent nature of our relationship. Me, nodding and grunting my "uh-huhs" rather than refuting his shit. I'd done it my entire life. He'd started with, "It's safe to say I'm being grievously misaligned by the women in our family, Brian." It seemed like he'd had some drinks. We hadn't talked since. If it was an attempt at reconciliation, some fatherly attempt at showing love or building allegiance, it was a shitty effort.

But today, my head jammed full of coals the way it was, on my way back home with this odd failure of a trip in my pocket . . . today felt different. I was halfway around the world. I was impervious, at least from him, his anger and contempt. Couldn't it afford me a moment or two of bravery?

It was ten-thirty or so in Arizona. As the phone rang, Brooke's terrible images zipped through my mind like tracers. Downward Dog, tan lines, the faint scars of breast implant incisions. Jesus.

"Hello?"

I cleared my throat. "Hi, Traci. I, uh, was hoping to speak to Brad."

A momentary pause. "Sure, can I tell him who's calling?"

"This is Brian."

Another pause. "Brian."

"His son, yeah."

"Okay." I could faintly hear the television in the living room of the Hauksdóttir house. "Well, I can try to find him for you. He should be out doing his laps at the pool."

I leaned my head against the wall. My father, sleek as a porpoise, nude in the community pool, sunlight knifing off the water. He'd been such an unhappy, private man, so many sharp, tucked-away corners to him. So distant from us all. Now he did the breaststroke naked in the community pool, traveled the emotional landmines of polyamory, lovingly traced Traci's implant scars while Scottsdale burned. Everyone was someone else. "Okay, thanks," I said.

But then Traci surprised me. "But do you think it's wise, Brian?"

"Sorry? Do I think what's wise?"

"Talking to him."

"Talking to my dad?"

"Aren't you all, you know, embroiled in a legal battle right now? Shouldn't you let everyone's lawyers handle things at this point?"

I let out a little laugh, incredulous. "I'd like to speak to my dad, Traci."

"I'm just saying, I think things might be kind of irreconcilable right now. He and your mom are in the thick of it, and he's upset. He might take that out on you when he doesn't mean to. You're the last person he should go off on, but you know how he is." This was Traci? This was the woman that Brooke spent hours concocting revenge fantasies against? Why, I suddenly wondered, would a twenty-four-year-old move to a nudist colony populated by people as old as her father? That was a loaded question, sure, but I considered the possibility that she might actually be in love, and able to find some avenue of tenderness or connection within the man that my mother hadn't been able to unearth.

I asked Traci to let him know that I'd called. That I was out of town but would be home in a few days. That I'd to talk to him when he was up for it.

Before we hung up, I said, "So what's life like out there?"

"Hot," she said.

"Does he really do the Sun Salutation with his balls out?"

There was a moment of silence on the other end. Then Traci said, "Goodbye, Brian," and hung up.

Sandoval, in the dining room, had the good sense to not say anything.

Ellis when I called was freer with his language. He picked up, wary at the international number, but once he found out it was me, unloaded with a seething, "Dude, *what the hell is wrong with you?* I've written you like ten emails! Not even kidding. Ten."

I've been afraid to get near a computer, Ellis. Sorry. "Sorry," I said. "Things have been crazy."

"Where the hell are you? You're seriously with Mark Sandoval?"

"Yeah. I can't really say."

"What, that NDA you signed?"

"Exactly," I said.

Ellis sighed. "Your sister's *pissed.* She came over here looking for you and just about blew a gasket when I told her you'd left the country. *Especially* with Sandoval."

I took a grim pleasure at this. "Did she know who he was?"

"Of course she did. I think your mom is pretty freaked, and Brooke's less than thrilled that she has to carry, you know, the banner of familial solidarity all by herself."

"She's used to it," I said.

"Seriously, where *are* you?"

"Can't say."

"You asshole. What're you guys looking for? Oh! Robert and I had some drinks and looked some up! Hold on, I've got a list right here. Is it Goatman?"

"I really can't say, Ellis."

"Loveland Frog? Momo the Monster?"

"You know what 'not at liberty' means, right?"

"Skookum! Old Yellow Top! Ogopogo!"

I said, "Even if you guessed it, I wouldn't tell you."

"Ghost deer."

"Nope."

"Unicorn," Ellis said.

I didn't say anything.

"Holy shit!" he crowed. "It's a unicorn! You're looking for a fucking unicorn with Mark Sandoval, oh my God!"

Mindful of Sandoval in the other room, I said, "Let's drop it, you're never gonna guess."

"Oh man, is he right there? He is, isn't he?"

I said, "Glad we agree on that."

"Gotcha. Okay, Brian. I will accept your apology for not answering any of my ten emails. *Wow.*"

"I am sorry about that," I said. "We've been busy."

"Call your momma, young man," Ellis said. "Call your sister. They're worried."

"I will."

"So have you officially just flamed out of school? Just crashed and burned?"

"Looks like it. But I'll be heading home tomorrow."

"Really? Did you find it? You must've found it! I know you can't answer that, but give me something, Brian. Grunt once for yes, belch twice for no."

In the dining room, I heard the various beeps that meant that Sandoval was cycling through the camera feeds on his laptop. "If Brooke gets in touch, just tell her I'll be home soon."

"So you're not going to reach out to her yourself, huh? Damn. That's cold."

"We've just got a lot going on here before we wrap everything up."

"Okay," Ellis said. "For Christ's sake, at least you called me. That counts for something. The second you get home, I want to hear everything, non-disclosure or not. Talk to you later. Safe travels, my dear."

That done, I picked up the receiver again, ready to call my mom. And then Liza's scream drifted from right outside the kitchen.

• • •

The children stood at the tree line at the rear of the house. Liza's yellow slicker shone bright in the gloom. She stood with her back to me, and Gunnar crouched beside her. I was out the back door as fast I could, and I could hear Sandoval's footfalls behind me.

I took Liza by the shoulders, gently, and crouched down. She turned to me, her face red, tears spilling off her chin. She tucked herself into me, tiny in my arms.

"What is it?" I said. "What's the matter?"

"Holy shit," Sandoval said behind me.

Karla came running out the back door in a robe, her wet hair in strings, eyes widened in panic. She called her daughter's name and Liza ran to her, buried herself in Karla's arms. I looked back and saw Sandoval and Gunnar crouched down before something in the churned mud.

I stood up and walked over to them. At their feet lay something that looked like clotted fabric, sheared in mud and moss. Something next to it: twigs, an old branch.

I should've known better, of course. Should've remembered the intricacies of a site, the careful way we cull the remnants of the past from the living world. And how, until we do that, the most striking remains can look like the blandest ephemera. A centuries-old pottery shard presumed to be a hunk of shale.

"Holy shit," Sandoval said again, and—in a move that eschewed every goddamned bit of education and training he had most likely ever received from Don Whitmer—hooked a finger in the fabric that sat half-buried in the mud and *pulled.*

Gunnar let out a sigh: half wonderment, half disgust.

"Brian," Sandoval said, still crouched. "Gonna wanna call the cops, bud."

"What *is* that?"

And then I saw the yellowed, atrophied hand coming out of the mud-clotted sleeve that Sandoval pinched between his fingers. The waxy nails, the worming green veins. Desiccated and skeletal and skin-tightened.

A hand lay buried there in the mud outside their house.

• • •

Constable Jónsdóttir and a slab-faced male cop pulled into the driveway twenty minutes later. He was massive, this other guy, his blond hair shorn so close I could see his scalp beneath it. He introduced himself as Leifsson, and as Jónsdóttir examined the remnants, he unloaded gear—shovels and tarps and little numbers on sticks to delineate evidence locations—and deferred to Jónsdóttir in everything else.

Leifsson rooted around with the shovel at her direction, and we watched as the hand became attached to an arm. We—Sandoval and I—were not permitted to participate and stood there like children watching someone else play with our toys, as screwed up as that may have seemed. The *actual* children watched goggle-eyed from the kitchen window until Karla eventually lead them away.

The arm ended in a ragged stump of shoulder, a yellowed knob of bone, the sleeve scorched stiff.

I saw the mud-smeared insignia on the sleeve, pointed it out to Jónsdóttir, who crouched low and held the arm, grimly turning it this way and that. Fearless, unbothered. Leifsson stood with his shovel at the edge of the divot he'd created, only the occasional tremble of his lips showcasing his troubles.

"You know what this is," Sandoval said to Jónsdóttir.

"It looks like an arm," she said drily.

"Look at that insignia. How old that thing is. It's skeletal."

"That's one of Karla's British soldiers," I said. "Right?"

Sandoval nodded. "You got it."

Jónsdóttir told Leifsson in Icelandic that they would need another car, two more officers. They'd be digging a while. He stalked off to the cruiser to radio it in.

"We can help," I said. "It's kind of what we do."

"No thank you," Jónsdóttir said, standing up and brushing the mud from her knees.

"Officer," Sandoval said, letting one of those flashbulb-bright smiles go, "would you mind if Brian and I took some photos? I'm working on a new book, and I'd be thrilled to include you in it, if you were interested. I'm thinking that what you're digging up there is at least marginally related to what's brought us here."

Again there was that curious type of celebrity at work—you could see Jónsdóttir wanting to say yes, but every notion of retaining a chain of evidence, of professionalism, flew in the face of it.

"I have some of your books in our car. My husband was hoping you would sign them."

"And I'd be happy to. So this is okay? If I go get my camera?"

"I—"

Which was when Karla leaned out the back door, her face taut with worry, and said, "Brian. You have a phone call."

I asked who it was.

"It's Vaughn Keller."

• • •

"What's up, buddy?" Vaughn crowed. "Sounds like you got some wild shit going on over there at Karla's place."

"I . . . How do you know that, Vaughn?"

"Oh hell, it's my day off. I listen to the police scanner when I'm bored. Nothing better to do. Nothing ever going on at the base, so if I need some action, I have to listen to Kjálkabein cops complain about drunks puking in the back seats of their cruisers. They found an *arm?*"

"They . . . Yeah, looks like it. Looks like it's one of the soldiers who had been stationed here during the war."

"Christ Almighty. Place is gonna be crawling with cops. You and Sandoval had better get the hell out of there unless you want to be pointlessly grilled for the next few hours about some Brit infantry asshole who's been dead eighty years. Which is what I wanted to talk to you about, actually."

I was reeling—a police scanner? Leifsson mentioned they'd found a human arm at the Hauksdóttir farm? Over the police scanner? And Vaughn was listening and decided to call us?

"Like, right now, you want to talk?"

"I can help you find what you're looking for. That's about all I want to say right now, but I strongly suggest you and Sandoval meet me for a drink at the same place we met last."

"Really," I said.

"It would benefit you greatly."

"I have to talk to Mark about it. I'm not sure if the cops will let us leave."

Vaughn coughed, and I heard the snick of a lighter. "Go talk to him. I'll wait."

I set the phone down on the island and walked out on the back porch.

Jónsdóttir was packing up the tarps, the shovel. Fury sparked off of her like static. Leifsson, looking ill, held the arm in a sheet of plastic. They walked around the side of the house.

"What's happening?" I said.

"They got called off," Sandoval said, his hands on his hips. He stared down at the riven mud where the severed arm had been. "They got some emergency call in Kjálkabein? That big blond cop just told the woman cop they had to go and she was *pissed.*"

"This isn't an emergency? Some guy's severed arm isn't an emergency?"

Sandoval shrugged. "I don't know. From the looks of it, he's probably not missing it, right?"

"Listen, Vaughn wants to meet us for a drink. He says he can *help us find what we're looking for.*" I did air quotes.

"Vaughn said that?"

"Yeah," I said. "What the hell is going on, Mark?"

Sandoval grinned. "We're getting close."

4

Keller sat at a corner table of the bar with a trio of pints and matching whiskey shots set out before him. Sitting with his back to the wall, he looked haggard and red-nosed, every inch the troll under the bridge. When he saw us, he smiled like he had a mouthful of safety glass. My skull throbbed like a siren.

Sandoval sat down, nodded at the glasses before him. He lifted his shot. "Thanks for the drinks." He hadn't drunk since we'd arrived in Hvíldarland, but I knew him well enough to know that there wasn't a bridge he wouldn't burn to get what he wanted. Internally or otherwise.

"Little early for me to be drinking," I said. I didn't like my back exposed to the bar like it was.

Keller rolled his eyes. "Just drink it, Brian. Come on."

We drank. The whiskey lanced through me, roiling and hot. Keller winced, exhaling loudly and pressing a fist against his chest. "Pisser," he rattled, and drank a third of his pint.

Sandoval lifted his pint glass and drank as well, wiped foam from his beard. "So, can we just get down to it? Without all the dancing around and grab-assing?"

Keller showed a mouth of little yellow teeth when he grinned. "Get down to what?"

"Whatever it is that you want to tell us. Whatever it is you think we're looking for."

"Well, I thought you were looking for a unicorn. That's it, right?"

Sandoval stood up. "Let's go."

Pointing a stubby finger with the hand holding the pint glass, Keller said, "You sit your ass down." There was a severity to it that I hadn't seen from him before, and I expected Sandoval to do anything except what he did: smirked and sat back down. He beat a little rhythm against his glass.

"Can I make a prediction?"

"Go ahead," Keller said.

"You're going to ask us to leave. You're going to say that we've become a nuisance, that we've worn out our welcome with the Hauksdóttirs. That it's time to go home."

Keller smiled at me. There was no humor there. "Give the man a prize."

"And how is that," Sandoval said, "exactly making it 'worth our while'?"

Pulling out a sheaf of papers from inside his jacket, Keller's eyes flat and snake-like while he did it, he pushed them over to me across the table.

A gold seal on the bottom, some official stationary. I leafed through them. "It's . . . an interview? With a General Stanley Brewster, Commanding Officer of . . . what's the Advanced Intelligence Threat Program?"

"That's me making it worth your while," Keller said, and turned to look at Sandoval. There was some dead-eyed staring contest between the two of them, while neither of them spoke.

"I don't get it," I said.

Without breaking eye contact, Sandoval said, "The AITP's an urban legend, Brian."

"What?"

"It's an Army program that was supposedly started after the Roswell crash in '47. They're the folks that've been backward-engineering all the technology from the wreckage for the past seventy years. The guys in dark suits and glasses in all the movies."

Keller said, "And Brewster's willing to talk to you for an hour. In a rented office, in a state far away from where AITP is stationed. No names, and there's a lot that he won't talk about. But there's a lot that he will. An exclusive sit-down with the head of the AITP. For *you*."

"I still don't get what this has to do with the unicorn," I said.

"It doesn't have anything to do with the unicorn, Brian," said Sandoval. "It's a bone that Keller—or Keller's people—are throwing our way."

"Here's the deal—" Keller said.

"There's just one problem," Sandoval said, and pushed the papers back across the table. "The Army's AITP program is a bunch of bullshit, and the unicorn is real."

Keller leaned forward. I saw his hands curl into fists on the tabletop. "Here's the deal," he continued. "You two have complicated things for that family. That farm's hanging on by a thread, and Karla's already a pariah around here, okay? Then you come in here with this unicorn thing? You're not helping."

Sandoval sipped his beer. "Who do you really work for, Vaughn?"

"This is the best deal you're going to get." Keller tapped a fingernail against the papers in front of him. "Exclusive access to a classified black project. That's a gift. That's a fucking book right there."

Sandoval turned to me. "It makes you wonder why, doesn't it, Brian?"

"Because," Keller said, "with that arm you idiots just exhumed—"

"That was just Gunnar playing around, actually," Sandoval said. "It'd have come up eventually whether we were there or not."

"It's true," I said. "Karla says the kids are always finding stuff around the property. Bayonets, cigarette packs."

"Jesus Christ, what is that between your ears? Can't you two listen? That poor family is gonna have cops all over the place now, and then there's *you* people looking for a made-up creature—can't you just leave them the hell alone? Just go home."

Sandoval gulped some more beer. He seemed to be enjoying himself now. "I feel like your altruism banjo's only got one string, Vaughn. I don't think you give a shit about Shane or about Karla Hauksdóttir or those kids."

Leaning back, Keller swiped a hand down his face. "You're not hearing me."

"Who do you really work for? Who are you?"

Keller held out a hand toward Sandoval, as if to implore me. "How many people have to tell you to get the hell out of here before you listen?"

"Here's the thing," Sandoval said, and then he lifted his glass and drained it, making us wait. I eyed the scars sneaking out the collar of his shirt. "The AITP was debunked as a hoax twenty years ago. There was never an AITP program to begin with. Anyone remotely involved with this stuff knows that it never got off the ground and was abandoned by '48. I don't know who Stanley Brewster is, but he's more likely your hair stylist—well, not yours, Vaughn, clearly—than he is a four-star general." He set the glass down. "You're treating me like I'm stupid, and I don't appreciate it."

Keller was gripping the table with both hands. "Every word you say—every minute you insist on staying here—is increasing the likelihood of getting a 5.56 round through your eye socket. And at some point, you're the only one who's responsible for it."

I went cold at that, and Keller noticed it and nodded grimly. "See? Brian gets it."

Sandoval said, "I thought you were just a poor little fobbit at a data station, Vaughn. Since when does a *data analyst* threaten US citizens with assassination?"

This was how quickly the world moved: Keller stood, his chair clattering to the floor, and that poor red-faced fool who'd gotten in my face the last time I was here, obviously a lifer, obviously a regular here, came up to him—he'd clearly been waiting for his shot with us, and looked to be bleakly drunk already—slurring something about Americans and their lack of respect.

Keller palmed the man's face and pushed him over a table. Glasses exploded, people scattered, the guy tumbled shoes-up out of sight behind the fallen table. I half-rose from my seat, and Keller walked behind the table and started stomping on the man, his leg pistoning up and down like he was trying to kickstart a chopper. Someone grabbed his shoulder, some kid, and Keller spun around and reached into his jacket. He pulled a pistol from a holster snug against his gut and jammed the barrel in the kid's face. The kid immediately cowered, ducking down with his hands in the air. Keller hoisted him up by his collar and marched him backward until he was pressed against a wall. He was just some kid in a puffy silver jacket, Adam's apple bobbing madly. He looked like any poor terrified fool would with a gun against his jaw.

In perfect Icelandic, Keller said, "*Hvað* núna, rassgat?" What now, asshole?

The kid turned his face turned away from the barrel, pressing his head hard against the wall. He blubbered "sorry" in Icelandic and English again and again, eyes cinched shut, spit shiny on his lips.

Keller took a step back, dropped the gun to his side, saw that the red-faced man had had the temerity to rise up on his hands and knees. Blood fell from the man's mouth in clots, and Keller stomped over and delivered a punt to his face that I'm sure would have killed him had Keller not been wearing office-guy wingtips. It might have killed him anyway. Someone screamed and the man dropped like he'd been unplugged. Vomit tickled my throat.

Keller put his handgun back in his holster, smoothed his hair back. He was breathing hard, chest heaving. His shirt had come untucked. The sound of cold Icelandic pop music filled the room but beneath that there was nothing. No one spoke. I could see the injured man's leg twitching, the heel of his shoe tapping arrhythmically on the floor.

Keller took the papers and put them back in his jacket. "People," he said, running a hand down his mouth and then jabbing a finger at us, "have been telling you to leave since day one. It's time to listen."

5

An hour later we stood in Karla's empty living room, riddled with nerves and watching television. The eyes of her long-dead ancestors glowered down upon us from their spots on the walls. She'd taken the children to run errands; I assumed finding a severed arm in your yard—whether or not it belonged to someone long dead—did not exactly warm the place up with the notion of familial safety. It was a good thing, too—it saved us from Karla's inevitable interrogation after seeing our ashen, shit-scared faces after the thing with Keller. We were waiting for Shane, and then we were going to the álagablettur, and then I was leaving.

An hour of this, I told myself, *and then you make your exit. Fobbit or not, Vaughn Keller has informed you that there are people on this island willing to end your life, and what exactly has happened in the past few weeks to make you think he's lying?*

Sandoval wore a balaclava rolled at the top of his head like a black condom. His NVGs rested on top of that, their lenses bulky and awkward-looking. He kept checking the equipment he had tucked in the many pouches in his jacket—it was a bulky tactical vest, another item he'd had delivered with the cameras—and amid the canned TV laughter and Sandoval's ceaseless snapping and unsnapping and Velcroing and unVelcroing, I just stood there with my hands in my pockets, feeling emotionally run-through. Gutted and ready beyond words to go home. It was time to admit I needed to take care of the headaches. Time to admit that I didn't understand what was real and what wasn't. That things had just gotten away from us.

It was time to go home, whether Sandoval was right or not.

"Why are we going into the woods with Shane again?"

"Because he knows the woods," Sandoval said. "And he's got a truck."

"You don't trust us on the bikes out there."

Sandoval looked up at me, surprised. "Do you?"

"No."

He went back to battery-checking and level-adjusting.

I said, "Do you think we're going to find something out there?"

"I do. You bet."

"Do you believe me now, that I heard someone say my name?"

He looked up again, and those eyes were clear and sober and all the more terrifying for it. "Yes. Oh yeah."

I roved through the channels on the television, knowing it would be on, and it was.

The lasagna dangled precipitously off the edge of the kitchen table, plate atremble, runnels of grease and cheese sliding to the floor. The son, shirtless, sat at the table, thumbing through a magazine and eating a cookie. He sat hunched over, his gaze glassy, like Sandoval's got at times. The lasagna's eyes wobbled and slid, its mouth oozed and sputtered in fear, clots of hamburger and cheese running off now. This was it. The lasagna was about to plunge to its death.

The boy, shoving the last wedge of cookie into his mouth, wordlessly pushed the plate back onto the table. He turned the page of his magazine.

The lasagna, safe, trembled and quaked.

The audience roared with relieved laughter.

"Seriously," I said, "what is happening to us?"

Sandoval battery-checked. Level-adjusted.

I turned the TV off.

We heard footsteps on the porch, and Shane came in without knocking. He wore a bright yellow parka that dripped with rain, his hair tied back in a ponytail.

He scowled at Sandoval. "What are you, a ninja?"

Sandoval looked down at his vest, nervously unsnapping a pocket. "What are you talking about?"

"Why are you dressed all in black?"

"This is just how I dress."

"Dude, no, it isn't. What's with the ski mask? You look like the bad guy in a Steven Seagal movie."

I held up a finger. "I actually technically don't think Steven Seagal makes movies anymore. I don't think so, anyway. Maybe in Russia? Didn't he move to Russia?" Nervous, nervous.

"You know what I'm talking about." He told Sandoval to take the balaclava off. "And those NVGs, too."

Sandoval said he didn't think that was going to happen.

"I'm serious, Mark. It's dark out there, dude. The goal is to be seen, not to walk around in the middle of the night like a goddamn vampire. You got it?" He pulled a roll of reflective tape out of his pocket and tossed it to me. I fumbled it, and the tape rolled under the coffee table. "Put it on."

A test of wills between them, all dependent on how much Sandoval wanted to tell Shane—about the álagablettur, Vaughn's threats, the arm, all of it—and how much he needed safe passage and access to the base.

He sighed, tossed the NVGs on the couch. "Fine."

• • •

Something pummeled out of the speakers. It sounded like a mating wyvern listing its dissatisfactions over a car being furiously dismantled in a chop shop.

"Who's this?" I asked.

"Rectal Dismemberment," Shane said.

"What kind of music is this?" Sandoval said. "*Is* this music? This is . . . a social exercise of some kind. A test or something."

"This is grindcore," said Shane.

"Does Gunnar listen to this?"

"Gunnar's ten, dude. I'm a dad, I'm not a lunatic. He listens to the soft stuff." The road unspooled on each side of us. Sandoval finally complained he couldn't hear himself think and Shane turned the stereo down. The trees ran in grim black stretches on each side of the road, and I tried to remember what it had been like that first time, riding our bikes back from the base. Had it been this endlessly bleak? Hvíldarland was full of this rough beauty, the whole island barren and windblown, but this part of it was different.

"We're gonna do ten minutes out here," Shane said, his cigarette wagging as he spoke. Smoke dragged itself out of the window. "I don't want you guys getting lost. We stick together."

"Would've been easier with the NVGs," Sandoval muttered.

"Yeah? How many pairs you have?"

"Two."

"How many of us are in this truck?"

Sandoval was silent.

"Exactly," Shane said. "I'm not walking around out there by myself while you two trip the light fantastic in your little fantasy commando goggles. You got that tape on?"

"Yeah," said Sandoval.

"That reflective tape? You got it on your coats?"

"Yes, Shane. Christ. Talking to me like a kid, that's not gonna work for me."

"What's not gonna work is us getting lost out here."

"You sound a little nervous," I said. Sandoval cast a glance my way; we hadn't told Shane yet about the arm, and I figured he hadn't heard about it from Karla. I assumed consoling his children would have trumped our little jaunt into the woods.

I was sitting in the middle of the seat, my knees flush against the dash, and Shane dug an elbow into my side. "Yeah, I'm nervous, Brian. I don't want to be responsible for the Camping Unicorn Babies when they get turned around communing with nature in the middle of the night."

"You think we're going to find anything?"

Shane snorted. "You'll be lucky if your feet touch ground, we'll be gone so fast. So take your pictures, get your *readings*"—his voice was rich was sarcasm—"and then I'll try my luck at getting you in for a quick tour of Camp Carroll, and you can put this whole goddamn unicorn thing behind you. I wouldn't hold my breath, though."

"Doubter," Sandoval said drily, then turned his face to me. "Another doubter, Brian. You surprised?"

"Sandoval, I worry about you," Shane said. "I worry about your brain sometimes."

"Your wife contacted *me*, remember?"

"To my huge disappointment, believe me."

"The video—" said Sandoval, and Shane flung his hand like he was shooing an insect, nearly spearing me in the eye with his smoke.

"The video? Always about the video! Gunnar could make something like that in ten minutes at school. Everybody knows CGI these days. Please, the video."

"Of course," Sandoval said. "You think it's fake. Of course you do." I watched him absently pick at a piece of reflective tape on his sleeve. Were the trees beginning to curl toward the windshield just a little bit? Was I imagining that? That familiar stutter of fear wormed its way into my heart, just a flitter of a thing. I understood then that you really could grow exhausted of anything—even terror.

"Look," said Shane, "you got a good deal going on with your books, Mark. It's a good business model, man. But this shit is not sustainable. There's *no unicorn*." He waved his cigarette at the expanse of forest in front of us. "There's no haunted woods. No ghosts of dead British grunts."

I looked at Sandoval and waited to hear what he was going to say. Anything from *Your son found a seventy-five-year-old arm in the mud today, Shane* to my personal favorite, *Who calls to me out here?* A veritable potpourri of insanity could have spilled from his mouth. Instead, he put his hand on the door handle and said, "Pull over."

Shane stared at him for a moment and then sighed and pulled into a rutted little clearing laced in deadfall. A branch scraped the roof and I hissed, ducking my head a little. And we sat like that for maybe a minute with the engine cooling, the truck suffused with Sandoval's martyrdom, my loneliness. Shane's cigarettes.

Then Sandoval pushed the passenger door open, his boots squelching in the mud as he jumped down. "Screw it," he said. "Let's just wrap this up. Here's as good a spot as any."

Shane rummaged through the toolbox in his truck bed and handed out flashlights. They lit the trees in stark relief. The swaths of tape on our clothes gleamed bone-white when the lights skated across them.

"Stick close together," Shane said. "And don't lose your flashlight. It gets cold as shit out here, and I don't want to spend the night looking for you."

We fanned out in the darkness. You had to, with the trees packed in the way they were. Roots ankle high, snarls of them at your feet. Leg-breakers. Waist-high impasses of brittle, spiky deadfall. I'd look down to step over a knotted whorl of roots and almost get speared in the eye with a branch when I looked back up, and all the while there was that fierce wind. A long stretch of ensnared darkness, these leafless reaching limbs lit in the beam of my flashlight—I was braced by people on both sides, only feet away, and it was still maybe the loneliest place I'd ever been.

"Ten minutes," Shane said again, and my heart leapt in my throat for how close his voice was. I scribbled him with the flashlight; he covered his face with a hand.

"Sorry," I said, and brought the light down.

I walked slowly, carefully, worrying my tooth-space with my tongue. My head pulsed, sickly and freezing. For a moment, when my flashlight beam passed over it, I thought I saw a face quickly rearrange itself in the bark of a tree; it became something like a crone or an old man, features twisting, and I nearly fell backward. But I shone the light on it again, ready to run, and it was just a tree, featureless and still. I could hear Sandoval occasionally muttering as he tried to ford his way through the darkness a few feet away.

I kept expecting to see some other visage speared in my flashlight. Some pale, dead-eyed face leering at me. Button-eyes sloughed in a sheet of desiccation. The stock image culled from every shitty horror movie ever made. Maybe it'd be a dead British infantryman. Face riddled with shrapnel, long-rotted. Missing an arm. Shambling toward me through this dark labyrinth of trees.

My head was a tuning fork for pain. I felt it in my teeth, my fingertips.

I stopped, put my hand against a tree and pulled it back; it felt moist, cold. *Like skin,* I thought wildly, and wiped my hand down my pant leg.

"Shane? Mark?" My voice was tight, small. If someone walked up and clamped on my windpipe with their pincered fingers, it would feel exactly like this.

"Guys," I hissed. "My head feels bad."

I stood still, blood loud in my ears. Slowly roving my light through the trees, I waited for the firecracker pop of dead limbs snapping underfoot, the frustrated curses of Shane and Sandoval as they also scraped themselves raw on tree branches. But there was nothing. I looked back, wheeled the light around where I'd come from, and Road Seven was gone. It was *gone*.

I stood in a sea of gnarled trees, alone, in tangles of underbrush swallowed by the night.

My flashlight flickered twice and winked out.

The world became a pure dark.

I started flailing, spearing my palms against branches, this kind of animal keening loosing from my throat. I zombie-stomped forward and the tip of a branch speared me in the cheek, broke skin. I was yelling their names, then just yelling. I pressed my hand against my face, felt the warmth of the blood, and then stood there in the dark, these big heaving breaths racking through my pinched throat. The pain in my head flared suddenly, sent me to my knees. It was so leveling, like a bomb blast, a return to infancy. I wanted my mother. I wanted to be back in my sister's car with the windows rolled down, the ghost of spring there, the hint of heated tarmac and cut grass. Brooke steering with two fingers, and her looking over at me and smiling. Had that ever even happened?

I vomited, fell to the ground. I felt the earth against my face, the loam and grit of the woods against my wounded cheek. I saw stars in my periphery, stars that then gathered themselves along the trees, that lit the parchment-skin of the tree trunks near me.

Eight or ten of them were floating above me.

The death-lights of those men.

Chest-high, floating.

I keened, full of loss, wounded.

I was a child again, tumored, broken.

Those poor British dead hovering around me.

• • •

There was the gunfire snap of breaking branches above my head, and I felt hands grip my collar and hoist me up, pull me somewhat back to life. I was weeping. The pain behind my eyes was nearly blinding. "Fuckin dude is heavy," someone grumbled above me.

"Shut up," said someone else. Pure Americana in these voices, not like the two on the road had been.

The world lightened; they dragged me to the tarmac and dropped me next to the rear wheel of Shane's truck. I groaned, rolled in the mud. Saw a number of black-clad legs in front of me.

"Pick him up," a voice said.

"He's not a light guy," someone said, and then hands grappled me again, pulling me up and leaning me against the side of the truck. I started to buckle and someone pushed me upright, the metal curving against my back.

"The hell's wrong with him?"

"I don't know," said Sandoval. He was next to me. He hooked my arm around his shoulder, and I felt another person do the same on the other side. Shane.

"Did you shoot him?" One of the American voices.

"No, we didn't shoot him. Shit. We *should.*"

"What's that hole in his face then? He's bleeding like hell."

In front of me stood a black-clad man with a great black bowling ball of a head and two ragged eyeholes cut out. A balaclava. Just like Sandoval had wanted to wear. There were three of them, three men wearing masks on this dark stretch of road surrounded by nothingness. No other vehicles here besides Shane's truck. Just three black phantoms following us through the woods? I turned my head and said to Sandoval in a ragged, dusty croak I didn't even recognize as mine, "I saw them. The lights. The dead soldiers."

My head rocked back—someone slapped me—and I started crying like a little kid with the pain of it. There was a scuffle, Sandoval and Shane loosening themselves from me, and I staggered forward and was pushed back again.

When I opened my eyes, one of them had a hand against Shane's chest and a hatchet reared back above his head. A little camping hatchet, something used to chop licks of kindling off a log.

"We're good," Sandoval said, his hands up. "Okay? Everyone's good." His breath plumed the chill air.

Someone lit a flashlight. I squinted, held out my palm, and the light lowered, lit the pebbled, glittering surface of Road Seven. I saw that all three of the men in front of us held hatchets.

The one with the flashlight played the beam under his jaw, drew the mask into something grotesque. I saw the traceries of red veins in his glittering eyes.

"You are entire worlds away from good right now," he said. Their voices volleyed through the fog I was living in. Even with an ax dangling over

211 · ROAD SEVEN

him, I felt the reassuring weight of Shane's hand at my back as he said, "Cool, sorry. We're gone. We're leaving."

And maybe it was because of my head, and that cowardice that roiled inside me for years. Maybe it just was the arrogance inherent in these men. The brash fuck-you *Americanness* of strong-arming us out of here. Maybe it was just because, failures or not, we'd been *asked* to come. We'd ridden across the island on bicycles too small for us; we weren't an invading force with sniper turrets and bombs and manned gates. We hadn't stayed for seven decades.

Someone had asked us for help, and we'd come.

"You know what?" I hissed, leaning forward, taunting and jolly and contemptuous through the red haze in my skull. "*No*. We were asked to come here, and we're staying." I was yelling. "You hear me, Lieutenant? You hear me, Curtinson? You chickenshits?" I spat in the man's face and felt an ugly, savage triumph rip through me.

"Stupid," Shane muttered under his breath, almost admirably, right before the fight started.

Six guys grappling in the scant moonlight. The flashlight went rolling right away, dimly lit up a piece of the woods across the road. Limbs, grasping hands, everyone lurching against each other. I grabbed an arm that was like concrete with fabric pulled over it. "Hold him," Shane gasped, and someone's hand ran across my throat, scratched my bleeding cheek with a fingernail. I punched a mask that felt like a stone, then punched harder. It was like running my knuckles into a house. I heard the clatter of a hatchet fall to the pavement and for a moment saw Sandoval in his coat starfished on the ground—Shane's stupid tape was going to kill us all, you could see every goddamn thing we were doing—and I hooked my arm around someone's throat and jumped on him. He staggered, huffed, backpedaled me into the passenger door of the truck. The back of my skull connected against the window, and I bit my tongue in what felt like two pieces. Someone said "fuck" and then Shane told me to move and I staggered out of the way, and he ran a black-clad head into the door of the truck. The guy bounced off, fell back onto the pavement and rolled around, clutching his skull. The other two pulled him up and they ran across the road, swallowed by the darkness in seconds. A single hatchet lay on the tarmac, and Shane growled like an animal and hurled it into the trees after them.

I saw Sandoval sitting on the ground, leaning against the rear bumper. The fingers of his left hand drummed an impatient beat in the gravel.

"Mark?"

"Present," he said irritably. I stood over him. He frowned down at his splayed legs with the look of a guy who'd noticed his license had expired and was dreading the upcoming hours in the DMV.

A hatchet was buried in his shoulder, bisecting perfectly a piece of that stupid reflective tape.

"Guy chopped me," he said. His eyes burned up at me through his ashen, pale face.

I didn't say anything, just stood there with my mouth open.

"I'll admit it," he said. "We probably should've left a while ago."

6

We slalomed through the darkness of the álagablettur.

As always, it was more forgiving as we retreated.

I sat with Sandoval in the back of the truck. The hatchet jutted from his shoulder like some crazy juxtaposition: like a wolf with running shoes on, or a hat made of smoke. That was Sandoval. The wind whipped my eyes, brought tears. The moon broke through a ragged patchwork of clouds. Every time we hit a curve, Shane's toolbox scraped from one side of the bed to the other. Sandoval was loosing these quick little breaths that puffed out his cheeks. We could hear Shane cursing in the cab, loud enough to be heard through the glass, over the machine-shop snarl of Decimated Rectum, or whatever it was.

"You okay?" I asked.

Sandoval huffed. "What, apart from the ax-inside-me part?" We hit a spot in the road and he pulled his teeth back and gasped. I ducked as branches raked the top of the truck. "I'm stellar. Where the hell are we going?"

"We're not going to the base," I said. "Thank God."

"Yeah, forget that." He turned to look at the hatchet, the rubber handle nearly touching his chin. "Holy lord. That is a trip."

I rapped my knuckles on the window and Shane waved his hand at me, shooing me away. "I think we must be going to the hospital," I said.

Sandoval's hand locked around my wrist. "I have to tell you something," he said. These big punched-in gray hollows beneath his eyes. "It's important."

"Hold on," I said, and rapped on the window again.

Shane leaned back and opened the window without taking his eyes from the road. "*What?*" he barked.

"Where are we going?" I said. "The hospital in Kjálkabein? There *is* a hospital there, right?"

"Sit your ass down, Brian. We're not going to the hospital, you kidding? 'How'd your pal get a hatchet in his arm? Oh, three men in the woods, you say? Ah, wearing masks? Oh, okay. Well, let's call the cops and get this straightened out.'"

Hours of interrogation. Coupled with the whole "finding a severed arm on the farm" thing? We'd probably be arrested. Definitely questioned. Indefinitely, maybe. Clearly the last thing that our new friends the Balaclava Fun Time Trio wanted. Or whoever had told them to go out there and meet us.

"Where are we going, then?"

"Just sit down, man," Shane said. "We're going to Karla's house."

"Well, I mean, is that really a good idea?"

Shane shut the window.

The woods thinned once more, giving way to the buttes and low-slung ditches that braced the road. Finally the Hauksdóttir house shone spectral and washed-out in Shane's headlights. Beside Karla's truck there was a silver car in the driveway—I had a flash of dread that it might be Keller's BMW—and gravel pinged the undercarriage when we screeched to a stop behind it.

Shane stepped out, put his hands on the side panel of the truck, and peered at Sandoval.

"You know what," he said quietly. "I'm gonna clean this wound, then stitch him up. And then you and the circus act here need to get to the airport."

I pointed at Sandoval. "That's a hatchet. Like, *in* him. In his body. You want us to fly from here to Iceland to the States with him like that?"

"I have some stuff in my bag that'll relax him."

"That's not really what I'm talking about," I said.

"Dude, they told you to go." He drummed his fingers on the panel of the truck. "You just gotta go. This has gotten too big. I'll stitch him up while you pack. Deal?"

"What do they *do* on that base? What in the hell have we stepped in here, Shane?"

And I'd have had to be a fool to miss the cloud that walked across his face at that. Everyone here was weighted with some secret.

• • •

The children were crying in the living room. They and their mother formed a frieze on the couch, Karla framed by her son and daughter, a half-dozen eyes reddened and puffy. When they took in Sandoval's pale face and then the hatchet jutting out of his shoulder, they shrieked and the children started weeping again, louder.

"My God," Karla said, standing up.

"It's a mess," Shane agreed.

Gunnar yelled, "We didn't want you to leave!" He rose from the couch and reached for me and stopped; my proximity too close to Sandoval and his wound. His hands fell to little fists at his side. "We wanted you to stay! We were having fun! And then we were going to do the band! I'm sorry!" He turned and ran to Karla, pressing his head against her waist and sobbing.

"We've got to get this taken care of," Shane said wearily, gesturing at Sandoval. It was a stark difference between the frenzy and panic that had surrounded me and my run-in with the tree. It felt safe to say we'd worn out our welcome in Hvíldarland.

Karla ran to a closet in the hall, came back with towels. "The kitchen?"

"No, let him lie down," Shane said. "I'll go get my kit from the truck."

"The children found an arm," Karla said and Shane froze at the front door, his hand on the jamb.

"Um. Okay," he said.

And then Brooke walked into the living room.

She took in the scene—me, Shane, gray-faced Sandoval sitting on the couch with a hatchet stuck in his shoulder.

"Brian," she said. "Do you have any idea—I mean any clue at all—the kind of trouble you're in?"

7

"An *arm?*" Shane said, laying gear out on the coffee table, his tackle box spread open before him. Quieter, he said, "Like an *arm* arm?"

Sandoval kind of sagged across the couch and Karla walked the children up to their rooms. Gunnar's eyes were wounded and pleading as he marched with his mother up the stairs—he stared me down the entire time, tears spilling down his cheeks. "What did he mean," I said, "that he was sorry?" Brooke got right in my face and put the fingertips of her hand against my chest and said, "I need to speak to you in the kitchen."

"I think Shane might need my help."

"I'm just gonna pull this thing out," Shane said. "It's not brain surgery, believe me." Sandoval groaned.

We walked into the kitchen, the window a flat black pool that reflected our faces back at us. Sometime in the past few weeks, she'd cut her hair. Her pink bangs were gone. Her skull was shorn to blonde fuzz. The kind of blasé annoyance I was used to receiving had been superseded by a kind of flat rage that Brooke usually reserved for our dad.

She pushed a paper across the island to me. A printout.

This, it seemed, was happening to me a lot.

It was the email response I'd been waiting for from Biosearch Industries.

"When did this come?" I asked. "How did you get this?"

Brooke tapped the paper with a glossy fingernail. "Who is Vaughn Keller?"

"How did you get this, Brooke?" I picked up the paper. It didn't take long to read the results.

"I am going to be asking questions, Brian, and you are going to answer them. I have not slept in two days. You are in serious shit. I don't even think you know how serious."

"It's crazy that you're here," I said.

Brooke ran a hand over her eyes and then drummed her fingers on the tabletop. All these minute changes in such a short expanse of time: she'd gotten new nails, green and white. Aliens? Dollar bills? I sat down on one of the kitchen stools, resisted the urge to lay my face to the wood and just succumb. Just sleep forever. Be done with it all.

"Are you missing a tooth, Brian? What happened to your face?"

"I ran into a tree," I said.

"Can you sit up, please? I don't even know where to start. Do you have any idea what is going on with Mark Sandoval?"

"Keep your voice down," I said.

"*Keep my voice down?* He's wanted for questioning in Portland for a *murder*, Brian. For a hit and run. They think he fled here to avoid it."

"Who?"

"The cops!" she hissed. And then her face crumpled and for a moment I saw that young girl that I'd grown up with—overwhelmed, scared, a child fiercely holding on to the skin of the world as best she could. She put a fist against her mouth and her shoulders trembled. "And you have a fucking *brain tumor?* Are you *kidding* me with this, Brian? What are you *doing* here?"

I sat up. I slid awkwardly off my stool to go and comfort her, to take her in my arms and salvage some meager vestige of our love, our shared familiarity. My sister. I reached for her, I did, and then Karla came into the kitchen, filling the room with her own sense of urgency, and I let my hands fall to my sides.

"The children wanted you to stay longer," she said, leaning against the refrigerator, folding her arms in front of her. It was a gesture of protection and insulation I'd never seen from her before. She let out a long, shaky breath. "They told a— They lied. They took some old costume jewelry of mine. I didn't even think to look for it. It should've been obvious to me."

"Brooke just showed me the results," I said. "It's okay."

"It's not okay," Karla said. "Nothing about it is okay."

Brooke rapped her knuckles on the island and we turned to look at her. "Who is Vaughn Keller?"

"He's a family friend," Karla said.

I said, "He's a . . . data analyst. I think. Maybe. Probably not."

"He sent me that," Brooke said, and tapped a finger against the Bio-search Industries report that noted the sample Sandoval had sent consisted of 100%, entirely organic, all-natural Hvíldarlandic horse shit, sythentic glitter, and costume jewelry. "That and your CT results, Brian, and plane tickets, and a thing from the police about your boss in there." Her face warped again, then drew back to normalcy. "And then there's something about an arm? This woman here said you found a severed *arm* out there today? What is going on here?"

"Keller sent you all of that? He sent you a plane ticket?"

"He did. For both of us. Okay? *Get your stuff.*"

I was always so far behind. "But Vaughn sent you *plane tickets?* How did he get your address? How does he know who you are?" I turned to Karla. "If this was fake, did you fake the video, too?"

"Of course not!" Karla said, her hand at her throat.

In the living room, we heard Shane say, "Dude, that's not a good idea," and then the sound of the front door closing, footfalls diminishing down the porch steps.

Shane walked into the kitchen. He had a fresh smear of blood under his eye. To Brooke, he said, "Who're you again?"

"I'm his sister."

"What the hell happened?" I said. "Where's Sandoval?"

He walked to the sink and began rinsing the red from his hands. "I gave him a painkiller and started to stitch him up, and then he left."

"He *left?*"

Shane shrugged and made a flitting motion with one hand, spattering the counter with pink droplets. "He heard you talk about the horse shit and how it was fake—and I would very much like to talk to the kids about that, Karla, because that is some devious, manipulative shit they pulled. And then he just stood up and walked out, man. Gone."

5

petitions

"My mind at first refused to acknowledge the matted fur, the yellow and unblinking eyes. The fetid, heaving breath that sent leaves rippling, that made dust cloud the air. I didn't want to be witness to what was in front of me."

—Mark Sandoval, *The Ghost in the Dirt*

1

There had been no fear the first time Sandoval had heard them call his name.

It had happened almost immediately after Brian had gotten hurt, had crashed into the tree. And it hadn't been the least bit frightening. It had been a harmony, a sweet ache. And he was rewarded with that same ache, that sense of envelopment and love, every time he walked into the woods that braced Karla Hauksdóttir's farm. There were times when he simply stood out there and listened to the quiet ebb and flow of voices around him. A chorus of voices that hummed in the bones—in his very bones, it was true. This quiet joy. This rapture.

He'd gone out some nights with his NVGs and tried to see them, to see the coruscation of lights that wavered among the tree limbs—they should have shone like stars in the viewfinder of the goggle, like flares. Like the eyes of God! But there'd been nothing there. But when he took the goggles off, they appeared again, blooming around him. He took comfort in them, and with the lights rose that blessed cyclone of voices that was also one voice:

Stay with us.

Stay.

It had not gotten easier to leave the trees as their time at the farm passed. The lights, the voices, they lulled him, promised a great number of things that no one could actually promise: safety, redemption, a relief from grief and guilt. He wanted to believe, felt he was sometimes on the cusp of belief. Of giving himself over entirely.

But away from the woods—working in his notebook or pedaling his bicycle to the villages along Road Seven, trying to interview the stoic, tight-lipped people that lived there, fording his messy way through the world of the living—the voices seemed tangential, crafted from smoke and falsehoods. It was maddening then, and yes, a little frightening. And yet they called like sirens; he could still hear them faintly, no matter where he was on the island.

They sang in his dreams, this song that thrummed inside him like some blood-mad tuning fork:

Stay with us!
Stay!
Even through the worry, the fear that he had become enrapt by something false, it was beautiful.

He was finally wanted.

• • •

He'd heard Karla's confession—horse shit and glitter. Brian had been right. They'd all been right. There was nothing there. He'd stood up from the couch, his shirt cut away, Shane rearing back with the needle and thread still in his hands.

Stepping down the porch steps into the lashing rain, the voices called out and he walked to the edge of the trees as if an automaton. He could have done it in his sleep, the pathway to the lights seemed so familiar.

The voices rose.

Branches dug into his arms, snarled among his ankles. The wind blew rain into his eyes. The pain in his shoulder was distant. Shane had worked quickly, shot him with a local and fed him pain pills. But the blade had been lodged in the bone and the pain, he knew, promised a dark return. He was still bleeding.

The pills made the voices distant, watery, and he recognized their irritation at this in the way the lights hummed and worried his head like bees. The voices howled with admonishment and demand.

Stay with us!
Stay!
"I'm sorry," he said, wicking rainwater from his face, leaning against a tree with his uninjured arm. "I can't."

The lights battered against him like moths. Furious, seeking entrance. He looked for faces in them, could find none.

• • •

A kind of freedom tore through him. Freedom like a body flung out of a window. A freedom like leaping, like the final frank acknowledgment of the pavement screaming up toward you. He had become untethered, and even this provided its own sort of choice.

The simplest equation: if the horse shit was fake, the video was fake, too.
Stay with us.
Stay.
Through the traceries of limbs above him, constellations of stars hung in

the sky like thrown salt. He was angry at the voices, at their animal insistence. He'd staked everything—career, reputation, freedom—on this one gambit, this fingernail of possibility, and lost. And lost, too, in a way that was shameful. He'd staked everything—*everything*—on a child's prank.

A unicorn walks into a bar, he thought, and cackled.

Fear was churlish, gnawing, pushing its way to the front. Fear was the guest that took ownership of the home.

He'd heard Brian's sister. The man had died. He'd killed the man.

He touched the phone in his jacket pocket. The phone he'd kept upon himself all these days, through all of this. A useless phone he'd still kept charged. A phone he'd maintained with the attention to detail that bordered on mania, the way he kept all of his equipment charged, checked, and cleared.

He had noted all throughout their time in Hvíldarland as icons appeared on the screen, each bringing with them their own stirring of dread:

New Voicemail
New Voicemail
New Voicemail

• • •

Stay with us.
Stay.

"Leave me alone," Sandoval said as he stood among the trees, and the voices damped to a petulant mutter. The lights flitted away, keeping their distance.

• • •

He heard his name called from the house. Could see someone—Brian, it had to be—standing on the porch, hands shoved in his pockets.

"Mark, you out here?"

The lights winked out like someone had flipped a switch.

Rain ran down his collar.

• • •

He took his phone from his pocket, shielded it from the rain with his jacket. The battery showed a full charge.

The screen was snarled with a crack. Pixels blurred, errant blues and pinks.

He listened to his messages.

(Were the lights making this possible? There was no reception out here.)

Stay with us.

Stay.

Tad Hemphill, speaking with an officiousness that Sandoval had never heard before, and also sounding old and weary: "Mr. Sandoval, this is your attorney. Events have transpired recently which we need to address as quickly as possible. You have my number and I *urge you*"—and here, some vestige of humanity returned to his voice—"to call me when you get this."

His editor: "Mark, you've got to give me some kind of progress report, otherwise they're asking for blood. Legal's drawing up the papers if we don't hear from you by tomorrow. Throw me a friggin' bone here."

Lastly: "Mr. Sandoval, this is Detective Sotamayor with the Portland Police Department. I was hoping to establish contact with you, just had a few questions about a somewhat urgent matter. Why don't you go ahead and give me a call at this number."

• • •

He was stoned and thankful to be stoned. After these weeks of abstinence his blood was crying out for some alteration. The world filled now with a grand sense of drift. Shane had given him the good stuff.

Fake jewels! Glitter! His life upended by materials in a kid's pencil box, in a mother's closet!

He wondered where Marnie was right then, and poor Viv. Viv with her altruism, her inherent faith in the good that people can wreak on each other. Poor Don Whitmer. All these people in the shattered periphery of his world, people he'd burned to the ground. He thought of the man he'd left like a bundle of rags behind his car half a world away. Remembered the clerk at the Greyhound station all those long years ago, giving him aspirin and Band-Aids.

Stay with us.

Had it ever even occurred to him to ask the roving lights, ask these poor dead men, *Why me? Why have you chosen me? Why not Brian? Why anyone?*

Had he ever thought to ask them, *Who are you? Are you who I think you are?*

Or are you something else entirely?

• • •

He sank to his knees, pressed his back against a knotted, moss-furred tree trunk. The house stood white and strong through the fractures of the black woods. Brian was gone from the porch.

"Are you helping me?" he said, and the voices returned, the lights swarming him, jubilant.

Stay with us.

He started to cry, but even through the anesthetic his shoulder began to throb and he stopped. He was just a walking collection of injuries now, wasn't he? Neither he nor Brian had escaped unscathed. Everyone's lives all stacked and snared within each other. Some ornate, terrible puzzle of half-truths and obfuscations.

He began dialing Marnie's number, and even with the broken screen, the phone operated as it should have. Five bars of reception.

"Are you helping me?" he asked again, and the lights boiled around him.

The phone number arose as muscle-memory even though he hadn't dialed it in years. Crazy the things enmeshed in us. What time was it there? Hvíldarland was seven hours ahead of the States. Her "hello" was marred through some distant undercurrent of static. She said it again. She sounded tougher than he remembered. All gristle and sand, her shyness long worn away. His fault.

"Hey, Marnie," he rasped, the words strange in his mouth. It had been so long.

There was another pause. Part of it was the lag in the signal, but mostly he imagined it was simply the sound of his voice. How confused she must be! *"Mark?"*

"Yeah, Marn. It's me."

"What . . . What's going on?" Another pause. "I mean, why are you calling me?"

"Uh," he managed. The forest around him hissing with falling rain. "I just got a wild idea, you know?" He pictured her in some bedroom, the blankets mussed. Her hair short and boyish, her body lean and small. A swath of sun falling across her legs. A cat on the bed.

Oh Christ, who knew where she was.

"Mark. Listen, I've got to get to class. I'm not really able to talk right now." Her voice carried the rushed cadence of someone unhappily caught by surprise.

"Oh," he said brightly, "you're going back to school. That's great. That's great, Marnie." He was just so tired.

"No," she said, "I'm teaching."

"Oh, shit. Sorry. That's even better. Wow, congratulations."

"Listen, Mark." In that moment before she spoke, any number of things could have happened to them. Any number of words could have left her mouth. If he could stay in that moment, anything would be possible.

But that wasn't how things worked. You act and the rest of the world's inhabitants react in turn. On and on, relentlessly.

"I don't want you to call me again," she said. Her words were level and slow and even. "Ever. I want no part in your life. I don't want to hear your voice."

"Okay," he said. "Sure." Thinking of the apartment, remembering her hippie candles. Her red knees. The way she'd curled the sleeves of her sweater over her hands, as if protecting herself from life's sharp edges. How he would sit down on the couch while she was reading and she would get up, not even closing her book, still reading it, and walk into the other room without a word. Their short, wretched stretch of a marriage. The life they'd shared was something he'd ruined, something he'd leveled like a drunk, grandly sweeping glasses off a tabletop so he could dance on top of it.

"I'm serious," she said. "I've been sober for fourteen years, Mark. You are the very definition of toxic to me, okay?" God, she sounded tough. It was glorious. Joy ripped through him.

"Okay," he said. "I understand." Marnie didn't even say goodbye, just hung up. He felt cleansed by it, beautifully hollowed out.

Stay with us.

Stay.

He dialed the other number, this one coming just as easily, he'd always been good with inane shit like this, and she picked up right away. "Hello?"

He tried to inject some joy into his voice. "Dani, hey. What's up, lady?"

Another pause. Ah, he was racking them up. "Mark?"

"Yeah, it's me." His voice was tinny in his ears. "How's things?"

"You sound weird. Are you okay?"

"I'm good," he said. "Totally, sure. You got the check okay? I know I sent it on a different day."

She snorted. "Yeah, I got the check, Mark. What is going on? You're breaking your own rule here, dude."

"I know."

Her voice became deep and mocking, a caricature of his own. "I think we need to get some distance until our *shared history* becomes a little less obvious, Danielle. Just to be safe. Let's try to keep contact to a minimum."

"I know."

"Those are your words, not mine."

"I know, Dani."

"You didn't want to 'arouse suspicion.'"

He shut his eyes. "I was thinking maybe it was time we reconsidered that."

There was a moment of silence, and then she exploded in laughter. It was mocking, joyless. "What, *now?* Just out of the blue?"

"Well, I mean, when I get back into the States—"

"Mark," she said, "are you kidding? You've kept me on a leash for fucking *decades.* You send me a check once a month to keep my mouth shut and to stay away from you, so that people won't put two and two together. I mean, it's fine, I agreed to it, but now out of the blue you want to, what—rekindle some flame? It's a joke. What's the matter? Dick getting soft these days? You're that hard up?"

He couldn't help it—he laughed. Dani was the only one who could talk to him like this, could so easily revive some ghost of their old banter. But then she told him to fuck off and he realized—too late—that she really was hurt, furious. All this fury held inside her for years.

That day she'd picked him up outside the church with those bags of soup! With those two pairs of sweatpants! He remembered it all with a photographic clarity. *Your plans got you wearing someone else's pants outside of a church in Dog Dick, Montana, holding a sack of Campbell's Chicken Noodle soup. You can't even ride the Greyhound without fucking up. Don't tell me your plans, Mark.*

"I miss you," he said, and the voices coveting him howled in outrage. "I was wrong."

Dani's voice was soft. "I'm sorry, hon," she said. "But you're years too late with that. There was a time when I'd have done anything for you, but you missed that window by a long shot. Whatever you're going through right now? It's your burden, not mine."

• • •

He rose, grunting and gasping, from his perch at the foot of the tree.

What was left? The only tangible thing to stack upon the nothingness of this endeavor was the new book.

The notebook.

He'd stumbled upon some kind of mystery after all. More importantly, he'd told the truth as best he could. *Was* telling the truth. There was still more to write. Still more chapters being written. He would pen the rest of this tale in prison. He would come out redemptive. The book would be a confession. He would scourge his lies clean.

He would tell the truth. For once.

Stay with us.

Stay.

"I have to go home."

The voices rose, a buzz almost insectile. A hive stirred, awakened.

Stay with us!

Stay!

How had this happened to him? What was the catalyst? What single thing had brought him here?

He'd tossed so many lives like kindling into a fire.

He walked out of the woods, the mud squelching at his boots, the windows of the house shining bright.

"I have to leave," he said, and again the voices clamored for him, called to him. Hot with jealousy and anger.

Stay with us!

Stay!

"I can't stay," he said. Imploring them to understand. "I can't. I have to go home. I've done so many . . . so many things wrong."

The voices settled, stirred and feathered against him, seeking purchase, and the lights wended about him. Cold comfort now.

"I'm leaving," he said. "I'm sorry that this happened to you all."

Say goodbye to us then, the voices said quietly, slyly. *If you won't stay, say goodbye to us.*

He was so tired.

"Goodbye," he said to them as he walked toward the house, and he thought, *I need to get Brian home.* At that moment the voices—which he realized in a heartbeat, an eye blink, were only one voice—it *changed, flexed,* the voice became something mirthful and ancient, its throat clotted with darkness, its writhing mask pulled back. As understanding flooded through him, he had time to think, *It's not* lost *at all, it* wants *to be here,* and he took another step through the darkened yard and felt something like a stone beneath his foot. And then the earth coughed beneath him, so strange, this dark rose of soil blooming in his vision. Curiously lifted, he heard glass breaking, heard what sounded like someone throwing a handful of stones against the side of the house.

His eyes were cast to the stars, then to the lights weaving among the trees, the lights of the singular and terrible thing that trod this place.

And then the death-lights and the night stars merged, became one.

Sandoval tumbled skyward.

6

monsters americana

"Greed, gluttony, temptation, selfishness, pride, anger. If there *was* a devil,
I was paving my own road toward a showdown."
—Mark Sandoval, *Devil in the Blood*

1

I put on my jacket to go find Sandoval. In the past hour he'd been attacked, had a hatchet pulled out of his arm and had his sole motivation for being here yanked out from under him.

"Tell me what you think you're doing," Brooke said.

"It can't be that hard to figure out, Brooke."

"We need to talk," she said.

Shane took his cue and walked upstairs.

We stood there in the kitchen, the two of us, my sister flown halfway around the world to find me.

"I want to talk about your tumor," she said. That shorn scalp; even right then, some minute part of me wished I had a hat for her. She looked so tough and small.

"Yeah," I said, "and I want to talk about how you got my private and confidential CT scan emailed to you, but I don't think I'm going to like your answers."

"Brian—"

"There are a lot of things at play right now, Brooke. A lot of stuff is happening."

And then she said softly, "Tell me," in a voice so surprisingly kind it was simultaneously a balm and a shock. "Tell me what's going on. Please."

And I did. And she listened. Both of us surprised each other, I think. I told her about the unicorn video and the destroyed room at the Hotel Magnificence, how almost immediately our arrival had ignited some strange factions that wanted us gone. I told her about the whispering voice in my ear after coming back from the base, how the trees seemed to lean toward us. Of Sandoval's strange and growing allure to the forest around the farm, the way the woods seemed to snare him. I told her about the two men in the car on the road, and then the ones who buried a hatchet in Sandoval's arm. I told her about Vaughn Keller and the way he'd pressed that pistol against the boy's eye in the bar.

Listing it like that, a litany, it sounded crazy.

It sounded, really, like one of Sandoval's books.

"I probably should have left a while back," I said a little bashfully, and Brooke grinned at me for the first time since I could remember, the first time in years. She laughed and ran a finger under her eye.

"Well," she said, "if I wasn't unbelievably pissed at you, I'd almost be impressed. You certainly broke out of your rut. You idiot."

And with a great, ugly, embarrassing rush, I started loosing these heaving sobs. My big sister, so much smaller than me, wrapped her arms around me and held me as I put my chin on the top of her head and gasped in sputtering, half-decipherable wails. I felt like I had been walking through the dark by myself for so long.

• • •

Sometime later I stepped out onto the porch, feeling lighter than I'd felt since the whole thing began.

"Mark?" I called out. "Mark, you out here?"

But there was just the rain falling from the eaves, just the sense that we had finally passed some point we couldn't return from. Sandoval had made his choices. Was still making them.

I walked back inside.

• • •

Brooke helped me pack. I insisted on organizing Sandoval's stuff as well. She muttered under her breath the entire time, shoving clothes into my pack, grabbing various field notebooks and throwing them into my messenger bag. We were in the dining room, separating random pieces of my life from Sandoval's, when she came across his notebook on the glass-topped table.

"That's not mine," I said. "That's Mark's."

She ignored me, flipped the pages; I saw blurs of blue ink, black ink. Tightly capped and crested penmanship. I recognized it as the handwriting from the ruined *Monsters Americana* manuscript, Sandoval a creature of habit. Brooke thumbed another page, frowning.

"Brooke, that's not mine. And it's sure as heck not yours."

Something had changed between us, a softening of our resentments or blockades. But that didn't mean Brooke was suddenly a puritan. She leveled a no-bullshit gaze my way. "You got diagnosed with a brain tumor and then flew across the country without telling your family. Yes or no."

"Brooke."

"Yes or no, dick."

"Yes," I said. Here was our family's love—somewhere between a caress and an elbow to the throat.

She turned back to the notebook. "Finish packing."

"I'm worried about Mark."

She didn't look up. "Don't ever worry about Mark again. Mark is on his own."

• • •

I was in the living room, reaching behind the couch and grabbing one of the Sharpied band shirts I'd drawn with Gunnar and Liza. (My made-up band name was called the *Relentless Percolators*, and our logo featured a coffeepot with a bunch of fire pouring out of the top. I felt a fierce pang when I saw it.) Karla walked downstairs and I stood up. We stayed there awkwardly—everything had changed now, irrevocably—and looked out at the flat expanse of night beyond the windows. She held a mug of tea to her stomach like some kind of shield. "I feel like I'm responsible," she said. "I brought you here."

"You thought the video was real," I said. "Mark thought it was real."

"I *still* think it's real," she said, almost pleadingly.

"Okay."

She started to raise the cup, then brought it back down. "I'm worried about him. This . . . we should be out there. He's hurt. None of this should have happened."

I thought of turning the television on. Knowing what I'd see. On one channel or another. Knowing that something here was aligned against us. Trying to tell us something. Insisting upon it.

Karla tucked a lock of hair behind her ear. "Should we call the police?"

I didn't say anything. I didn't know what to say.

"Do you think he's safe?" Karla said.

"No," I said. "But I don't know what to do about it."

• • •

I was separating Sandoval's notes and papers from my own various logs and notations on the glass-topped table. We'd both kept copious and detailed notes about the locales and operational hours of the cameras, especially once our second order had come in. I was parsing through them, putting all the paperwork in their respective piles, still willing Sandoval to walk back through the door, when Brooke came into the dining room and said we'd be leaving in twenty minutes.

"What about Mark?"

Brooke shrugged. "He's a killer."

"We don't know that."

She pushed a stack of my notes aside and dropped the notebook she'd taken on the table. With some of her old venom returned, she said, "Read this, Brian." She opened the cover. "Starting here."

"It's not mine."

"*Read it.* Please."

And I did, and learned a great number of things about Mark Sandoval that I never wanted to know. About what happened in Portland, and that memorial I saw underneath the bridge outside of Drill, and a lawyer named Tad Hemphill. I learned where Sandoval's scars had really come from.

This was what he'd been writing while he was here?

This half-assed confession?

And then something exploded outside.

Earth and stone rained against the front of the house—the big front window buckled into a maelstrom of glass shards and upstairs the children screamed, and we all ran, all of us, outside into the rain.

2

The truck bed sloshed with blood.

We sped along the curves of the álagablettur and the blood ran in drifts when we turned or slowed. It warmed my knees where I knelt above Sandoval and pressed a towel to the broken cave of his chest. Brooke was across from me; her tourniquet was drawn tight around the shattered stub of his left arm. I could hear the clicking sounds he made as he tried to pull air through the engines of his lungs. The fabric of his pant leg was keeping his left leg attached to the rest of his body. I had tied another woefully inept tourniquet there from a bungee cord found behind Shane's seat. One of Sandoval's eyes gleamed among a shrapnel-wetted face. Beneath me, his body thrummed like a tuning fork. His remaining hand flailed against my leg and when I grabbed it, he squeezed with a surprising strength.

Overhead, a low-hanging limb raked the back of my jacket. The álaga-blettur, serpentine, ever reaching.

It hadn't been a difficult choice. Shane—with a calmness I could never match, even if we somehow did this again a dozen times—said, "He'll bleed out long before we make it to Kjálkabein. There's a combat hospital at the Camp." And that was it. Karla and the kids, terrified and weeping, stayed back; I'd never see them again. We'd lifted Sandoval's ruined body into the truck bed. The crater, not even that large, really, was halfway between the house and the trees, a spot we'd walked hundreds of times. Metal shards pocked the front of the house like tossed darts. It smelled animalistic out there while we loaded him up, profane. Guts and shit and death.

Now we slalomed and curved along that terrible road and blood poured from Sandoval's insides. A tree branch broke against the driver's side window with a sound like gunfire and Brooke screamed. Splinters peppered my temple, just missing my eye. "Get down," I said, and Brooke hunched down. More branches snarled the top of the cab and Sandoval's mouth worked like he'd eaten something bitter. Blood ran into his ears. His grip didn't lessen in mine.

I saw wickers of flame through the windshield, scattered jewels of it spied through the trees ahead of us.

We finally cleared the álagablettur and I resisted the urge to shake my fist, to scream something in triumph as the trees fell back and the night opened up around us. And then we entered hell.

• • •

No, not hell, but a hellscape.

The soldiers were burning the woods back.

We drove past a dozen men in flame-retardant suits standing in a phalanx with flamethrowers; a sea of embers glowed on the charred ground; shrunken trees lay curled behind the men like blackened ribcages. Ash hung heavy in the air, red sparks whirling in the vacuum of night, batting at the windshield and then winking out. An ember fell on my sleeve and Brooke slapped it away, her eyes huge and terrified. They poured flames against the trees.

The forest groaned, retreated. We passed a second line of men in fire gear who advanced on the still-remaining trees, went at them with axes and chainsaws. The sound the álagablettur made at this, at the burning, the ax-strikes: it was like a scream that lived in your teeth, in the curvature of your skull. I smelled the greasy, gagging stink of wood smoke and diesel. My head flared suddenly, brutally, and I nearly passed out, almost falling on top of Sandoval. Brooke grabbed me by the shoulders, screamed something I couldn't hear. Her face was twisted and crone-like in the firelight. She pushed me upright, Sandoval's ruined body between us. An aneurysm felt inevitable. I'd be grateful for it. And then we passed the burning and the feeling—all of it, the pain, the animal-like roar inside my head—evaporated in seconds.

We passed the fire-makers in their suits, and Shane's headlights painted things lunar and strange, some photo sent back from a planetary rover. Everything was blackened and cratered, desolate. Beneath the smoke-stink was the burnt-wire stench of Sandoval's blood. As we approached the base, the searchlights dutifully sprang to life from their places on the fence line.

Shane braked hard in front of the gate, the snarl of rubber on tarmac. The side of Brooke's head smacked against the rear window. I watched her turn and vomit over the side of the truck.

A voice from the loudspeaker: "You need to leave. This is a military facility."

Shane screamed out his window, "We have a critically injured man here."

"You're not authorized. You must turn back."

"This is a United States citizen," he screamed. As if that could magically change the trajectory of any of this.

Sandoval suddenly flexed beneath us, his entire body going rigid, a pained *Errrrrrrrrrr* purling from deep in his throat.

This is when he dies, I thought.

He turned and looked at me. He was an animal then, surprised and hurt and dying. He worked his mouth but no sound came out, a fresh torrent of blood wetting his cheek and running into his ear. That one glittering eye roved over me. It was a wonder that he was still alive at all.

"Just hang in," I said stupidly. His grip loosened and tightened again.

And then I looked over the hood of the truck and saw the front gate opening with a rattle.

And there was Keller standing in the headlights.

He wore a dark jacket, slacks, a black tie against a black shirt. Keller in his work clothes. A death-angel. That bloated face, like an alcoholic under-taker. He walked backward, motioning us in with one hand like someone helping a U-Haul driver park in a tough spot.

Soldiers bearing stretchers erupted from a building, flanked by others bristling with guns.

Shane pulled the truck through the gate and Keller caught my eye and smiled. Ice ratcheted through my blood. From his hip, Keller pointed a finger at me like a pistol. He winked.

• • •

Sandoval was taken away on a stretcher. His remaining arm hung down and his fingertips scraped the ground until one of the soldiers lifted it and put it at his side. They took him into one of the low, boxy, windowless buildings, one as indiscriminate as any other. A soldier directed Shane to park his truck beside one of the hangars. I sat there in the bloody bed and chanced a look back. Beyond the gate I could still see the strange red glow of the men burning the álagablettur atop the hill, the tongues of fire leaping from the flamethrowers.

Keller walked over to us, his tie flapping over his shoulder, hands in his pockets. Wattles rolling over the collar of his shirt. He looked deathly in the cold incandescence of the searchlights. A true harbinger.

We hadn't saved the arm, I realized. Sandoval's arm was still sitting there in the churned mud in front of Karla Hauksdóttir's house.

We'd taken one, we'd left one.

"Let's go downstairs," Keller said.

• • •

Some of the buildings were punctuated here and there with small windows. All had steel doors, yellow stencils on them. *CROSS-CO-1. LAB-ACCESS-4. Authorized Personnel Only* signs everywhere, every door with a keypad. Keller took the lead. The sea mist was close enough to kiss our faces. The sound of the ocean was loud. The three of us were flanked by a handful of men with rifles. It was clear we were being escorted.

Brooke, wide-eyed, a swath of Sandoval's blood down one cheek, tried to say something to Keller. He looked back at her over his shoulder and frowned. "We'll talk inside, ma'am."

In front of one of the buildings a soldier thumbed the keypad and the door clicked. Keller pulled it open and then held out a hand for us to enter. He patted me on the shoulder as I passed.

It felt like the hallway of an office, a place you'd spend a day at a training seminar. Bland and functional. Ceiling tiles, buzzing fluorescents, office doors with no windows. The hallway was featureless and a tight fit; our escorts hemmed us in on all sides. "We've got a plane to catch," Brooke said, and no one responded. We turned a corner, the soldier thumbed open another door and we followed Keller down a flight of steel-mesh stairs. This led us to yet another door with a blank black square for a keypad. Stenciled *Clearance Level 7 Only.*

Someone had put a handwritten sticky note on it that said *Stay smart! Meat's meat!* There was a little smiley face at the bottom.

Keller saw me looking and clapped a heavy hand on my shoulder again. "More shall be revealed," he said. "More and more and more, Brian."

He was having a good time with all of this. He was having a blast.

"Where's Sandoval?" I said. No one answered. Shane looked over at me, and I could see the same thing on his face that I felt striding up my own spine: a panic trying to be contained.

"You gentlemen can go," Keller said over his shoulder, and our escorts, all of them, turned without a word, the sound of their boots reverberating up the stairs. Keller turned and placed his palm on the dark keypad.

• • •

I'd expected something else: walls of weeping rock inset with panels of blinking lights, the jittering overhead lights of a horror movie, a villain's lair from an old comic book. But it was more of the same: the doorway opened to a hallway, with regular office-style doors lining each side, a few of them with windows. A pair of heavy steel doors bracketed the hall at each end. But there wasn't another soul among us, or in the offices that I could see. Beyond the faint hum of the overhead lights, the place was tomb-silent.

Keller led us to a windowed office and once more entered a code on a keypad. Inside, there was a conference table lined with chairs, a corkboard studded with nothing but pushpins. White walls. He urged us all to have a seat. "Anyone want coffee, tea? Water?"

We were standing there in some Office Max version of an underground military bunker, a place scoured of ownership or identification. I was doused in another man's blood, listening to this. Brooke took one of the chairs and pushed it against the wall. She sat down and crossed her legs, lifted her chin.

"Vaughn," Shane said, his voice shaky, "thank you, man. Guy would've bled out if we tried to drive to the city. Thank you."

"Yeah," Keller said, "good thing you brought him here, buddy. Really good thing. When's the last time you were downstairs?"

Shane grinned, but it was more like an admission of fear, almost child-like. "Been a while."

Keller nodded. "That's about what I thought." At the doorway, he turned. "Just so you know—you're all in a restricted military facility. Shane knows this. I'm gonna need you all to sign NDAs, okay? Whatever you see on the base, you'll be legally bound to stay quiet. Everyone cool with that?"

Brooke said, "We have a flight to Reykjavík that we need to catch."

He bit his lip and pointed a finger at her.

"You, I'm trying to place."

"I'm his sister. I'm the one you sent to come and pick him up."

He brightened. "Oh! You made it! That was fast. Great." He scratched his nose and said, "Well listen, Brian's sister. Here's the thing. You're going to want to stop operating under the assumption that I—any of us here, really, in the entire building, but especially me—care remotely about your plans." He keyed open the door. "You're on my dime now, darling."

Keller's figure through the window became a warped caricature of himself, and then he was gone and it was just the three of us.

• • •

Shane sat in the corner of the room, his elbows on his knees. Brooke kept trying the keypad, kept visoring her eyes against the window with her hand, trying to look down the hallway.

I sat at the table, my hands laced over the white blankness of it. Trying to think.

"Hey," Brooke yelled suddenly, slapping the glass; a soldier was walking by, his rifle slung over his shoulder. Eyes zeroed straight ahead. He was followed by two men in white coats as they consulted some kind of digital pad. None of them looked up, or even flinched.

Shane said my name.

He looked up at me, a cigarette hanging from his lips. He lit it with a flourish and his hand trembled around the lighter. He let out a plume of smoke. He pulled his ponytail into a hank at his shoulder and let it go.

"It was me," he said quietly.

Brooke turned from the window.

"What was you?" I said.

He frowned, stared at the floor. "The video."

Three people frozen in a room. Drifting cigarette smoke the only movement.

"You're kidding."

"No. I made the video. I made it." He glanced at Brooke and then at me, fast, before his eyes fell to the floor again. "It was a thing I did for Karla. It was like a love note, right? It just . . ." He let out a shaky, pained little laugh. "It was a pony. I just grabbed a white pony from a field off the road. He walked right up the ramp into the trailer. Then I parked by the rocks and led him up the driveway, around the far side of the greenhouses, away from the house. Tricked him out with a fake horn I made. There's all kinds of wild horses out there. Even miniature ones." He sniffed, ran a hand under his nose. "And then I let him go."

"Jesus," I said.

"I thought Karla would recognize that it was *me*, you know? That it was totally something I'd do. I let him loose and then I picked him up a few hours later. I knew she hung out on the porch and snuck a few cigarettes after the kids went to bed." Staring down hard at his own cigarettes between his fingers, he said, "I didn't think she'd *film* it."

He took a long drag. "It was just a thing that I did for her, you know? I thought she'd call me and I'd be all, 'Yeah, that was me. I love you. I love the kids.' You know? And I sure as shit didn't think she'd film it and send it to *you* guys."

"We're *downstairs*, Shane. Vaughn brought us downstairs. Why?"

He blew smoke, stared at the wall. Ashed his smoke on the floor. Couldn't look at us. "I don't know."

"Bullshit."

"*I don't know, Brian.*" He cocked a leg on his knee, his boot going mad. And then, in a rush, "I just worked the roof, okay? Up top, surface-level shit. Did my enlistment, got out, met Karla. I never came down here.

Vaughn's a good guy, the kids know him, all that. He takes care of all his guys, looks out for us."

Brooke said, "What are you talking about? What's the roof?"

"I manned the gate, worked Supply or Comms or in the motor pool. I was one of the hazmats that toasted the woods back every five days. 'Giving the wolf a haircut,' we called it. I just did surface work."

"Are you saying . . . What *are* you saying?"

"Camp Carroll, it's not just data. Not just satellites."

"No shit," Brooke said.

"That's just the grift. The cover. We're downstairs now. Grunts that work the roof, up there, they're regular guys. They don't come downstairs."

Quietly, Brooke said, "So who comes downstairs, Shane?"

He shrugged, dropped his smoke to the floor and rubbed it out with his bootheel. He wouldn't look at us, but he said, "I don't know, man. But whoever works down here, stays down here."

• • •

Keller walked in and pointed a finger at me in a *Come on* gesture. It was impossible to tell how much time had passed. He'd taken his jacket off and rolled up his sleeves. I could see a fine dusting of dandruff on the shoulders of his black shirt.

"You I need to talk to," he said.

"We're leaving," Brooke said. She stood up from her chair against the wall. I was surprised when Keller sighed and stepped aside, putting his hands in his pockets and dropping his big shaggy head as she stepped into the hallway.

"If I'm not with you," Keller said, "you'll be dead by the time you hit one of those doors. There are measures in place."

"Then take us out of here."

He raised his head, frowning and smiling at me. "Jesus, I thought you were the dumb one."

"You're having fun with this," I said.

"Oh, that is far from the truth, believe me. I'm actually very pissed right now, Brian. Very. You and Mark Sandoval have thrown a serious monkey wrench in my program and I'm scrambling like a *beast* to clean up your mess. I'm not happy."

"Where is he?"

"Who, Sandoval? In the infirmary. We've got a trauma team taking care of him."

"He's not dead?"

Keller shrugged, wattles puffing out of his collar. "Not yet. Now, Brian? May we?" He bent at the waist, extended an arm toward the door.

"We're not getting separated," Brooke said. "We're staying together."

A little laugh, mostly silent, and Vaughn pushed back that gray lock of hair from his forehead. "Again, Brian's sister, I cannot reiterate strongly enough just how much I don't give a shit about the way you want things to happen. You had your chance to take him"—and here Vaughn pointed at me—"and leave, and escape consequences, and you spent the whole night dicking around at that farmhouse instead."

Brooke sneered, stepping back into the room. "We got a little sidetracked by someone stepping on a bomb in the front yard."

Shane said, "Vaughn—" and Keller sprang toward him with surprising speed, a big man in motion. He made as if he was going to slap him and instead pointed a blunt finger in Shane's face. "*You. You* have fucked everything up. Irrevocably. I hope you understand that. You have brought this whole flimsy house down. *Flowers* would have sufficed, right?" His wide-eyed, maddened face pinwheeled between Brooke and I, seeking agreement. "Dinner out somewhere! *A trip to Reykjavik for a fucking spa day! Something.* But you, you had to woo your ex-wife with a goddamn *unicorn.* Jesus Christ. I've kept you and your family at arm's length from this for a goddamn *decade.* And you undo it all with a fake horn on a horse's head, Shane. Good God." He made as if he was going to slap Shane and then he balled his hand into a fist and laid it on his chest instead.

Then he turned to me, eyes glittering with that ebullient rage that I had mistaken for good humor when I first met him. "Now. Let us sally forth, young man. The night draws near."

• • •

We went through a steel door, and another, and I soon lost my orientation. Maybe that was the point. All the halls looked the same: the occasional soldier or bland civilian ignoring us, innumerable doorways with keypads, windows that looked into desolate offices or uninhabited common areas. Everyone we passed had the same supplicating, downward stares. When I lagged behind, Keller would cast an annoyed glance over his shoulder and I sped up.

We finally stopped at a door—*L-L3* stenciled on this one—and he placed his hand over the black square. It opened and we started down another flight of steps, the walls cement here, more steel-mesh stairs, a turn and another flight. Deep down in the ground. We had to be well below sea level by now, or close to it, and then we came to a door.

This was the last door, I knew.

All doors were crafted with a single intention, but *this* door? This door was a dull matte steel and featureless save for the bulged rivets lining each edge. You could drive the cab of a semi into this door and walk away frustrated. Keller thumbed the intercom next to it.

Immediately, a brisk, chilled voice came from the speaker. "Unit clearance."

Keller leaned forward. "Fool's gold."

"Asset clearance."

"Bury me standing."

Internal locks clicked and tumbled. The door slid open, silent as some ghost.

Chillier down here, the chuff of recycled air being pushed through the place. The men and women in white lab coats walked in pairs, in threes, guys in ties with their shirtsleeves rolled up. Someone pushed a cart of boxed equipment past us. Here, troops in body armor stood in pairs, their weapons hanging off their chests like weird appendages. The disorienting part: it still had the hushed quality of a library.

Keller led me down another hall, and we entered a large, open room flanked on one side by a glassed-in enclosure inset into the wall. The glass was smoke-black. A steel floor and a tall ceiling capped with rows of halogens, a few closed bay doors off to one side. More lab coats walking by, maybe a half-dozen clusters of armed men down here.

The place was suffused with a sense of wrongness, that jarring sense of someone running a glass shard along your nerves. Everything was snared to a focal point on that black sheet of glass set into the wall. My head suddenly pulsed, and I turned my face to hide the wince from Keller and heard a few other people cough, a sound that popcorned throughout the room.

When he led me to a room on the opposite side of that big enclosure, opposite the glass, I was eager for it. Keller turned the lights on, and when we stepped inside and he shut the door behind us, that sense of ache and *wrongness* diminished a little. Four white walls, a white table. A window that looked out onto the bigger room. A half-dozen metal folding chairs.

Keller took a seat across from me and folded his red hands over the table.

I lifted my chin at the black-glassed enclosure. "What is that?"

Raising a hand, Keller said, "Hold on a second."

Some anonymous lab coat knocked and opened the door. Mustache, glasses. An earpiece. He looked like a cross between a biologist and a stage manager. He handed Keller a folder and left. Keller started thumbing through it, tossing pieces of paper in front of me.

My CT scans.

Copies from Sandoval's notebook.

Copies from his typewritten *Monsters Americana* manuscript, pre-bath-tub wetting, with the inked margin notes intact.

A blown-up image of my father's driver's license.

A grainy newspaper ad for the bar where Brooke worked.

A photo of the doorway of 341-B in Sunny Meadows.

By the time he shut the folder and pushed a transparent piece of plastic the size of a notecard toward me, I understood everything.

"You run the show," I said.

He steepled his hands in front of his face. "I run the show. Peel the backing off that piece of plastic. Lick your thumb and press it on there."

I had nothing to bargain with but the annoyance of my continued heartbeat. If I lived, I was a witness.

"And it's all interconnected," I said. "Right? The woods, those dead British soldiers, this base. The way Sandoval . . . drifted away the longer he stayed here. Somehow it all fits."

"You're asking questions when you should be peeling the plastic off of that sheet there and licking your thumb and pressing down on it."

"I want a lawyer."

Wearily, he said, "You don't need a lawyer, Brian."

"That's a picture of my father's license? My mom's apartment? I want a lawyer."

"Hear me out," Keller said, and scrubbed his chin with the back of his hand.

"How did you get Sandoval's notebook?"

"What, his big confession? Those are just scans. We've got a guy on Karla's harvest crew that freelances for us sometimes. He just walked into her house on his lunch break while Sandoval was out cavorting with the spirit world. Snapped some photos." Keller grinned. "It's a trip, right? Did you read it?"

"I read it," I said.

"It's crazy. That hit and run? The whole alien abduction thing being fake? How he just holed in up DC after a bad trip all those years ago? No mother ship at all, no little gray men. Just some PCP at a rest stop. Having his body-mod girlfriend starve him and scar him up in DC over the course of a few weeks? And then making up the whole 'I was abducted by aliens' angle? Wrangling it into a *brand*. He played that *symphonically* when you think about it. They made a blockbuster out of that guy's bullshit." He leaned back in his chair, tapped out a rhythm on the table. "But that's the thing about guilt; it takes a certain kind of guy to just slough it off, keep it buried. Most people can't do it. Sandoval couldn't do it."

"You're using the past tense," I said.

"I am."

"He's dead?"

"He's way dead, Brian." He let out one of those phlegmy, lung-rattling laughs. "He didn't have an arm or a leg! I mean, you saw him. Guy stepped on a bomb, for God's sake."

I nodded. "Did you put it there?"

Keller reared back in his seat. "The bomb?"

"Yeah."

"Did I . . . Let me see if I get this right. Did I put a World War II anti-tank round in the Hauksdóttir's front yard so that a drunken grifter could blow himself up and bring down a metric ton of unwanted scrutiny on my project? That's what you're asking?"

I kept silent.

"So that I could take a guy like *you* downstairs, Brian? So I could sweat a pissant like you, and threaten the life of everyone you love? That's what you're asking me?"

I was still fitting Sandoval's death inside me, trying to find room among everything else that had happened.

"Come on," Keller said. "Use your head. I never wanted you assholes here in the first place. I've been trying to get you to leave since day one. Done a remarkably shitty job at it, admittedly, and that's on me. But no, I did not plant a bomb in Karla's front yard."

"Who trashed Sandoval's room?"

"Viktor. Him and his nephew. I wanted someone"—and here he shuffled his hands around in front of him—"off-base. Plausible deniability. And they worked cheap. Orvar's a little thug, man. I was hoping that was all it would take to get you to go."

"And the guys in the woods. The guys that slapped me around in the car."

Keller grinned big. "Ah, all my guys. You just weren't taking the hint. I *do* want you to understand that if I hadn't told them to go easy on you out there, you wouldn't have walked out of those woods alive."

I thought, *One of us didn't, you asshole.*

"Anyway," he said, and tapped that sheet of plastic with a blunt fingernail. "Peel the coating, lick your thumb, press down."

"You're getting my, what? DNA?"

"See, you're getting smarter."

"I want a lawyer," I said again.

Keller chuckled and shook his head. "All you have is me. I'm all you get."

"Why do you burn the woods back around the base?"

He shrugged a shoulder. "The truth? Because they need to be burned back."

"What is happening here, Vaughn? What lives in the woods?"

And here he gazed up at the ceiling. Closed his eyes and inhaled: the look of a man on a beach somewhere. "Brian, it's something . . . You can't fit your head around it, my man. I mean, we've *got one,* we've had one for years, and we're still not sure what we have. It's a heck of a tough question, I'll be honest."

"So Sandoval just stepped on a piece of old ordnance."

"I guess so."

I put my hands in my lap. "He triggered an explosive after walking in a spot that people have been walking on for seventy years."

Keller scratched an eyebrow with his thumb. "Brian, we're running out of time here. Do you know anything about chemical fuses? Delayed timers? You familiar with rust accumulation on detonators? You familiar with how *any* of that shit works? The world's a volatile place. Someone fires a gun up into the air ten thousand times. Ten thousand times it falls back to earth, no big deal. Bullet lands in a pond. Lands in a field. But the time after that? Ten thousand and one? The bullet rises and then drops into someone's brainpan and kills him. Right? People break their necks getting out bed."

"I want a lawyer."

"No."

I held up my hands, pushed back from the table. "I can wait." If I lived, I was a witness. That's all I had.

Some heat was creeping into his cheeks. "It doesn't work like that, Brian. We're on a schedule."

"That's the only way this is going to work." I shrugged, looked out the window.

"I know you feel like you're doing what you need to do." Keller tucked his chin into his collar, spent some time examining his tie. "Like you're being brave. But things are going to change in just a minute, Brian. In a way that's going to haunt you. I don't say that lightly. I mean it. *It will haunt you.* You will feel remorse, and guilt, and ownership. So the best thing you can do right now, for yourself and everyone else, is peel that paper off and lick your fucking thumb and press it down right there. I could have one of these guys walk in and put a round through your eyeball, but I don't want to do that."

He wore the impassive, crag-like face of a loveless deity. A blown-out, blood-rimmed, heartless gaze. There was no pity there. Whatever animus it was that powered Keller—greed, power, loyalty—I could touch nothing inside him.

I peeled the coating off, licked my thumb, pressed it to the plastic.

I left a pale whorl of evidence of myself there, a few miniscule flakes of Sandoval's blood embedded in it.

"Thank you! Progress!" Keller took the plastic by the edges, put it in the folder. He pushed the pen and a new sheaf of papers across the table. "That's a nondisclosure agreement. A boilerplate form acknowledging that you'll keep quiet about what you've seen here today."

"You just threatened my life and you're having me sign, like, a corporate NDA."

"Just sign it."

"Why did you bring me here if you didn't want me to see anything?"

"For all that is good and holy, Brian, sign the fucking form."

I said, "We found that arm in the mud and then a few hours later we left Sandoval's arm there. I can't stop thinking about that."

Keller put his hands in his armpits, pushed back in his chair. The chair legs slowly screeched along the floor. Then he said, "Where are you, Brian?"

I said, "Hvíldarland."

"You're not thinking. Where *are* you?"

"Camp Carroll."

"Where?"

"Downstairs."

Keller lowered his head. "And what's downstairs?"

"I don't know."

He touched his nose and then pointed at me. "Go ahead and sign that for me."

I signed it. What else was there to do?

Keller scooped up the papers and motioned for his pen back. "Thank you. Now I need you to understand that this is me reaching down benevolently and placing the kiss of God upon your soiled, woefully stupid forehead. This is my blessing to you."

I looked out the window at the wall of smoked glass out there. "You had my sister fly out here."

"I did. She obviously loves you very much."

"She's your insurance policy, right?"

"No. She's your insurance policy."

Quietly, I said, "So you're not going to kill us?"

"No."

"Really?"

"This is the deal," he said. "I want you gone, Brian. I want you gone and

I want you quiet. I'm sending you and your sister home. Mark Sandoval is going to be seen in a few different places around the globe, spotted here and there. It's a big, bad world, and he's working on a book, after all. So someone will post something about seeing him in Myanmar, or Berlin, or somewhere in the Outback, and then it'll go quiet for a bit, and then he'll pop up somewhere in, I don't know, Zimbabwe. And eventually people will stop giving a shit. From what I can tell, he's a man who has not inspired much loyalty in others."

"I think you're miscalculating people's interest."

"You could be right. But thanks to you, this is the shitstorm we're working with. I'm coming in with my broom and dustpan, Brian. You can go ahead and mouth off to the *New York Times*, to the *Post*, to fuckin' *Fangoria* if you want. A juicy exposé about Mark Sandoval and how he died, how he pulled off one of the biggest hoaxes in modern history. You can talk about the secret military base in a little island country off the coast of Iceland. You can even tell people about what you're about to see, and how you could have stopped it if you'd just left when you'd been told." He held up the folder. "But remember: we have your DNA, my man. We have your fingerprints. We have your signed confession to a number of crimes. And we can be *vastly* creative with all that material, believe me."

I'd grown cold all over. Hands numb as stones. "I get it."

"We've already gathered up your stuff from Karla's place. Mark Sandoval's already caught a flight to Reykjavík, according to any records that anyone's gonna find."

"Okay."

"If your brain tumor doesn't eventually kill you, and you breathe a word of this, I will roll tanks through your life. I'll delegitimize you. I'll send detailed lists of child porn sites you frequent to your employer, to your family. You know the kind of pariahs that dudes in the sex registry are? Good luck with your PhD after that, Brian."

"What is it that you do here, Vaughn?"

"The IRS will audit you with a pair of tweezers. We'll get you on that no-fly list. *Allahu akbar* and all that. You'll never catch a flight again without being sweated in a room by a couple of roided-up TSA dudes with onion breath. You'll make a phone call to an ex-girlfriend or a buddy, hear a bunch of strange clicks. See the same guy in a different car parked outside of your house every day. Oh wait—you'll be on the registry, so count yourself lucky if you're still sleeping indoors by then. That'll be your life."

"I get it."

"And then we'll send someone to your sister's bar, right? Some guy that'll start following her to *her* car, okay? Knocking on her door, calling her, sending her emails. And worse. I mean, there's always room for worse, Brian. We haven't even *talked* about your mom yet, or your dad and his sweet thing. You think you're living some black helicopter shit right now, but you have *no idea*. You *will*, but right now, you think you've seen it all." He coughed. "The world is a fragile place, balanced on a *great number* of fragile beams, and you and Sandoval have just upended a lot of them. So now I have to clean up your mess."

"Okay. I'm sorry."

"People don't really believe in ghosts. Monsters under the bed, all that. They just like the idea of them, as long as they're safe. People just want to be protected, you know? 'I'm in here, the bad things are out there.' And that's what we do here, Brian. We protect people."

Another knock, and the same guy in the lab coat peered his head around the door. "We're on schedule."

Keller pushed his chair back with another squeal and bounced to his feet. "Excellent. Let's go." He'd grown jolly with fury, bristled with it.

My sister was in a room down here. She'd come to get me.

Keller led me back out into the cavernous, high-ceilinged room, his hand around my bicep. My head pulsed immediately and I almost buckled to the floor.

"Hurts, right?" Keller leered. He moved his warm hand to the back of my neck, squeezed. "You're gonna want to get some specialists for that tumor when you get home. I guarantee your stay here has exacerbated your situation. It messes with some people more than others, but some of my guys can't even be down here with a hangover. I need you to just hang in a little bit longer. You bought tickets to a show, after all. Hell, you *wrote* the show!" Next to us, the guy in the lab coat murmured something into his earpiece.

A siren blared once. It filled the room—a knife-zipping lighting along the cleft of my brain—and then trailed off.

Like supplicants, we all turned to the glass. I shut my eyes, afraid of what I would see.

The smoked-glass wall in front of us—Keller smacked the back of my head, told me to open my eyes—grew transparent.

This unknowable thing writhed behind the glass, lashed against it. Sinuous, wet, plated. A single eye passed across me and I felt something reach toward me, invite me.

"It's got a tug to it, right?" Keller grinned. "You feel that?"

"We're clear," the man murmured into his earpiece. "Send in subject one."

A panel slid open in the room behind the glass and there stood a small, trembling, pale horse. A pony, really. Eyes widened to show the whites, an animal so like the ones we saw in the fields along Road Seven, like the one I had spied in my night vision goggles. It might have even been the same one that Shane slapped a fake horn on, that had started this whole thing.

It immediately began bucking in terror at the indefinable thing that reached for it.

In my ear, Keller said, "You wanted to fucking see it, right? Right, Brian? You came here looking for a *monster*? Here you go."

I watched what happened to the horse. What was done *to* it. I struggled to comprehend what was happening, the way things were moving behind the glass, the jets of blood that doused the inside of the glass and ran down in rivulets.

Keller said, "This is on you. This is your show. Remember how fragile the world is, Brian."

The man in the lab coat cast a glance at Keller. Keller nodded.

Into his earpiece, the man said, "Subjects two and three are go."

The door behind the glass slid open again, and there were two nude figures standing there. I opened my mouth to scream—I thought it was Brooke, Shane—but Vaughn clapped his hand over my mouth and let out a throaty little chuckle. Into my ear, he whispered, "Believe me, you don't want to be making a lot of noise right now, Brian."

Constables Jónsdóttir and Leiffson, sent on some charade after finding the arm in the mud. Sent to some trap. Keller orchestrating it all. Naked and crouched there.

And so we watched. Keller's hand gripped the back of my neck. We watched as the thing behind the glass got to work on them as well. I wept.

"Open your eyes," Keller said.

"Open them," he said.

Jónsdóttir and Leiffson, paying for my sins.

7

quiet enough, and then loud enough

"And now, years later, here I am. Scar-heavy, gun-shy, but accepting of what's become of me. We aren't privy to all of the answers. We don't get to know. There are vast swaths of time where we're just riddled with uncertainty, with a lack of understanding. And I'm okay with it. After all, I'm here. I made it. I took the long way home, but I made it."
— **Mark Sandoval**, *The Long Way Home*

1

It's stiflingly hot in his little one-bedroom place in Kenton. The fan pushes fetid air around in the kitchen while a fly buzzes in unhurried, bumbling constellations against the window screen. Lawnmowers and the shrieks of children come drifting through the mesh, the lulling sound of some neighbor's radio.

Brian's entering grades into his laptop and sweating in his boxers when he hears the ding of an incoming email. He tabs open his mail program, sees the tagline, and goes cold. Easy as that. A deep cold, a bone-chilling cold like some ghost is settling down on top of his heart. Like some ghost-Brian is drifting into his same shape in the chair where he sits.

It's an email about a monster hunter.

Mark Sandoval spotted in Jamaica—and he's LOOKING for DUP-PIES? CLICK HERE!

He clicks on the link, viruses be damned, and is taken to a fringe website he's never heard of before. Bigfoot, alien sightings, sidebar ads for hair-growth creams and investment programs urging viewers to transfer their assets into gold before the oncoming and inevitable economic collapse. The article shows a blurry picture of a white man in sunglasses and a button-up shirt loose at the throat. The man crosses the street at a busy intersection. Are those the telltale scars on his neck? It's hard to tell. The article itself is a three-paragraph travesty about Sandoval being spotted in Kingston while potentially researching duppies—a term originating from the Caribbean, meaning the restless spirits of loved ones. Brian reads it. There is, of course, no mention of him, of Hvíldarland, Camp Carroll, or of anything remotely factual, as far as he can tell. He closes the laptop with a hand that doesn't even feel like his own. He takes a shower to obliterate the chilled sweat that's suddenly covered his body.

Summer is winding down, persistent and cloying. He dresses, steps outside into the heat shimmer of the afternoon, heads to his MAX stop.

On the way, he's met with the almost pleasant miasmic stink of blacktop and gutter-piss and cut grass. Since returning home, he's taught a single semester at the nearby community college, three classes: Anthro 101, Intro to Sciences, and Writing 65. Today he teaches his last class. He's just boarded the train, his bag snug over his shoulder, sweat already making the maddening journey down the crack of his ass again, when he realizes the email could've been sent specifically for him. That it's very likely. He realizes that Keller could've as easily as not planted some kind of bug or malware on his computer now, that the website might have been built expressly for this purpose. Tracking him, his searches and page visits. *Remember how fragile the world is.*

If your head feels like it is growing or is hot, the article had read, *you may be in the presence of a duppy. You can shame a duppy by using bad language or exposing your genitals.* He could picture it, Keller okaying the copy, grinning and scratching his nose. Grimly mirthful and mocking to the very end.

The MAX clacks and rolls beneath his feet. People sit, people stand with their hands laced around the poles, the overhanging straps; they all sway with the ululating rhythm of the train's movement. Everyone is sweating. Sunlight refracts off the angles of the outside world, dim knives of light behind the tinted windows.

His phone rings and he stares at it for a moment before accepting the call.

"What's up?" he says.

"Hey, I'm wondering, have you had these Soy You Later things? It's like they want to convince you it's chicken, when it's clearly not."

His father's voice is loud, brash; Brian's certain the people around him can hear the entire conversation. This would've mortified the pre-Hvíldar-land Brian as he skulked his way through the world. This Brian couldn't care less.

"Yeah, those are good," he says.

"Okay. So we've got fake-ass chicken, kale—Traci, you said kale, right?—green beans, salad, wine. Can you still drink wine?"

"Yeah, just until twenty-four hours before the surgery."

"So tonight's the last night you can drink," his father says.

"Yeah. I guess so."

A pause. "Okay." He clears his throat. "So, that's dinner for tonight. That work for you?"

"Works great, Dad."

"Okay," his father says, and there is an awkward pause where he clearly wants to say something more but doesn't. There are these vast swaths of unexplored topography between them; so far neither Brian nor his father has been quite willing to ford them. "Well, I had something I was gonna say, but I'll be damned if I can remember what it was. We'll be back in a few hours. I'm taking Traci to a movie, get out of the heat."

"Cool. I'll be home after class. You've got the key."

His father hangs up. Brian smiles at the evening's menu; Traci has been insistent on shopping for him before his surgery, and everything is antioxidant-rich, organic, vegan. This is the strange trajectory of his world now; his father, after learning of the tumor, has sold his condo in the nudist colony, and he and his twenty-four year-old girlfriend (twenty-five now! Time passes!) have returned to Portland to caretake for him after his operation. Assuming, of course, that the operation is successful and he lives, which his neuro team has solemnly informed him is not a given.

"Don't talk bullshit like that, Bri," his father had barked after Brian had mentioned to him of the odds of recovery. He'd been shocked to hear of Brian's reluctance to do the surgery immediately, and even more shocked when Brian had insisted on teaching an entire semester of classes while he decided what do. So much history sat wasted between them, so many stony, silent years. Traci and his father had gotten a room in a seedy hotel on Lombard to be close to Brian's house once he is allowed to come home. An air mattress sits on the living room floor; they will take shifts caring for him. It all seems excessive to Brian, but his father has reached for it like a man grasping for a life preserver.

The train slaloms gently around a curve. A cement wall faces one side of the tracks, a wall festooned in graffiti and hasty tags. It goes by in a blur.

Somehow, inexplicably, the article about Sandoval calms him—at least he knows where he stands. It affords him a type of clarity. It's clear that Keller means every word he said, and undoubtedly can do everything he's said he can do.

For Brian, it is simply a question of being quiet enough, and then being loud enough. This is a thought that comes to him often, as close to a mantra as he has.

Hvíldarland has taken on the blurry inconsistency of a mirage, something like a heat shimmer, until shards of it suddenly stick like slivers of glass in his heart. This usually happens in the half-lit world between waking and dreaming. He wonders what Shane is doing now, the children. Poor Shane, man. Poor Karla; he thinks he knows them well enough to know that both will blame themselves for the chasm between them, the chasm that Sandoval's arrival built and his death cemented. All based off of an attempt to salvage love. Everything birthed from this one tiny untruth and all the things that spiraled from it.

But maybe Brian's wrong. Maybe the family will be able to come together, to entwine their lives again.

Then again, maybe Shane is dead. Maybe Shane, too, was put behind the glass.

(How he's had to reframe his entire world around what happened behind the glass. Jónsdóttir and Leiffson and what he owes them. Even Sandoval. How the dead stack up in his mind, how he constantly calculates his indebtedness.)

The doors open to let someone off the train, and there above the chiaroscuro of buildings is the beginning of a sunset, drawn in strident bars of oranges and pinks, that practically cracks his heart to see, even as he can feel the heat roiling off the pavement, the diesel stink of evening traffic. He is nearly driven to his knees with entirely average shit like this now: the simple beauty of a sunset, or a drawing of a heart poorly scribbled in a bathroom stall, or a man anguished and gesturing to himself at the right angle of two brick walls. Every day, something threatens to undo him.

Writing 65 is held twice a week, evening classes, ninety minutes at a stretch. A mix of kids out of high school taking it for college minimums, older immigrants, and blue-collar folks who work during the day. He is proud of all of his students, the work they've done in the short time he's known them. It hadn't paid shit, this semester of teaching, but he made some extra cash freelance editing, got some pieces published here and there, and the shack in Kenton—labeled a "cottage" by the friend of Robert's who hooked him up with the place—sits in the shadow of a larger house and costs less than his old room.

The MAX stops at the college and Brian gets out. His phone buzzes. It's his father again.

"Hey, Dad. Everything okay?"

His father's voice is a little shaky. "The thing I wanted to tell you, Brian. I, uh— I'm pretty nervous." He laughs. "I'm a little afraid, to tell you the truth. I just wanted to let you know that."

"About dinner?"

"Yeah."

"Trust me, Dad. Brooke's as scared as you are."

"Oh, Jesus." His father laughs again, sniffs. "Your sister's never been afraid a day in her life."

"It's just dinner. An hour or two, and then she'll go home."

"And there's wine," he said, and lets out another honking laugh.

"And there's wine," Brian agrees. "It'll be over before you know it."

"Okay, bud," his father says, and Brian hears him blow his nose into the phone. He sniffles a few times and says, "Love you, bud."

"Love you, too, Dad," Brian says, feeling the grind in it, the difficulty, and feeling also the possibility that one day those words might not seem such a heavy stone to lift.

He makes it through the lobby and heads to the lower level of the school. Glossy floors, that lovely wonder of circulated air, only a few students roaming the halls given that the semester has wound down. Between the classrooms are banks of lockers, scuffed and dented, painted an industrial tan. Brian steps to one, looks at his phone to check the time, and then spins a combination.

Inside are a sheaf of printouts and a single notebook.

The notebook is much like Sandoval's had been—a thin black cardstock cover, bound in spiraled wire.

He has an hour before class starts. He takes the notebook and printouts and heads to the college's library.

The pair of students manning the front desk are strangers, but he loves the familiarity of the library. Loves coming to the school. Teaching now is different; there's an ease to it that had been missing. The weight was gone—that sense that every day doing this was a wasted day. Every day now has, after all, the potential to be his final day, doesn't it? Every day since Hvíldarland has been a gift.

Now, after Sandoval and Jónsdóttir and Leifsson and what he saw behind the glass, he is laden with both a purpose and a grand debt. He is armored with it.

The tumor is still nestled there in the dark of his skull, growing. That peach pit of rot within him. It still clamors and throbs. Today is Tuesday, and Thursday is the operation.

His phone rings again, and with a grimace of apology to the librarians, he walks out into the hallway.

Brooke says, "This is bullshit."

"It's dinner," he says. "That's all it is."

"I'll piss in his meatloaf."

"We're having soy chicken and kale, actually."

"God, if the tumor doesn't kill you . . ."

"Come on, Brooke. Dad's bringing wine."

She sighs. "The nutritionist is gonna be there?"

(This is progress. This is better than anything she's called Traci up to this point.)

"They're together, Brooke. It's a package deal."

"Ugh. I'll piss in her meatloaf too."

"We're having soy—"

He can hear her smiling when she says, "Shut up, Brian. God."

"See you at seven," he says.

"If Mom tells me not to go, I'm not gonna go."

"Mom is stoked that he's eased off on the lawsuits, Brooke. This is a good thing. We're doing better."

"Maybe," she says.

"Seven o'clock."

"Seven," she says. And then, quickly, she blurts, "I love you" and hangs up before he can say it back to her.

They haven't talked about Camp Carroll. About Sandoval. He prays— if that's what you want you call it—that she has no idea about the thing behind the glass. She said she'd bummed Shane's cigarettes in that room, and then they were taken back upstairs, and that was it. Like his father, Brooke had been furious at his reluctance to have the operation immediately. But she had afforded him a grudging respect when he said that he would get it taken care of, but he needed to get his affairs in order first. Brian, putting his foot down? It had bridged some gap between them, his quiet, steadfast insistence.

He walks back into the library, picks a table near the back of the fiction section.

He takes a pen from his bag, checks the time again.

His opens the notebook with the black cover.

And he starts writing.

It's free writing, really, something he has his Writing 65 students do for ten minutes at the beginning of every class. Occasionally he refers to a printout and crosses something out in his notebook and writes beneath it.

Something in him rejoices in this simple race against time. Against biology. Against his own limitations.

Against Keller and what he did.

The printouts are sacred things, imbued with sanctity. (Given his education, he is accustomed to sanctifying objects; it's second nature to him.) He cross-references timelines, expands upon the biographical and geographical facts he remembers from reading Sandoval's own notebook. He writes about the specific placement of the stairwells in Camp Carroll, draws maps, wracks his memory for the way that Keller's hand had moved on the doorway keypads, the patterns there. He writes down as many names of as many soldiers as he remembers during his brief stay in Hvíldarland. He writes about the bar they went to, about the distant, wistful tone that Karla took when suggesting they go there. He lists Gunnar's favorite bands. He writes about Constable Jónsdóttir, and how she had a husband, and how she and Constable Leifsson got a call after coming to the farm, a call undoubtedly orchestrated by Keller. He writes about the bending trees of the álagablettur, about Road Seven, about Orvar and Viktor, about the dizzying way the plane hung over the little island before they descended.

But mostly he writes about Vaughn Keller.

After class tonight, or tomorrow morning—he tries to keep it sporadic, without structure—he'll go to a FedEx office or a copy shop and use their internet. He'll pay for his time with cash. He'll visit websites and leave with a half-dozen printed pages, sometimes less. His sheaf of printouts will grow. The article he saw today reinforces the notion that he should be careful. It could even be a warning—knock it off.

Of course, it's all terribly flimsy, these paltry defenses, this insistence on grade school–level subterfuge. But Brian is banking on the chance that Keller has other things to worry about. The man has to get Sandoval away from Hvíldarland, has to continue to lay those breadcrumbs away from Camp Carroll and the thing behind the glass. Two dead cops? Brian saw the newspaper article in which Sandoval had been officially charged in the hit and run case, so Keller also has to keep the Multnomah County District Attorney off the trail. He's got to balance that with whatever he's done to appease or threaten the Hauksdóttirs, the Jónsdóttir and Leiffson families. The Kjálkabein police. Brian wonders if he already has enough information to make things happen. Before people do begin to forget about Mark Sandoval.

But for now, Brian, small and tumor-fat, is a little mouse. Quiet and not bothersome at all.

He hopes to still be alive on Friday.

He hopes the rot is removed from him.

He hopes.

So he's researching. He's building the foundation of his story. He's anchoring facts to footnotes. It's an old muscle, research is. Don Whitmer's three-armed embrace: theory, investigation, and review. It's a familiar, beloved, well-developed muscle that he's using now, even if the subject matter is a little out of his wheelhouse.

You can go ahead and mouth off to the New York Times, *to the* Post, *to fuckin* Fangoria *if you want. You think you're living some black helicopter shit right now, Brian, but you have no idea.*

He writes. He builds the foundation, solidifies the narrative. He names names. And meanwhile, time does what it does. Time is relentless. Time is a beast. He wishes he still had Sandoval's notebook, even his original, ruined version of *Monsters Americana*. Something. His phone chirps—the alarm going off. He has a class to teach. But hopefully not his last—he's found that he loves it. It's a good fit after all. He writes another paragraph, reluctant to stop, but then rises and shuts his notebook, gathers his pages.

He walks out of the library and puts his materials in his otherwise empty locker. It's all thin, wire-thin, the whole process. The gamble.

It's all so goddamn fragile, but he's trying.

He hopes.

He's found a few things about Vaughn Keller that he believes will lend credence to his story. He has the names of a few people who might be willing to talk about a small and mostly forgotten military base on a remote island near Iceland.

His classroom is on an upper floor in another building, and he smiles when he steps outside—the evening here is kissed with the scent of warmed cement and cut grass. The sky is a deep strident purple and, oh, it's glorious. It really is.

They are waiting for him, his students, with laptops or notebooks open on their desks. A few of them chat quietly with each other. He nods, smiles, walks up to his own desk and puts his bag down by his chair. A few minutes later, his classroom is full.

Who will he tell? Who will believe him?

When he's ready to talk, who will help him?

For now, it's enough to simply do the work.

It's enough to be quiet while preparing to be loud.

"Okay," he says, and smiles. Their expectant faces gaze up at him, waiting. "We made it. Is everybody ready to do this one last time?"

ABOUT THE AUTHOR

Keith Rosson is the award-winning author of the novels *The Mercy of the Tide* and *Smoke City*. His short fiction has appeared in *Cream City Review, PANK, Outlook Springs, Black Static, Phantom Drift, December,* and more. He lives in Portland, Oregon. More info can be found at keithrosson.com.